FORGOTTEN DESTINY

Recent Titles by Janet Tanner from Severn House

ALL THAT GLISTERS
HOSTAGE TO LOVE
MORWENNAN HOUSE
SHADOWS OF THE PAST
TUCKER'S INN

FORGOTTEN DESTINY

Janet Tanner

This first world edition published in Great Britain 2004 by
SEVERN HOUSE PUBLISHERS LTD of
9–15 High Street, Sutton, Surrey SM1 1DF.
This first world edition published in the USA 2004 by
SEVERN HOUSE PUBLISHERS INC of
595 Madison Avenue, New York, N.Y. 10022.

British Library Cataloguing in Publication Data

Tanner, Janet
    Forgotten destiny
    1.   Amnesia - Fiction
    2.   Young women - England - Bristol - Fiction
    3.   Love stories
    I.   Title
    823.9'14 [F]

    ISBN 0-7278-6095-X

Typeset by Palimpsest Book Production Ltd.,
Polmont, Stirlingshire, Scotland.
Printed and bound in Great Britain by
MPG Books Ltd., Bodmin, Cornwall.

*B*eneath lowering grey skies, the ship, towed by barges, came slowly up the narrow Avon Gorge on the morning tide. Above her, seagulls wheeled and mewed, beneath her bows the water, salt merging into fresh, became steadily more greasy and rubbish-strewn as she neared the wharf where the man stood watching.

In his fine coat, buckskin breeches and leather jackboots, he cut a handsome figure; to the casual observer, he might have been one of the Merchant Venturers, the elite society of rich Bristol traders, watching his vessel come in with her valuable cargo. But unlike most of them, he wore no powdered wig – his natural hair was braided into a pigtail beneath his Holland hat, and instead of an expression of satisfaction or pleasure, his features were set in grim, hard lines.

Soon the ship would dock, the grating to the hold would be lifted, and the hell beneath the creaking decks would be revealed to an uncaring world. The evil stench of sweat and fear, filth and disease would float up to mingle with the sickly sweet smell of sugar and alcohol, and the pervasive stink of an industrial port where, at low tide, the mud and sewage of the channel was exposed, bank on reeking bank with barely an eggcupful of brown water here and there to cover it. And from that hellhole the slaves would be dragged in chains – those who had survived the long and tortuous voyage from Africa.

They had been seized, those poor souls, by the slavers. They had been torn from their homeland and the arms of those they loved, herded with less care than would be afforded to valuable cattle, starved, beaten, made to dance barefoot for

1

the amusement of the sailors, then thrown back into the prison that was foul with their own vomit and excrement. They had seen some of their number exchanged for sugar in the great plantations of the West Indies, where they would be worked until they dropped like flies in the cruel conditions. And then it had been back to sea, shivering whilst the weather grew steadily colder, grieving for their friends who were dumped overboard when they succumbed to hunger and pestilence, terrified, hopeless. Now they would be sold for whatever the ship's owner and his partners could get for them, subjected to humiliations beyond imagination, whipped into submission. All resistance and hope would be beaten from them, their freedom lost for ever.

It had to be stopped, this barbaric trade in human life. The man was determined on it. Somehow it had to be stopped, and he would do everything in his power to see that it was. But the odds were stacked high against him and those who thought as he did. The trade was too profitable, those who benefited from it too powerful. They held Parliament in their pocket, and here, in a port such as Bristol, a man could be lynched for airing such revolutionary beliefs, let alone acting upon them. Going against those who grew fat on the evil trade was a dangerous business. Already his convictions had cost him that which he had held dearest in all the world, but still he refused to allow himself to be deterred. If anything he was the more determined – Rowan's life must not have been lost in vain. And besides, to fail to do what he could would be to betray his principles, make him no better than those who made fortunes from the degradation and suffering of others.

The commotion on the dockside grew; men shouted, chains rattled, the ship's prow ground noisily against the quay. He turned away, sickened, and the resolve hardened in him, rocky and unmoving as the deep lines in his face.

He would see an end to this barbarity, one way or another. And if the men who dealt in it were ruined, so much the better. But the task that lay before him was monumental. He raised his eyes to the heavy grey skies and prayed that he was equal to it.

One

It is one of the great mysteries of life to me that sometimes one has a premonition before a momentous event occurs – a dream, perhaps, only half-remembered, that leaves one with a pervasive feeling of sadness or great joy, or simply a sense of fate unfolding – whilst sometimes one's world as one knows it can change in a twinkling and one is given no warning at all.

That was the way it was for me that spring afternoon in the year of 1786 when my grandfather called me to his study. I had spent the day thus far as I had spent every day since I had recovered from the terrible accident which had, so my grandparents told me, claimed the life of my mother, and so very nearly claimed my own life too. I had helped my grandmother with the household tasks which, in grander establishments than ours, are taken care of by an army of servants, but which, in a country rectory, fall to the rector's wife, no matter that she is no longer a young woman. And when the noonday meal was over and the dishes cleared away, I had taken off my apron and repaired to the parlour with a pile of darning which my grandmother's failing sight no longer allowed her to do in the neat, precise way she would have wished.

I was there, sewing diligently, when the carriage drew up at the front door, and I heard voices in the hallway before the door of my grandfather's study was firmly closed, cutting them off, but I thought nothing of it. Visitors frequently called at the rectory, both the poor and devout, and the great and the good of the parish and beyond. Often the latter came by carriage, for my grandfather's living covered a sprawling

3

area of rural Gloucestershire, in a fold of the Cotswold Hills. It simply did not cross my mind that this particular visitor had anything whatever to do with me, much less that he held my entire future in his hands. And so I simply went on with my sewing, giving no thought at all to what might be taking place behind the closed door of my grandfather's study.

I was startled, and puzzled, therefore, when a half an hour or so later the parlour door opened and my grandfather put his head round to ask me if I would join him in the study.

'There is someone I wish you to meet, Davina,' he said in his precise tones, overlaid with just the faintest burr of a Gloucestershire accent. 'Someone who has a most important proposition to put to you.'

I frowned. 'What sort of proposition?'

My grandfather smiled thinly. 'It would be wrong of me to discuss it with you until he has had the opportunity of meeting you,' he said. 'Suffice it to say I think it will provide the answer to all our problems.'

'A position,' I said, my hands very still suddenly on the piece of linen I was darning. 'He is going to offer me a position.'

'I'll leave it to him to tell you himself,' my grandfather said. 'But, Davina, your hair is coming loose from its pins. I suggest you tidy it before you join us. It is important you create the right impression of a well-brought-up young lady, not some wild ragamuffin.'

The censure was there in his tone, just as it always was when he made oblique reference to the life I had led before being taken in by him and my grandmother, and I felt my cheeks grow hot as the familiar defensiveness flooded through me. Whatever my grandfather might think, I felt sure my mother *had* raised me properly, and it was no one's fault but the good Lord who made me that my hair was wild and unruly, refusing to be restrained no matter how many combs and pins I put into it, and falling into long, curling tendrils on my neck and about my face.

But although I wished my grandfather would not cast aspersions on my poor dead mother, at the same time I knew

4

he only said the things he did for what he considered my own good. My mother had caused him and my grandmother such shame and heartache with her wild ways, and they lived in fear, both of them, that I might take after her and follow in her footsteps.

It was one of the reasons, I know, why Grandfather had recently been making enquiries with a view to securing me a position as a governess with some respectable and well-set-up family. That, and the fact that having to keep me was a constant drain on their meagre finances.

I was not, I must admit, overly keen on the prospect. I had heard that governesses often had a hard time of it. Not quite a servant, nor one of the family either, they were isolated and looked down upon, overworked and lonely. Often the children made things difficult for them, behaving in a fashion they would never dare to with their parents, and knowing that they could get away with impertinence and sometimes outright disobedience because the governess was, in so many ways, inferior to them.

But I could not remain dependant on my grandparents forever. They were growing older; one day soon my grandfather's health would force him into retirement, and their income would be depleted still further. Already they had done far more for me than I had any right to expect. Now it was time for me to make my own way in the world. And, it seemed, the moment had come.

Obediently, I tucked the offending curls back into their pins, though I had little hope of them obliging me for long, and followed my grandfather across the hall, where the afternoon sunlight lay in golden bars on the flagged floor, and into the study.

A man was there – a *gentleman*, I should say, for his standing in society was immediately apparent. From the top of his powdered wig to the toes of his buckled shoes, everything about his attire spoke of quality. His face was a little red-veined, as if he partook regularly of spirits rather than porter, and a concertina of chins and a rounded stomach beneath the tight-fitting silk of his breeches suggested that he

5

kept a good table and did not stint himself of the pleasures it afforded.

'Mr Paterson.' My grandfather came close to genuflecting before him. 'May I present my granddaughter, Davina. Davina, this is Mr John Paterson of Bristol. A member of the City Corporation, and also of the Association of Merchant Venturers. You know what the association is, don't you?'

'Yes, of course.' I could hardly live within twenty miles of the City and Port of Bristol and not know of the existence of the Association of Merchant Venturers, the elite band of businessmen who held the trade, and the city itself, in the palm of their hand. I did not know exactly what they did, of course, only that they were both wealthy and powerful.

So, I thought, if this Mr Paterson were indeed to offer me a position, I would have to leave the beautiful Cotswold countryside and move to the city. But at least, judging by his appearance, the house I would live in would be a fine one, and perhaps the children would not be so bad. I could not imagine this Mr Paterson allowing them to run wild. In fact, I could scarcely imagine Mr Paterson with children at all – or certainly not ones young enough to be in need of a governess. He must, I thought, be forty-five or so if he was a day; for one thing he looked it; for another I felt sure that it took time to reach the kind of station in life he had clearly achieved. But then, perhaps he had married late, to a much younger wife . . .

As I tried to avoid staring at him, I suddenly became aware that he was equally fixated on me. He was, in fact, looking me up and down with a frankness that surprised me, his eyes narrowed and speculative, his full lips half-smiling.

'Miss Grimes,' he said. His voice was rich and rolling. 'I am indeed honoured to make your acquaintance at last. I have heard so much about you from your Cousin Theo.'

Cousin Theo. Son of my grandfather's older brother, Charles, who was himself a merchant in Bristol, though not quite of the standing of this gentleman, I thought. Theo had followed his father into the trade, and was now managing all his affairs. It must be he who had put my name forward for this position.

'Mr Paterson,' I responded, hoping that the colour that had risen in my cheeks under his scrutiny was not too plainly obvious. 'The honour is mine.'

'Yes. Well.' For another long moment his eyes dwelt on my face, then the half-smile broadened into a full smile of apparent satisfaction, and he turned to my grandfather. 'A charming young lady indeed. Yes, I am well satisfied.'

'I'm very glad to hear it.' My grandfather was smiling too, the benign expression I had seen him turn on rich parishioners after an Easter Sunday service, at once gracious and ingratiating. 'Davina is a beauty, is she not?'

My colour heightened; this time I felt sure it must be noticeable. But what, I wondered, had beauty to do with anything, even given that it were true? Personally, I always thought that my mouth was too wide for beauty, my nose too short and tip-tilted, my eyes too slanting. But whatever, I could not see that such things were of any importance in the order of attributes that were necessary, or even desirable, in a governess. I had expected questions as to my suitability to teach children to read, write and do sums, and perhaps even some discussion as to the values I would try to instil in them, but not an assessment of my physical appearance.

'Yes,' Mr Paterson said, playing with his malacca cane. 'Yes, I think we shall get along very well. And what are your feelings on the matter, Miss Grimes?'

'I have scarcely had time to form any,' I replied frankly. 'I have to admit to a lack of experience, but I am more than willing to apply myself to learning the skills required of me.'

I saw my grandfather's jaw drop. Surely he had not expected me to pass myself off as an experienced governess? I thought. In my opinion, honesty was the best policy by far.

'A forthright woman!' Mr Paterson said. 'Admirable! It certainly makes a pleasant change from some of the simpering females of my acquaintance, who would sooner die than call a spade a spade. The girl is a credit to you, Reverend. You have done a fine job with her.'

'I think Davina's demeanour is more the result of her mother's influence than mine,' Grandfather said stiffly. 'She has been with us a mere two years, and was already nineteen years old when she came into the care of her grandmother and me.'

'Well, whatever.' Mr Paterson mopped his face with his lace-edged handkerchief; above it, his eyes were still focused on my face. 'So, my dear Miss Grimes, I take it that you are happy with the arrangement?'

I lifted my chin, meeting his gaze levelly. 'You are offering me the position, then?'

He frowned slightly. 'Position . . . ?'

'Of governess,' I said.

His frown deepened, then, to my utter bewilderment, he threw back his head and laughed.

'Oh, my dear Miss Grimes! We seem to be talking at cross purposes here! I thought it was unusual, to say the least of it, for a lady, however liberated, to answer me in the vein you did! You are under the impression that I am interviewing you with a view to taking up a post as governess?'

'Well yes, certainly . . .' So confused was I, I did not know what to say.

'Oh no, I'm afraid you are much mistaken! The late Mrs Paterson and I were, unfortunately, never blessed with children. She was never strong. No, I am not looking for an employee, my dear. I am seeking a wife. It's not a job I am offering. It is a proposal of marriage.'

In all my life, as far as I can recall – though, heaven knows, that is not far – I have never swooned. But in that moment I believe I came close to it. The blood rushed to my face and drained away again; the familiar study, lined with shelves of theological books, seemed to swim before my eyes. One hand went to my throat, with the other I steadied myself against my grandfather's desk, scattering the pile of papers that comprised, I think, an unfinished sermon.

The shock was enormous, and yet, foolishly, uppermost in my mind was the shame at having made an utter fool of myself. The bald statement I had made, about being inexperienced but willing to learn, echoed in my ears, and I wished the floor would open up and swallow me.

No wonder Grandfather had looked so horrified! No wonder Mr Paterson had laughed! Though what there was to laugh at in a young woman apparently behaving in a quite shameless manner, I could not imagine! The blood ebbed and flowed in my face, though my legs felt as cold as ice. I felt sick, and weak with horror.

'Davina? Are you ill? Perhaps you had better sit down . . .' My grandfather's voice seemed to come from beyond the roaring tide, very faint.

'Well, well!' That was Mr Paterson. 'I don't believe I have ever had such an effect on a young woman before!' And then, as my grandfather eased me into the visitor's chair, which occupied the opposite side of the desk to his own: 'Is it as a result of her accident? Does she suffer these turns often?'

'Oh no, no! I have never seen her like this before. Her recovery seems complete, I assure you!' my grandfather said hastily. He seemed anxious to reassure Mr Paterson as regarded the state of my health, I thought, as if some defect had been uncovered in a brood mare he was selling at market. To my embarrassment was added a sense of outrage that they could discuss me thus, just as if I were not here at all.

And clearly this was not the first time that I had been under discussion! Without my knowledge or consent, marriage had been talked about – marriage between me and this stranger! First, presumably, with Cousin Theo and perhaps Great-Uncle Charles too, and then with my grandfather. I had been brought to the study for this Mr Paterson to look me over, and all without a word of explanation! In order to save my feelings, presumably, had I failed to pass muster! Oh, the indignity of it!

Somehow, the rush of pure anger at the position in which I had been placed brought me to my senses. I jumped to my feet, scattering the pages of Grandfather's sermon.

'Really, Grandfather, I do think you could have acquainted me with the true purpose of Mr Paterson's visit!' I cried passionately. 'Your reticence has placed me in an intolerable position! I know that women are regarded as no better than chattels, but even so, I do think you could have been honest with me. As for you, Mr Paterson . . .' My eyes flared green fire at him. 'If you think it is amusing to allow me to think I was being interviewed as a prospective governess when in fact you were measuring whether I was good enough to become your wife . . . well, I think it quite despicable! And I should tell you that, when I marry, it will be to a man I love, not someone old enough to be my father, however rich and influential he may be.'

I paused for breath, and Mr Paterson, to my outrage and disbelief, laughed again.

'Bravo, Miss Grimes! You are a spirited woman as well as a beautiful one – if not perhaps as liberated as I first thought! I think you would make me an excellent wife – and one who would certainly raise an eyebrow or two in Bristol society. I can see you are not much taken with the idea just now, but don't be in too much of a hurry to turn my proposal down. Old enough to be your father I may be, but marriage to me would not be without its advantages. Think about it, talk it over with your grandparents, and let me have your answer when you are ready. I have waited a good long while to replace my dear departed wife. I can wait a little longer.'

Before I could withdraw my hand, he took it and kissed it, his lips moist and fleshy on my skin.

'I very much hope, Miss Grimes, that you will give my proposal your favourable consideration. Your grandfather is, I know, fully aware of the advantages such a move would afford you, as are your Great Uncle Charles and Cousin Theo. Well, clearly so, since they brokered the arrangement. I hope you will come to see the advantages too when they have been fully explained to you. In the meantime . . .' He kissed my hand again. 'I shall have to content myself with fervent expectation and try to be patient.'

He left the room, and my grandfather went with him. I could hear the rise and fall of their voices in the hall, but the roaring in my ears prevented me from hearing exactly what was said.

I merely sat motionless, still in too great a state of shock to be capable of any coherent thought.

'You could scarcely hope for a better match, Davina,' my grandfather said.

And: 'Your grandfather is right, my dear,' my grandmother added.

I would not have expected her to say differently. She was a meek soul, who always agreed with every word he uttered, as if each and every one carried the same weight as the Bible texts he quoted from the pulpit at Sunday services.

'Mr Paterson is a far better prospect than ever we could have hoped for,' Grandfather went on. 'You know that we cannot afford much by way of a dowry, but that is of scant importance to a gentleman of his means. It is company he seeks.'

'And a wife young enough to improve his standing among his peers,' I said, a little sharply, for I was still too shocked to think about guarding my tongue.

'Do you want to remain a maiden lady forever?' my grandmother asked. 'It's no life for a woman, Davina. Believe me, no life at all.'

'I had hoped to marry for love,' I protested.

My grandmother gave a small, strangled gasp, and my grandfather shook his head despairingly.

'That was your mother's ambition – and look where it led her! To a life of poverty and hardship and an early grave.'

I could scarcely argue. I knew nothing whatever of my mother beyond what they had chosen to tell me, and I felt sure there was a great deal they preferred to keep hidden. But it did not stop me from longing, deep down, for a match with a man who could make my heart beat faster; a love that, for all I knew, existed only in fairy tales.

'How could you have taken things this far and never so much as mentioned it to me?' I demanded of my grandfather. 'Can you not imagine the shock it was to me to be suddenly

11

brought face to face with a man I have never set eyes on before and to be inspected for marriage as if I were a prize heifer going to market?'

'We thought it was for the best,' my grandfather said stubbornly. 'We thought that until Mr Paterson had seen, and approved of you, we should not raise your hopes.'

I laughed shortly. 'Hopes! I would never hope for marriage with such a man!'

'Davina, you are being foolish and short-sighted,' my grandfather said. 'As I explained earlier, Mr Paterson is a member of the Merchant Venturers of Bristol, highly respected in every way. It is very fortunate that Theo happened to hear that he was seeking a wife, and naturally he thought of you at once.'

'Why *naturally*?' I demanded. 'I thought Theo and I were friends! Now, it seems, he thought of me as a stray puppy for whom it is necessary to find a home!'

'What nonsense, Davina!' Grandfather said. 'He knew your grandmother and I had hopes of making a good marriage for you, that's all.' I pursed my lips, and he went on: 'We want to see you secure and settled. You are twenty-one years old, Davina. You should have a home and a husband, not waste the best years of your life buried here in the countryside with only ourselves for company. That way lies trouble . . .' He broke off, and I knew that once again he was thinking of my mother.

'But we would only approve a marriage that was truly in your best interests,' he went on after a moment. 'And this . . . This truly is a wonderful opportunity. Mr Paterson has a fine house, well above the city and overlooking the gorge. Until recently he was a neighbour of Charles' in Queen's Square, but he has had this house built especially. The new trend, it seems, is to move away from the docks to where the air is much fresher and cleaner, and Mr Paterson blamed his first wife's ill-health, and even her death, on the situation of his previous residence. Now, why, up on the Heights, you would think yourself still in the countryside.'

I said nothing. I could not imagine the air in an industrial

12

port could ever smell as sweet as the breeze that blew, grass-scented, from the Cotswold Hills.

'He is a wealthy man,' my grandfather went on, ticking off Mr Paterson's assets on his fingers as if he were praying with rosary beads. 'He has a fleet of ships, a thriving business trading sugar and spirits and other marketable commodities. He has more money in the bank than most men could dream of, with ready access to credit should he ever need it. And as to his lifestyle . . . he has fine carriages and servants. He has connections in high places right up to ministers in government. Socially he mixes with the landed gentry, so you would be invited to grand balls and even, in the season, to London itself. You would want for nothing, Davina.'

I pressed my fingers to my temple where a little ache had begun, throbbing like a dull echo of the terrible, debilitating headaches that had consumed me in the months following my accident.

What of love? I wanted to say, but did not. I had already dared to mention love and seen how little my grandparents trusted such a naive aspiration.

'I do not know,' I said instead. 'It's such a huge step. To agree to be the wife of a man I scarcely know . . .'

I broke off, the enormity of what I would be entering into dawning on me in dizzying waves like the rush of an incoming tide. If I agreed to this match, which my grandparents were clearly so set upon, I would be setting the course for the whole of my life. There could be no turning back. Any hopes and dreams I had cherished must be set aside for ever. Duty and obedience would rule me – and, of course, Mr Paterson. He had seemed pleasant enough, and certainly it was true I would be well taken care of. I would have security. I would have my own home and my position in society. But could that ever compensate me for the things I would have to eschew? Could it ever be enough?

'Davina.' My grandmother caught my hand, holding it between her own small work-worn ones. 'You are apprehensive, dear, of course you are. But truly, your grandfather and I think it is an opportunity you must not allow to pass you

13

by. We worry about you so much. We are getting older, and we shall not always be here for you. Can't you understand the sense of responsibility we feel?'

'Yes, of course,' I said. 'But I could take care of myself. I don't want you to feel responsible for me.'

I sensed her withdrawal, and knew I had hurt her.

'I'm grateful, of course – so grateful. If you had not taken me in, I don't know where I would be now – the poorhouse, I shouldn't wonder.'

'If you had survived at all,' my grandfather said grimly. 'When I think of the long hours your grandmother sat beside your bed, willing you to recover – and the prayers we said together. When I think of how she tended you – washed you, fed you as if you were a baby, provided for your every need . . .'

'I know.' Love and gratitude washed over me in a warm flood tide, and with it a sense of guilt that I could scarcely explain, even to myself. 'I do know. And I shall never be able to repay you adequately.'

'We do not need repaying,' my grandmother said. Her lip trembled. 'It was as if Elizabeth had come back to us. As if we had been given a second chance . . .'

'Oh, Grandmama . . .' The guilt was sharper now; I knew then that I was bearing it for my mother, who had caused them so much pain. 'What can I say?'

'You can say you will wed Mr Paterson,' my grandfather said grimly. 'We shall know then that you, at least, are settled and set up for life. We shall be satisfied that at least we did not fail in our duty to *you*.'

'It would set our minds at rest,' my grandmother added softly. 'We could sleep easy in our beds at night. And oh, Davina, we should be so proud of you!'

That, I supposed, was the crux of the matter. My mother had brought them nothing but shame and heartache and they were not only afraid that I would do the same, they also wanted to hold their heads high and feel pride.

I looked at them, sitting there in the fading light, and noticed for the first time how old they looked. Older by far

14

than when I had first come here two years ago, and more frail. My grandfather might bluster and preach damnation, but the fire had gone from him. And my sweet grandmother looked so fragile and vulnerable, her bones no bigger than a bird's, her little face creased into pouches and hollows, the hair beneath her cap snow-white and fine as threads of cobweb.

I had not known them at all until I was nineteen years old, so many years lost that could never be regained, but I had learned to love them. They had taken me in, cared for me, nursed me back to health. And now they were begging me to make them proud, where my mother had brought them only shame. Their peace of mind was in my hands now.

'Very well,' I heard myself say. 'If you think it is the right thing . . .'

'Oh Davina, we do!'

'I can send word to Mr Paterson that your answer will be yes?'

I nodded.

But in my lap I clasped my hands together so tightly that my nails dug crescents into the skin, and a dark abyss seemed to be opening up before me, an abyss of trepidation and uncertainty, an unknown future as well hidden from me as my past.

I had no memory, you see, of the first nineteen years of my life. None whatsoever. For all I could remember, I might have drawn my first breath when I eventually regained consciousness in the cold little bedroom at the Cotswold rectory where I had, apparently, been taken following the accident.

I had, the physician said, suffered severe injury to my head as well as to my body, and though, with time and my grandmother's tender care, my bruises had faded and my broken bones healed, the damage to my mind had been lasting. I could remember nothing of the accident itself, and that, I suppose, might be merciful. But it was distressing to me that neither did I have any memory of my previous life.

15

No warm memories of childhood, no recollection of how I had spent my growing years, no joys, no sorrows, no friends, no enemies. Sometimes there came the briefest snatch of haunting recollection – a perfume that stirred some deeply buried joy or sadness, a glimpse of a face seen through a mist, a sensation I seemed to have experienced before, a place that felt vaguely familiar. But always it was gone like a fading dream before I could grasp hold of it, leaving me wondering if it was real or merely a figment of my imagination, and for the most part there was nothing. Nothing at all. My life, as I knew it, had begun and ended with my grandparents; all I knew about myself was what they had told me.

And they had, quite frankly, been unable – or unwilling – to tell me very much at all. It was painful for them, I knew, and beyond the bare facts they preferred not to talk about the great sadness, and shame, which my mother had brought on them.

They told me, because they had to, no doubt, how she had run off with a strolling player, who was, presumably, my father. He had, it seems, a wife already, so he was unable to make an honest woman of her, a fact which added to their shame. They claimed not even to know his name, though that may rather be something they preferred to forget. They knew of my existence, but had never seen me – either they had cut my mother off, or their obvious disapproval had so alienated her that she stayed away of her own volition, I was not clear which. However it had come about, our lives had run on quite separate courses until the fateful day of the terrible accident.

As with so much of the detail of my former life, my grandparents had been able to tell me little. All they knew, they said, was that the carriage in which my mother and I had been travelling had run off the road and rolled down a steep incline. My mother had been killed instantly, they said, and I had been found senseless and badly injured in the wreckage.

'But how did you come to hear of it?' I had asked. 'How did you know that the injured girl was me – your granddaughter?'

16

They had answered vaguely – the accident had occurred not many miles from my grandfather's parish, at Brocksbury Hill, and someone who had come upon it had recognized my mother. As soon as they heard of it, my grandparents had me brought home. But I sensed their discomfort talking of it, and it had crossed my mind to wonder if they were indeed telling me all they knew.

Pursuing the matter was useless, however. I simply ran up against the blank wall of their reluctance to discuss it, and I was left with many unanswered questions.

Since the accident had happened locally, was it possible my mother had been on her way to try to mend her bridges with her parents? Or had we already been to see them and been turned away? Who was my father – and where was he? Why had he not appeared on the scene to care for me and mourn my mother – bury her, even? Her grave was in a quiet corner of my grandfather's churchyard – to my knowledge no one ever visited it but my grandparents and myself.

Sometimes I would go there to lay flowers and sit for a while in silence whilst the sun splintered through the branches of the tulip tree which overhung the grave, and the wild bees droned lazily in the long grass, and I would try to communicate with her, feel her presence, find some answers to the myriad questions regarding my former life.

But nothing came. Not even a sense of peace. The questions only plagued me more urgently, and the feeling of utter desolation was the greater. A name on a tombstone – that was all that was left to me of the mother who had given me life and raised me.

Elizabeth Grimes. Thirty-six years. Dear daughter of Winifred and the Revd Joseph Grimes.

So little. So very little! I could not even remember her face, though, from a likeness my grandparents had of her, painted when she was a young girl, I could see that I had taken after her, and now, two years later, when I pictured her, it seemed to me that I remembered her face as being very like the one that I saw when I looked into my mirror.

I had loved her, that much I knew, but had there been others whom I had loved too, and forgotten completely? There must have been, surely, but where were they now? Why had they abandoned me? The wondering was a pain in me that refused to go away, though I had learned to live with it.

As for me, I had no real sense of self, for, with no past, it is difficult to be whole in the present. Perhaps that is one of the reasons I was prepared to agree to the match my grandparents had arranged for me. How could I, with my impaired brain, be capable of deciding for myself? Easier to go along with the judgement of those who have a lifetime of experience upon which to draw.

But mostly, I knew, it was because of guilt and gratitude. I owed my grandparents everything; it was my duty to do as they wished and make up, in some small way, for the pain my mother had caused them. My debt was hers as well as my own. They wished me to marry Mr Paterson; to please them, I would do so.

Because the only love I had ever known was the love I bore for them.

Two

The moment I had signalled my agreement, it seemed, things were set in motion with frightening speed. Whatever he might have said, Mr Paterson was not a patient man. Though I assumed he had to wait long months for his ships to return home from their voyages to Africa and the West Indies, in his personal life, once a decision had been reached, he believed in acting upon it.

'There's no point in shilly-shallying,' he said with his customary bluntness when he next came to discuss arrangements. 'I'm a man of action and I have always found it pays off. Take my new house – I bought the land on impulse, for I liked what I saw. Now everyone else of any note is following suit. The price of land has risen fourfold – they all want to live off Park Street or in Clifton. And it's the same with marriage. I've no time for long engagements – and I don't want to give Davina the chance to change her mind, now do I?'

He smiled slyly, patting my knee in a manner I found overfamiliar – and I noted that he had progressed very quickly to calling me by my given name too. He had even asked me to call him 'John', but it did not seem proper to me, and I could not believe I would ever be able to think of one so much older than myself as anything other than 'Mr Paterson'. But I must, I supposed, just as I would have to accustom myself to other liberties, such as I preferred not to think about.

'Davina will certainly not go back on her word,' my grandfather said, interrupting my thoughts. 'She has agreed to be your wife, and your wife she will be.'

'Good. Good!' Mr Paterson patted my knee again, and I

managed to move towards the corner of the sofa, out of his reach, without, I hoped, it being too obvious.

'I think,' he said, 'that Davina should come to Bristol at once.'

'Before the marriage takes place?' My grandmother looked shocked. 'I'm not sure that would be proper.'

'It would be much easier to make the arrangements if she was there,' Mr Paterson pointed out. 'She'll want a new gown especially for the occasion, I expect – I never yet heard of a woman who didn't want a new gown on the slightest excuse, never mind her own wedding. And she will be able to make the acquaintance of some of my friends, so that they will not be strangers to her on the great day. I really feel it would be for the best. Could she not stay with Charles in Queen's Square? He and Theo rattle around in that great house – there must be room for one pretty little one!'

'I'm sure he would be agreeable to that,' Grandfather said, clearly anxious to fall in with whatever Mr Paterson suggested.

'But she cannot go alone,' my grandmother put in, surprisingly firm for her. 'She must have a chaperone. Perhaps Linnie could accompany her.'

Aunt Linnie was my grandfather's sister, ten years and more his junior. She was a spinster lady, a little, chattering, bird-like woman, and in my unkinder moments it did seem to me that she had been hidden away behind the door when brains were handed out. But she was kind-hearted and cheerful, and I could well imagine she would leap at the opportunity to spend a few weeks in Bristol, since she had scarcely set foot outside rural Gloucestershire in the whole of her life.

'That would seem to be the answer,' Grandfather said, satisfied. 'I'll write to Charles and ask if Davina and Linnie can stay with him.'

'Why not put pen to paper now?' Mr Paterson suggested. 'I can deliver the letter to him in person.'

Grandfather nodded. 'As you wish.'

'Oh yes, I wish.' Mr Paterson glanced at me again, and

20

the look on his face made me squirm with discomfort. No, whatever he might say to the contrary, he was not a patient man. And with all my heart I wished I had not agreed to this union.

I had never before been to the house in Queen's Square, and I had no memory of ever having been to Bristol. I had wondered if anything about it would jog my memory, and indeed, as we drove through the busy cobbled streets, they did seem vaguely familiar to me, as did the awful, pervasive smell that hung over the city. It came from the river and the docks, I supposed – the stench of garbage and filth all overlaid with sickly sweetness from the cargos of sugar. It turned my stomach, that smell, and I thought that perhaps it was something I might well have wanted to forget, if indeed I had known it.

I glanced at Aunt Linnie, wondering what she was making of it. She had a lace-edged handkerchief pressed to her lips, but, above it, her eyes were bright with excitement.

'Isn't it thrilling!' she exclaimed from behind the handkerchief. 'Oh Davina, I've never had such an adventure before! I want to see everything there is to see whilst I'm here! There will be time, won't there, between your dress fittings and other appointments?'

I smiled faintly. 'Yes, Aunt Linnie, I'm sure there will be plenty of time,' I assured her.

The problem, as I soon discovered, was not time, but transport.

Great-Uncle Charles – a crusty, sharp-spoken version of my grandfather – had sent his carriage to Gloucestershire to collect us but he quickly made it clear it could not be spared on a regular basis.

'I'm not wealthy enough to be able to keep two carriages on the go,' he complained. 'I don't have the wherewithal of some. John Paterson will have to send a carriage down for your use – or pay to hire one. He can afford it.'

I could not help but notice the bitter resentment in his

tone, and wonder at it. To my unpractised eye, it seemed Great-Uncle Charles was very well off indeed, with far more than his brother, my grandfather, had ever had or could hope for. The house, built of buttery yellow stone and overlooking a central green, was furnished with good-quality furniture and decorated with the sort of artefacts that came from trading in foreign parts, there were several servants, and the wine flowed free as we dined off the fat of the land. But, I supposed, the more one had the more one was inclined to want, and envy was not confined to those who had nothing at all.

'I'm sure Mr Paterson will provide for anything we need, Uncle,' I said. 'The last thing I want is to put you to any inconvenience.'

He humphed and hawed a little at this, as if we were indeed putting him out simply by being there, and I found myself wishing Cousin Theo was at home. He was, it seemed, away on business, and would be gone for at least a week.

Though I did not know Theo very well, I had always found him to be very good company. He had a ready, and rather wicked, sense of humour, unlike all my other, rather straight-laced relatives, and, almost unfailingly, he could make me laugh. It was always good, too, to have the company of one so much closer to me in age than the rest of them, particularly when he was as personable as Theo.

The moment the matter of the carriage was mentioned to Mr Paterson, however, he agreed to put one of his own at our disposal.

'Least I can do,' he said magnanimously. 'My future wife must travel in style, eh, Davina? You shall have the new landaulet – just right for you and your aunt – and Thomas to drive you. Thomas will look after you well. I'll bring him in to meet you, if that meets with your approval, Grimes.'

'Oh yes – yes . . .' Great-Uncle Charles said, but the resentment was there again, burning in his rheumy eyes. He turned to Aunt Linnie as Mr Paterson left the room. 'You'd better prepare yourself for a shock, Linnie,' he said, his lip curling a little.

I was puzzled; I had no idea what he meant by that.

But when Mr Paterson returned with Thomas, I understood.

Thomas was black; the first black man I had ever seen in my life.

I had known, of course, that there were black people in England, brought here from their native land to be sold as slaves. I had heard that it was most fashionable in London society to have a black butler or a little pageboy, and some families even took piccaninnies as playmates for their own children. But such modern ways had not reached the wilds of Gloucestershire. And though I knew Great-Uncle Charles, Theo and Mr Paterson sailed their boats to Africa and the West Indies, it had never occurred to me that they might be involved in the trade.

On the few occasions when I had thought about it at all, I had found myself instinctively repelled by the idea that human beings could be bought and sold like sugar and spirits, but when I had said as much, Grandfather had pointed out they were heathens, and more likely to be saved here in a Christian country than if they remained in their own uncivilized land. Since there was nothing I could do about it, I had taken the coward's way out and put my misgivings to the back of my mind. Now, however, they all came rushing back as I looked at the tall, fine-looking man with sculpted features and a cap of iron-grey woolly curls, a little too gaunt, but proud and upright in his royal-blue livery.

Great-Uncle Charles had been right, however, to anticipate Aunt Linnie's reaction. Her eyes went wide and she jumped back half a dozen paces, her soft little face contorting into an expression of pure terror.

'Oh!' she gasped with what breath she had left. 'Oh, my life!'

The man called Thomas stood motionless, eyes dark as coals, returning her frightened gaze with something which might almost have been disdain.

'Don't be alarmed, Miss Grimes!' Mr Paterson said heartily. 'There's nothing to fear.'

23

'But . . . what is it?' Aunt Linnie squeaked.

'A fully grown African male,' Mr Paterson replied. A corner of his full-lipped mouth was ticking, as if he were trying to control a desire to laugh. 'I assure you he is fully house-trained, Miss Grimes. And he speaks very good English. My late wife taught him herself.'

'Oh, but I never saw such a thing!' Aunt Linnie exclaimed. 'I feel quite faint with shock! Why, he looks like a joint of meat left too long in the oven!'

Mr Paterson did laugh then, unable to contain his mirth a moment longer.

'You hear that, Thomas? You spent too long in the sun before the slavers came to rescue you,' he chortled.

I suppose there was something quite funny about Aunt Linnie's small, horrified face, but I failed to find it amusing. I saw only a proud man who stood impassive in the face of such indignity, his dark eyes burning with something like anger, yet managing to retain his dignity. He did not look like a savage to me, and my sense of unease that people like him could be taken against their will and owned, body and soul, by people like Mr Paterson, made me turn away, ashamed.

'Have no fear, Miss Grimes, if Thomas fails to afford you the respect you deserve, he will be soundly beaten,' Mr Paterson said carelessly. And to the slave: 'You hear that, Thomas? If I hear one word from these ladies that you have frightened or upset them in any way, you will be beaten and chained in the cellar for a week. Savvy?'

'Oh my life!' Aunt Linnie said again, but I said nothing at all.

I resolved to treat this black giant as I would any other human being. Certainly Mr Paterson would not hear one word against him from me, for I was uncomfortably certain that Mr Paterson was not given to making idle threats.

Again I found myself wishing with all my heart that my grandparents had not been so set upon this match. Again I wondered if I should have protested against it more vehemently. But none of my reasons for going along with it had changed one jot. I had made them happy by my acquiescence, and I should try to be happy too – or at least take comfort from knowing it.

And in any case, it was far too late to go back on my word. I was to marry Mr Paterson, for better or for worse, and that was all there was to it.

The days passed by in a whirl of fittings and appointments interspersed with leisurely sightseeing and social gatherings, when I was introduced to Mr Paterson's friends and their wives, all of whom, it seemed, were to be guests at the wedding. The very thought of what a grand occasion it was to be began to make me feel more nervous than the marriage itself. I was not used to being the centre of so much attention and never had been, I felt sure, for the prospect of walking up the aisle of the cathedral before so many curious eyes made me feel sick with apprehension.

I did not take after my father, clearly, I thought wryly. If, as my grandparents had said, he had been a strolling player, he must have enjoyed appearing before an audience! No, it must be that I followed after my mother in temperament as well as appearance. And yet . . .

That was not right either, I thought. My mother had possessed the courage to go against my grandparents' wishes and follow her heart. For the first time I thought of the enormity of what she had done, leaving all that was comfortable and familiar, and running away to be with my father. For the first time, instead of feeling ashamed, I saw her bold action as romantic and brave, and I could not help feeling that she would not have approved of me meekly marrying a man I did not love, and could not imagine I ever would, simply to please my grandparents. Or had she lived to regret her headstrong behaviour? What sort of a man had my father turned out to be? Perhaps he had led her a merry dance and she had, in the end, decided to return home and try to make peace with the family she had shamed and abandoned. Perhaps that was the reason my father had never come looking for me – because he

25

had turned out to be the no-good wastrel my grandparents had always thought him.

My head ached just thinking about it, that persistent throb at my temple that could sometimes still send a jab of searing pain like a red-hot bolt being driven into my skull, and I tried to banish the fruitless, worrying conjecture just as I tried to banish my trepidation at marrying Mr Paterson, and concentrate instead on the arrangements, and on being pleasant to his friends.

They were a strange crowd, I thought. The men were bluff, confident, and a little arrogant, as only those who are used to success and the respect that comes with it can be. One or two were real gentry, a lord here, a sir there, and the others aped their demeanour, so that they gave the appearance of gentry too. But I sensed a rough edge hidden beneath the surface, and a certain ruthlessness. These men had made their fortunes in a hard world, most likely walking roughshod over anyone who got in their way, climbing on the shoulders of lesser men. And they would not be prepared to relinquish a penny piece, if anything, they would do whatever was necessary to grow ever richer. I sensed this ruthlessness in Mr Paterson too. He was just the same. And was I not living proof of it? Mr Paterson had wanted to marry me, and Mr Paterson had got his way.

As for the wives of his friends, I liked them even less than the men. They were very much given to airs and graces, and forever trying to better one another with the latest fashions, both in their dress and in the furnishing of their grand houses. This seemed to be their sole aim in life. That and spending their husbands' money!

But perhaps some of my dislike came from feeling they looked down upon me, a country mouse with no dowry to speak of and no knowledge of the finer points of how society conducted itself.

Well, I thought, I would show them! I would show them all! I might be apprehensive about that walk down the aisle, but none of them would see it. I would carry myself with pride, knowing that, in the watered-silk gown that was being made for me by the finest dressmaker in Bristol, I was the equal of any of them, and looked far nicer. And if my hair came out of its pins, as it almost always did, I would hold my head high and pretend it was the latest fashion. And not one of them would know that inside I was shaking with nerves and heavy of heart.

I would make my grandparents proud of me if it was the last thing I did!

'I should very much like to visit the hot well and pump room, Davina,' Aunt Linnie said.

It was a fine, bright morning, and today we had no appointments to keep, no fittings to attend, nothing but the day spread out before us to do as we pleased.

I frowned. 'I didn't know that Bristol had a spa,' I said.

'Oh yes! It's a wonderful place, I've heard. And the water is so beneficial! I think it might cool these hot flushes that have been troubling me . . .' Aunt Linnie pressed her fingers to her cheeks, which certainly looked a little rosier than usual.

'It would do you good to have a glass too, Davina,' she ran on. 'You have been very pale these last few days, not at all yourself. Are you not sleeping, dear?'

I was not sleeping well; I was troubled by improbable dreams and then waking with the first pale light of dawn to lie tossing and turning whilst the chaotic thoughts chased one another around my brain. But I was not about to admit it to Aunt Linnie – nor to drink so much as a drop of the spa water if I could help it! Once, when I had been recuperating from my accident, my grandparents had taken me to the pump room in Bath with the idea that the waters would benefit me, and, frankly, I had found the taste of them quite disgusting.

'I'm perfectly well, Aunt,' I said. 'But, of course, if you would like to go to this hot well, then we shall.'

'Oh Davina, you are such a good girl! Mr Paterson is a very lucky man. You are so very different from your mother! Oh, but she was a wild creature! She cared for no one but herself, you know . . .' She broke off, the flush in her cheeks deepening. 'Oh, I'm not supposed to talk about your mother.

27

I promised Joseph I would not. There are so many things I am not supposed to talk about, it quite makes my head spin!'

I frowned. 'What things?' I asked.

'Oh . . .' She fluttered helplessly. 'Things, Davina. Just things. Don't press me, please. You confuse me, and if I told you what they were, then I'd have broken my promise already, wouldn't I?'

'Aunt Linnie . . .'

'No – no!' She hurried to the door. 'We shall have to send for Mr Paterson's carriage, I suppose. It's such a nuisance Charles didn't provide us with one. Why he is suddenly pretending poverty I don't know. He has always had nothing but the best.'

'Perhaps he liked you to think he was better off than he really was,' I suggested.

Aunt Linnie did not respond to this. 'I do think it would be best if we went to the pump room nice and early,' she said. 'It's less likely to be crowded. And in any case, we want to make the most of the day. I think it could turn thundery later on. My head feels quite tight, and that is always a sign.'

She fluttered out, leaving me puzzled and frustrated as to what she had meant by her remarks about 'things she had been asked not to talk about'. That Grandfather had not wanted her to discuss my mother with me, I could well believe. He was always reluctant to so much as speak her name. But Aunt Linnie had said that there were other things. She had never made mention of them before – but then, until she had accompanied me to Bristol, I had never spent any time alone with her, and, since we had arrived, she had been so full of her 'adventure' that she had thought of nothing else. Now . . .

Oh, it was typically Aunt Linnie, of course, enjoying her little secrets and getting everything wrong. But I was not entirely convinced. A little simple she might be, but there was something she had not wanted to tell me. And with the blank wall of memory loss shutting off the whole of my previous life, I was anxious indeed to know what it might be.

*   *   *

28

Mr Paterson's carriage arrived at the front door of the house in Queen's Square within the hour. Thomas, the handsome black slave, was driving it. He was as polite as ever, but equally unapproachable, with that silent dignity which almost suggested that he felt himself superior to us despite the fact that he was owned, body and soul, by Mr Paterson. His chiselled features might almost have been carved from stone, I thought, as he handed us courteously into the carriage and resumed his place in the driver's seat.

Very soon we were beside the river. The tide was out this morning, leaving thick banks of mud, and the smell I found so offensive wafted on the gentle breeze. But the sun glinted on the white limestone cliffs of the Avon Gorge, and the thick woodland on either side was lush and green. As we drove along the little road which hugged the bank, I saw a riverside walk, shaded by trees, and a colonnade of shops, built of red brick and fronted by white pillars.

'Oh, we must look at the shops!' Aunt Linnie cried excitedly. 'Everything here must be the height of fashion, I'm sure!'

I did not have any great interest in fashion – so long as I looked presentable, that was good enough for me, and the endless fitting for my wedding gown and my trousseau had used up any enthusiasm I might otherwise have had. But it would have been cruel to deny Aunt Linnie her fun. All too soon she would be buried in the wilds of Gloucestershire again, whilst I . . .

I pushed the thought aside, and called to Thomas: 'Thank you. We'll walk from here.'

He pulled over and handed us down, then followed discreetly as Aunt Linnie and I walked along the colonnade of shops, Aunt Linnie exclaiming in delight at the pretty goods she saw in the windows – hats, gloves, accessories to grace the grandest occasion.

Beyond the shops was the pump room itself, much smaller than the one at Bath, but busy nevertheless with invalids come to take the water for the good of their health, and social visitors, laughing, chatting to friends, and promenading.

When I had paid the entrance fee, we went inside, where a string quartet was entertaining the visitors.

'Oh will you listen to that music!' Aunt Linnie cried rapturously. 'This could be the very same quartet Mr Paterson has engaged to play at your wedding breakfast, Davina!'

'I should hardly think so. I imagine they are fully occupied here,' I said shortly.

'But isn't this place owned by the Merchant Venturers?' Aunt Linnie persisted. 'Mr Paterson might well have arranged for them to play at your wedding instead!'

I said nothing. I was feeling dreadfully claustrophobic suddenly, as if the music had suddenly transported me forwards in time to the day of my wedding. The quartet would not be the same one, I felt sure, but it would be very similar, and the haunting strings seemed to scrape on my nerves, evoking something close to panic.

The throbbing pain was there again, too, in my temple, fiercer than it had been for some time, making me a little nauseous and blurring my vision.

'Davina?' Aunt Linnie said. 'Are you sure you are well? You really are very pale . . .'

'I'm perfectly well,' I said, but my voice seemed to come from a long way off.

'Oh dear, I do hope you are not going to have a relapse!' Aunt Linnie said, with some agitation. 'I have heard of the effects of a blow to the head returning long afterwards, with dreadful consequences . . . Dreadful! And, of course, none of us knows what illnesses or accidents you may have suffered as a child . . . It's most worrying, Davina. I really think it would be of benefit to you to take a glass of the waters . . .'

The memory of that strange metallic taste made me feel even more nauseous.

'No,' I said. 'It's just that this place is so stuffy. It's fresh air I need.'

'But we've only just arrived!' Aunt Linnie said petulantly. 'There's so much more to see! And look – isn't that Mrs Jotham who used to live at Uley? It is, I'm sure! She moved to Bristol to be near her son after Mr Jothan died. Yes, it is her! I'd so much like to speak to her! She will be so surprised to see me here, and I can catch up on all her news!'

It was so typical of Aunt Linnie, I thought, professing concern for my health one minute, running off at a tangent the next. It was impossible for her to concentrate on one subject for any length of time – particularly if it was something she found uncomfortable or distressing. Aunt Linnie liked everything to be pleasant and undemanding.

'Stay as long as you like, Aunt,' I said. 'Talk to Mrs Jotham, take the waters, listen to the quartet, whatever pleases you. But I have to go outside, in the fresh air.'

'Alone?' Aunt Linnie sounded scandalized. 'Oh Davina, I'm not sure you should go out in the street *alone*.'

'No harm will come to me, I'm sure,' I said. 'Thomas is nearby with the carriage, in any case. He followed us down here and will be waiting. If I should need him, I only have to call.'

'I suppose so . . .' Aunt Linnie's look told me she still did not entirely trust Thomas. 'Oh, Davina, he does make me feel so dreadfully uncomfortable! He's so big. And so black!'

'All the better to take care of me,' I said a little sharply, for Aunt Linnie's twittering, as well as the wretched pump room, was grating on my nerves. 'Mr Paterson would never have entrusted us to his care if he were not perfectly reliable. And in any case, I'm quite used to looking after myself.'

The moment the words were out, I did not know why I had uttered them. In the last two years I had scarcely been allowed out of my grandparents' sight. Could it be that unwittingly I was referring to my life before the accident? Was this how memory would eventually return to me, in tiny fits and starts, until one day everything fitted together like a puzzle? For though it made no sense, and I could not recall a single instance, yet I had the strangest feeling that I had spoken the truth – I *had* been quite used to looking after myself.

'If you don't go and speak to Mrs Jotham soon, you'll miss her,' I said to Aunt Linnie. 'I'll be quite safe, I promise. And I'll see you outside when you're ready to leave.'

31

'If you're sure . . .' But already Aunt Linnie was starting in the direction of her old friend, and I turned and made my way through the thronging crowds to the door.

It was the most enormous relief to emerge into the sunlight and feel the fresh breeze on my cheeks, even if I could still smell the pervasive river stink on it. I could see the carriage drawn up and waiting in the shade of the trees, with Thomas holding the horses, but I turned in the opposite direction. He made me uncomfortable too, though for quite different reasons than those of Aunt Linnie – guilt that another human being could be owned by my future husband, and shame for the outrage that had been perpetrated against him.

In something of a daze I walked towards the shops. Even here, out of earshot of the music of the string quartet, I seemed to hear it still, mournful, painfully sweet, precursor of a future I did not want. A sob rose in my throat. I did not want to marry Mr Paterson, but I was trapped. Trapped by duty. Trapped by guilt. Trapped by honour. Trapped by love . . .

'Rowan!'

It was a man's voice, startled, yet somehow commanding. It must have been commanding, otherwise why would I have taken even the slightest notice of it, preoccupied as I was, and when it could not possibly have anything to do with me. Yet for a brief moment I checked, quite frozen, as if every nerve in my body, every pore, was listening. Then, as suddenly as if it had never happened, I moved on in the direction of the shops.

'Rowan!' the voice called again, and a hand caught at my arm.

This time I could not help but stop.

I turned my head and saw him. And in that moment the most dizzying wave of emotion washed over me. Surprise. Confusion. Joy. Yes, most of all, the greatest sense of joy I have ever experienced. And something else, something I could not put a name to, something half-seen through a mist, like those dreams from which I woke with the frustrating sense that I had almost, but not quite, glimpsed my long-lost past.

Then, just as suddenly, it was gone. All gone. The man was just a stranger to me. A handsome stranger, it was true, but a stranger none the less. And there was nothing left but a feeling of loss so dreadfully overwhelming that I wanted to weep.

I lifted my chin. My eyes met his, hazel eyes, deep-set in a rugged face. His hair was unpowdered, the clothes he wore suggested quality, but no great interest in fashion. He looked a little like a sea captain, as if that face had been weathered by stormy winds and those hazel eyes were used to staring out over the vast and rolling expanse of the oceans. But just now they were fastened on mine, and the expression in them might almost have been disbelief.

'I'm sorry, I think there must be some mistake,' I said.

'Rowan!' His voice was raw with urgency. 'For God's sake, don't play games with me!'

I shook my head. My heart was beating too fast; blood was roaring in my ears.

'My name is not Rowan,' I said. 'My name is Davina. I think, sir, that you have mistaken me for someone else.'

'Oh no!' His hand tightened on my arm. 'I couldn't make such a mistake. Dear God, but I thought . . .'

I was beginning to be frightened. Panic swelled in me, the little pain in my temple was suddenly the red-hot bolt of the early days following the accident, blinding me, almost, with its intensity.

'Please . . . !' I whispered. 'Let me go!'

'Never!'

'Please . . .'

'Is this gentleman bothering you, Miss Grimes?'

Thomas! He must have seen me accosted and come to my aid. Relief flooded me. The big, handsome African was no longer a slave, someone to make me faintly uneasy, but a friend.

'Yes,' I said. My voice was shaking, along with my knees. 'Yes, he is. He seems to think he knows me, but that is quite impossible.'

33

'Unhand the lady.' Thomas spoke quietly, but with an authority that would not be denied.

'Rowan, for the love of God . . . !' For a moment longer the stranger's fingers bit into my flesh, hard enough to bruise it, and there was something like desperation in that rugged, weatherbeaten face.

Somehow I managed to stare him out defiantly, and suddenly, with an oath, he released me.

'Do you truly not know me?'

'I have never met you before in my life. And I told you, my name is not Rowan, but Davina. I'm sorry, but I am not the person you thought me to be.'

'If I am mistaken, then I, too, am sorry. But I am not mistaken! How could I be! I thought her dead, but you . . .'

He was still staring at me, staring as if he were seeing a ghost. Suddenly I could bear his scrutiny no longer.

'Thomas,' I said. 'Please find Aunt Linnie and tell her I am waiting in the carriage. I want to go home.'

I turned and walked away from the stranger, but I could feel his eyes following me. At the carriage step I turned back. He was still there, tall, handsome, enigmatic – and totally disconcerting. For a brief moment I wanted desperately to run back to him, ask him exactly who he thought I was. But my heart was pounding too fast, the pain in my temple was too sharp, I was too afraid.

Yes, most of all, without understanding why, I was afraid. And the fear swallowed me up, draining my strength, robbing me of coherent thought.

I sat in the carriage waiting for Aunt Linnie with the world around me fluid and nebulous, a kaleidoscope of ever-changing patterns and formless emotions. When I dared to look around again, the man was gone.

Three

I could not forget him. Try as I might, I could not forget him. As I sat in the carriage waiting for Aunt Linnie I seemed to see him still, his tall muscular frame, his rugged, weatherbeaten face, his eyes – yes, most of all those hazel eyes, regarding me with surprise that bordered on disbelief and yet, at the same time, seeming to reflect that stab of pure joy which I had experienced in the first moment when I turned and saw him. As we drove back to Queen's Square through the busy streets, I seemed to hear his voice in every hawker's cry.

Rowan.

The name, as well as the voice that had spoken it, seemed to stir some echo deep within me. But for what reason? I was not Rowan, whoever she might be. I was, as I had told him, Davina Grimes. Of course I was! And yet . . .

I had only my grandparents' word for that. Dear God . . . a shiver of ice ran across my burning skin. I had only their word for it that they *were* my grandparents, or indeed any relation to me at all! The whole of my life before I had opened my eyes in the bedroom of the Cotswold rectory was a complete blank to me. They could have told me anything, anything at all, and I would have believed them because I knew no different.

But why would they do such a thing? Certainly they had nothing to gain by it – if anything, taking me in and caring for me had cost them dear. They had nursed me with loving kindness, they had kept me, and I had been a drain on their meagre resources. And I had been able to give them nothing in return. No, it made no sense that they would take a desperately sick and penniless stranger into their home, give her a new identity and feed her a pack of lies about her past. No sense at all, even if I could believe them capable of such a deception. I was who they said I was – Davina Grimes, the child of their own disgraced daughter. I had to be! It was the only identity I knew. If I did not trust them, then who in the whole wide world could I trust?

But still the doubts niggled at me, flapping around and around inside my head like a flock of wheeling ravens. And my grandparents' evasiveness worried me. They had, when it came down to it, told me very little about my past. Was it possible they knew more, far more, than they were willing to admit to?

I thought again of the strange conversation I had had with Aunt Linnie just this morning when she had referred to things she was not supposed to discuss with me. I had put it down to Aunt Linnie being Aunt Linnie – enjoying game-playing as much as any child, finding a sense of self-importance in having secrets that she must not share with anyone, least of all me. Now, instead of seeming amusing, if frustrating, her reticence seemed to me to be almost sinister. She knew something she must not tell. But what?

Could it be that once I had been a girl named Rowan? And had I known a tall, weatherbeaten man with challenging hazel eyes? A man who had evoked a strong, if unidentifiable response in me, brief, yet frighteningly powerful, before it flickered and was gone like a lantern light in the fog?

Who was I?

For the last two years I had had no past, and I had almost grown used to it. Now, suddenly, I felt as if I could no longer be sure, even, of those two years. The whole of my world had shifted beneath my feet once more. I felt as if I stood on quicksand and it was sucking me in.

Somehow I had to learn the truth. Somehow I must find the weatherbeaten man and ask him just who he had thought I was. Maybe by now he would have realized his mistake and I would find I had simply run into another blind alley.

But if he had *not* made a mistake . . . A tremor ran through

36

me, and the pain in my temple was so piercing it almost made me cry out.

Perhaps I was on the verge of discovering the truth about my past. A past my grandparents – if indeed they were my grandparents – had been at great pains to keep from me. And I must find out before I married Mr Paterson. I owed it to him. And, more important still, I owed it to myself.

The carriage came to a stop outside the house in Queen's Square. Thomas handed us down and went to ring the bell for the maid to let us in.

About to follow Aunt Linnie into the palatial tiled hall, a feeling of panic suddenly overcame me, a feeling that, if I went inside the house, the door would close behind me, not just against the outside world, but also against the opportunity this morning had offered me to discover my lost self.

I turned and ran after Thomas, who was climbing back up on to the driver's seat of the landaulet.

'Thomas!' I called urgently.

He paused, looking down at me.

'Thomas . . .' I hardly knew how to begin. 'Thomas, the man who accosted me outside the pump room . . . Do you know who he was?'

For a brief second Thomas' dark eyes narrowed and an expression that might almost have been wariness flickered over his sculpted ebony features. Then: 'No, Miss,' he said.

'You've never seen him before?'

'No, Miss.'

Disappointment flooded me. Why, oh why, had I not pursued the matter when I had had the chance? But the man had startled me so – and, to be truthful, frightened me. Now it was too late.

'Will that be all, Miss?' Thomas asked respectfully, and on an impulse I heard myself ask: 'Was he a sea captain, do you think? Do you think if you drove me back to the docks we might find him?'

'I do not think Mr Paterson would approve of that,'

Thomas said. His face was as expressionless as ever, but the disapproval in his voice was unmistakable.

Aware, suddenly, of how far I was straying beyond the bounds of propriety, I felt the colour flood my cheeks.

'No. Of course not. Yes, that will be all. Thank you, Thomas.'

He inclined his head slightly, a small, majestic tilt, and turned to climb into his seat. Confused by my own churning emotions I, too, turned away, and walked back towards the house. But the throb in my temple was sharper than ever, and the fog that surrounded me had never felt thicker or more impenetrable.

The front door still stood ajar, though both Aunt Linnie and Johnson, the maid, had disappeared inside. I went into the hall, shrugging off my thin wrap, and heard voices coming from the parlour. Great-Uncle Charles' thin, reedy tones, and another voice, much younger, which I recognized instantly, and with a rush of pleasure.

Theo! Theo was home!

I started towards the parlour door to greet him, then stopped in my tracks.

'Damnation, Theo, how could you be so stupid!' Great-Uncle Charles was saying, his querulous voice high and shrill as a girl's. 'If this got out it could ruin us!'

'It won't get out,' Theo returned. He sounded angry – and defensive. 'You make such a song and dance of everything, Papa.'

'Is it any wonder?' Great-Uncle Charles railed. 'I have spent my entire life building this business, and I won't stand by and see you destroy it! I might be old now, but I still have my wits about me. You, on the other hand, seem to have lost yours!'

'You handed the reins to me, Papa,' Theo said, and I could tell his anger was barely under control. 'You handed the reins to me because you had lost your nerve and *that* was leading to certain disaster. Now you seek to blame me for doing what I must. Well, I won't have it. You must allow me a free hand.'

'To go against the law of the land?'

'To save what little remains of our capital! It won't be for long – just until my other plans bear the fruit I expect them to.'

'Oh Theo, sometimes I find it hard to believe you are my son!'

'And often, I promise you, I wish that I were not . . .'

Throughout this angry exchange I had stood transfixed, unwilling to intrude upon it, yet somehow quite unable to tear myself away as I knew I should. All families have their quarrels, I supposed, especially where business is involved. Always there will be conflict between the old lion and the young one in a pride when the balance of power changes hands.

But elements of this quarrel went further than that. All was not well with the trade as far as the Grimes dynasty was concerned, it seemed – the reason, no doubt, why Great-Uncle Charles had not had a carriage to place at my disposal. And beyond that, and more disturbing still, Theo was involving himself in something illegal in an effort to put matters right. No wonder Great-Uncle Charles was so upset! Like my grandfather, he was a man who lived by a strict moral code. But surely what Theo had done could not be so terrible?

I should not have stayed to listen, of course. I was a guest in the house, and what went on between Theo and his father was no business of mine. Guilty, I began to move away to take myself upstairs to my room until things had calmed down, as Aunt Linnie no doubt had done, but I had left it too late. Before I managed to reach the staircase, the door to the parlour was thrown open and Theo came storming out.

He checked when he saw me, his eyes widening with astonishment.

'Davina!'

Flustered, I tried to smile as if everything were perfectly normal.

'Theo! You're home, then!'

Theo rolled his eyes heavenward.

He was a good-looking man, perhaps the most handsome I have ever set eyes on, with perfect, regular features and a ready smile that could charm the birds from the trees. He dressed well too, in the height of fashion, but just now his cravat was a little awry, and the colour high in his fair-skinned cheeks.

'I'm home, yes – and I might wish I were not, but for the pleasure of seeing you!' He gestured towards the parlour, and added in a low voice: 'Why do men become so contrary in old age, Davina? Answer me that!'

I had no intention of being drawn into taking sides in the quarrel between Theo and his father.

'I expect everyone has the right to be a little contrary with age,' I said lightly. 'Aunt Linnie . . .'

'Oh, of course, she's here too, is she not?' He glanced around as if expecting Aunt Linnie to materialize as if by magic. 'How is she? As simple as ever, I expect.'

In spite of myself, I could not help but laugh. Theo had that effect on me.

'You should not say such things!' I protested. 'You are terrible! Aunt Linnie is very sweet.'

'And simple-minded, as I said. Oh, come and take a walk with me in the garden, Davina. You can tell me how the arrangements for the wedding are proceeding.' Theo took my arm. 'Come on now, don't refuse to keep me company. After the castigation I have just received from my father, a little chat with a lovely young lady is exactly what I need!'

What could I do but go with him?

The garden at the rear of the house was small but perfectly laid out; the heavy scent of the roses and lavender all but banished the faint, pervasive smell of the river, and when we sat down on a little bench covered with camomile, the perfume from the crushed stems rose in a sweet cloud all around us.

But, as I answered Theo's questions, acquainting him with the arrangements that had been made, my head was still full of my encounter with the strange man and the compulsion I felt to try to learn what it meant before I could embark on a future that I wanted less with every passing day.

Dare I tell Theo how I felt? I wondered. But, of course, I did not. Instead I heard myself describing the floral arrangements we had ordered for the cathedral, where the ceremony was to take place, and for the grand reception that would follow, for all the world as if I were a normal, happy bride, excited about her forthcoming nuptials.

As for the quarrel I had overheard, not another word was said about that, and it was banished to the back of my mind. Already I had far too much that directly concerned me to think about without paying attention to things that were of no concern to me at all.

Or so I thought then. For I had not the slightest notion that the two subjects were more closely linked than I could ever have dreamed.

When we had eaten a light lunch of soup, cheese and cold meats, Theo said he had to go out on business and took his leave of us. Aunt Linnie and Great-Uncle Charles both retired to take their afternoon naps and I was left alone.

It was always a relief to be given a rest from Aunt Linnie's ceaseless prattle, and never more so than today. For it had occurred to me that no one would miss me if I went out in search of the stranger who just might hold the key to unlock my hidden past. He had looked like a sea captain, I thought, or even an ordinary sailor – though I rather thought he was too well dressed for that – and the most likely place to find him would be the docks, which I knew were within walking distance of Queen's Square. And it was to the docks that I planned to go.

I knew I should do no such thing, of course. Mr Paterson would certainly not approve of me wandering the streets on my own, and Grandfather and Grandmama would be scandalized if they knew. But the little imp that had made me tell Aunt Linnie I was quite used to taking care of myself stirred in me again. Why, the very excursion alone would be a sort of test to discover if there was any truth in that or whether

41

it was simply something that had come into my head, and the prospect of uncovering such a little thing about myself was exciting. I could not think I would come to any real harm, and in any case, it was a risk I was prepared to take. If the man was indeed a seaman he might sail on the next high tide and with him would go my chance to discover why he had mistaken me for a girl called Rowan, and who she was.

A terrible sense of urgency filled me. If I could not find him I would burst with the not knowing. And besides . . .

I *wanted* to see him again. I wanted once again to experience that moment of heady joy. Wanted to see that weather-tanned face and those hazel eyes . . .

Frightened suddenly by the longing which filled me, I tried to push the thought aside. I had no business feeling that way. I was engaged to be married to Mr Paterson, and that was that. But at least perhaps, if I could only find the man again and talk to him, I would be able to put behind me this stupid notion that was suddenly obsessing me – that I was not Davina Grimes at all, but an unknown girl named Rowan . . .

I fetched my wrap and, trembling with my own daring, let myself out of the house.

The afternoon sun filtered through the plane trees as I walked quickly across Queen's Square, past a fine statue of a man on horseback, in the direction of the masts of the sailing ships that were clearly visible above the roofs of the buildings ahead. One or two people glanced at me curiously, a woman alone in the city, but no one bothered me. As I came closer to the river the stench grew stronger, that nauseating stench of filth, of effluent, of rotting material, all mingled together with sugary sweetness. I had wondered why at times it was much worse than at others, and when I reached the wharf, I knew.

The tide was out, and the ships that were in port sat clumsily upon a thick bed of mud and slurry. The garbage that slopped lazily around their hulls was the main cause of that disgusting smell, undiluted by the sea water that flowed in at high tide to meet the freshwater trickle of the river.

My stomach turned, but I pressed a handkerchief to my

nose and mouth and hurried on while the mean-looking half-timbered dwellings and gin shops gave way to impressive warehouses.

The dock was busy. Costers and hawkers bawled their wares, barrels rolled noisily over the cobbles, men worked to repair sails and rigging, shouting to one another – and, occasionally, to me. I ignored them, mustering what dignity I could and hoping desperately they would not think me a lady of easy virtue and molest me for favours. And all the while I scanned every group of men I could see for the one I was looking for. Once I thought I saw him and hurried eagerly forward, but when the man turned around, though similar in build and attire, I could see that he was much older, with a pockmarked face, one of his eyes covered by a velvet patch. He gave me a long, curious look with his one good eye, and, disappointed and embarrassed, I turned away.

A ship was unloading a little further down the river – or, at least, the gangplank was down and hands milling back and forth. I felt a little surge of hope. The ship must have come in on the tide; judging by how low the water was now, that must have been this morning. Could it possibly be that the man I was looking for was her captain? I wondered. I had no idea whatever of the routine of seafarers, but, eager as I was to hold on to the faintest glimmer of hope, it seemed to me quite likely that after many long months at sea a man might very well make a visit to a spa bath to wash away the dirt and sweat of a voyage and make himself presentable again.

I hastened towards the ship – and then stopped short in my tracks.

Down the gangplank came a line of black slaves. I knew at once that they were slaves, for they were manacled together by means of a chain passing through neck collars – men, women, even little children, ragged and unkempt, bloodied and bowed. As I watched, horrified, yet unable to tear my eyes away, one man stumbled, his legs no doubt unsteady from many months at sea, and the slave master, who was driving them like cattle, raised his whip and brought it cracking down on to the poor slave's bare back. He made no sound, or if he did, it was lost in the hubbub of the quayside, but he raised his head, throwing it back on his shoulders, teeth bared, gaunt features contorted in a mask of pain, humiliation, terror – and despair.

I stood motionless, for I do not think at that moment my legs would have carried me a single step. My horror paralysed me; I could scarcely believe that one human being could treat others so. No, not even if they were savages, as Grandfather had said. And Thomas was certainly not a savage! Had he once been manacled and driven in this way? Had his first sight of English soil been these greasy cobbles and swirling filth? It must have been! Small wonder that his gaze now was impenetrable and hostile. How he must hate the white race who had inflicted on him such degradation and suffering!

All these things passed through my mind in less time than it takes to tell, yet there was, at that moment, no real coherence to them. I was conscious only of utter revulsion – and shame. Shame that I belonged to a race who could practise such atrocities, shame even for standing and watching. And still I could not move away. Still I stood there, transfixed, as the trade in all its raw horror became reality for me.

The line of slaves was dragged across the cobbled wharf and herded, with shouts and blows, towards an arched doorway that led into one of the dockside warehouses. They disappeared from my sight and still I stood, no longer even aware of that terrible stink, for my senses had been overloaded and I was, I think, in shock.

But there was yet more to come. When at last I tore my eyes away from the doorway into which the poor slaves had disappeared, and took a few steps along the quay, the name of the ship that had brought them here, emblazoned boldly on the sloping bows, came into my line of vision.

The *Swallow*.

I froze again. All my great-uncle's ships were named for birds. Grandfather had joked about it, that his brother had never forgotten his country upbringing. The *Swift*. The *Martin*. The *Swallow*. This ship, which had plied its terrible trade from Africa to Bristol, was owned by my own flesh and blood. The suffering I had just witnessed was what put the food on our table and paid for the roof over my head.

Great-Uncle Charles and Theo did not only deal in sugar and rum.

They also dealt in slaves.

'Davina!'

This time the name, and the voice calling it, were familiar to me, yet, stunned as I was, it was a moment before it registered with me, and I turned to see Theo coming towards me.

He had emerged, I supposed, from the same doorway through which the slaves had been taken, and he approached me with a look of scandalized horror clouding his handsome features.

'Davina! What do you think you are doing here?'

For the moment, all thought of my purpose in coming to the quay was forgotten. I could think only of what I had just witnessed – and my outrage that my own family should be behind it.

'Those poor people!' I said foolishly.

Theo frowned, bemused. 'What are you talking about?'

'The black people. In chains.' I could not bring myself to use the word 'slaves'. 'They came from your ship, Theo!'

His frown deepened. 'What of it?'

'They were in torment!' I cried passionately. 'They looked so cowed – so sick! And the man driving them took the whip to them when they stumbled.'

Theo shrugged. 'He was only doing his job. They have to be controlled, and the whip is the only language they understand.'

'But it's so cruel!' I cried.

'Oh, don't be foolish! They are not like us.' His tone was disdainful.

I thought of Thomas: proud, dependable – and quick to come to my aid when he had thought I was being threatened.

'Not so different, surely?' I said. 'Oh, a different-coloured

45

skin, perhaps, but underneath it, not so different. How can you condone what is done to them, Theo? Taking them, all unwilling, from their homes, and treating them so?'

'It's business,' he said coolly. 'A perfectly respectable trade.'

'It's barbarous! I can't believe you can profit from trafficking in human life!' A thought struck me. 'Does Mr Paterson trade in slaves too?'

'John? He did, of course. All the great merchants of this city did.'

'Did?' I repeated. 'You mean he does not do so any longer?'

'He has no need to. His fortune is made. Now he can afford to undertake the shorter voyages only – to the West Indies. There's less risk of losing a ship than on the dangerous passage between there and Africa. And in any case, Liverpool is ruining our trade.'

Well, that at least was of some small consolation, I supposed. But even so, all the luxuries I was to enjoy as Mr Paterson's wife had been bought with the lives of poor wretched souls such as I had just witnessed being treated with less respect than a man treats his horses.

'I don't know why you should look so disapproving, Davina,' Theo said. 'You have always known we are merchants, and merchants take their profits where they can.'

Into my mind shot the quarrel I had overheard between Theo and his father. But it could not have been slave trading to which they had been referring when they had talked of breaking the law. Slave trading was perfectly legal, if immoral, as I was beginning to believe.

'You still have not explained what you are doing here, Davina.' Theo had taken hold of my arm as if he were afraid I might suddenly make a break for it and disappear among the dock workers and hawkers. 'It's not proper for you to be here at all – much less alone. Dear God, it's not even safe!'

'No one has harmed me!' I retorted.

'And thank God they have not! John Paterson would never forgive us for not taking better care of you if . . .'

46

His jaw tightened. 'Don't you realize the danger you have put yourself in with this foolishness? You could have been attacked, robbed . . . or worse! You could have been taken by white slavers . . . oh yes, they exist, and not only in popular fiction! A beautiful girl like you would fetch a pretty price . . .'

'Well, I wasn't taken by slavers!' I said mulishly, though I have to admit the very notion made my blood run cold and made me aware, suddenly, of the extent of my recklessness. 'Unlike those poor souls . . .' I looked meaningfully towards the warehouse door, which had now closed.

'And never mind the danger – what of your reputation?' Theo went on. 'I hope to God John doesn't get to hear that his future wife was walking the quay like a common fishwife – or a harlot plying her trade. He'd call the wedding off, as like as not.'

I was beginning to lose my temper. 'And perhaps that is just as well!' I snapped.

An alarmed look crossed Theo's handsome face. 'What are you talking about?'

'I don't want to marry him anyway!' I declared. 'I never wanted to. I'm only doing it to please Grandmama and Grandfather.'

'Davina!' Theo looked thunderstruck. 'You can't mean it . . .'

'You wanted to know what I am doing here,' I went on. 'Well, Theo, I'll tell you. I am searching in vain for the answers to some very pressing questions. Answers that *you* may well be able to give me. And I swear that, until I have them, I cannot – will not – marry John Paterson, or anyone else!'

Four

I must have spoken with great conviction, for Theo seemed to believe me.

'What questions, Davina?' he asked, his eyes, narrowed and wary, searching my face.

A man rolled a barrel so close past us that some dirty water that had lain in a puddle on the cobbles splashed up and splattered my skirts.

'Look where you're going, can't you!' Theo shouted at him angrily, for it was clear the man's attention to his job had been quite overtaken by his curiosity at seeing a merchant and a lady arguing there on the quayside.

'Do we have to talk here?' I asked. 'Isn't there somewhere more private?'

'Yes. You're right.' Theo's hand tightened under my elbow, steering me towards the door through which the poor slaves had disappeared, and my throat tightened at the thought of seeing them once again. But once inside I found myself in a narrow passageway, on one side of which was a heavy door, presumably leading to the cellars, and ahead of us a staircase. The slaves had been driven into the cellar, judging by the sounds that came from behind that door, and it was towards the stairway that Theo was leading me.

The stench of the river seemed to have permeated the very walls, and after the bright sunshine outside it was very dim in the building.

'We'll go to my office,' Theo said.

He led the way up the steep staircase and into a small room which overlooked the quayside. The windows were grimy, but enough light found its way through them for me to see a desk, two or three chairs, and shelves lining the walls, stacked with ledgers. More ledgers lay on the desk, together with writing materials. Theo indicated that I should sit in one of the chairs, and he sat himself down opposite me with the desk between us.

'So, Davina,' he said, leaning back in his chair and looking at me narrowly. 'What are these questions that are troubling you?'

Now that the moment had come, I scarcely knew where to begin.

'You know that I have no memory of my past life beyond the last two years,' I said, knotting my hands in the folds of my skirts and glancing down at them.

'Yes.'

'And you must realize that it is very important to me that I should regain at least something of what happened to me in the first years of my life.'

'Yes. But I'm afraid I can be of little assistance, Davina. Your mother played no part in our family life during those years. The first time I ever set eyes on you was in our grandfather's rectory, and that was just two years ago. I am sure our grandparents can tell you more than I. You will have to ask them.'

'Well, I have asked, of course,' I said. 'But they are very reticent. So much so that I cannot help but feel they are keeping something from me. Why, I am not sure any more that the little they have told me is the truth.'

'Oh, surely . . .' But there was something guarded suddenly in his eyes. 'What makes you think such a thing, Davina?'

I glanced towards the window, where a bluebottle buzzed impotently against the sooty glass. Just so was I trapped. Trapped by commitment. Trapped by duty. Trapped by the lack of any real sense of identity.

I looked back at Theo; caught again that strangely guarded look on his face.

'Something very strange happened this morning,' I said hesitantly. 'Aunt Linnie and I were visiting the hot well and a man spoke to me. He seemed to recognize me, and thought that I should recognize him.'

'And did you?' Theo asked.

'No, not really. I don't remember having ever seen him before in my life. And yet . . .'

'Yes?'

'There was something. For just a moment . . . there was something.'

Theo regarded me narrowly. 'But why should such an encounter make you doubt what you have been told?' he asked.

'Because . . .' I took a deep breath. 'Because he did not call me Davina. He called me Rowan.'

Theo sat forward in his chair, elbows on the desk, very alert suddenly.

'What did he look like, this man?'

'Tall, perhaps thirty-five years old, it's hard to say, for the lines on his face could have been caused by exposure to the elements. I thought he looked like a seafarer – that is the reason I came to the docks this afternoon. In the hope of finding him again. But you have not answered my question. Does the name Rowan mean anything to you?'

'I have never heard you called anything but Davina,' Theo said levelly.

I let my breath out on a long sigh, disappointment and frustration flooding through my veins. But, in all honesty, what had I expected? That Theo was going to tell me that I was not Davina Grimes at all, but some unknown girl who had been given her identity for some inexplicable purpose? It was fantasy, sheer fantasy, born of a desperate desire to find a hidden past and escape a future I did not want. Nothing but fantasy. And yet . . .

'There is something,' I said stubbornly. 'They are keeping something from me, I'm sure of it! And before I can marry Mr Paterson, or anyone, I have to know what it is.'

For a long moment Theo looked at me. Then he rose, crossing to the window and turning to lean himself against the sill.

'Very well, Davina, since it is clear you are aware you have not been told the whole truth, and it is worrying you, I will tell you all I know. It is not much, but it may well explain to you why your grandparents have been reticent.'

My nerve endings were all alive suddenly, pricking beneath my skin, and breath caught in my throat. So – I had been right! They *did* know more than they had told me.

'To begin with, there was a little more to your accident than you have been made aware of,' Theo said carefully. 'It was no mere accident in the sense of a misfortune or a piece of bad driving on the part of the coachman. He survived the crash long enough to impart the information that he had been held up by a highwayman. The scoundrel ordered you and your mother down from the coach, thinking to relieve you of your valuables, no doubt, and the coachman did his best to save you. Shots were fired, the horses took fright and bolted. It was then that the carriage left the highway and overturned, killing your mother and badly injuring you.'

I frowned as a tiny shard of recollection stirred deep within me. Fear. A shot. Yes, for a brief moment in time it felt right, and I thought the mists were about to lift. Then they descended again, impenetrable as ever, leaving me once more frustrated.

'Why did they not tell me that?' I asked slowly.

'They believed it would cause you more distress and that, if you did not remember, then there was no advantage in your knowing.' Theo pulled a kerchief from his pocket and mopped his forehead where tiny drops of perspiration had gathered beneath the line of his wig. 'Whether they were right or wrong to keep it from you, I couldn't say. But that was their decision, and they requested that the rest of the family should support them in it.'

I was silent for a moment. This piece of information, though curious, took me no closer to learning any more about myself.

'The coachman,' I said at last. 'Who was he?'

'He had been hired, I believe, from somewhere in Somerset. I don't remember the name of the place. It was probably never mentioned. In any case, as I already said, he died from his injuries, so he would not be able to tell you anything, even if you could find him.'

'Somerset. That is another of the counties that borders Bristol, isn't it?' I mused. 'So if the accident happened in Gloucestershire, then we must surely have been on our way to visit my grandparents.'

'You had already been to visit them,' Theo said. 'Your mother had fled to them to ask for their help, and they had turned her away. I don't suppose I need to explain why they were unwilling to tell you that. Naturally, they blame themselves for what occurred. If they had taken you in, as she asked, then you would never have been on that road on that fateful night. Your mother would still be alive, and you would not have suffered the injuries that have left you with this terrible memory loss.'

Again I was silent, thinking. Yes, I could well imagine how much my grandparents must blame themselves. No wonder they had lavished such love and care on me. They had been making a belated effort to put things right. But what had my mother done that was so terrible that they had refused her shelter in her hour of need? And why, after all the long years that she had been estranged from them, had she been so desperate that she had hired a coach to take the two of us to the only sanctuary she could think of, without even being certain of the reception she would receive?

'Did you never hear the reason why she needed my grandparents' help?' I asked. 'If she had the wherewithal to hire a coach, then we could not have been destitute, surely? Unless she hoped Grandfather would pay the coachman. But, in that case, he would not have been driving us away again. He would have parked himself on the rectory doorstep until he got his money.'

Theo sat down again, leaning towards me across his ledger-strewn desk.

'It seems, Davina, there was trouble with a man.'

'A man? My father, you mean?'

'Not your father, no. I don't know what became of him.

52

Dead, perhaps. Or maybe he abandoned you and your mother. He was a strolling player, as I think you have been told, and they are a notoriously fickle breed. No, there was another man she had taken up with. A dangerous man – and one who had led her a merry dance. She had stayed with him, she told her parents, because she had no choice. Well – no choice she cared to make, anyway. Leaving the security he offered would have meant the poorhouse – or going on to the streets to make enough to buy a crust and put a roof over your heads. To be honest, I think there may well have been more to it than that. He was, by all accounts, an attractive devil, as his sort so often are. I believe she was in his thrall, and could not bring herself to leave him. Until . . . until for your sake she felt she had to.'

'*My* sake?' I repeated, puzzled. 'What do you mean – for *my* sake?'

Theo took out a cigar. He did not light it, but rolled it thoughtfully between his fingers as if he needed some prop to allow him to continue.

'It seems, Davina, that this man, who had to all intents and purposes been a father figure to you, suddenly became aware that you had grown into a beautiful young woman. He transferred his affections from your mother to you. He became totally obsessed with you. Your mother was very afraid of what harm he might do you, and at last tried to escape his lecherous clutches. But he became deranged, saying, even, that if he could not have you, then he would ensure that no one else did. Afraid for both your lives, she fled to her old home.'

'But my grandparents refused to forgive her and take us in.'

'That is so. They told her that her troubles were of her own making. I believe they feared, too, that this man might follow and find you, and they would become embroiled in yet more scandal of the kind that had shamed them so, all those years before, and which they had tried so hard to live down.' He hesitated. 'You must not blame them too much. Good reputation matters to them so very much. Their lives are nothing without the respect of your grandfather's parishioners.'

'I know,' I said. My head was spinning with all that Theo had told me, and with trying to remember. 'But he never came, this man, did he? He never found me.'

'I'm not so certain of that,' Theo said.

I looked up at him, puzzled – and frightened suddenly.

'What do you mean?'

Theo set the cigar down on the desktop and spread his hands.

'I have wondered, sometimes, if the man who held up your carriage was in reality a highwayman at all. I have wondered if perhaps . . .'

'You think it was him?' I whispered.

'Yes. Oh, I have no proof, of course. But it could be that he followed you – and when he held up the carriage, his intention was to make off with you.'

'But . . .'

'Things went amiss. Shots were fired, the horses bolted and the carriage went over the side of the hill. Two people died that night, Davina. It could well be that he believed you had died too. God only knows, it was a miracle you did not. And if he believed you died, then that would have been an end to it. He would not have come looking for you again. But now . . .'

'Dear God!' I whispered as his meaning dawned on me. 'And now you think . . .'

'That this man and the one who accosted you this morning may be one and the same. Yes, Davina, that's the way my thoughts are leading me, and that is why I felt I should acquaint you now with as much of the truth as I know. You might well be in danger from him if you were unaware of the threat he posed.'

'Oh!' My mind raced back to my encounter with the stranger outside the hot well. I thought of the proprietorial way he had caught at my arm; of his words, spoken so harshly: *Don't play games with me!* Certainly there had been something close to aggression in his manner and in

54

his tone, certainly he had looked like a man who might, with reason, be described as 'dangerous'. And yet . . .

In that first moment my instinctive reaction had not been fear or loathing, but joy. I could remember it still, with every fibre of my being, that brief singing happiness that had suffused me before the mists descended once more and I knew nothing but confusion and alarm. It made no sense. None at all. And besides . . .

'But why should he call me Rowan?' I asked, more of myself than of Theo. 'If I truly am Davina, and if he knew me once, then why would he use another's name?'

'I was not entirely honest with you, Davina,' Theo said.

'What?' I looked up; saw the indecision in his face.

'I did not lie to you,' Theo said, 'but I did not tell you the complete truth either. I never have heard you called anything but Davina; it is the name your grandparents always refer to you by. But I have heard them say your mother called you by another name. I never heard what it was, only that, in your grandmother's words, it was 'quite unsuitable for a young lady'. They decided you should be known as Davina, I believe, and that the other 'unsuitable' name should be laid to rest with your rather insalubrious past.'

'And now you think . . .'

'That the man who accosted you called you by the name he knew you by. Yes.'

'Rowan.' I said it softly, listening to the sound of it, waiting for it to strike some chord of familiarity within me. Surely – surely! – if it was indeed my name, I should feel something? And perhaps I did – a faint echo of sweet sadness in the mist-filled caverns of my mind. Or was that simply wishful thinking, a fervent hope that something was stirring my lost memories? I could not be sure. In fact, I could not be sure of anything.

'Oh!' It was a cry of sheer desperation, frustration, anger, even, at myself for my own feebleness, my inability to find what I was seeking. I balled my hands to fists, beating them against my thighs, and the tears ached in my throat. 'It's hopeless! Hopeless! What am I to do, Theo?'

I meant, of course, what was I to do about my stubborn foggy brain, but Theo, typical man that he was, took my question to relate to the practical, the danger this unknown man posed to me if he was indeed the one who was obsessed with me so much that he had attempted to abduct me, and thereby caused the terrible accident.

'The first thing to do,' he said, is to get you away from here. If I am right, he now knows that you did not die in the carriage accident. You were fortunate this morning that you had a worthy champion in Thomas, ready to come to your aid. And even more fortunate that you did not run into this man when you came down here to the docks, alone, this afternoon. If he is, as I believe, a seafarer, he may well still be in the vicinity. If you had found him, or he had found you, I dread to think what might have become of you. I shall accompany you home at once, to ensure you are safe, out of his reach. But do not think of creeping out alone again, I implore you. For if you do, you could once again be in his clutches – the very thing from which your mother was trying to protect you when she met her sad end.'

'Oh Mama . . .' The tears were there in my eyes suddenly for the mother who had died for me, but was nothing but a sweet shadow in the dark recesses of my mind and senses.

'Thank God you will soon be John Paterson's wife,' Theo went on. 'His name alone should protect you. He is a powerful man – the one who goes against John Paterson would be a fool indeed.'

His words reminded me of my imminent marriage – the marriage I wanted so little – and the tears pricked again at my eyes.

'Theo – I don't think I can go through with it,' I said urgently. 'The thought of marrying Mr Paterson . . .' I bit my lip, fighting to regain my composure and failing. Suddenly it was all too much for me. And after the confidences Theo had just shared with me, he felt like an ally. Surely I could share some confidences with him too? But as I opened my mouth to speak, I saw Theo's expression. His jaw had set, his eyes narrowed.

'You are not going to change your mind, are you, Davina? You are not going to renege on the agreement? This marriage is of the greatest importance – to all of us.'

'What do you mean?' I asked.

'Mr Paterson is a very important man in this city. If we were to get on the wrong side of him it would mean ruin for our family,' Theo said. 'You cannot do this to us, Davina!'

'But . . .'

'And besides, it would break your grandparents' hearts,' Theo said, and it was only afterwards that it occurred to me that he had realized he was on safer ground, with a stronger argument, if he brought my grandparents into it, for though he was a cousin of sorts, and Great-Uncle Charles was Grandfather's brother, Theo must have known that I owed no great allegiance to them. 'Your grandparents feel so guilty already, and want so badly to see you settled,' he went on. 'Why, I think it would be the death of them if you were to bring down more disgrace on their heads by calling off your marriage at this late stage. Don't think of such a thing even for a moment, I beg you!'

A solitary tear rolled down my nose. I wiped it away.

'Come on now,' Theo said, more encouragingly. 'It won't be so bad. You'll want for nothing ever again. And you'll see as much of us, your family, as you wish. It can't be as bad, surely, as being shut away in a country rectory in the Cotswolds with no company but an ageing cleric and his wife? You'll have fine clothes and servants, you will be mistress of your own house – and a grand house at that, in the finest part of town. Everyone who is anyone will live in Clifton soon – why, I'd like to think I shall live there myself, well away from this stinking river. And I will, too, if everything goes according to plan!'

His arguments were the same ones I had heard so many times before. Each one of them was valid, yet they did nothing to convince me. How could they, when they were all founded on reason, and my objections came from my heart?

'But I don't love him,' I said wretchedly. 'And I never will.'

'Never is a long time,' Theo said. 'Love, as you mean it, is a fickle and fleeting thing; the kind of love that comes from sharing a life together is worth far more. John Paterson will treat you with kindness and consideration, I'm sure, and in time you will grow to love him.'

'Why, then, have *you* never married, Theo?' I asked archly. 'Could it be because you have never met a woman you loved in the way you speak of with such disdain?'

He smiled suddenly, reverting to the charming man I had come to know.

'Touché, Davina. But it's different for a man. And if I were to meet a woman who could offer me all the advantages John Paterson can offer you, I might well be prepared to overlook the fact that she might be plain and dull.'

'I don't believe you,' I said.

'I don't know why I am trying to talk you into this match,' Theo went on, teasing me with his eyes, 'when I ought to be persuading you into marrying me instead. Now, you and I, we'd make a handsome pair. But I'm prepared to make the sacrifice and let the better man have you. Noble of me, I think.'

'Theo . . .' I protested, feeling the colour flood my cheeks.

'You think I jest, Davina – and perhaps I do, a little. But if things were different I'd sweep you off your feet, I promise you, and John Paterson – and any other man – would not stand a chance.' He reached over and took my hand and his face grew serious again. 'Don't talk any more of calling this wedding off, there's a good girl. It's pre-marriage nerves, that's all.'

The shutters, through which just a little light had briefly glimmered, slammed tight shut again, the bars of the cage that held me were secured once more.

'At least you'll be safe from that devil,' he said. Then he stood up. 'Come on, Davina, I'll take you home.'

The conversation I had had with Theo played itself over and over in my mind from beginning to end and end to beginning. But although of course I could not help wondering about his motives in his obvious eagerness for me to marry John

Paterson, it was the things he had told me about my past that mostly claimed my attention.

From what he had said, it sounded as if the life I had lived with my mother had been rackety indeed. Small wonder my grandparents were so concerned to see me settled into respectability now. Though they had not been concerned enough to risk trouble and scandal when my mother had brought me to their door in search of refuge!

I must not blame them for that, though – I felt sure they could hardly blame themselves more, and they had done everything in their power to make it up to me. What I could not help blaming them for was that they had not told me everything they could. Perhaps they had withheld what they knew with the best of motives, but I still felt they owed me the truth. And was there more? Things Theo had not heard about? I resolved that at the first opportunity I would question them further, prompted by the little Theo had been able to tell me.

And then the man who had accosted me this morning was on my mind once more. Was it as Theo had suggested and he was the same man my mother had tried to protect me from? Had he been the cause of the accident, with its terrible consequences? Was I in danger from him still – now that he knew I was not dead, but here in Bristol?

Around and around in my head it ran, until I thought it would drive me mad. Around and around. And always, hanging over me like a dark cloud, my obligation to marry Mr Paterson.

It was hardly surprising, perhaps, that I dreamed that night. And all the elements of my waking confusion were in the dream, thrown together in a pot-pourri that made no sense at all. I tossed and turned as if I had a fever and when dawn broke I pushed aside the covers and went to the window, looking out over the roads that criss-crossed the green expanse at the centre of Queen's Square. But I could not remain there for ever; it would be some hours before the rest of the household rose, and so, at last, reluctantly, I returned to lie down in the great, ornate bed.

Though I had not expected to, before long I fell asleep

once more. And this time, when I dreamed, there was more form to the dream.

I was in a carriage, and my mother was there. I felt her presence very strongly, smelled her perfume – the scent of lavender, sweet and haunting, and though I could not see her face clearly I knew it was a mirror image of my own, and, strangely, not a day older, so that it seemed to me that we were more sisters than mother and daughter.

But we were not alone. There was someone else in the carriage with us, someone whose presence was every bit as strong as my mother's, but whom I could not see at all. Whoever it was was hidden behind a veil. In my dream I reached out my hand to move the veil aside; it rippled, nebulous beneath my fingers, and remained exactly where it was. I tried again and again, increasingly frustrated, for I had the compelling feeling that it was vitally important for me to see who it was the veil hid. At last – at last! – it began to dissolve like mist in the sunshine. My heart beat fast with expectation. But there was no one there at all.

My disappointment was so fierce, so all-consuming, that I began to weep. It was more than mere disappointment, it was a feeling of complete and utter desolation, of loss so great that my whole body ached with it. I wrapped my empty arms around myself and sat staring at the last swirls of the mist that hid someone so dear to me I could not bear to be without them, and yet hid no one at all.

And then, quite suddenly, I heard the horses that pulled the carriage whinny, loudly and shrilly, as if something had caused them terror. The carriage rocked to an abrupt halt, and through the little window, I saw in the moonlight a dark-cloaked figure in a tricorn hat. His face, too, was hidden to me, yet I experienced a moment's sharp bewilderment as I looked out at him. *What are you doing here?*

Then a pistol shot cracked in the stillness of the night, and another, making my ears ring. The carriage lurched forward, throwing me back into my seat, and gathered speed with terrifying momentum. Someone must have opened the carriage door, for now it swung wide on its hinges, banging against the frame with the crazy rocking of the carriage, and the horses' hooves were like thunder on the hard rutted ground.

I screamed out in terror, yet my greatest concern was for whoever it was who had been hidden by the misty veil, but was not there at all. The carriage was swaying dangerously and I somehow knew what was going to happen next, but was powerless to prevent it. A jolt and an awful grinding sound and we were at a crazy angle. I was thrown into the corner of the velvet-covered seat, my head cracking into the side of the carriage, and then the world was revolving about me, dragging me with it, over and over, and I was thrown again, like a pea in a barrel. I heard the crack of splintering wood and the terrified screaming of the horses. And then nothing. There was stillness, silence, broken only by the sounds of staccato sobbing and a muffled cry that I thought might have come from my own lips. And the blackness came down, covering everything, and I was trapped. Trapped in a wrecked carriage. Trapped within the prison of my own mind.

I woke then, and the dream was still so real I could almost touch it. The aura hung over me still, and my face was wet with tears. I lay unmoving, reliving every moment of it again, just as vividly as before.

Had it simply been as a result of Theo's terrible story playing on my mind? I wondered. Or had it been more than that? Could it be that those few bare facts had unlocked one of the doors inside my mind and allowed me to peep inside? Were the feelings I had just experienced – which still hung over me – not imagination at all but the feelings I had truly experienced on that night? The terror, the bewilderment – and the terrible aching loss for I knew not who? And if they were, who was it that had been in the carriage with me and my mother, hidden by a veil that not even my reawakening consciousness could lift?

But the mists had come down again and I had no answers. There was nothing to hold on to but the tears on my face and the empty ache in my arms – and my heart. I could only pray that if the door had opened just a little once, it would do so again. And next time I would learn a little more of the circumstances of my lost past life.

Five

My conversation with Theo had made me forget for the moment the awful scene I had witnessed when the cargo of slaves had been dragged and driven from the hold of the ship which I knew belonged to my great-uncle. Under any other circumstances, I feel sure, their torment would have haunted me, and the knowledge that their suffering was putting the food I ate on the table, and the roof over my head, would have played dreadfully on my mind. But, selfishly, thoughts about my own situation had taken precedence.

Next morning, however, when Mr Paterson's carriage arrived to take me for a final fitting of my wedding gown, and I saw Thomas in his smart blue livery sitting on the driver's seat of the landaulet, it all came rushing back.

As he climbed down, tall and straight, a vision flashed into my mind of him half-naked and in chains, and I seemed to see his proud, impassive face contorted in agony as the face of that new arrival's had been when the slave master brought the whip stinging down on to his bare back. When he handed me up into the landaulet it was all I could do not to shrink from his touch, so great was my discomfort.

Well, at least Thomas did not have such a bad life now, I comforted myself. There were plenty of English people who were worse off, living in hovels, wearing rags, and never having enough to eat. But, for all that, they were in their own homeland, surrounded by their families. And they were free. Thomas, for all his fine livery, was a slave. He belonged to Mr Paterson and could be bought and sold for whatever he would fetch. And he had been trained and tamed as one might train and tame a wild animal. It was not right. It could never be right. But what could I do about it? I could remonstrate with Great-Uncle Charles, and beg him not to take part in this dreadful trade, but he would take no more notice of me than Theo had done. And even if he were to take notice, there were hundreds of other merchants up and down the country who would still carry on, for it was not just Bristol that gave safe harbour to the slavers. Had not Theo said that Liverpool was now an even busier slaving port?

No, there was nothing I could do. But that did not mean I had to like what was going on. And when the fine silk gown whispered over my head and fell in ivory folds about my hips, I could not help but feel it was tainted by the blood, sweat and tears of these poor, misused Africans.

Since I had come to Bristol I had seen surprisingly little of Mr Paterson. He was, clearly, a man with a great many calls on his time. Now that Theo was home, I thought that, very likely, he saw more of my future husband than I did, for the merchants took many of their meals together in the coffee houses near the quay, doing business and socializing both at the same time.

I mentioned it once to Theo, joking: 'You merchants seem to find trading a most pleasurable pastime!'

At once his face darkened. 'The Venturers, perhaps. I've never been invited to join that elite band.' Then he added, with that quick, rather wicked smile: 'But I'm hoping that will change now that you are to be Mrs Paterson. I can't think that John would wish his wife's family to be seen as the poor relations.'

I frowned, beginning to feel uncomfortable.

'Would it make such a difference to you, then?' I asked, and he threw back his head and laughed, the laugh of a man confident that his circumstances were about to change for the better.

'It most certainly would! Insurance for our voyages would be cheaper and easier to come by – the Merchant Venturers band together to insure one another. We'd have free use of the crane for loading and unloading, and most of the port fees I have to pay now would be waived too. The Venturers, between them, own Bristol. Oh, it certainly would make the most amazing difference to my overheads. And I'd be invited to dine at the top table in the coffee house, where respect is taken as a matter of due.'

'Theo!' I said, half joking, half serious. 'I hope you are not marrying me to Mr Paterson so that you can get better service for your breakfast!'

And: 'Well, of course, you have it, Davina!' he joked back. 'Some say a woman's price is beyond rubies. I say it is beyond a dish of fine coffee and a wad of best tobacco!'

I found it beyond me to raise so much as a smile, and he reached out to tweak a strand of that unruly hair of mine behind my ear. 'If I become a Merchant Venturer, Davina, I, too, may be able to afford to run the shorter voyages instead of dealing in slaves to make a decent profit. Given your objections to the slave trade, I'd have thought you would be glad of that, at least.'

I said nothing. If I had said anything at all, it would most likely have been something I would later have regretted. And I did not want to cross swords with Theo. In spite of his somewhat dubious motives for wanting me to marry Mr Paterson, he was still the closest thing to an ally that I had.

'So, you think you do not see enough of your future husband?' he went on, in the same jocular tone. 'Perhaps you have a secret fancy for him after all!'

'Not at all!' I did not in the least mind not seeing very much of Mr Paterson. In many ways it was a respite. I could not help feeling that before too long I would be seeing rather too much of him.

I was not much looking forward, either, to the first great occasion when I was to appear on his arm and he would present me formally as his future wife to everyone who was anyone in the city of Bristol.

It was to take the form of a reception which Mr Paterson was hosting at his house in the Clifton heights. I had a new gown for the occasion, hastily made for me by the same dressmaker who had been charged with making my wedding gown, and when the great day came and I put it on, freshly shaken out from the box in which it had been delivered, my appearance in the long dressing mirror at least gave me a little much-needed confidence.

The gown was straw-coloured satin, which looked well with my dark hair, and fell gracefully from a high waist, which emphasized the curves above it and my slim hips below. A white fichu decorated the plunging neckline and provided a perfect picture frame for the beautiful pendant, suspended from a velvet ribbon, which Mr Paterson had sent me as a betrothal gift, and which Johnson, the maid, had fastened around my neck when she helped me to dress.

At least, I thought, I would be able to hold my own with the finest of the ladies I would be meeting tonight, and Johnson encouraged me further by her frank admiration.

'Why, Miss, you will be the belle of the ball, and no mistake!' she said, standing back, hands on hips, to get a longer view of me. 'There's not a man in Bristol who won't wish it was him you were going to marry, mark my words!'

The carriage was brought to the front door – Uncle Charles' carriage this time, since he and Theo were to accompany me and Aunt Linnie, and we climbed into it, Aunt Linnie so fluttery with excitement that she could scarcely sit still.

'For heaven's sakes, Linnie!' Great-Uncle Charles chided her. 'Contain yourself do! You'll frighten the horses!'

That quietened her down for a little while; Aunt Linnie was rather nervous of horses at the best of times, and his words awakened an echo of apprehension in me, too, as I was reminded too sharply for comfort of the terror I had felt in my dream when I had been trapped in a rolling, swaying carriage that was no longer under the control of the driver.

We drove up Park Street at a sedate pace, leaving the stink and squalor of the city behind, and drew up outside the house that was soon to be my home.

From the first moment I had seen it, I had well understood Theo's ambition to move to Clifton too. The house overlooked the gorge, which rose, thickly wooded, from the

65

river. The tide was in this evening, and the river was busy with traffic. Little tugs guided a majestic sailing ship in, and a ferry boat crossed and recrossed the river. The late sun sparkled on the water, lending it a silvery hue that could not have been more different to the dark and filthy effluent I had seen slopping around the hulls of the boats when I had visited the docks, and I thought that the whole, dramatically beautiful, scene scarcely looked English at all, but almost as if it had escaped from an Italian painting. Certainly I could live here without complaint. I only wished it did not have to be with Mr Paterson . . .

He came to the door himself to greet us and stood there, smiling broadly, his thumbs tucked into the pockets of his trousers so that his coat was pushed aside to reveal the impressive expanse of his stomach.

'Very glad you could be here good and early,' he said. 'I want Davina on my arm to greet my guests.' He turned to me, his eyes narrow and appreciative in his florid face. 'And what a picture she makes too! I'm a lucky man indeed to be marrying such a beautiful wife!'

He took my hand, pressing his moist lips to it, and Aunt Linnie giggled, part scandalized, part envious.

'Linnie! Would you do me the honour of allowing me to kiss your hand too?' Mr Paterson asked, and for the first time I had a glimpse of the kind nature that lay behind his rather bombastic exterior.

'Oh, Mr Paterson, I'm not sure!' Aunt Linnie, all a-flutter, pressed a hand to her throat. But she quickly extended her other hand before he could change his mind, and as his lips touched it, a pink flush suffused her cheeks. 'Oh, Mr Paterson!'

'Two charming ladies!' he said, still holding her hand between his. 'I swear if I were not already promised to Davina, I would be hard-pressed to choose between you!'

'Oh my! Oh my!' I thought Aunt Linnie might be going to swoon clean away with pleasurable excitement.

'Come on, Linnie, don't make a fool of yourself now!' Great-Uncle Charles admonished her.

66

We went into the magnificent hall. It was tiled in the Italian fashion, and the late-afternoon sun, slanting in through the stained-glass panels around the door and windows, threw patterns of opaque light across it. Further light came in through a cupola in the ceiling, and the scent from a jug of tea roses which stood on a heavy oak bureau filled the air.

Mr Paterson led us through into the long room, running the whole depth of the house, where the reception was to be held. This room was decorated on an Oriental theme, which I had heard was quite the vogue, with rich draperies and vases in fine porcelain, with a great Chinese urn on a plinth taking pride of place. This room, too, had been filled with flowers – yet more roses, lilies, and some long stems of exotic bloom that I imagined must have been brought from hotter climes as cuttings and lovingly cared for in a hothouse, for they were not of a strain that could ever have grown to their magnificent best in our English climate, however clement the summer.

'Oh my goodness!' Aunt Linnie had not seen this room before. Now she stood in the centre of a huge Eastern carpet, clasping her hands and almost dancing with delight. 'Oh, it's so *grand*! And the flowers . . . A treat indeed, Mr Paterson!'

'I'm glad you like them.' Mr Paterson beamed. 'I had them brought in especially for this evening's gathering. The house must be a worthy setting for my beautiful bride.'

He glanced at me, awaiting my approval.

'They are wonderful,' I said. 'I have never seen the like.'

'I think,' Mr Paterson said, 'that I shall order more for the cathedral on the great day. And for the reception, too, if enough are available. I shall speak to the florist tomorrow and acquaint her with your wishes.'

'Oh, please don't upset her on my account!' I said hastily, all too aware of all the thought that had gone into the planned arrangements, and the trouble the florist had gone to already to fulfil our every whim.

'Nonsense!' Mr Paterson said. 'I'm paying her well enough – she must be ready to put herself out a little on our behalf. Now – I've arranged for a trio – you like music, don't

67

you, Davina? They will sit here . . .' He indicated three spindle-legged chairs set up at the far end of the great room, with space in front of them for music stands. 'I do think a little light music calms the nerves and assists the digestion.'

'Oh, Mr Paterson!' Aunt Linnie turned a little pink; talk of digestion seemed to her a little indelicate, no doubt.

Theo laughed, rather ingratiatingly, I thought. 'You have thought of everything, I see, John.'

'I hope so, my dear fellow. I certainly hope so! Now, shall we relax with a glass of good porter until it's time for the guests to arrive?'

'That is most civil of you, John,' Great-Uncle Charles said in his quavery voice, but Aunt Linnie squealed.

'Porter? Oh, not for me, Mr Paterson!'

'No, indeed not! A dish of tea for you, perhaps? Or can I tempt you to a nice fine Madeira?'

Aunt Linnie giggled. Actually giggled.

'Madeira! Do you know, Mr Paterson, since this is such a special occasion, I think I just might!'

I took a glass of Madeira too, since I thought it might help to steady my nerves, and sure enough, by the time the guests began to arrive I was feeling the effects of it – a warm glow that I hoped was not showing in my cheeks, and ever so slightly light-headed.

As we welcomed them the trio was playing, very softly, so as not to make conversation difficult, and I floated through, greeting those I had already met and being introduced to those I had not in a pleasant haze. Once, as I made polite small talk with a fat, pompous alderman and his even fatter, even more self-satisfied wife, I caught Theo's eye and he winked at me. I was forced to look quickly away, for I feared that I, like Aunt Linnie, might giggle, and I did not think that giggling, whilst talking to such important folk, would be looked upon favourably.

Little morsels of food were served by no less than three black slave boys who had been brought in especially for the occasion and who wore silver collars upon which their names had been engraved – Zion, Melchior and Job. The wine flowed freely, and though I tried to sip sparingly, my glass was replenished so regularly that I dreaded to think how much had actually passed my lips.

A cold table had been set in the dining room and we had repaired there to fill our plates with slices of meat and game pie when a manservant came to whisper to Mr Paterson that there were more guests arriving. Since we were at the time engaged in conversation with yet another dignitary, Mr Paterson left me talking with them whilst he went to greet the latecomers.

'You must come and take tea with us the moment you can spare an hour,' Mrs de Vere, the dignitary's wife, was gushing.

'Thank you, that would be very nice,' I replied politely, though my heart was sinking, for the thought of long afternoons of stiff socializing did not appeal to me in the least.

And then, over her shoulder, I saw Mr Paterson returning with the new arrivals, and my heart seemed to stop beating.

One was a grand lady, of indeterminate age, bewigged, bejewelled, imposing. But it was the other who had my full attention; the other who made the breath catch in my throat.

Tall, weatherbeaten, good-looking in an unforgettably rugged way.

The man who had accosted me outside the hot well. The man I had sought in vain. The man Theo had warned me against.

Here, in Mr Paterson's house.

They were coming towards me, picking their way through the little knots of guests. My heart began to beat again, very fast, very unevenly, and a dozen confused thoughts raced through my brain all at once – *What was he doing here? How had he come to be invited? Who* was *he?* – and my emotions churned. Shock, nervousness, given that Theo had warned me he could be dangerous – and that same sense of joy I had experienced when I had first seen him on the quayside. His hazel eyes were on my face, his mouth a set, unsmiling line. There was a calculation in those eyes now, which had not been there before, and it unnerved me.

Mr Paterson caught my hand, tucking it through the crook of his arm, and smiling beatifically.

'Lady Avonbridge, I am proud to present my future wife, Miss Grimes. Davina, may I introduce Her Ladyship.'

The grand lady extended a hand, which sparkled with precious stones in ornate settings, and I took it. Under normal circumstances I would have been overawed – I had never before, to my knowledge, shaken the hand of a member of the aristocracy, never even been in such close proximity even. But the sight of the man at her side had wiped all else from my mind.

'And I must introduce you to my friend,' Lady Avonbridge said with a slight smile. 'I hope, John, that you will forgive me for having taken the liberty of asking him to accompany me this evening. This is Mr Richard Wells. You may be familiar with his name.'

'Indeed.' Mr Paterson extended his hand, but his lips had tightened a shade, and I thought there was a certain lack of warmth in his tone. 'I am honoured to make your acquaintance, Mr Wells.'

'Richard, please.' He took Mr Paterson's outstretched hand. 'I am delighted to make your acquaintance at last.' He returned his gaze to me, level, disconcerting. 'And yours, Miss Grimes.'

Because convention called for it, I extended my own hand, which trembled slightly. His fingers touched mine, holding them firmly, and a tremor ran through me, a tremor as sharp as if I had been struck by lightning. For a brief moment in time some emotion twisted in me, unfamiliar, yet half-remembered, and was gone.

'Mr Wells.' There was a tiny tremor in my voice too; I hoped desperately that neither he nor Mr Paterson would notice it.

Richard Wells released my hand; I pressed it against my skirts, seeming still to feel the touch of those fingers, cool, firm.

70

'You are indeed a lucky man, Mr Paterson.' His eyes never left my face as he said it. Nor when he added: 'Davina reminds me very much of someone I once knew. Someone—'

'Who broke his heart,' Lady Avonbridge interjected. She was looking at me, too, I realized, my discomfort growing. Her eyes were sharp, and there was a slight twist to her mouth which might almost have been amusement.

'Do please allow me to furnish you with a drink,' Mr Paterson said.

They moved away and I closed my eyes briefly, trying to compose myself. Richard Wells *had* known me, I felt sure – why else would he have engineered this opportunity to see me once again? For that, I felt certain, was what he had done. And something was telling me that I had known him too, though I had not recognized him and could not recollect a single fact about our acquaintance.

But whoever he was, I did not think Mr Paterson had been very pleased that he was here. Though polite, his manner had been distinctly frosty. Was that because Richard Wells was indeed the 'dangerous' man of whom Theo had spoken – the man from whom my mother had sought to protect me? I had to know.

I looked around for Theo and saw him entering the dining room deep in conversation with a man I recognized as another of the Merchant Venturers. Clearly he was taking advantage of the occasion to further his own ambitions. But there would be other opportunities for him to socialize with the great and the good of Bristol; my need to speak to him was more pressing.

I made my way through the guests, fielding their attempts to engage me in conversation with a polite smile and all the determination I could muster.

'Theo!' I touched his arm urgently. 'Can I speak with you?'

'Davina!' He excused himself from the merchant and led me to a corner of the room. 'What is wrong? You look dreadfully flustered.'

71

'He's here,' I said. 'The man who accosted me near the hot well.'

'The devil he is!' Theo exclaimed. 'Where is he?'

'Over there.' I nodded in the direction of the cold table. 'That's him, with Mr Paterson, and a grand lady by the name of—'

'Richard Wells!' Theo exclaimed, following the nod of my head. 'Good Christ! How did he come to be on the guest list?'

'I don't think he was,' I said. 'He arrived with Lady Avonbridge. I don't think Mr Paterson was very pleased to see him.'

'I'll wager he was not!' Theo said with feeling.

'So – who is he?' I asked.

'He was a sea captain, I believe. Now he meddles in things that do not concern him.' Theo's tone was grim. 'And you are certain he is the man who spoke to you and called you Rowan?'

'Of course I'm certain!' I returned with asperity. 'I might remember nothing of my past, but there's nothing wrong with my faculties when it comes to recalling what happened a few days ago!'

'Well, it's a surprise to me, and no mistake!' Theo said. 'But in some ways it fits well enough. I told you the person involved with first your mother and then you was a dangerous man – and Richard Wells certainly fits that description.'

'But why? What has he done?' I asked.

'Oh, it's a long story,' Theo replied vaguely. 'And not one that I care to go into now. But you'd do well to steer clear of him, Davina. Now I know who he is, I'm even more convinced of it. He might well pose a real threat to you.'

'He can hardly harm me here,' I argued.

Theo took my arm urgently. 'He is a devious man as well as a dangerous one,' he said grimly. 'And he has the nerve of the very Devil. To inveigle his way in here tonight . . . That tells you something about how ruthlessly determined he is.'

'To see me,' I said, and perversely something that was part pride and part joy stirred within me.

'I told you the man in question was obsessed with you, Davina,' Theo said harshly. 'Now you must see for yourself that I was not exaggerating. Stay close to me, there's a good girl, and take no chances.'

A tiny shard of resentment prickled, along with all my other confused, conflicting emotions. The man who might be able to tell me something about my lost past was here, in the very same room as I was. If I let the opportunity to speak with him slip away I would later regret it, I felt sure. And yet . . .

If he *had* molested me, if he *had* followed my mother and myself and perhaps even held up our carriage in order to abduct me, then he was indeed dangerous. A man who would do such a thing would stop at nothing. And besides . . .

For the first time, it occurred to me that perhaps I might learn things I would prefer not to know. Could it be that the veils that obscured my memories of my past life had remained so stubbornly closed for a reason? Was it that they hid something so terrible I could not bear to face it? Was my memory loss not a curse, but a blessing, something that had occurred not just because of the accident, but as a device to save my sanity?

I shrank inwardly suddenly, afraid, terribly afraid, of what it was that was hidden from me. And still the compulsion was there, battling with the fear that Theo's warning had awakened in me. A compulsion to learn the truth, however terrible. And a compulsion that drew me inexorably to Mr Richard Wells.

Six

It was, perhaps, approaching eleven o'clock when I missed Aunt Linnie.

Somehow I had gone through the motions of acting as hostess, and the performance of my duties and the demands of the guests had taken from my hands the decision as to whether or not I should seek out Richard Wells and try to answer some of the burning questions that troubled me. I had, I think, taken a little too much wine, but that was not a bad thing, for I felt after a little while that I was floating, rather than walking on trembling legs, and the world was floating around me; nothing really seemed quite so important any more.

Good as his word, Theo had remained close to my side, though Mr Paterson had left me to my own devices whilst he circulated amongst the guests and made frequent visits to the morning room to smoke a cigar with his male friends.

When I noticed Aunt Linnie's absence, I was a little concerned. I hoped that *she* had not taken too much wine, for she was as unused to it as I was, and not nearly as young and strong.

Theo had relaxed a little in his scrutiny of me and was chatting to yet another merchant, and I managed to slip unobtrusively away. For the moment I did not want to mention my concern for Aunt Linnie to Theo in case it should turn out that she was indeed a little the worse for drink, for she would be mortified, I knew, if Theo were to witness her in such a state.

I went through to the great hall, where the trio were still playing; I could not see her amongst the people there. I looked in the dining room, again with no success, and then in one of the ante-rooms. And there I found her.

I think she must indeed have had a little too much wine, or perhaps excitement at the grand occasion had overcome her, for she was sitting on a small chaise, fast asleep. Her wig had fallen slightly askew, her mouth was wide open, her eyes closed. I shook my head, smiling to myself at the picture she made, and stood wondering whether or not I should waken her. She would not want any of the other guests to see her so, I felt sure. But she looked so peaceful sitting there that it seemed it would be a crime to disturb her.

As I stood there, undecided, I suddenly became aware of someone in the doorway behind me.

I spun round, and came face to face with Richard Wells.

Breath caught in my throat; my limbs seemed to freeze. I tried to speak; no words would come. Richard Wells took my arm, drawing me into the room and closing the door behind him.

'Rowan,' he said.

His tone was low and urgent; the flickering light from a candelabrum on the mantle shelf illuminated his face, those hazel eyes darkened now, deep shadows marking the lines that ran between his nose and the corners of his mouth. He towered over me, a powerful figure, all coiled strength and hard muscle.

'I have to talk to you,' he said. 'You can't avoid me for ever.'

Somehow I found my voice.

'Who are you?' I whispered. 'What do you want with me?'

His hand tightened on my arm as if he thought I might run from him – and indeed I almost might have done if there had been an ounce of strength left in my trembling legs.

'Do you truly not remember me? Dear God, Rowan . . .'

'Why do you call me that?' I asked.

'Why, because it's your name! I cannot believe you do not know it, even if you don't know me! I thought, when I first saw you at the hot well, that I was going mad! I had thought you dead, and when you told me your name was Davina—'

'It is,' I said stubbornly.

'It's the name they are calling you by, I grant you. And at first I thought you must be her double, come back to haunt me. But that's not so – I know that now. And so must you.'

'I don't,' I said. 'I don't know anything. I was injured in a carriage accident two years ago. My life prior to that is a complete blank. And you are a stranger to me.'

'A stranger!' He uttered an oath. 'Are you telling me you remember nothing? Nothing at all?'

'Nothing but my grandparents nursing me back to health, and my life with them.' I drew a trembling breath. 'But you still haven't told me who you are.'

'I am . . .' His tone was harsh. 'I am the man who loves you. The man you loved when you were Rowan Gillespie.'

'Rowan *Gillespie* . . .' I repeated. The name stirred in the depths of my memory like a summer breeze through the leaves of a birch tree, bringing with it some faint, haunting scents from another place, another life, and the feeling that I stood on the very brink of remembering. The sensation was awesome; it frightened me as I recalled the idea that the past might be something so dreadful I had *chosen* to forget.

'Did you come here tonight on purpose to see me again?' I challenged him.

He nodded. 'I have to admit I did. With the assistance of my good friend Lady Avonbridge.'

'But how did you know . . . ?'

'That I would find you here? Oh, that was easy enough,' he said roughly. 'I recognized your carriage by the hot well. Everyone in Bristol knows John Paterson's landaulet, and Thomas who drives it, dressed up in that blue livery as a child might dress a doll, with that disgusting silver collar around his neck. I thought perhaps you were working for John Paterson in some capacity. I could scarcely believe it when I learned that you are to *marry* him!' His fingers tightened on my arm again; his features in the flickering candlelight were grim. 'You cannot go through with it, Rowan! I won't let you!'

76

'I have to,' I said. 'My grandparents . . .'

'Your grandparents!' He swore again.

'Don't speak of them like that!' I said sharply. 'They are good people, and they love me!'

'*Love* you?' His tone was scornful. 'How can they *love* you, and do what they have done?'

The fear was back, prickling over my skin, and this time I faced it.

'What do you mean?'

'Pshaw! It's a strange sort of love that robs you of your identity and hides the truth of your past. A strange sort of love that tears you away from those who care most for you and need you, then marries you off to a man old enough to be your father, for the sake of his wealth and position—'

'That's not so!' I protested.

'Isn't it? Oh, I think it is! Theo Grimes and his father have been trying for years to infiltrate the company of the Merchant Venturers. In you they have seen their chance. They are using you, Rowan, for their own ends, just as they use everyone – without scruple – if they see the slightest benefit in it.'

'No!' I protested again, unwilling to hear my family slandered so by a man who was, after all, a stranger to me whatever he might say.

Richard Wells' face darkened. 'You don't love him, do you?' he demanded.

I could not answer. I could not betray Mr Paterson with the truth, but neither could I lie.

'You can't love him!' Richard Wells sounded aghast, as if the possibility had never occurred to him before, and now he was facing the unthinkable. 'No, I don't believe it! If you think you love him, Rowan . . .' The hand on my arm slipped to my wrist, jerking me roughly towards him. 'I'll remind you what love is. This!'

Before I could move a muscle in my own defence, I found myself pressed against him so close I could scarcely breathe. With one hand he still held me by the wrist, the other was around my back, his fingers like rods of steel digging into my skin through the thin silk of my gown.

I gasped with the last of my breath, and as I did so, his mouth came down on mine hard, trapping my lips with his as his hands trapped my body.

I felt a moment's utter panic. And then, unbelievably, my lips were responding to his, and instead of trying to push him away or beat him off, my hands were on his upper arms, feeling the hard ridge of muscle there, holding him at first tentatively, then firmly. And something was stirring within me, some primeval urgency that was painful and sweet, both at the same time. There was warmth, there was desire, there was a magnetism so strong that without any thought I moved closer, so that my hips were pressed against his. And it felt right, so right!

I clung to him with no thought beyond a need I had never before knowingly experienced and yet which felt as familiar as the drawing of breath. And with it, the joy. Unbridled joy, a sense of coming home.

My lips parted, for all the world as if they knew exactly what to do, and I tasted his tongue. Closer, closer, but I wanted – needed – to be closer yet, and the urgency was a fire in me, chastening me, blotting out all conscious thought.

And then the door flew open, brighter light flooded the little room, and, as if from a long way off, I heard Theo's voice.

'Faith! What is happening here?'

The spell was broken; I tried to pull away, but Richard Wells' arms held me still.

'You vermin! How dare you . . .' Theo was, I could tell, beside himself.

Richard Wells released me; I spun round. Theo caught my wrist, pulling me away behind him, out of Richard's reach.

'Don't touch her!' he grated out. 'And get out of this house.'

'Who do you think you are, Grimes?' Richard's tone matched Theo's. 'You are not master here.'

'No, but John Paterson is, and it is his intended wife you are molesting,' Theo returned. 'When he knows what you have done, he'll have you hung, drawn and quartered. So,

78

if you value your life, you'll go now, before I make him aware of it.'

'And if *I* make him aware of a thing or two?' Richard Wells said. His voice was low and threatening. 'If *I* were to tell him he has been taken for a fool, what then? His intended wife, as you call her, is not free to marry him – and well you know it. And there's more I could tell him, too, that would not please him – your dealings, to begin with.'

'You know nothing of my dealings!' Theo raged.

'I know enough, and I'll know more yet. But at this moment, it's Rowan who concerns me. I will not see her wed John Paterson, or anyone else. She is mine!'

So shocked was I by my encounter with Richard Wells, Theo's abrupt intervention and Richard's furious tirade, that I had not had the wit to wonder about the things he was saying. But Richard's retort cut sharply into my conscious mind. The words were an echo of what Theo had said to me before – that the 'dangerous' man from whom my mother had sought to protect me had threatened that, if he could not have me, no one else would.

A knot of panic deep inside me seemed to swamp all my other churning emotions. Suddenly, all I wanted was to run away from the angry voices, the claustrophobic room, the uncertainty, the pressures that had been brought to bear on me. My nerves were jangling, my legs trembling beneath me, the pain sharp as a bolt throbbing once again in my temple.

'Stop it!' I cried. 'Stop it, both of you! I can't bear it!'

'Rowan?' Richard Wells sounded alarmed; but it was Theo whose arm went around me, supporting me.

'Now see what you have done!' he grated at Richard Wells. 'Davina has been very sick. Do you want to bring on a relapse?'

'I want only for her to remember!' Richard Wells returned harshly. 'The choice she is making is no choice at all when she does not know what it is she is losing! She must be told the truth, and then—'

'The truth!' Theo exclaimed. 'That's rich, coming from you! The truth is not something you are familiar with, Wells!

79

Davina's family saved her from you once and we'll do it again, if I have to kill you!'

'Oh please!' I cried. 'Don't begin again! Don't . . .'

'I'm taking her now to her future husband,' Theo said. 'And you had better stay away from her, Wells, if you value your life.' He started with me towards the door, but with a movement surprisingly swift for such a big man, Richard Wells was there before us, blocking the way.

'Then let her tell me first that she does not want to know what was between us . . . what will always be between us. Let her tell me first that she is prepared to sacrifice everything for marriage with John Paterson.' He looked directly at me. 'Rowan?'

'I have to marry him,' I whispered wretchedly.

'Because your so-called family have told you that you must! They don't care a tinker's cuss for you, Rowan, except for what you can do for them! For God's sake, listen to me!'

'Stand aside, Wells, and let us pass.' Theo's voice was low and threatening. 'If you do not—'

'You don't love him, Rowan!' Richard Wells said urgently. 'If you can remember nothing else, think of the kiss we just shared. Does he kiss you that way? Would you want him to? No! And you must not tie yourself to him for the rest of your life! Can't you see that, at least?'

Tears had gathered in my eyes, tears of panic and confusion, tears for a past I could not remember and a future I dreaded. But: 'I have to marry him!' I repeated. 'I am promised.'

'Rowan . . .'

'Oh please!' I cried. 'Just go away and leave me alone!'

For a moment longer he stood there, barring our path, then he moved abruptly, throwing open the door.

'Very well, if that's what you want.' His tone was cold now, cold as ice. 'I hope, Rowan, you will not live to regret it. But I know you will, if memory comes to you too late.'

He turned, and was gone.

My trembling legs threatened to give way beneath me;

the tears ran in a hot flood down my cheeks. I turned to Theo, burying my face in his shoulder and crying out all my confusion and despair into the fine wool of his coat.

On the chaise, totally oblivious to the drama that had unfolded, Aunt Linnie slept.

I do not know how I managed to get through what was left of the evening, but somehow I did, with not one of the guests, nor even Mr Paterson, realizing the turmoil that raged within me.

When at last I was able to stop crying, Theo lent me a kerchief to wipe my face and we emerged from the ante-room, leaving Aunt Linnie to her wine-induced slumbers.

The party was still in full swing and no one seemed to have missed me. But of Richard Wells and Lady Avonbridge there was no sign. They must have left, I thought, immediately following the altercation. And a good thing too, for if they had still been in the house, I dreaded to think what Theo might have done. Yet a perverse little bit of me regretted it. The chance to glimpse my past had been there, close enough for me to reach out and touch it, and now it had gone, very likely for ever.

But more, far more than that . . . Oh, I could feel yet the touch of Richard Wells' lips on mine, the urgency that had ached and throbbed in me when I was in his arms. I could see his face, strong and shadowed in the candlelight. Hear his voice, urging me not to marry Mr Paterson.

'What did he mean, Theo?' I had asked when my tears had stopped sufficiently to allow me to speak. 'What did he mean when he said Mr Paterson was being taken for a fool – and that I was not free to marry him?'

And Theo, striving without much success to contain his impatience in an effort to calm me down, had replied: 'He'd say anything, Davina, to try to put doubts in your mind. Forget about it. It meant nothing.'

But it worried at me still; that, and the intensity of my response to him.

I was ashamed, too. Ashamed that I could have behaved in

such a wanton way, ashamed, even, of the feelings of desire he had awakened in me. My cheeks burned as I remembered it, and the pain in my temple burned so fiercely I could scarcely bear it. But somehow I kept it all within myself, somehow I hid it and smiled at the guests and made foolish conversation, which they seemed to think was charming. And not one of them, I think, was aware of the turmoil raging within me. Not one, except perhaps Theo, who remained by my side, watching me closely through hooded eyes. And when the last guest had left and Mr Paterson, a little the worse for drink himself, pulled me close, with an arm about my waist and a rum-soaked kiss that mercifully missed my mouth and landed on my cheek, it was Theo who said: 'I think it's time we took Davina home, John. You'll have her all to yourself soon enough.'

'Indeed, and I cannot wait!' Mr Paterson said. 'You were a triumph tonight, my dear. A veritable triumph!'

I smiled at him with stiff lips and went with Theo to the carriage, where I was sandwiched in between him and a still-tipsy Aunt Linnie, whilst Great-Uncle Charles sprawled on the seat opposite, Malacca cane held unsteadily between his bony knees.

I had known Richard Wells in my other life; I now had no doubt of that. There had been something between us. But whether it had been something good or something so evil that I was better off not remembering it, I did not know. The questions were still there, more troubling than ever, questions I might have to live with, unanswered, for the rest of my life.

Only one thing was certain. I was promised to Mr Paterson, and by this time next week I would be his wife. Unless I chose to renege on the agreement. But that would cause the most enormous upset and bring great distress to the only people I could remember showing me love and affection.

I turned my face towards the carriage window, looking out on the dark streets of the city that was now my home, and felt nothing but confusion and utter despair.

*   *   *

The dream came again that night, and it was just as before. The carriage, occupied by myself and my mother and that mysterious someone who was hidden from me by a veil. The abrupt halt, the face at the window, my feeling of surprise, the shot, the wild, terrifying charge into the blackness of the night, the sense of impending doom, the crash, the edge of all-enveloping darkness. But this time, at the moment when the dream stopped and the darkness began, I cried out a name. And I thought that name was Richard.

With every day that passed, bringing me closer to my wedding day, my doubts increased, if such a thing were possible. Yet I could see no way out. No way at all.

I talked with Theo again, but the talk got us nowhere; we simply went around in circles. Theo apologized, it is true, for his behaviour on the night of the reception.

'I'm sorry if I frightened you, Davina, but I could think of nothing but protecting you from that devil. How he had the brass nerve to gatecrash the party, I can't imagine – but it is clear proof, if proof were needed, of the lengths to which he is prepared to go. Sweet Jesu, when I think of what might have happened . . . ! Why, even as it was . . .'

He broke off and I knew he was thinking of the scene he had walked in on, but could not bring himself to mention.

I did not wish to mention it either. I felt too much shame. In one respect at least, I had no doubt Theo was right. It was not safe for me to be alone with Richard Wells. Never mind that I was afraid, in the light of what Theo had told me, to trust him. I did not trust myself!

What would have occurred had Theo not come bursting in? I wondered. Oh, I did not think Richard Wells would have harmed me, but there are other things to fear besides physical harm. As it was, I had disgraced myself and dishonoured Mr Paterson. And with the strong feelings which had robbed me of my self-control and sense of propriety, heaven only knows where the encounter would have led me.

My grandparents arrived, taking another of the guest rooms in Great-Uncle Charles' house, and, whilst I was glad to see them, their arrival brought home to me more clearly than ever the finality of the course I was set upon. And made it more difficult than ever for me to even think of changing my mind.

'Oh Davina, I know this is the right thing for you,' Grandmama said.

She was not excitable about the coming nuptials as Aunt Linnie was, but she had a serene look about her, a glow that came from her obvious relief that my future was secure and she no longer had to worry that I might follow my mother and end up living a rackety life, far removed from the respectability they set so much store by. I did feel, however, that I must raise with her the fact that they had not been entirely honest with me.

'Grandmama,' I said, when we were alone. 'Theo has told me something of the circumstances surrounding my accident.'

'Oh!' The serene look was gone from her face, replaced by a look of consternation, and, it has to be said, displeasure. 'He should not have—'

'He only did so because I pressed him,' I said. 'I realize you were only thinking of my best interests in keeping it from me, but it is very important to me that I learn everything I can about my past. Not knowing is dreadful; it plays constantly on my mind.'

'Perhaps it is better that way,' Grandmama said stubbornly.

'Perhaps, but nevertheless . . .' I hesitated, then: 'Theo told me we had been to visit you just before the accident occurred,' I continued. 'He said that we were seeking refuge from a man who was a threat to me. I know this is painful for you, but is there anything more you can tell me about that man? What Mama said to you about the reasons she thought he was a danger, for instance?'

My grandmother shook her head. There was a tight, closed-in look to her face now.

'Nothing.'

'But surely . . . she must have said something by way of explanation! *I* must have said something!'

'I can tell you nothing because there is nothing to tell,' Grandmama said. 'We never saw you and your mother that day. We were out, visiting one of your grandfather's parishioners who was dying. Your grandfather was administering the last rites to him, and I went along with him in the hope that I could be of some comfort to his poor wife, who was soon to be a widow.'

'But Theo said . . .' I hesitated, confused. 'Theo said you turned us away, and that you felt terrible guilt at having done so . . .'

'Then Theo is mistaken,' Grandmama said firmly. 'It happened just as I said, Davina. We were not at home. It was only later that we learned you had come to us – George Hickley saw the carriage at the rectory gate, and you and your mother knocking at the door. He recognized your mother, of course. He had known her as a young woman, before . . . before she went away. The guilt we bear is that we were not there in her hour of need. She had swallowed her foolish pride, come back to seek our assistance, and we were not there. That is all I can tell you.'

Her face had crumpled, her lip trembled, and she twisted a small square of white lace kerchief between her fingers.

I was filled with disappointment and the all-too-familiar feeling of frustration. Once again I had come up against a blank wall. I was not sure who to believe as to the rights and wrongs of the story, Grandmama or Theo. But one thing was quite clear. I was going to learn no more, no matter how hard I pressed Grandmama.

'It's all behind you now, Davina,' Grandmama said urgently, recovering herself a little. 'Your future is secure now, that's all that matters. You must look forward.'

'But . . .' I wished I dared say in no uncertain terms that I did not want to marry Mr Paterson. But whilst I sought for the words, Grandmama took my hand in hers.

'We do feel guilt, Davina.' Her lip trembled again. 'Though it was fate that we were not at home that day, we still wonder if things might have turned out differently if we had been there. To have seen Elizabeth again, after so many years, would have meant so much to me – and to your grandfather, too, though he would never admit it. He is a proud man, and she had hurt him so much. But we did our best to make up to you for what had happened, you must believe that.'

'I do, of course,' I said.

'Everything we did, we did with your best interests at heart,' Grandmama said, and it was only much later that it occurred to me that her choice of words was strange to say the least of it. 'Everything. And now . . . now we know your future is assured. You will be happy with Mr Paterson, I know – and we will be happy knowing it. So now, show me your wedding gown, dear, and let us forget about the sad times and the troubles, and look to the good times that lie ahead.'

What could I say? What could I do? There was nothing for it but to let go this conversation that was clearly distressing to my dear, sweet grandmama. And before I knew it, I was once again being carried along on the tide of preparations for the wedding.

It dawned, my wedding day, bright and clear, like most of the other days that summer. But there was no sunshine in my heart, only a fog as thick and dark as the one which clouded my mind.

Grandfather was to assist the bishop with the ceremony and Great-Uncle Charles was too tottery to give me away, so it was Theo who rode beside me in the carriage, Theo who lent me his arm as we stood at the back of the cathedral and looked down the long aisle to where Mr Paterson waited.

The cathedral was full, a sea of faces turned to look at me, but I did not look at them. I saw nothing but Mr Paterson waiting for me, and even that was tinged with a sense of unreality. I heard nothing but the pounding of blood in my ears. I felt nothing. I was too numb.

Theo smiled at me encouragingly as we started the long walk, and squeezed my hand, which lay in the crook of his arm. But I could not smile back. For the life of me, I could not smile back.

'You must be the loveliest bride this cathedral has ever seen,' he murmured in my ear. 'I wish it was me you were marrying, Davina.'

I could have wished it too. Though I was no more in love with Theo than I was with Mr Paterson, at least he was closer to me in age, at least he was able to make me laugh, at least we shared some sort of rapport. But he could not wish it all that much, I thought, since he had arranged this marriage. All very well for him to say he desired me: he desired the advantages my union with Mr Paterson would bring him more.

And so we moved down the aisle with a ripple of admiration following, and I took my place beside my future husband at the altar rail.

When the bishop spoke the words asking if there were any just cause or impediment to the marriage taking place, I caught my breath, remembering Richard Wells' assertion that I was not free to wed. But no one spoke; one could have dropped a pin and heard it fall in the hush that descended on the packed cathedral. And then we were making our vows, Mr Paterson in a firm, rolling voice that must have carried to every lofty corner, me in a low whisper. And the bishop was proclaiming us man and wife and asking God's blessing on our union.

It was done. Nothing could save me now. My legs trembled beneath the ivory silk of my skirts, my heart was heavy. But somehow I held myself erect, somehow I forced a smile to my lips, somehow I managed not to lean too heavily on Mr Paterson's arm as we made our way back down the aisle to the door of the cathedral.

We came out into the bright sunshine to the clamour of pealing bells and the excited congratulations of the guests.

And then I saw him. A tall, weatherbeaten figure standing on the opposite side of the street, his face, in contrast to all the smiling ones, grim and drawn.

For just a moment our eyes met, and that tantalizing twist of emotion stirred in me, a sense of longing so great that I wanted nothing more in the whole world than to throw down my wedding bouquet and run to him. And as I stared at him,

87

my heart seeming to reach out to his across the width of the street, he bent down so that for a moment he was lost to my view behind the crowd of onlookers that had gathered. Then he straightened, and to my astonishment I saw that he now held a child in his arms. A little girl, not much more than a toddler, whose hair shone bright gold in the sunlight.

Breath caught in my throat. The sight of Richard Wells – the brooding, wholly masculine man whom Theo had described as 'dangerous' – with a child in his arms startled me so that I had not a single coherent thought. The way he held her, as if he was perfectly comfortable with doing so, the way her small fair head leaned so trustingly against his dark one, was so surprising I could only stare, open-mouthed, whilst emotions I could not identify raged through me like forest fire through dry brush.

Mr Paterson said something to me – I scarcely heard him, and then a crowd of smiling guests enveloped us and a cloud of rose petals obscured my vision of the man who called to me with every fibre of his unknown being and the child he held in his arms. And when they cleared, he had gone.

Frantic suddenly, I scoured the street for them: they were nowhere to be seen. I wondered for an insane moment if I had imagined it – that he had not been there at all and he and the child were just a product of my fevered imagination. But I knew I had not imagined it.

Richard Wells had come to the cathedral to see for himself whether I had gone through with the marriage he had sought to prevent me making, and when he saw that I had, he had slipped away.

But who was the child he had brought with him? And why had he brought her? Simply to see a bride in all her wedding finery, because he knew the spectacle would please her? Or for some other, inexplicable reason? I did not know, and in all likelihood, never would.

I was now Mrs John Paterson, my life changed for ever. I was tied, till death us do part, to the man who was now my husband.

Seven

I remember very little of the wedding breakfast but the simpering, gushing and weeping of the female guests and the unashamed imbibing of copious amounts of liquor by the men. I remember even less of changing from my wedding gown into my new travelling outfit, helped by the girl Mr Paterson had engaged to be my personal maid, and watched, misty-eyed, by Grandmama.

'You look beautiful, Davina,' she said, and I suppose the outfit was very likely finer than any she had ever seen, and more fashionable by far than any that the ladies of Grandfather's parish wore to church on Sundays. It consisted of a redingote gown in pink, rucked at the hem and neck, and a short black double-breasted jacket with wide lapels and sleeves. To complete the ensemble the milliner had made me a green felt hat with pink ribbons which matched exactly the colour of my gown, and pink gloves.

'Beautiful,' Grandmama said, brushing an imaginary speck of dust from my shoulder and tweaking the buttons, quite unnecessarily, since Perrett, my new maid, had done an excellent job. She had been trained in a most aristocratic household, Mr Paterson had told me, and came to me with excellent references.

'And now,' Grandmama said, leaning close so that she could speak softly, 'Now, at last, you will be safe, my dear.'

Safe. The word reverberated with a hollow echo in the mists that had descended to envelop me. *Safe* – but from whom? From the so-called 'dangerous' man who had stood to watch me emerge from the cathedral, tenderly holding a child in his arms? How could such a man pose any real threat to me? The now familiar compulsion ached once more in me, the longing for I knew not what, but which was so strong it was an almost physical pain. And with it the fear of what it might be that I longed for with every fibre of my being.

Safe from myself and my dangerous desires. No – not safe from my desires – they were with me still. Safe from where they might lead me, yes. Safe, as a bird in a cage is safe when all freedom is lost. I had briefly glimpsed what might lie beyond the bars that had contained me for the past two years since I had awoken to find myself in the small, dark bedroom at the rectory, where the creeper grew thick around the window and the branches of a great sycamore tree blotted out the sun, and now it was lost to me again. Even if memory returned to free my mind, yet still I was a prisoner, bound by the vows I had made in the presence of God and the assembled congregation.

The knowledge pressed down on me like a great weight and I retreated once more into the hinterland where thoughts and feelings were disconnected from reality, whilst I went through the motions of what I must do.

Mr Paterson had planned a wedding tour to celebrate our marriage. We were to travel to Weymouth and spend the night there before setting sail for France. When he had first talked of it, I had imagined we would sail out of Bristol on one of his own ships, but he had other ideas. For one thing, his fleet were all tied up with his various trading enterprises; for another, he was concerned that, since I had never been to sea before, the crossing should be as short as possible.

'Seasickness can be very unpleasant,' he had said. 'It disappears as if by magic the moment one sets foot on dry land again, but whilst it lasts, the sufferer truly believes his last day has come. I want you to have happy memories of the first days of our marriage, my dear, not nightmarish ones. We'll travel down to the south coast and set out from there, on a ship better equipped for the comfort of passengers than my own.'

And so it was that, as soon as I was ready, we climbed

into the carriage – not the landaulet, but a much larger and grander vehicle – with Thomas in the driver's seat and all our trunks and the servants who were to accompany us packed into another carriage behind.

The entire assembly came to wave us off, with the exception of Great-Uncle Charles, who had imbibed a little too much wine but was blaming the leg pains he said he was plagued by for his inability to walk steadily.

Grandmama and Aunt Linnie were tearful, Grandfather silent and a little disapproving of what he saw as excessive sentiment. As if to distance himself from the proceedings, which, in his opinion, detracted from the solemnity of the marriage rites, he stood a little apart, head bowed, hands clasped, and I had to make a small detour in order to kiss him goodbye. And then we were in the carriage, pulling away, and Mr Paterson's moist palm was covering my hand, lifting it to rest on his plump, silk-covered thigh, and beaming with satisfaction.

'A good day, Davina. Everything went off without a hitch, exactly to plan. Did you enjoy it, my dear?'

'Yes,' I lied. 'It was wonderful.'

'And that is only the beginning of your new life. I intend to spoil you shamelessly. You will love France and Italy, I know. Though the French are a strange people – and quarrelsome – they can be hospitable, too, once we get away from the cities and into the countryside. Or perhaps it's just that they know a good thing when they see one!' He laughed, and patted his money pouch. 'Money talks, Davina, never forget it. Money can buy respect and friendship as well as fine wine and good food.'

And a wife, I thought bitterly.

'And it's something you won't have to be short of ever again,' he went on. 'Whatever you fancy, my dear, just name it, and it's yours. Whatever. Don't be afraid to ask, now, will you? It's been a long time since I was party to a woman's whims, and I can't pretend I ever understood them very well. So don't be shy. Just appraise me of your desires, and I'll see you're not disappointed.'

'Thank you,' I said quite formally. 'You are very kind.'

'Kind? No!' He chuckled. 'It's myself I'm thinking of. If you're happy, then I shall be happy too. And I assure you, I shall not hesitate to make my desires clear to *you*, my dear. Honesty in a relationship is by far the best policy, don't you think?'

His plump, moist fingers tightened over my hand and moved it a little higher on his thigh, closer to his groin. Some nerve tightened inside me, and every muscle seemed to shrink away from him. This was what I had been dreading, the enforced intimacy of the wedded state; my side of the bargain. But I forced myself to remain immobile, willed my fingers not to tremble, and sought not to think about the duties I would soon be called upon to perform.

I had no choice, and repellent though the very idea was to me, I did not want to hurt Mr Paterson's feelings. He had shown me nothing but kindness; it was not his fault that he was old and fat. It was not his fault that I did not love him and never could. It was not his fault that he was not . . .

Again I saw the tall lean figure of Richard Wells in my mind's eye; again I felt a pang of longing for some half-remembered delight, and, with an effort, closed my mind to it. Tonight I must lie with my husband in some strange bed and submit to his embraces. And somehow I must hide my revulsion and behave as a good wife should.

It was my duty now. Pleasure did not enter into it. I had entered into a solemn and binding arrangement. And I must fulfil my part in it, whether I wanted to or not.

In the event I was spared the worst of what I dreaded, that night at least.

By the time we reached the inn where we were to spend the night, it was late. We were shown to our suite of rooms on the first floor, and Mr Paterson declared his need for a jug of good porter and went off downstairs to sup it in the public bar.

When Perrett had helped me undress and put on my nightgown, I went to the window and threw it open, for

92

the room was hot and airless. There was a smell of salt in the breeze that came wafting in, and I could hear the lap of the sea, rhythmic and somehow somnolent in the still darkness, and it stirred some distant memory of forgotten happiness and went some way to calming my shattered nerves.

After a little while I went to the bed and lay down on the lumpy mattress, pulling the sheets up to my chin, and I was drifting towards an exhausted sleep when a tap on the door brought me back to full consciousness.

'Are you still awake, my dear?'

It was Mr Paterson.

I lay still and silent, hoping he would think I was asleep and not wish to disturb me, but it was not to be. A board creaked and I saw his heavy form silhouetted against the moonlit window.

'Now, now, Davina, I know you are teasing me,' he said playfully. His voice was a little slurred. 'You are a naughty girl to arouse an old man so and leave him cold. You *are* awake, aren't you? Come, it's no use pretending!'

'Mr Paterson . . .' I murmured faintly, trying to sound sleepy and a little bemused, as if he had just woken me.

'John!' he insisted groggily. 'How often do I have to ask you to call me John?'

'John,' I repeated obediently.

He was getting undressed now, rather unsteadily, stumbling around somewhat as he pulled off his breeches and shirt and let them drop on to the floor. For a moment I had a glimpse of his vast, naked body, and then he put on a voluminous nightshirt,which he must have collected from his own room on his way to mine, for it was certainly not there when I had retired. Although it made him faintly ridiculous, I felt a moment's sharp gratitude that I did not have to endure the feel of him completely naked. Then the bed dipped alarmingly as he lowered himself on to it and pulled me into his arms.

His mouth was wet and slobbery on mine, his breath smelling of the porter he had lately consumed; he scrabbled up my nightgown and his own and rolled on top of me. I gasped as the weight of him forced the air out of my lungs, and waited apprehensively for the pain I had been led to believe I would feel when he entered me.

It did not come. Just the discomfort of his heavy body thrashing about on mine and the rather unpleasant sensation of something soft and flabby between my legs. For an eternity, it seemed, I waited. Then, with a groan, Mr Paterson rolled off me and I could breathe again.

'I'm sorry, my dear.' He sounded regretful, awkward almost. 'It seems I must disappoint us both. Too much wine and porter, I expect. Oh well, there will be other times, and plenty of them. A good night's sleep, a dose of sea air, and I'll soon be myself again, no doubt.'

I said nothing; what was there for me to say?

'Do you want me to sleep beside you, or would you prefer me to retire to my own room?' he asked.

Relief at my reprieve and a sense of duty made me magnanimous.

'Whichever you choose,' I whispered.

'Oh, better my own room, I think,' he sighed after a moment's hesitation. 'I snore like a pig when I've had too much to drink, or so I'm told.'

He climbed off the mattress. 'You get your beauty sleep, little one,' he said, his voice still slurred. 'You'll need it, and your strength, for the voyage tomorrow.'

He leaned over and kissed me again, almost losing his balance as he did so. Then, leaving his clothing where he had dropped it, he staggered from the room and I was alone.

I lay for a moment, unmoving. I could still taste the porter from his mouth, still smell the faint rancid odour of his sweat on the sheets. Then the wretchedness washed over me in a great, relentless tide. I turned my face into the pillow and wept soundlessly.

I think I must still have been weeping when exhaustion finally overcame me and I slept. But my last conscious thought was of a man with a child in his arms, my last feeling an ache of emptiness both deep inside me, and in my huddled arms.

*   *   *

We sailed on the morning tide. In spite of the feeling of depression that had been with me when I woke, and which remained whilst we breakfasted and made ready for the voyage, I felt my spirits lift a little with the fresh, salty smell of the harbour, so different to the river stench which pervaded Bristol, and with the excitement of seeing the sailors, nimble as monkeys, swarming up the double masts to unfurl the sheets of canvas sail. In spite of everything, it was something of an adventure, and as I stood on deck with Mr Paterson, watching the waves swirl around the hull and the land recede until it was little more than a blur on the horizon, I thought that perhaps my new life did, after all, have its compensations.

We went to the bows then, and for an hour or so I stood entranced, watching the endless procession of the waves and enjoying the keen cut of the wind on my face. My wilful hair had long since come loose from its pins, blowing about and whipping my flushed cheeks, but I could not care, and Mr Paterson did not seem to mind either.

'You look a little windswept, my dear,' he said with a smile, taking one long strand and curling it round his fingers, and I did not even flinch.

Mr Paterson was in good humour this morning, and he made no mention of last night's fiasco. As for me, I put it to the back of my mind too, determined to make the most of this new experience. The night ahead, and all the nights to come, seemed a long way off. I schooled myself not to think about them, and lived merely for the moment.

I do not know when I began to feel unwell. It crept up upon me, that queaziness, vague at first, a malaise I could not quite identify, a feeling that the swell of the waves and the bobbing of the boat were no longer quite so pleasant or enjoyable, and then I realized I felt very sick indeed.

'I think I should like to go to my cabin,' I said.

Mr Paterson, who had been leaning on the rail, the better to watch the surging waves, turned to look at me, and shook his head when he saw my face, which I imagine was quite green.

95

'Oh dear,' he said. 'Oh dear, Davina, is it not suiting you?'

A wave of nausea washed over me.

'No,' I said. 'I really want to go to the cabin.'

'You're better off up here,' he advised. 'In the fresh air. Be sick over the rail if you must.'

'Please!' I felt quite panicky. Bad enough that Mr Paterson should be talking of it; to actually be ill in his sight, and that of the other passengers and crew, was too humiliating to even contemplate. 'I must go to the cabin! If I can only lie down . . .'

Mr Paterson sighed. 'Very well, if that is what you want. But it won't do you any good, I fear.'

He was right; it did not. When I lay down upon the bunk, I felt worse than before, for the room seemed to go up and down around me, and my stomach pitched with it. The heaviness in my chest was no longer just wretchedness but physical sickness; when I could bear it no more and tried to get up, it rose in my throat and I had to run for the basin, where I retched violently. I should, I supposed, call for Perrett; I was a lady now and should not expect to clean up after myself even if I was fit to do so. But I could not bring myself to call for her; I was too ashamed of my weakness, and in any case, for all I knew, she had been made as ill as I by the relentless rocking motion. Again and again I heaved into the basin, and once, when I was too slow getting to it from my bunk, I vomited on to the floor and down the front of my smart new gown. And I felt so weak and ill I was almost past caring.

After an hour or so, Mr Paterson returned.

'Oh dear, Davina, I told you it would do no good coming below,' he said.

'Oh please – make it stop!' I begged, like the child I seemed to have become. 'I can't bear it! Make it stop moving about, please!'

Mr Paterson laughed – actually laughed!

'I'm not God, Davina! Only God can stop the waves. And it's raining now, too, and growing dark, so I cannot even suggest you go back on deck either. You'll just have

96

to put up with it, I'm afraid, until you get over it or we reach France, whichever is the first.'

My first reaction was that he was quite heartless, but I suppose it was just his way to call a spade a spade, and all the platitudes in the world would not have made me feel one jot better.

And for all that he had no word of sympathy for me, still he washed my face for me and called for Bray, his manservant, to dispose of the unpleasant contents of the basin, for, as I had suspected, poor little Perrett was, it seemed, suffering as much as I was. And he stayed with me, too, for a little while, sitting in a chair beside my cot, until I could bear him there no longer and told him to go and get his dinner and have a drink – if he had the stomach for it.

'Well, if you are sure you will be all right, my dear,' he said doubtfully.

'Yes – yes I'm sure,' I snapped, too sorry for myself to engage in any niceties.

'I'll look in on you later then.' He crossed to the door, steadier, in spite of the rocking, than he had been last night on dry land. 'Try to get some sleep.'

As if I could! I did not think I could ever remember feeling so ill, not even when I had first recovered consciousness after my accident. I had been weak then, and plagued by the pains in my head, but oh, I had not felt as I felt now, surely! This . . . this was a sickness so all-consuming I felt I must die of it.

But at least, I thought wretchedly, Mr Paterson would not be able to attempt to consummate our marriage tonight. It was some small compensation – a tiny crumb of comfort to hold on to as the ship bucked and rolled and my stomach, my every sense, bucked and rolled with it.

Mr Paterson had been right about one thing. The moment our ship docked in France and the surging waves became once more a gentle rhythmic swell, my sickness disappeared as if by magic. Though I still felt weak and my temple ached dully, I was able to swallow some soup and a cup of hot coffee, and by the time we were on our way south, I was myself again and even able to take some pleasure in the countryside

97

through which we were driving. It was such an enormous relief not to feel so dreadfully ill that for the moment all my doubts and anxieties seemed lighter than before, as if, now that I was well again, I would be able to deal with anything.

It was, of course, a euphoria that was illusory and short-lived. That night, when we stopped at an inn, I was no longer able to avoid doing my wifely duty by Mr Paterson.

I knew I must expect the inevitable when he paid me a great deal of attention over dinner, patting my hand and making little jokes, even laying his hand on my knee in the manner I could not help but find repugnant. Each time I laid down my fork and looked up, his eyes were on me, and there was a gleam of anticipation in them, mingled with just a trace of apprehension. He was anxious, no doubt, that there might be a repeat of the debacle of his first attempt to consummate our marriage. Certainly he drank very sparingly of the good French wine during the early part of the evening, and then, when we had almost finished our meal, he quaffed the entire remains of the carafe in one fell swoop, his need for fortification overcoming his caution.

This time, however, it did not impede his performance. Perhaps wine is less debilitating than porter, I do not know, but certainly it tasted better on his breath.

And when it was over and he lay beside me, exhausted and puffed up with self-satisfaction, I had to admit that perhaps it had not been as bad as I had anticipated. There had been no real pain, just a little discomfort, and it had been finished quickly enough, far more quickly than I had imagined. Yes, I had found it distasteful – a messy, awkward business – but, oddly, having to touch and hold Mr Paterson's flabby body caused me more disgust than his violation of my own. That was the easy part, lying immobile whilst he worked in me. I found I was able to divorce myself from the gruntings and thrusts as if I were no more than a casual observer floating on the ceiling above the marriage bed.

'So, now we are truly man and wife,' Mr Paterson said when his breathing had become regular enough to allow him to speak. 'It wasn't so bad, now, was it?' I think you even enjoyed it a little.'

'Yes,' I replied dutifully, though I had certainly not enjoyed it at all.

'I thought so,' he murmured happily. 'I know it's not considered proper for a lady to admit to it, but you are a warm-blooded girl, and the pleasures of the flesh are nothing to be ashamed of. Well, we shall do it again, as often as you like, and the next time, you will enjoy it even more now that you are no longer a virgin.' He paused, then asked, as if it had only just occurred to him: 'I didn't hurt you too much, did I?'

'No, not at all,' I answered, this time truthfully.

'Good.' His tone had become self-satisfied once more. 'That is where experience counts, you see. Some of these young bucks . . . virile they might be, but they are overeager. They rush and snatch and think of nothing but their own pleasure.'

'Please . . . !' I said. This discussion was even more repellent to me than the act itself. 'I'm very tired . . .'

'Oh my dear, of course you are! You sleep, and I shall lie here and remember the delights.'

But in fact it was Mr Paterson who fell asleep, replete and satisfied, snoring almost as soon as the words were out of his mouth, and I who lay staring into the darkness of the unfamiliar room, feeling the small protesting aches in my stomach and a slight burning sensation between my legs, and trying not to think of a stolen kiss that had set my whole being on fire, and an unknown man who could possess my thoughts and instil in me a bittersweet longing that I did not understand, but was powerless to ignore.

We travelled to Bordeaux on roads that I thought were more rutted, less well made than English ones, through villages where the houses had roofs of blue slate, and the sun, shining through the branches of the trees, seemed harsher than the one that had shone on the soft countryside of home. We dined well, on food scented and flavoured with garlic, and accompanied by fresh bread whose texture and taste was quite different from the bread I was used to, but was none the less delicious, and washed it down with wines made from local grapes. I saw carefully tended, yet dusty, little gardens, and tall old church towers, unfamiliar-looking trees and patches of wild flowers growing at the wayside, and there was a faint air of unreality to it all. And I became more used to Mr Paterson's fumblings and gruntings as he exercised his marital rights, and resigned myself to them as my part of the bargain, an inevitable element of my new life.

I looked forward, however, to my monthly bleed, since I thought it would give me a little respite from Mr Paterson's attentions. But it never came. And then one day the same nauseous feeling I had experienced at the beginning of my bout of terrible seasickness returned. At first I thought it was the swaying of the coach, carrying us now towards the Italian border, then, almost in disbelief, it occurred to me there might be quite another reason for my feeling of malaise.

I was with child.

Quite suddenly I knew without a shadow of doubt that it was so. For some days afterwards, perhaps as long as the next two weeks, I tried to tell myself there might be some other explanation – the seasickness I had experienced, or even the trauma of the weeks preceding the wedding, might have upset my cycles. Yet in my heart I knew it was not so. And in spite of everything, I could not help but be glad. I would, I knew, be even more tightly bound to Mr Paterson, if such a thing were possible, for soon there would be not only my marriage vows and my duty to my grandparents to hold me, but the welfare of a living, breathing child. A child who would need the security of a loving home where his happiness was assured, as well as his material needs.

There was all that to think of now. And there was also some apprehension deep within me which I could not understand. I was young, I was strong, I had survived a terrible, life-threatening accident – surely I could survive bearing and giving birth to a child? Then why did I feel this inexplicable fearfulness? In the small dark hours of the night, lying in some strange bed under foreign skies, I tasted something close to panic.

And yet at the same time I could not help but be glad.

I did not tell Mr Paterson of my condition at first. I hugged it to myself – my secret – and there was something strangely familiar about the keeping of it. But when he found me retching into the basin one morning and asked me anxiously what ailed me, I could keep it from him no longer.

I told him, and never have I seen a man more delighted.

'A child?' His ruddy face, which the hot suns of the continent had made redder than ever, was incredulous. 'We are going to have a child?'

'Yes,' I said. 'It will be born in the spring.'

'Oh Davina!' There were tears in his eyes, but his smile told me they were happy tears. 'I never thought that I would be a father!'

I could not help but laugh.

'Surely you must have known the likely outcome of the marriage bed!' I said, a little shamelessly, I dare say, but since I had left my grandparents' rather restrictive household I had discovered I had perhaps less modesty than might be seemly.

'Well, of course! But all the years I was married to the first Mrs Paterson, there was no such outcome!' he said. 'I suppose I got out of the habit of expecting there might be. But there you are – I am a very foolish man. I should have realized you are different. Well – I knew that, of course! I know that you are young and beautiful, and that you make me happy and very proud when I have you on my arm. I imagine other men thinking, *How is it that an old goat, such as he, can have such a lovely young wife?* But now – to be a father too! Davina, you have made me the happiest man alive!'

'I'm glad you are pleased,' I said.

'Pleased? I'm more than pleased! But I can see I shall have to take better care of you than ever. I think I should get you home to England at once. We'll cut the tour short and make our way back.'

'There's no need for that,' I protested. 'I am quite well really – apart from this wretched sickness, and that seems to pass as the day wears on.'

'There is every need!' Mr Paterson insisted. 'I want you under the care of a physician I can trust – not these foreign johnnies. And consider how poorly you were on the voyage out – you'd do better to make the return voyage before the risk of winter squalls – and before you are too far gone. Just supposing delays occurred, and you were forced to give birth on this side of the Channel! I want my child born in England, not France!'

I laughed again – really, there was no stopping him in his enthusiastic delight. And deep in my heart I knew, too, that I would be glad to be back on English soil. The tour had been a hiatus, a dash of unreality in my troubled life. But now, without doubt, I was ready to go home.

We set out at once, recrossing France and heading for the channel coast. When we boarded the ship, I waited with dread for the sickness to begin and worried very much that, if I was terribly ill, it might have some bad effect on the baby. For all Mr Paterson's pontificating about it being best to get the voyage over early, and my own desire to be back in England, I could not help but feel it might have been better to wait patiently until the middle months before putting my body through the strain of the *mal de mer*, as I had heard the French call it.

But I need not have worried. Surprisingly, the crossing had little effect on me. It was as if, having suffered so dreadfully once, I had found my sea legs. The morning nausea was no worse than it had been on land, and, if anything, the fresh salt air braced me.

We spent the night after we landed at the same inn as we had spent our wedding night – to give me a chance to gather my strength, Mr Paterson said. He was treating me with the utmost consideration and there were certainly no fumblings to endure that night, as there had been on our previous visit. Then, next day, we journeyed back to Bristol.

The weather was not as hot now as it had been when we left, and the tide was in, so the stench of the river was less overpowering. Though it was not now raining, it was clear there had been at least a sharp shower, for the cobbles gleamed wetly and when we reached the house in Clifton the leaves of the rose bushes near the front door were dripping, dark-green against the last overblown flowers.

The door was thrown open at once and we went in. I felt only relief that the journey was over at last, though I had no sense of coming home. Why would I? I had never yet lived in this great house; I was mistress in name only.

We washed off the dust of travel in our own rooms and I changed into a fresh gown. A dish of tea would be waiting downstairs, I knew, and I was more than ready for it.

As I descended the staircase, I saw Thomas in the hall below, and was surprised when he came towards me, waiting deferentially until I reached the last little flight. There was something almost furtive about his movements, which was unlike him, since he was usually so proud and erect, and he glanced over his shoulder, then peered past me as if to be sure I was alone.

'Thomas,' I said.

He extended a thin ebony hand; I saw he was holding an envelope, which he thrust in my direction.

'This came for you, Mrs Paterson.'

'For me?' I echoed, surprised.

I took the envelope. It was indeed addressed with my name, but the writing, bold, and in black ink, was quite unknown to me.

'I would open it when you are alone,' Thomas said. Then, without another word, he turned and glided back in the direction of the servants' quarters.

I stared at the envelope, puzzled. Who would be writing to me, and why had Thomas urged me to open it when I was alone? Curiosity almost got the better of me, then I heard footsteps on the flight of stairs above me and instinctively thrust the letter into the folds of my skirt. Mr Paterson was coming down.

103

'My, but it's good to be home! You are ready for a dish of tea, I'll warrant, my dear!'

'Yes, but first I must fetch a kerchief. I quite forgot to bring one with me . . .'

'Perrett can fetch it for you.'

'No, there's no need. And the exercise will do me good!'

I passed him, keeping the letter guiltily concealed and feeling as furtive as Thomas had looked. Back in my own room I closed the door and stood with my back against it. Then, with fingers that trembled slightly, I tore it open.

There was just a single sheet of paper inside. I read what was written upon it, in the same bold black hand, and gasped.

Just a few lines, but so startling the world rocked around me.

Rowan. Did you not know our daughter? She is two years old and she needs you. So do I.

And it was signed: *Richard Wells*.

Eight

I was back in the maelstrom. I could not think a single coherent thought. I could scarcely breathe. What did it mean? Was this some new trick he was playing to get me back into his clutches, this 'dangerous' man my mother had sought to protect me from, and the thought of whom disturbed me so? I looked at the paper again, and the words leaped out at me.

Our daughter.

The little girl outside the cathedral, presumably.

Our daughter.

His child – and mine, if this madness was to be believed. But it was not possible! How could I be the mother of a child and not know it?

She is two years old.

Two years old. Two years ago I had lain unconscious in my grandparents' house.

It must be a trick. It *must* be! And yet somehow there was a rightness to it, a rightness that had no foundation in logic, but came from the heart of me, from somewhere buried deep within my being. My thoughts whirled around and around as I stood with my back pressed against the wood panelling of the door to support me, staring alternately into space and back at the letter.

A tap on the door made me start violently; the paper fluttered from my nerveless hands to the floor.

'Mrs Paterson?' It was Perrett's voice, thick with a soft West Country burr. 'Is everything all right, Mrs Paterson?'

'Yes, thank you, Perrett.' I was afraid the turmoil I was experiencing would be evident in my voice, but to my amazement it sounded reasonably normal.

'Is there anything you need?' Perrett asked. 'Can I do anything for you?'

'No – no, I'm perfectly fine. I'll be down in just a moment.'

'Very well, madam.'

I waited until I heard her footfalls disappear along the landing before I risked moving away from the door to pick up the letter from where it had fallen. Then, without stopping to look at it again, I quickly folded it and placed it inside my bodice.

I must join the others downstairs. Mr Paterson must already be concerned about me and the time I had taken, or he would not have sent Perrett up to seek me out. If I did not go down to the parlour, and quickly, he would no doubt come looking for me himself, afraid that the voyage and carriage journey had taken its toll on me.

For a wild moment I wondered if I should pretend that I was indeed unwell and gain a little much-needed privacy. But it might not work out like that. Mr Paterson, in his present mood, might very well insist on sitting at my bedside, smoothing my brow and holding my hand, and if he did that I thought I would go quite mad! Better to act normally, as if nothing out of the ordinary had happened at all.

And besides, there were things I wanted to do that I could not do if I was confined to my room. Pressing things, such as getting Thomas alone and asking him just how he had come by the letter and how he had known that its contents were best discovered by me when there was no one with me to witness my shock. It would not tell me anything about Richard Wells' outrageous assertions, but at least it would be a start.

Taking a deep breath and composing myself as best I could, I went downstairs.

The condition of pregnancy, I suppose, covers a multitude of sins. It can be used to excuse any peculiar behaviour, and everyone who witnesses it simply nods sagely, exchanging knowing glances and smiling indulgently. If I had not had my pregnancy to hide behind, heaven alone knows how I would have managed to get through the day without anyone suspecting something was not simply troubling, but obsessing me, or even worse, deciding that I had, whilst out of the country, gone stark raving mad.

I could not concentrate on any conversation – and there was plenty of that, for Mr Paterson had sent to invite his good friends Sir Harry and Lady Amelia Bell to dine with us. He maintained it was to enable him to catch up on any important developments that had transpired in his absence, concerning the Merchant Venturers; I suspected it was, more likely, to give him the chance to boast about his forthcoming fatherhood, for he wasted no time in imparting the news to his friends.

'Wonderful news, Paterson! Wonderful news indeed!' Sir Harry clapped Mr Paterson on the back. 'This calls for a toast, does it not?' He raised his glass. 'To your son – if son indeed he be! And may he be the first of many!'

'Oh Harry!' Lady Amelia remonstrated. 'You'd be less ready to say such a thing if you were the one who had to bear a whole brood of children and bring them into the world!'

She turned to me, kissing me on the cheek and adding more softly, for my ears only: 'Congratulations, my dear Davina! And don't worry about what I said. It's not so bad – at least, the worst of it is quickly forgotten in the joy of holding your baby in your arms. And the first is the worst by far – the others follow much more easily.'

The first. But perhaps this was not the first child I had borne, if the outrageous claim in Richard Wells' letter was to be believed. At once I was back in my reverie, my thoughts racing, and I could only mutter nonsensically in reply.

I could not eat. The food – a good piece of roast beef, especially prepared by Cook for our welcome-home meal – stuck in my throat and I pushed it around my plate, staring at it as if it might miraculously provide the answers to my whirling questions, and cutting it into tiny pieces which were still too much for me to swallow.

Their voices were nothing but a background hum, like a swarm of angry bees; occasionally I realised with a start that

107

someone was speaking to me and dragged myself out of my private world to make reply. But for the most part I was lost, drowning in confusion and churning emotion.

I thought the nightmare would never end, that I would be trapped for ever in this web of social nicety. It was, I think, the most claustrophobic evening I have ever endured, forcing myself to go through the motions whilst my thoughts raced, chaotic and totally disconnected. But at last Lady Amelia touched her husband's arm and rose.

'I think it is time we were leaving, Harry. Davina is looking very pale.' She smiled at me. 'You must be exhausted, my dear, and the last thing you need now is to overtire yourself. You have the little one to think of, too.'

The little one. A girl with hair turned gold by the sunshine . . . ? But no, of course, she meant the baby I was carrying. Mr Paterson's baby.

'I *am* tired,' I said. 'I admit it.'

'Of course you are! This travelling is all very well, but now you need your rest. Harry! Do finish your drink, my dear, so that we can be on our way. You have to be up early, too, remember. There's a breakfast meeting of the Merchant Venturers, or so you told me.'

'Oh, I suppose you're right.' Sir Harry drained his glass and stood up, to my enormous relief. 'You'll be there, too, of course, Paterson. It's a good thing you're back. I had thought to brief you this evening with regard to developments, but in the event it seemed a pity to spoil a good dinner with business.'

'Developments? What developments?' Mr Paterson asked, and my heart sank, thinking they were going to begin all over again and my release from this unwanted company would be delayed yet further.

To my relief, however, Sir Harry seemed as unwilling now to talk business as he had been earlier.

'Too late to go into it now. That troublemaker has been at it again, stirring things up on every level, but I think we've enough parliamentarians on our side not to have to worry too much about him. Those that represent us know on which side their bread is buttered. But it seems there's been some law-breaking, with Bristol ships involved. You'll hear all about it tomorrow.'

None of this made any sense to me; I was twanging with impatience now for them to be gone.

'Come along, Harry!' Lady Amelia insisted.

As if by magic, Thomas appeared with Lady Amelia's cape and Sir Harry's cane; perhaps he had been listening at the door, I thought, anxious as I was for them to take their leave so that he could get to his bed. He looked at me gravely as he helped Lady Amelia into her cape, but the expression in his jet-black eyes was quite unreadable. And, of course, there was no opportunity for me to ask him the questions that were burning on my tongue.

Then, thank heaven, our visitors were gone, and Mr Paterson was summoning Perrett to help me get undressed, and bidding me goodnight.

'I think I'll stay down a little longer, my dear – have another brandy,' he said, and then, to my intense embarrassment, reached out and patted my stomach. 'No point coming to bed with you tonight, I dare say. And no need either!'

I must have blushed, because he added apologetically: 'I'm indelicate, I know, my dear. But then, I'm just a rough trader at heart, and you'll have to become accustomed to my ways.'

Mr Paterson's indelicacy was, at that moment, the least of my worries. I retired to my room, glad to be alone at last, but knowing there was no escape from myself or from my chaotic thoughts and churning emotions.

When at last I fell into an exhausted slumber, the dream came again. My mother and I in the carriage, rocking along the rutted road. And the other – the one I could not see, hidden by the veil. As before, I reached out to move it aside. And this time it fell away. And behind it I saw the little girl with the sun-bleached hair; the little girl Richard Wells had held in his arms.

I reached out for her and she came to me, round and

baby-soft, firm, sweet-scented. Her little arms went round my neck, her head, with that fine cap of hair, rested trustingly against my chest. And an overwhelming feeling of joy welled up in me and the tears were wet on my cheeks.

I knew the dream would continue as before, relentless as a stormy tide, and I could do nothing to stop it. Panic and a feeling of utter helplessness replaced the joy as the galloping runaway horses dragged the carriage behind them to disaster. And I held on to the little one as tightly as I could, desperate to keep her safe. Then we were rolling, over and over, and I knew the darkness was coming and that when I opened my eyes she would be gone. For there was still nothing I could do. Nothing at all.

I woke with a start. My arms were empty, empty and aching with the emptiness. My face was wet with tears, my body bathed in a fine mist of perspiration.

It was real, that dream, so very real! And in it the child had indeed been mine, not a doubt of it. But it was, of course, all nonsense, the product of my fevered imaginings. The child could not possibly have been in the carriage with me at the time of the accident. It had occurred more than two years ago and she was, according to Richard, only two years old now. In my dream she had looked exactly as she had looked when he held her up to see me – or for me to see her – outside the cathedral. Just the same. Not a babe in arms, but a pretty little girl.

What in the name of heaven did it all mean? Was I being deceived – and deceiving myself into giving credence, for even a moment, to his claims? Or was I really a mother already, without knowing it?

I thought of the ease with which I had conceived, of the lack of any real pain when Mr Paterson had consummated our marriage. Might it be that I had not been the virgin he had thought me? But would he not have known? Surely such a thing would be obvious to a man? But Mr Paterson had been so concerned about his own performance, or lack of it, that he might well have given little thought to me.

With a little shock I remembered what Richard Wells

had said in anger on the night of the reception – that Mr Paterson was being taken for a fool, and that I was not free to wed him. Could it be that was because I already had, not only a child, but a husband? Was that what he had meant? But if so, then why had he allowed the marriage to take place at all? Why had he not come into the cathedral and interrupted the service? Why had he not been there to object when the question had been asked of the congregation whether anyone knew of any just cause or impediment why I might not become Mr Paterson's wife? Instead, he had lurked outside with a child in his arms and done nothing to intervene at all.

None of it made any sense – none of it. But they could use me as a plaything, all of them, because I had no memory beyond the past two years, no way of knowing if I was being told the truth. So far, I had accepted everything I had been told; now I knew that someone was lying to me, for the stories were no longer compatible. Someone was lying – but who? And why?

When I had undressed, I had slipped the note Richard Wells had sent me out of my bodice before Perrett could see it and slid it out of sight beneath my pillow. Now I took it out, crossed to the window, where bright moonlight shone in to make it almost light as day, and unfolded the paper.

Did you not know our daughter? She is two years old and she needs you. So do I.

'She needs you.'

The words tore at the strings of my heart and again I felt the firm little body clasped tightly against mine as I had felt it in my dream.

I had to know. Somehow, I had to know the truth. I could not live my life with the uncertainty.

But how could I discover where the truth lay? And when I had it, what would I do with it?

I stood at the window in the moonlight, empty arms wrapped around myself, shivering a little as the air cooled with a pre-dawn chill. I knew I would sleep no more tonight.

*   *   *

111

With all that was on my mind, I had quite forgotten that Mr Paterson was to take breakfast at the coffee house with the Merchant Venturers. Though I had thought I would not sleep, I must eventually have dozed after returning, cold and aching with tiredness, to my bed, for, the next I knew, Perrett was pulling back the curtains and setting a cup of chocolate beside my bed.

'Here we are, Mrs Paterson. Cook's sent up a lovely drink for you. And there's hot water in the jug for you to wash when you're ready. Oh – and Mr Paterson said to tell you he's left already for his meeting and didn't want to disturb you.'

'Thank you, Perrett.'

I felt drained, as tired still as if I had not slept at all, with eyelids that burned and a mouth that felt thick and furred, but it was an enormous relief to hear that Mr Paterson had already gone out. The thought of having to make some sort of sensible conversation with him when I felt so dreadful, and my brain was still so full of billowing cobwebs, was a daunting one.

'You take as long as you like before you get up,' Perrett said in her soft West Country burr. 'You've nothing to do today but spoil yourself. And I think that's what you should do. Just ring when you want me.'

I managed a smile. During our weeks abroad I had become very fond of Perrett. She was a cheerful girl, and most reliable. And I thought she rather liked me too. She had confided in me one day that her previous employer had led her a dreadful dance and been impossible to please. 'I shall try not to be like her, then,' I had said, and Perrett had replied: 'Like her, Mrs Paterson? Why, you couldn't be if you tried! You're more like us.' Then she had clapped her hand over her mouth, horrified at her outspoken indiscretion. 'Oh, I didn't mean—'

'I *am* like you, Perrett,' I had said then. 'I never had a maid before – I might have become one myself if I had not married Mr Paterson. And can't I call you by your given name? It would be much more friendly. What is it?'

But: 'Oh no!' she had replied quickly. 'That wouldn't be proper at all! It's Becky, if you want to know, but you mustn't call me by it. That wouldn't be proper at all!'

112

So Perrett she had remained, but the warmth continued between us too.

Now I thanked her for bringing me my chocolate and enlisted her help.

'Would you ask Thomas to make the carriage ready for me?' I asked. 'I should like to call on my family. I haven't seen them since the wedding.'

The idea had occurred to me during the wee small hours. For one thing, it would give me the opportunity to speak to Thomas alone; for another, I wanted to question Theo. He knew more than he had told me, I felt sure, and even if he did not, he was in a better position than I to make enquiries.

When I had finished my chocolate, Perrett returned to help me dress, and I managed a little breakfast, though I felt knotted up with nervousness. The landaulet drew up at the door with Thomas, immaculate as ever, in the driving seat. He gave no sign that anything unusual had occurred between us yesterday, and I waited until we were safely out of sight of the house before I asked him to pull over.

'Thomas, I have something to ask you,' I said, my voice tight with apprehension. 'It's about the letter you handed me yesterday on my return.'

'Yes, ma'am.' He was not looking at me, but staring out over the horses' nut-brown backs. His handsome profile gave nothing away.

'How did you come by it?' I asked.

Thomas glanced at me, his features still implacable.

'Mr Wells asked me to deliver it to you, ma'am.'

I frowned. I do not know what I had expected, but it was most certainly not this.

'He came to the house, you mean?'

'No, ma'am. Not to the house.'

'Then how . . . ?'

Thomas's face was inscrutable. 'I'd rather not say, ma'am.'

'I don't understand . . .'

'He simply asked me to see that you received it as soon as you returned from your wedding tour, and to tell you that it would be best if you opened it in private.'

I could tell I would get no more from him as to where he had encountered Richard Wells.

'When was this?' I asked.

'The day after you left, ma'am. I told him you were expected to be away for some time, but that I would do as he asked as soon as I was able.'

'I see. And if I were to ask you to take him a reply, would you be able to do that?'

'I would, ma'am.'

'Or tell me where I could find him?'

'That might be more difficult, ma'am.'

'I see.' There really was no more to be said. 'Thank you, Thomas. Drive on.'

He did so, and I stared unseeingly at the grand new homes we were passing in Park Street, more confused than ever.

I was not entirely hopeful of finding Theo at home. When I had been staying at the house in Queen's Square he had often been out on business during the day, and in any case it had occurred to me that, if he had been accepted into the Association of Merchant Venturers following my marriage to Mr Paterson, he might well be at the very same meeting that my husband had left early to attend.

When I rang the bell, however, and Johnson answered it, she was able to tell me that he was indeed at home, though Great-Uncle Charles was confined to bed with an unpleasant cough and wheezy chest. She showed me into the parlour and shortly afterwards Theo joined me there.

I could tell at once that he was in an ill humour, though he greeted me pleasantly enough.

'Davina! It's good to see you! How was your trip?'

'It went very well,' I said. 'Apart from the voyage out, when I was dreadfully sick. I enjoyed France very much, and Italy too, though we were there only a very short time. It is very picturesque.'

'Yes, I'm fond of Italy myself,' Theo said. 'Though I am less enamoured of France. Such a quarrelsome nation,

I always think. But you are home sooner than you planned, surely?'

I felt my cheeks grow a little hot.

'That is because I have some news,' I said. 'I am going to have a baby in the spring, and Mr Paterson thought it best we return to England before my pregnancy was too far advanced.'

'Oh, that is capital news indeed!' Theo enthused. 'Whoever would have thought it – old John Paterson a father at last!'

He spoke, I thought, rather disparagingly, and to my own surprise I found myself rushing to my husband's defence.

'I really don't know why you should find it surprising, Theo. Babies are a part of marriage, surely?'

'I dare say, but . . .' Theo snorted, an explosion of ill-concealed merriment. 'Well, there's life in the old dog yet!' He must have become aware of my disapproving expression, because he made an effort to straighten his face and change the subject. 'You should have let us know you were coming to visit, Davina, and I'd have laid on the fatted calf.'

'It was a spur of the moment decision,' I said. 'I only decided this morning that I'd call on you. I wasn't even sure I would find you at home. I thought you might be at the docks, or even the meeting of the Merchant Venturers.'

Theo's face darkened. 'Chance would be a fine thing.'

'You haven't been invited to join, then?'

'No – and it's beginning to look as though I won't be,' Theo said shortly. 'Not that I'd want to, mind you, if it were not for the financial and business advantages it would bring. I can't say I relish the thought of having to be charming to a lot of pompous asses who while their days away scratching one another's backs. They are not my idea of the sort of company I would choose to keep.'

So – we were back to sniping at Mr Paterson and his partners. Theo's disappointment at not being invited to join the association was making him bitter, I thought, whether he admitted it to himself or not.

'Great-Uncle Charles is not well, I understand,' I said.

'His chest is playing him up,' Theo said rather carelessly.

'It's a familiar enough problem for him, but it does not usually strike him down until winter, when we've had a spell of cold, wet weather. It's early in the year for him to have to take to his bed. We shall have trouble later on, I shouldn't be surprised.'

'What does the doctor say?' I asked, concerned.

Theo shrugged. 'Oh him – he'll say anything so long as it means he can get more money out of us! He thinks Papa would be better off living up on Park Street, or in Clifton, but there is fat chance of that unless the blamed Merchant Venturers decide to look on us more kindly.'

'Perhaps I can go up and see him before I leave,' I suggested.

'As you like. He'll be asleep, though, I shouldn't wonder. He seems to sleep most of the day away.' Theo shot me a quick, rather wicked look, a little more like his usual self. 'You've seen me, anyway. Isn't that what you came for?'

Ignoring his implication, I grasped my opportunity.

'Actually, yes,' I said guilelessly. 'I wanted to talk to you, Theo. Something very strange has happened.'

His eyes narrowed. 'Strange? In what way strange, Davina?'

I hesitated, my courage almost failing me. Never had Richard Wells' assertion seemed more outrageous than it did to me at that moment, when I was faced with putting it into words for my cousin. It seemed to make a fool out of me that I should give it credence for even a fleeting second. Yet, at the same time, it accused me, for if it were true, then it meant that either I was a wanton woman or a bigamist. The realization, which had not previously occurred to me, shocked me to the core, filling me with shame – and fear.

But I had come this far – there could be no going back. And in any case, whatever heartache or disgrace lay ahead, I had to know the truth. For the sake of my sanity, I had to know the truth.

'You remember the man who accosted me outside the hot well and called me Rowan,' I began hesitantly, choosing to skirt around the night of Mr Paterson's reception, when Theo

116

had surprised us in such a compromising situation, and the angry altercation between them which had followed.

Theo grunted angrily. 'How could I forget? But I hoped that you might have done, Davina.'

'That is more easily said than done,' I ventured, still, I think, delaying the moment when I must tell him the reason I had begun this conversation.

'He won't bother you any more, now that you are wed to John Paterson,' Theo asserted with misguided confidence. 'He knows you are a married woman, and one with a husband who is most influential in Bristol.'

'But he has,' I said quietly.

Theo swore. 'The swine! Will he never realize you are lost to him? But I thought you said you returned only yesterday. What possible opportunity can be have found to accost you again?'

'I have not seen him,' I said, biting my lip. 'There was a letter waiting for me on my return. A letter which has disturbed me greatly.'

'He dared to write to you at John's house? Did John not intercept it?'

'He did not know it had come,' I explained. 'And I have to tell you, he still knows nothing about it.'

'You are deceiving your husband? By Jove, Davina, you are treading on dangerous ground!'

'I know it,' I said, shamefaced. 'But I wanted to talk to you first about the contents. And in any case, I don't want to cause trouble for Thomas, who acted as his messenger. Mr Paterson might well be very angry with him if he knew Thomas had passed the letter to me behind his back. He's threatened before to have him whipped, and I think he might well be capable of carrying out his threat.'

'And Thomas would well deserve it!' Theo said roundly. 'So – he's involved, is he?'

'Involved?' I repeated, remembering suddenly Thomas's reluctance to divulge any information whatever regarding Richard Wells or his whereabouts. 'Involved in what?'

'Oh – it doesn't matter.' Theo moved impatiently. 'So,

117

what did it say, this letter, that has upset you so? Why did you wish to talk to me about it?'

I could avoid the nub of the matter no longer. I licked my dry lips and met Theo's gaze squarely.

'It claimed that I am the mother of his child.'

If I had struck him, I do not believe Theo could have looked more thunderstruck. For a moment the colour left his face, then returned in a rush, ruddying his cheeks, and his expression was one of utter shock. And then the anger began to creep in.

'Dear God, will the man stop at nothing? How dare he lay such a charge at your door? Why, Davina, surely you must know such a thing could not possibly be true?'

'But that's just it,' I said desperately. 'I can remember nothing of my past – you know that.'

'And so, damn him, does he!' Theo swore again. 'He's seeking to play on your loss of memory for his own ends!'

For some reason I felt, not relief, but an ache of disappointment.

'It's not true, then?' I asked in a small voice.

'I certainly hope it is not!' Theo exclaimed. 'I can't speak for what happened before you came into the care of your grandparents, of course, but . . .'

'He said she is two years old,' I said.

'Well there you are then! It can't possibly be true, can it? Two years ago you were safely in Gloucestershire – and confined to your sickbed.'

I knotted my hands in the folds of my skirts, unable now to meet his angry, disbelieving eyes.

'I have only their word for that,' I said softly.

'What do you mean?' Theo demanded.

'I have only their word for the exact date when I was taken to them,' I persisted. 'I don't know for how long I lay unconscious, and even when I did come round, things were very hazy for some time. Suppose I *did* have a child, Theo. Suppose that was the reason Mama was taking us to my grandparents – to seek succour and protection, not for me, but for the child. I have this dream, you see, about the accident,

118

and there is someone in the carriage with us. I've never before known who it was, but last night I saw her clearly. The little girl . . .'

'What little girl?' Theo asked, looking puzzled.

'The little girl he brought to see me at the cathedral. The little one he claims is *our* little girl . . .'

'He did what?' Theo exclaimed. 'He paraded a child in front of you on your wedding day? Sweet Jesu, the man is more devious – and more ruthless – than even I imagined! He must have borrowed her from someone. Richard Wells has no child of his own that I've ever heard of. He's a trickster and a charlatan, Davina. He is seeking to play with your mind, and by God, he's succeeding! How old did this child appear to be?'

'About two, I should think, exactly as he said.'

'Well, there you are then! It's quite impossible she can have been in the carriage with you – and if she had been, doubtless she would have been killed. Your mother was, remember.'

'And the coachman,' I added automatically.

'Oh yes – the coachman. I'd forgotten him. And you were terribly injured, as well you know. A babe would have been most unlikely to survive. No, take it from me, Davina, the child he is using to lure you back to him, whoever she is, cannot be the child in the carriage in your dream. Unless she's a ghost!' He laughed almost insanely at his own joke, but I could not see that there was anything even remotely funny about it.

But he was right, of course. I had known already that it made no sense. Theo had only put into rather cruel words what I had deduced for myself.

And yet I was still not satisfied. Perhaps it was this inexplicable ache of disappointment within me that made me reluctant to let go of the idea, perhaps it was sheer romantic fantasy, a desire to have something more in my life than a brief past in a country rectory and a tedious future with a man I was not, and never would be, in love with.

But I knew in that moment that I could not give up my

quest for the truth simply because I had come up against a stone wall in Theo.

Perhaps Richard Wells was a charlatan and an adventurer as Theo claimed he was. Perhaps he was using the most dreadful deception to get me back into his clutches. Perhaps I was deluding myself when I thought it might be different. But I had to pursue it. I had to know.

What I thought I could do about it, of course, if any of it proved to have a foundation in fact, was something else again. As Theo had pointed out, I was a married woman now – and one who was with child. But that really had no bearing for the moment on what I felt compelled to do. It was the uncertainty I could not live with.

Thomas had said he knew where to find Richard Wells. If I saw him, spoke to him face to face, then surely I would know if he was lying.

Nine

I spoke to Thomas as he drove me home. I asked if he would kindly arrange a meeting for me with Richard Wells, striving to sound as if it were an everyday order, such as making the carriage ready or asking Cook to prepare boiled mutton for supper, and he agreed in much the same spirit. Though we were, in fact, conspiring, yet neither of us acknowledged the conspiracy. There was no need even for me to ask him not to mention my request to Mr Paterson; I knew he would not. Then there was nothing I could do but wait. And in the waiting period my nerves were so on edge I did not know what to do with myself.

I was dreadfully afraid that my agitation would be apparent to Mr Paterson, but if he noticed it at all, he must have put it down to my condition. Ever since I had told him I was with child, he had treated me with the utmost consideration – but then, when had he ever done anything else? Nothing was too good for me, and his kindness made me burn with guilt to know that I was deceiving him.

Two days went by, then three, then four, with no news. I prowled the house like a caged tigress, and whenever I encountered Thomas I had to steel myself not to ask if he had yet had the opportunity to pass on my message. I did not wish to appear too eager. But it was all I could manage, especially on the morning after I had by chance seen what looked like his impressive figure stealing along the side of the house and disappearing in the direction of Park Street. He should not have been out at night, I knew, and I could only think that he had gone on my errand, and pray that his absence would not be noticed.

At last I could contain my impatience no longer. When I heard him clearing the salvers from the breakfast room, I slipped in after him, making sure no one was within earshot.

'Thomas – have you yet had the opportunity . . . ?'

He raised his eyes to mine, dark, inscrutable as ever, and said nothing at all.

'Mr Wells,' I said urgently. 'Have you spoken with him yet?'

Thomas picked up the dish containing the remains of the griddled kidneys.

'I thought to see him last night.'

So – I had been right!

'And . . . ?'

'He was not there,' Thomas said flatly. 'Word was that he has met with some kind of an accident.'

My heart seemed to stop beating. My hand flew to my throat.

'An accident? What kind of an accident?'

'Word has it he was set upon by ruffians.'

'By ruffians!' I repeated stupidly. 'Is he . . . Was he badly hurt, do you know?'

'I couldn't say, ma'am.'

Daltry, the housemaid, came in then with a scuttle of coal to make up the fire – the weather had the bite of autumn in it now, and, since we had returned from our wedding tour fires had been lit in all the reception rooms each day, though not yet in the bedrooms – and I could ask no more. Thomas went out, carrying the salver of kidneys, and I was left frustrated and dreadfully anxious.

My last question to Thomas was the one uppermost in my mind – how badly had Richard Wells been hurt? Quite seriously, I imagined, if he had not been wherever it was Thomas had expected to find him. Why, he might even have died of his injuries! Such a thing was not beyond the bounds of possibility if he had been set upon by a gang of ruffians. The docks area crawled with them by night, drunken seamen who would pick a fight with anyone, as well as rogues looking

122

for a man to rob. They would steal their victim's watch and money and tip him into the docks so badly beaten that he would likely drown if no one came to his aid, and it was a brave man who would take on not only a gang of rough and ready thugs, who might well be armed, but also the filth of the water that slopped against the quayside.

But surely Thomas would have known if the worst had happened? Even in such an unruly society, murder was still a serious enough occurrence to be talked about. More likely by far that the attack had stopped short of murder and Richard Wells had been confined to bed to nurse whatever injuries had been inflicted upon him.

And that, heaven alone knew, was bad enough! I thought of that handsome face beaten to a pulp and closed my eyes against my imagining. I wondered if his ribs had been cracked or his limbs broken. He was such a strong man, and the thought of him damaged was unbearable. And somehow quite out of keeping . . .

The thought occurred to me that he was not really the sort of man thugs usually set upon at all. He was not overtly wealthy, and he certainly did not look an easy victim. He looked like a man who could take care of himself, who would not give in without putting up a fight. Ruffians usually picked on the soft and the weak and the nervous. Who, I wondered, would have chosen to attack Richard Wells?

I did not have to wait long for my answer. Theo came calling, ostensibly to tell me that Great-Uncle Charles was somewhat recovered and would like to see me. But as soon as we were alone he made it clear that there was another reason behind his visit.

'I don't think Richard Wells will be bothering you again in a hurry,' he said, rather smugly.

I was so startled it was all I could do not to give away the fact that I had already heard he had been subjected to an attack.

'What do you mean?' I asked.

And Theo smirked. Actually smirked.

'I've had him taught a lesson he won't forget in a hurry.'
I stared at him, horrified. 'What?'

'There are those I know who will show a man the error of his ways for a small payment,' he said lightly. 'A good beating in a dark alley will soon show a dog who is master, especially if the reason for his misfortune is explained to him. Let us simply say that Richard Wells met with a gang of thugs who would have done it for the sheer pleasure of it, as like as not, even if there had not been a purse of money for them at the end of it. And the message was that if he continued to bother you it would be worse next time, and there would be a body found floating amongst the garbage in the river.'

'Theo!' I gasped. 'Are you saying you had Richard Wells attacked because of me?'

'It's the only language scum like him understand,' Theo said carelessly. 'Writing letters to you secretly, trying to frighten you into returning to him with all kinds of wicked nonsense . . . He had to be stopped, Davina.'

'But to beat him senseless . . . !' I cried. 'Oh, Theo, that cannot be right!'

'Don't waste your pity on him, Davina,' Theo said shortly. 'This is the man, remember, whom your mother died to protect you from. The man who might even have been directly responsible for her death, if my suspicions are correct, and it was he, and not some highwayman, who held up your carriage. Your mother's murderer, Davina – think of that if the idea of him taking a little of his own medicine offends your sensibilities.'

'But . . .' I could find no words to express the turmoil I was feeling.

'You will be free of him, that is what matters,' Theo went on. 'God alone knows what trouble he would have made, just when your future is secured. Mr Paterson would not take kindly to hearing such derogatory rumours, I am sure. He might begin to wonder about just what sort of wife he has married. And besides, you should not be upset when you are in such a delicate condition. You have the child to think of now, and causing you such distress might do your baby untold harm, even if he stopped short of something worse.'

'Something worse . . . ?' I seemed unable to do anything but repeat Theo's words like some sea captain's parrot.

'I believe he tried to abduct you once,' Theo said. 'He may well do so again. and if he is thwarted . . . well, as I've said before, he is a dangerous man, Davina.'

He took my hand. 'Come now, let's forget all about Mr Richard Wells. He's had his warning; he knows now what he can expect if he cannot curb his obsession with you. He knows there are those who will protect you better than your poor mother could, and will do it, by God!'

'Theo,' I said, suddenly finding my voice. 'I don't want harm to come to Richard Wells, or anyone, because of me. I don't want beatings and murder laid at my door – I could not sleep at night if I thought such a thing was likely. You must promise me you will never do anything like this again.'

Theo shrugged. 'It's in his own hands.'

'No. Promise me!'

'Oh, very well.' He half turned away, and added softly: 'I promise at least not to tell you of it.'

'Theo!'

'But you must promise too,' he said. 'You must promise that if ever you come face to face with him you will cut him dead and never place yourself in a position where he might be a threat to you.'

'I do not cut people dead,' I said. 'Not even Richard Wells. It is not my way. But if, as you say, he has been given such a stern warning, I should think it very unlikely he would risk repeating the experience. Now, are you going to take me to see Great-Uncle Charles or not? Because, as far as I am concerned, this conversation is at an end.'

I could not, of course, forget it. As we drove down to Queen's Square, as I sat beside Great-Uncle Charles' bed, making polite conversation and uttering platitudes about his state of health, which was still, as far as I could see, very precarious,

I kept thinking of what Theo had arranged to be done in my name, and cringing.

He had, I suppose, only been thinking of my good, for he was clearly convinced that Richard Wells was a danger to me, but all the same, he should not have done such a thing. Civilized people did not behave so, and I could not think that Richard Wells was such a threat that he deserved to be beaten, or worse, to protect me. Yet Theo seemed to think that he was. Why, he had even accused him of being the 'highwayman' who had tried to hold up the carriage and had caused the terrible accident, and all for the purpose of abducting me.

A sudden thought came unbidden into my mind, a thought that in all my confused wonderings had never occurred to me before, but which now caused me to go rigid with shock.

The child. The child he claimed was our child. The child I had dreamed had been in the carriage with me that terrible night, though I accepted it was not possible that she could have been more than a baby.

Supposing – just supposing – that Richard Wells had seduced or even raped me, and I had borne him a daughter? Supposing my mother had been taking us to the only sanctuary she could think of to keep the little one out of his clutches? Supposing it had not been *me* he had been attempting to abduct that night, but my child? Supposing he had succeeded? Why, he might even have fired the shot deliberately to frighten the horses, so that he could get away with her without fear of being followed . . .

The blood drained from my face, and indeed, I believe, from my body, for suddenly I was icy cold and trembling from head to foot. I swayed where I sat – had I not been sitting, I would almost certainly have fallen. Great-Uncle Charles' quavery voice was a faraway humming in my ears like a swarm of somnolent bees; the walls of the room seemed to close in around me.

'Davina?' I think I heard him speak my name, querulous, concerned, but I could not answer. Then I became aware of

126

the urgent ringing of his bell, lifted my misted eyes, and saw his hand on the rope.

'Great-Uncle Charles, there is no need . . .' I heard myself say, but my voice did not seem to be my own. And then Theo was in the room, taking me by the shoulder.

'Davina? Davina, are you ill?'

'No,' I said, just as faintly. 'No, there is nothing wrong with me at all. I am perfectly well . . .'

But I knew I was not perfectly well. The world was spinning around me. I did not think in that moment that I would ever be perfectly well again.

Theo took me home. I went to my room and lay down, and the milling thoughts came to me as if from a long way off. Reason seemed to have entirely deserted me. I had turned too many thoughts and ideas over and over in my head during the past weeks; now they were more jumbled than ever, nothing but whirling demons, and I thought I was going quite mad.

When Mr Paterson came home and found me there, he was most concerned and insisted upon sending for the doctor, though I tried to dissuade him. I knew no doctor could put right what ailed me. But he sent for him all the same.

When he arrived, within the hour, I was surprised by how young he was, not much older than me, and certainly no more than his early thirties. His name was Andrew Thorson. He examined me and pronounced that all was well with the baby, but suggested that perhaps I should take a dose of laudanum and rest.

I did not want to take a dose of laudanum. I had been given it after my accident and I remembered how befuddled it had made me feel even when I was not actually sleeping. Heavens, I was befuddled enough already, without a drug to make things worse! I wanted to be able to think more clearly, not lose myself altogether in a dream-filled haze.

'Is something troubling you?' he asked, sitting beside my bed and looking at me with soft brown eyes that were full of concern.

For a moment I was tempted to tell him everything, to

unburden all my worries on to this stranger with the kind face. But I knew I must not. Mr Paterson would be paying his bill; he might feel duty bound to share my confidences with him, Hippocratic oath or no Hippocratic oath. And in any case, I was frightened and ashamed. There were secrets in my past, I was sure of that now, dark and guilty secrets that condemned me. Until I knew what they were, I must keep my own counsel.

'No,' I lied in a whisper in answer to his question, but I could not meet his eyes.

He sat there quietly for what seemed like an eternity, waiting, I think, to see if I would change my mind. Then his breath came out on a long sigh.

'Whatever it is,' he said, 'you must try to put it to the back of your mind for the sake of your baby. That must be your first concern now, or it will be the worse for you.'

He rose, taking a phial of laudanum from his bag and placing it on the table beside my bed.

'I'll leave this in case you change your mind. Two drops in a warm posset at bedtime would help you to sleep, and a good night's sleep is a great healer for body and mind alike.'

In the doorway he paused, looking back at me.

'Don't hesitate to send for me again if you need me – or if you need to talk to someone. I gather that you have few friends here in Bristol and I am a good listener, even if I have a great deal to learn before I am a good doctor.'

'Thank you,' I said faintly, and indeed it was a comfort to me to think that there was someone I could confide in if I could bring myself to do so. He was quite right, I was very alone, and especially after Theo's revelations concerning the beating of Richard Wells. I had thought Theo was my friend and ally, but he had resorted to sickening violence as a result of my confiding in him.

A sudden thought struck me. 'Dr Thorson!' I said urgently.

Half out of the doorway, he turned back, head cocked to one side expectantly.

'You were not by chance called upon to treat a man named

128

Richard Wells who was set upon by a gang of ruffians a few days ago?' I asked.

His eyes narrowed; he came back into the room.

'You are acquainted with Richard Wells?'

'I've met him, yes,' I admitted. 'You did treat him, didn't you?'

'He is a patient of mine.'

'Is he . . . is he badly hurt?' I asked. 'I suppose you think it's strange that I should be concerned when I scarcely know him, but . . . well, I don't like to thing of *anyone* being attacked in such a way, and it has been on my mind . . .'

There was a sharp awareness in those soft brown eyes now, and I knew I had said too much. Then a corner of his mouth lifted.

'He'll live,' he said.

'And . . . will it be long before he is up and about again?' I simply could not stop myself asking, no, not even if he guessed that Richard Wells was part of the confusion that was ailing me.

'Not long, I think,' Andrew Thorson replied. 'He's a strong man and a healthy one when he is not suffering the effects of a bad beating. He'll mend without much help from me, I should think.'

'Will you be seeing him again?' I asked impetuously.

'I'm sure I will. Even if not in my professional capacity,' Dr Thorson said carefully.

'Then will you please tell him I was asking for him?' I said.

Andrew Thorson nodded. 'I'll pass the message on, certainly.'

And then he was gone and I was alone. I had spoken rashly, I knew, and perhaps unwisely. But at least I knew now that Richard Wells had not suffered any lasting damage as a result of the attack by Theo's hired thugs. For the moment, it was the best I could hope for.

I had wondered if, now that he had been warned off in such a scurrilous manner, I would hear no more from Richard Wells.

129

But I rather thought he was not the man to bow under pressure, rather that it might make him all the more determined, and I was to be proved right.

One morning Thomas came into the breakfast room, where I was lingering over coffee for want of something better to do. I scarcely looked up, since I thought he was there to clear away the salvers as he usually did, and was surprised when he moved soundlessly to stand at my side.

'The carriage will be waiting at eleven as you instructed, ma'am.'

I frowned, on the point of asking what he could mean; I had not asked for the carriage to be made ready for me this morning. Then my heart began to beat very fast as realization dawned.

'You mean . . . ?'

Thomas made no reply and his sculpted features gave nothing away.

'Thank you, Thomas,' I said. He glided away and I was left alone with my tumultuous thoughts.

I was ready well before eleven, so anxious was I that I should not be late. Somehow I had run over the day's menus with Cook, though I had not a single thought for what would be appearing on the table, somehow I had allowed Perrett to help me dress, though I was very much afraid she would notice that I could not keep from trembling. I had chosen a simple blue redingote and bonnet which I thought suited me, but was not too grand, since I felt I would be more confident if I looked nice, but did not want it to appear that I had taken too much trouble. My stomach was churning as if it were inhabited by a million butterflies, I was excited, nervous and downright fearful, but nothing could have prevented me from keeping the appointment I felt sure Thomas had arranged for me.

How did he know Richard Wells? I wondered. How was he able to make contact with him and Mr Paterson not know of it? But I did not wonder for long. I had too many other things on my mind.

'Where are we going, Thomas?' I asked when I was

130

seated in the landaulet, and he replied: 'To the home of Lady Avonbridge in the Clifton Woods, ma'am.'

Lady Avonbridge. The grand lady in whose company Richard Wells had come to Mr Paterson's reception just before our wedding. Well, at least I could not see that I would be in any danger there – I had been a little afraid that our meeting might be going to take place on some lonely road or in one of the dark, oppressive warehouses on the docks. But I supposed that, given Theo's violent warning to him that he should have no more contact with me, Richard Wells was anxious that the meeting should be well away from the curious eyes of anyone who might gossip or report back to Theo that his cousin had been seen in questionable company.

The carriage descended to the river, crossed a bridge, and began climbing again. The smell of burning lime over-powered the stench of the river as the road rose steeply, flanked on either side by thick glades of trees. Then we were turning into a drive between gateposts topped with magnificent stone eagles, and up to the door of an imposing mansion.

Thomas helped me down; my knees were trembling so much I feared they would not support me. I looked towards the house. The great door stood open.

And then I saw him, standing there waiting for me. And for a single mad moment I forgot all my doubts, all my fears, and felt nothing but that shaft of pure, unadulterated, heady joy.

He came towards me. He walked, I noticed, with a slight limp, and an angry bruise discoloured one side of his face. Otherwise there was little to show for the beating Theo had arranged for him.

His eyes were guarded; no reflection now of my crazy joy, which had been swallowed up, in any case, by a dreadful attack of nervousness.

'You came then, Rowan,' he said.

'Of course I came!' I returned shortly. 'How could I not, when you wrote to me in such riddles?'

131

He glanced at Thomas, nodded abruptly in acknowledgement, and placed his hand on my back, causing a shiver to run through me as if I had been struck by a bolt of lightning.

'Shall we go inside? This conversation is for no ears but our own.'

I stepped into the great hall, which was filled with the scent of late roses, arranged in a bowl on a spindle-legged table. No one else was in evidence, no sign of Lady Avonbridge, and no servants either. A door to our left stood open; he indicated that I should go into the room beyond it. I did so and found myself in a richly furnished drawing room where the walls were hung with paintings of aristocratic-looking ladies and gentlemen, ancestors, I supposed, of Lady Avonbridge or her husband, if she had one.

Richard Wells indicated a chaise set at an angle to the windows, which overlooked the drive and the woods beyond.

'Shall we sit down?'

'Thank you, I'd rather stand,' I said. Though my knees would scarcely support me, I felt somehow safer standing, more in command of myself and in a better position for flight, or to call to Thomas for assistance if it proved necessary. 'I don't intend to stay long,' I warned him. 'But I think you owe me an explanation. The letter you sent me . . .'

A corner of his mouth twisted. 'Which you went running straight to Theo Grimes about.'

'I had to speak to someone!' I returned defensively. 'I had to try to discover if there was any foundation for it.'

'And you thought Theo Grimes would tell you the truth? A truth that would put an end to all his carefully laid plans? Pshaw! He's a liar and a scoundrel who wouldn't know the truth if it jumped up and bit him! And he has some very disreputable friends, too.' His anger was palpable, and considering what Theo had had done to him, I supposed that was not surprising.

'I am very sorry about what happened to you,' I said. 'If I'd known what he would do, I would never have told him about the letter. But, however wrong it was, he was only trying to protect me.'

'Protect you? Protect his own interests, more like! Oh – '
he gestured dismissively – 'don't trouble to apologize. I've
taken beatings before and no doubt I'll take them again –
yes, and give them too. And I know, without you telling me,
it was not your doing. The Rowan I knew had too soft a heart
to condone the whipping of a mad dog, never mind the man
she once loved.'

I lowered my eyes, biting hard on my lip. *The man I
once loved . . . Had* I loved him, this hard, handsome man?
Something deep inside me was whispering that I had . . . no,
more – that I still did! Why else would I have reacted as I
had done to his kiss on the night of the gathering? Why else
would I feel this crazy desire just to see him, speak his name,
be in his presence?

Yet my conscious mind was full of the warnings I had been
given that he was a desperate, dangerous man, and the sheer
improbability of the claims he had made in his letter in order
to persuade me – a married woman and a mother-to-be – to
meet with him in secret.

'I find it very hard to believe I once loved you when I do
not even remember you,' I said tersely.

'So do I, Rowan,' he said bleakly. 'So do I.'

'And—' I took a deep, shuddering breath – 'It's even
harder to believe that I could have forgotten that I had a
daughter.'

There. It was said.

A wary look came into his hazel eyes, wary – and sharp.
'You saw her.'

'I saw a little girl in your arms when I came out of the
cathedral,' I said. 'But I fail to see how she could possibly
be mine. Even if she is yours, which I doubt.'

'Who do you think she is, then?' he demanded.

'I don't know. A child you borrowed, perhaps, in order to
deceive me. One thing I am sure of, though. Two years ago
I was lying critically ill in my grandparents' house. So you
see, it doesn't add up, does it? You must think me a fool,
Mr Wells.'

'Not a fool, Rowan.' He took a step towards me. 'Never a

133

fool. And what do you think I am that I should seek to deceive you so? No, don't bother to answer that. You have come here today because you have doubts about what you have been told. And you are right to have them. But now, about what I have told you. The child is indeed your daughter. Yours and mine. Her name is Alice, and as I told you, she is two years old. She was born at your grandparents' house when you lay, as you so rightly say, critically ill following the accident.'

'So why do I not know of it?' I demanded. 'Why have I no memory of her birth? And why is she with you and not with me?'

His face darkened.

'Are you sure you do not want to sit down? It's a long story, and not a pretty one. But as God is my witness, Rowan, it is one I intend to keep to myself no longer.'

Ten

I sat. Truly, I do not think my trembling legs would have supported me any longer. It was not true. It could not possibly be true! But I had come to hear what Richard Wells had to say, and hear it I must. Then, and only then, could I begin to weigh up the things I had been told and the things I had yet to hear, and decide, if such a thing were possible, where the truth lay.

'Perhaps,' Richard said, 'it would be best to begin at the beginning.'

'Yes,' I said faintly, 'perhaps it would. You told me once that you knew me as Rowan Gillespie.'

'And so you were. Does the name mean nothing to you?'

I gave a small, almost imperceptible shake of my head. I did not want to admit yet that it had stirred some chord of familiarity deep within me. It might indeed have been my name; Theo had more or less admitted it.

'What makes you so certain that I am she, and not someone who looks like her?' I asked. 'You had thought, after all, if I remember rightly, that Rowan Gillespie was dead.'

'I had been told she was dead, yes.'

'In a . . .' My voice wavered. I controlled myself with an effort. 'As a result of a carriage accident?'

'Not in a carriage accident, no,' he said, 'but we will come to that later. As to how I knew you were she and not some double. . . do you really think I could make such a mistake after all we had been to one another? At first, it's true, I could scarcely believe my eyes. But the moment you spoke, I could be in no doubt. Your voice, your gestures, your expression, everything about you . . . oh, I knew you were she, though in the light of what I had been told – what I had believed – it seemed impossible. You were . . . you *are* Rowan Gillespie. And the fact that your loss of memory leaves you unable to disprove it is further evidence, if any were needed.'

'Theo admitted to me that my grandparents may have changed my name,' I said quietly. 'He said they had decided Davina was more suitable.'

'As they decided so much else,' Richard Wells said grimly. 'Oh, believe me, Rowan, they have a great deal to answer for. But let us go back, as we agreed. Let us set the scene the better for you to understand why I have pursued you and refused to be deterred, no matter what your so-called family may do in their attempts to stop me.'

His hand went to his ribs, holding them gingerly for a moment and grimacing with pain, and I guessed they had been damaged in the attack.

'Are you badly hurt?' I ventured, but he interrupted me with an impatient gesture.

'There's nothing wrong with me that won't mend. In the physical sense, anyway. Let's not waste precious time talking about it. I was telling you who you are, and hoping against hope that some of it might reawaken that confounded memory of yours.'

'So,' I said. 'Tell me about Rowan Gillespie. I'm not saying that I believe she and I are one and the same – don't think for a moment that I am. But tell me about her anyway. Where did she live? How did you come to know her?'

'Very well, that's how we'll play it if that's the way you want it.' He crossed to the sideboard, poured some brandy into a glass and took a swig.

'For medicinal purposes,' he said with a crooked smile. 'Do you want one?'

'Indeed not!' I said, shocked. 'Why should you think I would? Rowan Gillespie did not drink brandy before noon, surely?'

'Not to my knowledge.' The crooked grin flashed again. 'But she would not have been afraid to had she so wished.'

'She was a wanton creature, then.'

136

'Not wanton, no. Like her mother, she was uninhibited.
And why not? There's too much adherence to what is
considered proper – it causes a great deal of trouble. No,
Elizabeth Gillespie was a free spirit, and she raised her
daughter to be the same. They travelled the country with
a band of strolling players, living and loving and enjoying
their freedom.'

A nerve twisted deep within me. That much my grandparents had told me, that my mother had run off with a
strolling player. How could Richard Wells have been aware
of that if he had not known us then – unless, of course, in order
to practise his deception, he had familiarized himself with
facts that would not be difficult to come by. But no . . . I was
allowing my thinking to become confused. From what Theo
had said, Richard Wells had certainly known me. It was the
details of the nature of our relationship which were at odds.
And whatever the truth of that, at least I could gain some
insight into the previous life which had been lost to me.

'Did Rowan Gillespie not have a father?' I asked.

'I never knew him.' Richard Wells took another drink of
the brandy and refilled his glass. 'He had died when Rowan
was just a little girl – as a result of some bizarre accident,
I believe. He was run through by a sword in a stage fight
that went wrong, and died from his injuries. A good way, I
suppose, for an actor to go, doing what he loved best and with
an audience to boot. But a tragedy, nevertheless. Elizabeth
was heartbroken, I believe – certainly I never knew her to so
much as look at another man.'

That, then, went against what Theo had told me.

'What did she do then, she and Rowan, after she was
widowed?'

'Whilst Rowan was small, she took domestic jobs from
time to time, I believe, in order to survive and keep a good
solid roof over her child's head. Then, later, she returned to
the stage. She was a pretty woman, and a fine actress and
singer. And Rowan took parts in the plays too.'

'Did she have a talent for it?' I asked.

His eyes smiled at me over the rim of his brandy glass.

'Now you are fishing for compliments.'

'No!' I flashed. 'I simply want to know!'

'And so you shall. Rowan was good enough, I think, though perhaps more from having learned her craft at her parents' knees than from natural ability. But, in my eyes, she was the greatest actress who ever lived. I would have watched her even if she had been as wooden as the boards she trod, and still acclaimed her a talent beyond match.'

A little colour rose in my cheeks; I felt it, and returned hastily to the more practical issues. To seek information as to Rowan's accomplishments was indeed mere foolish vanity.

'So how did you come to meet them?' I asked.

'I happened to attend an open-air performance in the courtyard of an inn. I was impressed – ' the corner of his mouth quirked again – 'both by the performance and the players.'

'My mother,' I said, then hastily amended my words. 'Elizabeth, I mean. You took a fancy to Elizabeth.'

'Elizabeth?' He frowned. 'No, not Elizabeth, though I grant you she was still a very handsome woman. No, it was you who took my eye, Rowan. Some romantics would say that I fell in love the moment I clapped eyes on you, but I don't know whether such a thing is possible. What I do know is that I wanted you – wanted you so badly I could think of nothing but meeting you, talking with you – and seeing you again. Not so easy to achieve, since the troupe was to move on the very next day.'

'So – how did you manage it?' I asked.

'By hiring the company to perform for my father – entertainment for a private party at his house. He was a little startled, I admit, when I told him what I had done and asked for a stage to be constructed in the great hall, but I think he was impressed.'

'Your father has a house with a great hall large enough to erect a stage?' I exclaimed, surprised.

'It's not so unusual, surely? Your husband was able to do the same for that reception he gave in order to introduce you into Bristol society.'

'Yes, but . . .' I broke off. Somehow I had not thought of Richard Wells as coming from a wealthy family. 'Well, I had never seen such a house before that night,' I finished lamely.

'You cannot *remember* having seen such a house before. I assure you, you most certainly have, on a number of occasions. Anyway, you came to my father's house.'

'Which is where?' I interrupted.

'In rural Somerset. My father inherited the family home, Covington Hall, along with the title, when his elder brother, the Earl of Covington, died in a hunting accident. Prior to that he was a Bristol merchant, very like Mr Paterson, but that is another story.'

'Your father is an earl?' I exclaimed, amazed. 'But your name is Wells . . .'

'The name I use. The family name. One day I suppose I shall be the Earl of Covington, God willing, though I can't say I relish the prospect. In the meantime, I am plain Richard Wells, and that is the way I like it.'

I gave myself a little shake. This truly was beyond belief, though I suppose the aristocratic background explained Richard Wells' acquaintance with Lady Avonbridge, the reason he had been able to persuade her to bring him as a guest to Mr Paterson's reception, and why we were here, now, in her drawing room.

'So – we came to perform at Covington Hall,' I said, returning to the story he was telling me. 'What then?'

'Why, I wooed and won you.' He took a long gulp of his brandy. 'I acquired a little house for you and your mother in Watchet, an idyllic little Somerset port. Elizabeth was glad enough now to leave her nomadic life with the strolling players, for her health was not as robust as once it had been, and she was glad, too, that you had the promise of something better than she had ever been able to provide for you.'

'You mean Rowan was . . . your mistress?' I could scarcely bring myself to speak the word.

'Mistress? As you mean it, no. I had too much respect for you for that. We were to be married, Rowan. I was the

139

happiest man alive – and you were happy too. But there was something I had to do first – a voyage I had to make. I don't want to go into details now, it would take too long, and I'm not sure if we have the time. Suffice it to say it was something I had to do.'

'A voyage . . . You were a sea captain, then?'

'Not by that time, though I had been. But, as I say, the transposition from my former life as a sea captain to what constitutes my raison d'être now – and at the time I planned to wed you – is another story, and would only cloud the important issues with which I need to familiarize you. The simple fact is that I left you in Watchet to travel to the West Indies. And before I left, we allowed our emotions to get the better of us. We became lovers.'

A nerve twisted deep inside me, bittersweet, haunting, and yet incredibly immediate. *Lovers*. The word caressed me. I looked at the powerful figure of the man before me, the man who tossed back brandy as if it were water whilst still, almost unconsciously, keeping a hand pressed against the ribs that had been injured because of the outrageous claims he persisted in making, and found myself almost wishing for a moment that it could be so. It was as if some deep unthinking part of me remembered what it was like to be held by those strong arms, loved by that lean, yet powerful, body, and yearned to experience it once more.

Lovers. Oh, Richard! *Lovers!*

With an effort I dragged myself back from the magical place I wanted to be, grasping the thread of the story he was telling me, following it to its inevitable conclusion.

'And this is how, according to you, I . . . that is, *she* . . . came to bear you a child?' I said, measuring each word.

'I did not know the situation when I left for the West Indies,' Richard said. 'If I had known, then I would never have left you, Rowan, without making proper provision for you or ensuring your safety. I did not even expect to be gone so long. Under normal circumstances I would have been home long before the child was born. But my ship was caught by a sudden storm and suffered enough damage to delay us for many weeks whilst it was repaired. And it was whilst I was there, stranded in the West Indies, that I learned that you were with child. You wrote to me, sending the letter with an old acquaintance of mine, another sea captain, who was on his way to Africa, in the hope that, if he did indeed encounter me and pass the letter on, I would make fast tracks for home.

I could not do that, of course, until my ship was repaired. There was nothing I could do but wait – and believe me, boat builders and craftsmen in that part of the world work at an even more leisurely pace than they do here. Can you imagine it? Can you imagine how I felt, knowing that you were having our child and I was many hundreds of miles away and unable to be with you – caring for you, making an honest woman of you, even? I was beside myself, but what could I do? My only comfort was that you were safe – or so I thought – in the house I had bought for you, and your mother was with you. She would not blame you, I knew, though there were plenty of others who would. The life she had chosen had been outside of the normal conventions; she would not accuse you, and she would not burden you down with shame either.'

He paused, looking at me, expecting, perhaps, some reaction, but there was nothing I could say. I was feeling it now, that shame – the shame of an unmarried woman who has lain with a man and is left to bring his bastard alone into a harsh, condemning world. Perhaps my mother – *Rowan's* mother – had not been the cause of it, though perhaps again she had been. Perhaps, with a life lacking any respectability behind her, she had been so disappointed that Rowan was no better, that she had hit out at a love that had been unprepared to wait for the marriage bed. Or perhaps the shame had been all Rowan's . . .

'But she took me to my grandparents,' I said, abandoning any pretence that the story was anyone's but mine.

'Not to begin with. I don't think she intended that you should do other than remain in Watchet and wait for me. But the months went by and I did not return. I had not been able to get a letter back to you, and I expect you thought I was dead – drowned, or murdered, or dead of a fever. And then something terrible happened. The house where you both lived was burned to the ground.'

'A fire.' Suddenly I had one of those tantalizing glimpses of something buried deep in the mists of my memory. Just a glimpse, only a glimpse – the acrid smell of smoke in my nostrils, a taste of fear. Then, once again, it was gone. 'A fire. The house burned down.'

'Yes. It was, apparently, a terrible conflagration. You and Elizabeth were lucky to escape with your lives. As it was, or so I was told on my return, you were left homeless and with not a single possession but the clothes you stood up in.'

'But . . . did we have no friends who would take us in?' I asked. 'Was there no one who would offer us shelter?'

'I am sure there was, but for some reason your mother had the idea it was no longer safe for you to remain in the area,' Richard said. 'She had, according to my information, been anxious for some time that there was someone who meant one or the other of you harm, and she was convinced that the fire was no accident. I believe she thought her only course of action was to seek sanctuary well away from whoever it was she feared.'

I frowned. 'But who would do such a terrible thing as to try to burn us in our beds – and why?' I whispered.

'I don't know,' Richard admitted. 'I have never found anyone she was prepared to confide in – only that she feared for your lives. Maybe it was my fault – the business I am engaged in has made me many enemies. Maybe they were trying to get at me through you. I don't know – and believe me, I have left no stone unturned in trying to discover who it might be. But whatever. Your mother took you, heavily pregnant, and fled to what she believed would be the safety of Gloucestershire. But she was not safe – and neither were you.'

'Are you saying that the carriage going out of control was no accident?' I asked. 'That whoever had fired our house followed us and—'

'I don't know that either,' Richard said. 'It could be that it is pure coincidence that, only days after the fire which

142

failed to claim your lives, this second catastrophe overtook you, killing your mother and damned near killing you too. But I am not a great believer in coincidence. If you ask me what I think, then I think there is the possibility that whoever it was your mother feared caught up with you and finished what he had started. An accident in Watchet which could have killed you both and did not, another in Gloucestershire that proved fatal for your mother, at least.'

'Dear God!' I pressed a trembling hand to my mouth.

'I told you it was a terrible story, Rowan,' Richard Wells went on, 'and it is not finished yet.'

'The child,' I said in a whisper.

'The child,' he repeated. 'When you were found unconscious and badly hurt in the wreckage of the carriage, you were taken to the home of your grandparents.'

'And they did not turn me away,' I said.

'They would have had to be monsters to do so,' Richard said harshly. 'Though I think what they did later was monstrous enough.'

'They did not turn me away,' I repeated, hanging on to that fact. 'Grandmama said they did not. She said that, when we first arrived at the rectory, she and Grandfather were out visiting a dying parishioner, and, if they had not been, my mother and I would never have been on the road that night . . .'

'Well, that's as maybe.' Richard Wells' tone was hard. 'I couldn't say, though it wouldn't surprise me if they took one look at their wayward daughter and their granddaughter, soon to be an unwed mother, and decided their respectability would never recover from the disgrace of it.'

'But . . .'

'I cannot get inside their minds, Rowan. I am not in a position to know what they did or did not do, or what they planned. I can only tell you the facts as I know them. I returned at last to England just a few short weeks after your flight – I had missed you by so very little. As soon as I was told you had gone to Gloucestershire, I set out to find you – knowing nothing, of course, of the accident which had occurred. I came to the rectory—'

'You came to the rectory!' I exclaimed. 'You came to my grandparents' home?'

'Well, of course – what else would I do? I intended to marry you at once, before our child was born a bastard, as I thought, and set up a home for us and your mother too. Instead I was greeted with the news that you were both dead. Your mother in the accident itself, you in childbirth, immediately following. But the child, they told me, had survived. A little girl. And they would be much obliged if I would relieve them of the care and responsibility of her.'

His voice was hard and angry now, the words clipped, and they carried all the more weight for it. I was glad I was sitting, for all the strength that remained in me seemed to leave my body in a rush, and for a moment my mind was a terrifying blank.

'They said what?' I whispered.

'That you had survived the accident, but died in childbirth,' he repeated. 'That they were caring for your baby, but had no wish to continue to do so. That if I was the father, the responsibility for it was mine. Somehow they must have kept her existence a secret, I suppose, and they saw their chance to be rid of her so that they would never be forced to admit to what, I suppose, they saw as the evidence of your disgrace. I think they were even afraid I might refuse to take the babe, and they would be left with somehow explaining her away to your grandfather's parishioners and their friends. But they need have had no fears on that score. Devastated as I was by the terrible news of your death, the baby was undoubtedly mine, and I had not the slightest intention of leaving her with what were, to me, strangers. She was my flesh and blood – and besides that, she was all I had left of you. The woman I had loved, and thought I had lost for all time. When I left that accursed house, I took our baby with me.'

His words seemed to hover in the air between us, in the vacuum that was my conscious mind. It was beyond belief, all of it, and yet it had the unmistakable ring of truth. I felt it in every bone. Why should he invent such a story if it were not true? And it all fitted together, like pieces of a puzzle falling into place. My grandparents' reluctance to tell me anything about my past. Aunt Linnie's mysterious allusions to things she was not supposed to talk to me about. The family's eagerness to marry me to a suitable man. And, terrible though the thing they had done was, yet I could believe it of them. They would not have thought it so terrible. They were so concerned with propriety and respectability, they would no doubt have seen it as saving me from myself, from a life ruined by scandal. *It is for the best*, I could almost hear my grandfather explaining himself, and Grandmama adding: *We were only thinking of what was best for you, Davina*. Oh yes, they were quite capable of persuading themselves that what they did, they did for my sake, when in reality it was for their own.

But even given that I accepted the story thus far, yet it raised so many unanswered questions.

'Why should they tell you I was dead?' I asked in a whisper. 'Why did they not pass on the responsibility for me, as well as the baby, to you?'

Richard Wells lifted his shoulders in an impatient shrug.

'You will have to ask them that, Rowan. I imagine they thought I was the man who had ruined you, and you were better off without me. That you would have a fresh start in life. It was very convenient for them that you had no memory of me – or having given birth either.'

'But how could I have given birth and not know it?' I gave a small, bewildered shake of my head. 'Childbirth, from what I have heard, is very hard work, as well as being painful. If I were unconscious . . . ?'

I broke off, aware that ladies did not talk of such things with gentlemen, even gentlemen with whom they were intimate – and for all that Richard Wells claimed we had been lovers – and I believed him – I had no memory of it at all, nothing beyond our recent brief encounters. But surely what he had told me meant there were more important things than the conventions my grandparents had schooled into me. And did

I want to be like them? So inhibited that I was prepared to do anything, sacrifice everything, so as to be seen as respectable in the eyes of the world?

'If I were unconscious, how could I manage to bring the baby?' I finished, my cheeks turning pink as I spoke the words.

Richard Wells did not appear to be in the least discomfited by my indelicacy. He did not even appear to notice it.

'I've wondered that myself, Rowan. I can only think you were not unconscious at that time, or at least had periods when you were not. You were in the black hole, but able to obey the commands of your body – and whoever delivered your baby.'

'But . . .' The thought occurred to me that if my memory loss had been caused by the accident, then, if I had been conscious, even for a short period, at the time of giving birth, I should be able to remember it. But the fact was I could not, and there were more pressing questions at the moment. Questions about the child. *My* child, if this incredible story were to be believed.

'What did you do?' I asked. 'How were you able to care for an infant?'

'I followed the same instinct as your mother did,' he said evenly. 'I looked to my own parents for assistance. But I was more fortunate, as I knew I would be. My parents are not narrow-minded and hypocritical as your grandparents are. They are not ashamed to admit to a child born out of wedlock.'

'Perhaps they can afford to care less about the opinions of others,' I said, strangely, perhaps, in the light of all I had been told, flying to my grandparents' defence. 'When you have money and position, it's easier to flout public opinion. My grandfather's standing depends on him being seen as a moral man, who lives a life beyond reproach.'

'I would hardly have thought his behaviour in keeping with Christian morality or Christian charity,' Richard Wells said coldly. 'Lying, turning over his own flesh and blood to a man he clearly thought a rogue and a scoundrel, is scarcely what one would expect of a man who truly tried to lead a good life. But then, I dare say it's not uncommon for men of the cloth to care more about appearances than substance. Better to be thought pious and perfect than to be honest and flawed. I'm sorry if I sound harsh, but I cannot be as magnanimous as you seem to be, Rowan. I shall never be able to forgive them for what they did. Not for foisting Alice on to me – she has been a joy and a blessing, and I dread to think what might have become of her if I had not knocked upon the rectory door that day. But to tell me you were dead, when in fact you lay sick upstairs, and to separate you from your child and never even make you aware of her existence – no, I can never forgive them for that.'

'And she has thrived with your parents?' I asked. 'She is well and happy?'

'She is indeed,' he said. 'She is a delightful little girl, sunny-natured and pretty as a picture. But you saw that for yourself on the day of your marriage.'

'And can I . . . may I see her again?'

'Oh Rowan, you don't know how good it is to hear you say that!' He set down his glass, sat down on the chaise beside me and took my hands in his. Warmth ran through my veins from where his fingers touched; for a heady moment I thought he was going to take me in his arms and kiss me as he had on the night of Mr Paterson's reception.

He did not. Instead his eyes, narrowed and serious, sought mine.

'Are you prepared, then, to leave Mr Paterson, defy convention, and come to live with us? As my wife, and Alice's mother? As a family?'

Breath caught in my throat; a great void seemed to be opening up before me.

'Are you, Rowan?' he persisted. 'Before I take you to her, I must have your word.'

I was slipping, sliding, the earth on which I stood nothing but loose pebbles beneath my feet. Behind me, a mountain, steep, impassable. Before me, the chasm.

The certainty that he was telling the truth was gone,

suddenly, as if it had never been. Was this all an elaborate ploy to get me back into his clutches? Was he playing on my emotions, using the most primal instincts of any woman to win me back? Could he be that ruthless, as Theo had claimed he was? Ruthless and evil? Oh, I found myself attracted to him, there was no way of denying that, and perhaps I had been attracted to him before. Perhaps that was the root of all the trouble. For just because I was attracted to him – even if I had loved him – that did not mean I had given my heart wisely.

And now he was issuing me with an ultimatum. I must agree to leave Mr Paterson and go to him; he would not allow me to see the child he claimed was mine unless I did so. Evidence, surely, that possessing me was the most important thing to him.

I wanted to see her, of course, with every fibre of my being, this child of whom I had no recollection at all beyond that brief glimpse of her in his arms. I ached to see her with a longing that was physically painful. But I was also afraid, desperately, paralysingly afraid. Of the strength of my own emotions. Of the strength of his. Of the enormous step into the unknown that he was asking me to take, blindly, suddenly, with no opportunity to consider the implications. And heaven alone knew, with a new life beginning inside me, there was much to consider.

'That is terribly unfair!' I burst out. 'You can't expect me to give you my word on something so momentous just like that!'

'Surely it's simple enough?' he demanded impatiently. 'Either you want us as we want you, or you do not. And as for being unfair, do you think it would be *fair* to Alice to come back into her life and then disappear again? She may at present lack a mother, but at least she has security and stability. I won't see that eroded. That is why I am insisting on some commitment from you before I can allow such a meeting.'

'But she need not know who I am for the present,' I said desperately. 'She need know nothing. I could be just a friend. But oh, I do want to see her so much!'

His face hardened; those hazel eyes bored into mine for a moment, and I thought he was about to refuse me, point blank, unwilling, no doubt, to give up the bargaining position into which he had manoeuvred himself.

I, in my turn, held my ground. I could not give him such a momentous undertaking without having time to consider; he could not expect it of me. Why, I was still not altogether sure that what he had told me was nothing but a tissue of lies. And I had not only myself to think of, but my unborn baby. Nothing was as clear-cut as he was trying to make out.

And so I held his gaze stubbornly, and after a long moment he dropped my hands and stood up, pacing the length of the room. Then he turned to face me once more.

'You would be prepared for that? To give her no sign that might indicate you were anything other than a casual acquaintance?'

I swallowed on a huge lump of nervousness that had risen in my throat.

'Yes,' I said. 'Only, please let me see her.'

'Very well,' he said harshly. 'Perhaps then you will know what it is you have to do.'

The weight seemed to slip away from my heart. For a moment I forgot all the remaining problems in my eagerness.

'When can I see her?' I asked.

And Richard Wells replied: 'Why, now of course. She is out in the garden with her nurse. I will take you to her.'

Eleven

M y heart seemed to stop beating.
'She is here?' I repeated senselessly.

'Why should she not be?' He raised an eyebrow sardonically. 'I, at least, spend as much time as I can with my daughter.'

The remark cut me to the quick. That, too, was unfair, inferring that I was deliberately neglecting her. But this Richard Wells was a man who could be cruel in his determination to achieve his objectives; that much I had realized already. Any tenderness in his nature was well hidden, though his concern for his child's welfare, if indeed she was his child, was to his credit.

'Well, are you coming to see her or not?' he asked harshly.

I stood up. My legs felt weak and trembling; no, not just my legs, my whole body, like one of the milk jellies Grandmama had fed to me when I was convalescing after my accident. Richard Wells had picked up his brandy glass to drain what little remained in it and suddenly, though I had declined a drink earlier, I felt the need of something to give me courage.

'Could I have just a little?' I asked.

He frowned. 'And have Alice smell it on your breath?' he said censoriously.

'Oh, I didn't think . . .'

And perhaps in my condition I should not be drinking, in any case!

'Oh, I suppose she smells it on mine, and she's not old enough to know it's different for a lady.' He took

150

a glass, poured some brandy into it and held it out to me. 'Here.'

'No,' I said. 'You are quite right – I should not. And it would most likely make me cough.'

'Go on,' he said impatiently. 'I've poured it for you now. And in any case, as I said myself, it's medicinal. You are very pale. I shouldn't like you to faint away in front of the child.'

I took the glass. The smell of the brandy was strong in my nostrils; it awakened some deeply buried memory. I associated that smell with feeling very ill, I realized; I took a sip and my stomach turned, and I seemed to hear someone say: *It will make you sick, or it will pick you up. Either way you will be better.* And my own voice, childlike: *But I don't like the taste!* And that other voice, soft, loving, cajoling: *Just a sip, my darling! For me.*

It startled me, that sudden, unexpected smidgen from my forgotten past. I thought that for the first time since my accident I was hearing my mother's voice. Obedient to it, I put the glass to my lips and sipped.

I did not like the taste, any more than I had liked the smell, and the strong liquor burned my throat. But as it slipped down and went into my veins I did indeed feel a little better. I set the glass down on the table and took a determined step towards the door.

'I'm ready now.'

'Good. Your colour is coming back certainly. Now, remember, not a word to Alice about who you really are. This way.'

Richard Wells led me along a passage to where a door at the rear of the house led out into a herb garden. As I followed him nervously along the narrow path, I smelled sage, rosemary and thyme, and once again, to my newly attuned sense of smell, the scents seemed evocative, though of what I did not know. The path led to an archway, covered with a climbing rose that had showered yellowing white petals into a thick carpet, and beyond the archway the garden opened out on to a wide lawn, surrounded by trees.

And there I saw her. She was crouched down on the lawn, closely examining something in the grass, small fair head bent over so I could not see her face. Lady Avonbridge and a woman I took to be Alice's nurse sat on a rustic bench close by, but I had no eyes for them. I saw nothing but the child. The little girl Richard Wells maintained was my child.

She looked up at that moment and saw him, and in an instant whatever it was on the ground that had interested her so was forgotten. She was on her feet and running towards him, her little legs beneath her petticoats moving as fast as they would go.

'Papa! Papa!'

She threw herself at him, winding her arms round his buckskin-clad legs, totally oblivious of everyone but the man who was undoubtedly her father.

'Steady, sweetheart!'

He reached down and swung her up into his arms. His face had softened; there was no anger now, only love and pride in those weatherbeaten features.

'Papa, look – look what I found! A flower!' She was holding it up to him, crushed in her chubby little hand.

'That's not a flower. It's a clover,' he told her.

'Clover,' she repeated experimentally.

'And the leaf has three parts to it – look. One, two, three. Sometimes, just sometimes, you might find one with four parts, and if you do, that's lucky. A lucky four-leaf clover.'

'Lucky,' she repeated, looking from him to the clover and back again.

Her face, I saw, was small and serious and round, perfect Cupid's bow lips, small straight nose, fair, delicately arched eyebrows. And beneath them, fringed by long dark lashes, her eyes were hazel. His eyes. She had his eyes, then, and to be truthful, I could see nothing of myself at all. But my heart was pounding against my ribs and I could feel tears gathering in my eyes.

'Alice,' Richard Wells said. 'Here is someone I would like you to meet. She is a friend of mine and her name is – ' he hesitated – 'her name is Mrs Paterson. Won't you say good day to her?'

She gave me a quick, cursory glance, then returned her attention to her father.

'Papa . . .'

'Say good day to Mrs Paterson, Alice.'

Another cursory glance. 'Day.' She buried her head in his shoulder, feigning shyness.

'Alice! You can speak much better than that when you want to,' he chided her.

She wriggled in his arms, little legs kicking impatiently against his ribs. I saw him wince, but he did not put her down until she said: 'Papa – find me a clover with . . . with . . .' Her small serious face was screwed up with the effort of remembering what he had told her.

'With four lucky leaves? I doubt I can do that, sweetheart. It has to be a very special day before you find one.'

'Try! Please try!'

As he set her down, his eyes met mine over the top of her small fair head, and they were full of meaning. This could be Alice's special day, they seemed to say, and ours too, no matter whether we find a four-leaf clover.

'Look for yourself, Alice,' he said. 'You can easily count to four. Why, you can count to ten and beyond when you put your mind to it.'

'Papa . . .'

'I'll help you later,' he promised.

Something moved in the bushes at the far end of the lawn – a streak of ginger fur.

'Bessy!' Alice exclaimed. The clover leaf dropped from her plump little hand, forgotten already, as she set off as fast as her legs would carry her in pursuit of the cat.

'So now you have met your daughter,' Richard Wells said, almost carelessly.

I could not reply. My heart was too full and I could only stand there on the lawn in the warm autumn sunshine watching the small scampering figure and feeling the whole of my being melt with love and tenderness.

'Rowan – or should I say Davina?'

So engrossed had I been in little Alice, I had not noticed Lady Avonbridge coming towards us. The bright sunlight accentuated the deep furrows in the brow beneath her powdered wig, and the folds of skin drooping around her jawline, so that she looked older than when I had first met her at Mr Paterson's reception, but just as imposing.

'Lady Avonbridge,' I murmured dutifully.

Her hooded eyes flickered towards the bushes, where a flash of blue silk was all that was now visible of Alice.

'She is a charming child, is she not? If a little too fond of poor Bessy, who she torments mercilessly with her attentions whenever she comes to visit! All Bessy wants to do is bask in a pool of sunshine, all Alice wants to do is hug her, poke at her eyes and pull her tail. All in the name of love, of course.'

'The cat won't scratch her, will she?' I asked, alarmed.

'Oh, I shouldn't think so. The worst she'll get is a flea,' Lady Avonbridge said carelessly. 'A mother's concern is beginning to assert itself then? Well, I must say I'm glad – for all your sakes. And glad that I was able to play my part. I'll be vilified for doing so, no doubt, in polite society, but I've never been one to pay much attention to what people say about me.'

'It may not ever become public knowledge,' Richard said tersely. 'Rowan has not yet agreed to leave Mr Paterson.'

'Ah.' Lady Avonbridge raised an eyebrow, so that her expression was more arch than ever. 'But now that she has seen Alice, surely . . . ?'

At that very moment, for the first time, I felt my unborn baby move. Just a tiny tick, high in my waist, yet unmistakable, nevertheless, serving to remind me that I had other responsibilities than the ones that were tugging now at my heartstrings. I pressed my hand to the place where I had felt my baby move, and caught my lip between my teeth, overwhelmed by the impossibility of the choice I was being forced to make, swamped by conflicting emotions.

Richard's eyes were on me, narrowed, observant.

'I think perhaps Rowan should leave now,' he said. 'I don't want Alice upset.'

Lady Avonbridge touched my sleeve.

'Flouting convention takes a great deal of courage, my dear,' she said. 'But I think you may well find it worth it.'

Her words struck me as deeply ironic. My mother had flouted convention – and look where that had led! But I said nothing of it. I took my leave of her and let Richard lead me back towards the house. In the doorway I paused, looking back. Alice was emerging from the bushes, still pursuing the luckless Bessy, a small bundle of fair hair and blue silk. Then she was gone from my view. My heart went with her.

'Well?' Richard said. 'Has meeting Alice made up your mind for you? Will you come back to us?'

I shook my head, which was spinning. 'This has all been such a shock. You must give me time to think . . .'

'What's there to think about?' he demanded. 'I can understand that I am not the catch Mr Paterson is. My whole life is a gamble. But how can you turn your back on your own child, Rowan? Surely she is worth more to you than a fine carriage and a houseful of servants?'

'Oh, it's not that!' I cried passionately. 'But it's not so simple!'

'Why not?'

'Because . . .' I could keep it to myself no longer. 'Because I am with child! I am carrying Mr Paterson's child!'

Richard Wells stiffened, his features, his whole body, going as frighteningly still as if he had been turned to stone.

'What?'

'It's true,' I said wretchedly. 'So, you see, whatever decisions I make about the future are not for me alone.'

'I see.' If I had thought him cold and hard before, I had seen nothing. He had gone from me. Utterly. Completely. Suddenly, more than anything in the world, I wanted to reach for him, throw myself into his arms, let him make the decision for me. But I knew I could not, must not, and even if I did he might put me from him as ruthlessly as he had attempted to reel me in. The knowledge of my pregnancy had hurt him in a way my marriage had not; the shock of learning of it had made him withdraw into a place I could not reach.

155

'You don't want me now – now that you know I am carrying another man's child,' I said recklessly.

And he replied: 'It puts a whole new complexion on things, certainly.'

He strode ahead of me down the passageway. A maid appeared, ready to open the door for me; he waved her aside, opening it himself.

I turned, looking at him imploringly, not wanting to leave him like this. Not wanting to leave him – or Alice – at all.

'If you want to talk to me again, Rowan, you know where to find me.' His tone was as remote as his face.

'You'd take me back?' I whispered. 'You would still take me back even though—'

'Let us say we both have a great deal to think about, Rowan,' he said in that same cold tone.

Thomas, who had been waiting outside with the carriage, stepped forward. I bowed my head in an effort to hide the tears that were filling my eyes, and walked towards him.

At the carriage steps, I looked back. Richard Wells had disappeared and the great front door was closed. A great black despair filled me. Had I learned today something of the truth of my past, or was it all a great deception? And if it was the truth, had I learned it, only to lose it again?

I had hoped that when we returned to Clifton I would have some time alone. More than anything I wanted to retreat to my room, throw myself down on to my bed, and weep. A cowardly and useless attempt to retreat from reality, perhaps, but the well of tears aching inside me was preventing me from thinking of anything but controlling them; they needed to be spilled, and in private, before I could move on.

It was not to be. Mr Paterson was at home and the moment I walked through the front door, he called me into the parlour.

'Davina, my dear! You have been out! Where have you been?'

Guilt washed over me. I could feel the colour rising in my cheeks and the tears still pricking behind my eyes, and I felt sure he must notice.

156

'Visiting,' I said vaguely.

'Ah! Good! I'm pleased you are beginning to make a social circle,' he said, without bothering to ask who I had visited, and not appearing to notice my lack of composure either. 'I have a surprise for you, my dear.'

He was looking pleased with himself, I thought.

'A surprise?' I repeated, striving to sound normal. 'What sort of surprise?'

'I thought we could do with more help in the house,' Mr Paterson said. 'With a new baby on the way there will be extra work, and if one of the maids should leave to marry, as they have an unfortunate habit of doing, we should be left shorthanded at quite the wrong time.'

'You have taken on another maid?' I said, wondering why he thought this would be a treat for me, especially since it was usually the prerogative of the mistress of the house to oversee the engagement of servants.

'Better than that!' He was beaming proudly. 'We'll have no trouble with this one leaving to wed, or for any other reason. I've bought a little black girl for you.'

My first and immediate instinctive reaction was horror.

'A slave!' I exclaimed. 'You have bought me a slave?'

'I think you'll be pleased with her,' Mr Paterson said with satisfaction. 'She's a pretty little thing – very pretty indeed for what she is. She was brought to England as a child and the family who bought her have taught her to speak excellent English. We can soon have her trained up in our ways and to our standards, I'm sure. It will give you something to interest you when you're confined to the house and not able to go out on these visits of yours.'

I did not know what to say. I had not the first idea of how to set about training a slave in our ways, and no stomach for it either.

'You can even choose her name,' Mr Paterson went on magnanimously. 'You'd like that, wouldn't you?'

'Doesn't she already have a name?' I asked shortly.

'Well, yes, I suppose she does, but I don't know what it

157

is, and it's of no importance anyway. What we call her is up to us now that she belongs to us.'

All my own confusion and unhappiness suddenly metamorphosed into anger on behalf of this poor unknown girl, and I was furious, more furious than I could ever remember being.

'You bought a slave and you don't even know her name!' I exploded. 'And you expect me to be pleased at the prospect of deciding what she should be called, as if she were a pet puppy dog! Her *name*, John, is very likely the only thing she has that she can call her own!'

His jaw dropped in surprise, both at my angry reaction and the fact that I had, for the first time outside the bedroom, when he cajoled me into it, called him by his own given name. Looking back, I think I did so because it was somehow important to me at that moment to be his equal. At the time, of course, I was thinking of no such thing. My only concern was the dignity of this girl on whom I had not yet even set eyes.

I half expected Mr Paterson to be angry with me in return, both for criticizing him and for my lack of gratitude. But he merely threw back his head and laughed.

'My, Davina, but pregnancy is making you fiery!'

'It is not a laughing matter!' I snapped.

'No, and not one to get upset about either. The remedy is simple, my dear. Ask her what her name is and call her by it, if that's what you want to do. But, if I were you, I'd settle for the one her last owners knew her by. The African one she was given by her parents will be a mouthful of mumbo-jumbo, if I know anything about it!'

He crossed to the bell pull and gave it a few sharp tugs; a moment later Daltry answered it.

'Bring the new slave in, will you?' he instructed. 'Mrs Paterson wants to see her.'

I did not want to see her. More than ever, I wanted the privacy of my room. But I could do nothing but wait. It was my duty as mistress of the house, my duty as Mr Paterson's wife.

158

A few moments later and Daltry was back, pushing the poor little girl into the parlour as if she were a heifer being taken to market. It was, I suppose, Daltry's way of exerting her one little bit of superiority. She was a housemaid, with only the scullery maids beneath her in the pecking order of servants, but at least she was free. She was paid a wage – albeit a meagre one – and she had her days off when she was free to visit her mother. The slave girl would not be paid and she would have no days off unless I could persuade Mr Paterson to allow it, which I thought was unlikely. He would be too afraid she might try to run away. Daltry knew all this, and was glad to have someone she could order about, someone who made her feel important.

The new slave was even younger than Mr Paterson had led me to expect, little more than a child, though I suppose her slight, underdeveloped frame, lost in the too large dress that had been found for her, and her big frightened eyes may have heightened the impression. But even so, I did not think she could be much past thirteen or fourteen. If she had already been in England long enough to learn the language, she must have been snatched and put on a slaving ship when she was very young indeed. And she certainly was very pretty, her features clear and smooth beneath her cap of tight black curls.

'Thank you, Daltry, that will be all,' I said, thinking the slave child might feel less uncomfortable if she was not under the baleful, rather mean, and certainly triumphant eye of the housemaid. Daltry's expression turned to one of disappointment, but she bobbed dutifully and left.

'Straighten up, girl,' Mr Paterson said sharply. 'We don't have slouches in this house. Now, this is your new mistress, Mrs Paterson. I expect you to do as she tells you, and show her the respect she deserves, or it will be the worse for you.'

The poor little girl looked so overwhelmed by what was happening to her, so small and lost, I could not imagine her doing anything else.

'Don't be frightened,' I said gently. 'I won't harm you.'

She caught her full upper lip between her teeth, standing

there as still as a rabbit caught in the light of a poacher's flare, her little body shrinking still further inside the voluminous dress. I would get something to fit her better as soon as I was able, I decided.

'What is your name?' I asked.

Her mouth worked as if she were trying to speak, but no words came.

'Come on, girl!' Mr Paterson said impatiently. 'Your mistress asked you a question. Don't you understand it? I was told you speak our language.'

'Yessuh.' It was just a whisper.

'So, what do they call you? Your English name, if you please.'

The jet-black eyes fell from his face to fasten on a spot on the carpet.

'Dorcas, sir.'

'That's better. Now, answer any other questions Mrs Paterson may have for you properly. Savvy?'

I could not think of a single thing I wanted to ask Dorcas, and I hated hearing him speak to her so. I wished I could put my arms around her and comfort her, but of course I could not, and in any case my touch would have been no solace to her. I was an alien being, a white woman who lived in a grand house and wore fine clothes, a white woman who owned her, body and soul.

'Have you been shown your room yet?' I asked. 'The room where you will sleep?'

'She can sleep in the cellar,' Mr Paterson said. 'We'll have a bed made up for her there.'

'The cellar!' I exclaimed. 'But it's dark there, and cold in the winter.'

'She can have a candle, and it's bone dry down there,' Mr Paterson said. 'I had it built to the strictest specifications.'

'But . . . the cellar . . . !' I was horrified.

'She's used to far worse, I'm sure,' Mr Paterson said dismissively. 'And it's not right for the maids to have to share with one of her kind.'

We'll see about that! I thought furiously.

160

'You won't have met Thomas yet,' I said to the girl. 'But I think you will find you have a friend in him. Like you, he was brought here from Africa, but he has been here a very long time and he's quite accustomed to our ways, so I am sure he will help you to settle in. He's kind, too, and . . .'

Mr Paterson snorted his derision. Trusted though Thomas was, he was still a slave.

I ignored him. 'And you are not to be afraid to come to me if anything is troubling you,' I said. 'I want you to be happy here, Dorcas.'

Mr Paterson snorted again. He would, I felt sure, remind me of my position the moment the little slave was not there to hear him. He would tell me the feelings of the servants were secondary to running a good efficient house and the feelings of a slave were certainly beneath consideration. He would tell me that if I wished to retain their respect, I must be certain to assert my authority, not mollycoddle them and give them credit for emotions they almost certainly did not have, since they were, after all, savages. He was going to be cross with me, I could tell, and I did not care. If I could bring a little comfort, a little relief, into the life of this poor child, I would do it, and the devil take the consequences.

But all the while I knew there was no real comfort or relief I could offer her. She was a slave, I was the mistress, and whatever I said, she would continue to be afraid of me until I could prove to her by my actions, not mere words, that she had no need for fear.

I had no time, the whole of that day, to be alone with my thoughts, though of course they whirled constantly as I went through the motions of normal living. I seemed to hear in snatches all the things Richard had told me, not in the ordered way he had related them, but jumping out at me higgledy-piggledy, one aspect engaging me completely for a while, only to be replaced by another, just as perplexing, just as unsettling, just as all-consuming. The life he said I had led, the love he claimed we had shared, the birth of a daughter of whom I could remember nothing at all, the deception my

161

grandparents had practised upon me, their heartlessness – for I could see it as nothing less, even though I knew they would have done whatever they did with my best interests in mind. That, as much as anything, had rocked the foundations of my world, for they had been the only constant since my accident, the only people I had felt sure I could trust.

And all the time, whether I was thinking of her or not, the ache of longing for Alice never left me. Some deep force was drawing me to her, much as I had felt drawn to Richard Wells, yet it was stronger, even, than that, instinctive and primal. It was in every breath I breathed, in every beat of my heart.

What was I to do? What could I do, torn as I was? On the one hand was my forgotten past, which even now I wavered between believing and not believing, my lover and my daughter, my longing for them adulterated by my fear that not only was Richard Wells deceiving me for his own ends, but I was deceiving myself. And on the other, my marriage vows to Mr Paterson, the baby I undoubtedly carried – his baby – and my overwhelming sense of duty to them both. Mr Paterson had never been anything but kind to me; he did not deserve to be hurt and shamed. And my baby needed security, a loving home, an assured future. Should I follow my heart, or my head? Whichever, someone was bound to be hurt. And did I even have a choice any more? I remembered Richard Wells' face when I had told him that I was with child – hard, cold, shocked. Perhaps he no longer wanted me. Perhaps the door to that other world was already shut and bolted. Perhaps it had never existed at all outside his imagination – and mine.

The confusion grew in me until I thought I would burst with it. And still I went about my duties in the house and carried on a social intercourse of sorts, and no one, unbelievably, seemed any the wiser.

That night, though I had thought I would not, I slept, exhausted, no doubt, by a day of worrying and wondering. And when I slept, the dreams came.

At first they were jumbled, all mixed up with the events of the day – most poignantly, I saw Alice on the lawn, searching in the grass for something, but when I asked her what it was she was looking for, she replied not, *A four leaf clover*, but, *I am looking for my mama*. And then, incongruously, the new slave, Dorcas, was there, little and frail in her too large dress, and she said: *I am your mama. And Thomas is your papa.* And I felt bereft, and also surprised that I had not realized it, though since Alice was fair-haired and fair-skinned, and Dorcas and Thomas both black as ebony, I supposed it was unsurprising that I had not. But now, of course, it was clear, crystal clear; I could not doubt it, but it made me dreadfully sad all the same.

As I slept more deeply, the dreams became more lucid, and overlaid with a strange sense of reality. It was almost as if I had control of these dreams, as if I were floating above myself, looking down, and could know what was coming before I lived it again in that strange and slightly distorted hinterland.

For a horrid moment I thought I was going to find myself in the carriage again, rattling and rocking towards oblivion, but as if by an effort of will I stopped it and moved further back in time.

I was on the cobbles beside a harbour. The sun was warm on my face, the water, unlike the filthy Bristol docks, blue and sparkling and lapping gently around the hulls of the ships that rode there at anchor. Their sails were white against the clear blue of the sky; semi-furled, they flapped lazily in the gentle breeze. But, for all the peace and beauty of the scene, there was an ache in my heart. I was not alone yet, but soon I would be.

I felt strong arms around me; I looked up and saw Richard Wells' face, not hard and angry as it had been this morning, but tender and loving. He reached out and twisted one of my curls, which had come loose in the stiff breeze, around his finger.

'Don't look so sad, Rowan,' he said. 'I'll soon be home again.'

'I know you will,' I said. 'But I wish with all my heart that you did not have to go at all.'

'You know I must.' His arms were about my waist, holding me tightly. I could feel the hard strength of his body with the whole length of mine and I pressed closer still, so that there was no part of us that was not touching, and shivers of awareness ran through the deepest parts of me. But the sadness in my heart would not allow me to enjoy them, as I knew I had when we had laid, the night before, in one another's arms. It was more than sadness; it was dread, a black cloud encompassing me.

I wanted to plead with him but I knew it would do no good. Not just because his ship was being made ready at this very moment, but because I knew there was some strong reason for his voyage, something that must take precedence over his love for me, something that, in his own words, he had to do, though I could not for the life of me remember what it was.

The sailors were swarming and sweating, ropes, curled across the decks of the ship, the sails filled and billowed. *Time to go!*

He turned towards the shout, answered by raising his hand, pulled me close once more. He kissed me deeply; my lips clung to his lips, my body clung to his body.

Take care, my love.

Then he was gone, striding up the gangplank, and I was left to watch the ship depart, growing smaller and smaller until it was no more than a speck on the horizon where sea meets sky, and I was alone. And still I stood there, on that small, neat, clean, bustling quay, with the fishing boats unloading their catch, and the old men sitting in the sun to mend their nets.

And I pressed my hands to my waist and felt the tiny tick there, first sign of a new life, and there was joy and sorrow both at the same time mixed up in me, and tears wet on my cheeks.

Dream and wakefulness were blurring; the little harbour merging into my bedroom in the house in Clifton. As I returned to the real world, I found that my hands were indeed pressed to my waist and I could indeed feel the tiny tick of new life beneath them.

And my face was indeed wet with tears.

Twelve

I dreamed a good deal in the nights that followed and I was unsure whether the dreams were my interpretation of the story Richard Wells had told me, or memory beginning to return whilst I slept, jogged by his revelations.

I saw a little house with roses round the door and the sea just a short walk away across the gorse-covered cliffs, I heard my mother's voice, I even once dreamed I was in a barn, lit by flares and filled with people, and a man on a makeshift stage, dressed in a strange costume and with an ass's head in place of his own, was reciting lines whilst other players gambolled around him.

Once, terrifyingly, I dreamed of fire. The smell of acrid smoke was in my nostrils, I could hear the sharp crack of burning timber and see the flames dancing like the cauldrons of hell against the black night sky. The feeling of fear was so intense it would not go away when I woke; I had to get up and light a candle because the darkness was full of it, and I stood for a long while at the open window, breathing deeply of the cool night air before the vision faded sufficiently to allow me to go back to my bed.

Often I dreamed of nights of love, my body entwined with another's, who I knew was Richard Wells, though, strangely, I could not see him. I felt his lips moving over my body, soft as a whisper, the way our moist skin clung, the hardness of him on me and in me. And the exquisite soaring joy that came from being in his arms. Those dreams sustained me, leaving me with the taste of a loving I could not remember ever having experienced, but also sad, with the same sadness I had felt when I watched his ship disappear into the blue haze from the harbour wall, for I doubted I would ever experience such glory in reality again – if ever I had.

By day I went through the motions of life whilst my conscious mind ran in wild circles and I wrestled with indecision, tempted to throw caution to the winds and follow my heart, yet all too aware of the momentousness of such a thing, and the consequences, not just for myself, but for others.

Should I go to visit my grandparents and confront them with what Richard Wells had told me? I wondered. Should I speak to Theo again? Should I go to Watchet and see if the place resembled that of my dreams, or if I remembered anything, or if anyone remembered me?

The one thing I could not do, I knew, was seek out Richard Wells again until I had reached a decision. He had made his position clear – I was to have no more contact with Alice unless and until I made a commitment. There was nothing to be gained by seeing him again unless it was to say that I was leaving Mr Paterson and going to him.

Not that I was even certain it was an option that was open to me any more. Though surely if he loved and needed me as he said he did, he would be prepared to take me back whatever my circumstances?

And then fate took a hand. Great-Uncle Charles took a turn for the worse and a message arrived early one morning to say he had died.

I was shocked, I admit it, and though I had not been close to Great-Uncle Charles, his death seemed to add another dark layer to the feeling of nightmare unreality.

I went straight away to the house in Queen's Square. The curtains were drawn in the parlour, and already Great-Uncle Charles had been laid out in a coffin which rested on trestles.

I went in to pay my last respects and was standing beside his body, thinking how small and shrunken he looked in death, when I became aware of someone in the room behind me.

It was Theo.

'Oh, Theo, I am so sorry!' I said. 'Poor Great-Uncle Charles!'

'Well, at least his worries are at an end now,' Theo said. 'And mine are just beginning.'

'What do you mean?' I asked, shocked.

'Things are bad, Davina,' Theo said. 'Papa was never a good businessman, I'm afraid. Oh, he managed well enough in his own small way, but he would never expand when the chances were there, and he tried his best to stop me from doing so when I took over the reins. The result is that I am finding it very difficult to make the books balance. We are overstretched in every way – and the debtors will soon begin to press. Now, just to add to it, the doctor will be sending in his bill, no doubt, and then there's the funeral to be paid for. I'm in a pretty pickle, I can tell you – and that damned husband of yours won't raise a finger to help. If he had proposed me for a Merchant Venturer, as I felt sure he would once we were family, it would be a different story. The Merchant Venturers have everything sewn up to their advantage, and they always look after their own.'

'Oh Theo, I had no idea!' I said awkwardly. 'Is there anything I can do? Speak to Mr Paterson, perhaps?'

Theo shrugged. 'I doubt he'd listen. And for God's sake don't tell him just how desperate are my straits. False confidence is my only chance of saving the day. And at least now I'll be able to do what I think best without Papa constantly finding fault and interfering.'

I found myself remembering the quarrel I had overheard between Theo and his father when I had first come to Bristol, and Great-Uncle Charles' warnings to Theo that the course he was set upon would lead to ruin. I still did not understand what he had meant, of course – I knew nothing of the intricacies of the trade, for all that my family and my husband were engaged in it. But I could not help feeling a little frisson of alarm that now there would be no one to curb Theo's plans.

'You won't do anything reckless, Theo, will you?' I cautioned. 'Whatever difficulties you are in, don't do anything to make things worse.'

Theo snorted. 'It's a little late in the day to worry about that, Davina. Anyway, things may yet work out. I'm a born optimist. And it's good that you are with child. If it's a boy, the day may yet be saved.'

'What on earth has my child to do with it?' I asked, startled.

167

'Oh, it will mellow old John no end. He's proud as punch already, from what I hear of it, boasting to anyone who'll listen that he is to be a father at last. It's the talk of the coffee house, with everyone congratulating him and him basking in it.'

'I see,' I said, my heart sinking. Quite aside from the fact that I did not like to think of my condition being the talk of the coffee house, it only made my burden the heavier.

'You are looking bonny, anyway,' Theo said. He was noticeably more cheerful all of a sudden. 'I only wish the babe was mine – I should have married you myself, Davina, instead of arranging for you to wed John. Why did you turn me down so cruelly?'

'What nonsense, Theo! The question never arose!' I said tartly. 'And I am not at all sure this is a suitable conversation in the room where your poor father is lying dead.'

'Oh, maybe not,' Theo said carelessly. 'But you know what they say. One in, one out!'

'Theo!' I chided him. 'That is a dreadful thing to say!'

'Oh, it's no use getting maudlin,' he said breezily. 'He's had a good life. And this baby of yours will have a good life too, no doubt. And bring a good deal of joy, and some much needed relief to our lives, if I'm not much mistaken.'

I shook my head. He really was incorrigible. Charming and great fun he could be, but there was also a side to Theo I really did not care for at all.

That very night Mr Paterson came to my room.

Since I had become pregnant, he had refrained from bothering me, anxious, no doubt, not to do anything which might cause me to lose his longed-for child, and it had been a great relief to me not to have to endure his attentions. I had begun to think – and to hope – that he would leave me alone at least until after the baby was born, and perhaps longer, if I provided him with the son he wanted so badly, for I could not see that he could get much pleasure from his hasty fumblings and not-infrequent failures either.

But that evening I began to notice the warning signs. There

were the little leers and the staring at me over dinner, there was the way he sat rather too close beside me on the chaise afterwards, his plump thigh resting against mine, and the way he patted my hand and let his fingers play with my wrist as he expressed his condolences over Great-Uncle Charles' death.

'I'm sorry he's gone,' he said. 'Another familiar old face we won't see again – the port won't seem quite the same without him. Ah well!'

It struck me that this might be a good opportunity to solicit on Theo's behalf.

'Yet you never invited him to join the Merchant Venturers,' I mused. 'Nor Theo neither. If you valued him, surely it would be a nice gesture to invite Theo now.'

Mr Paterson looked at me in surprise; I had never before spoken to him of anything concerning business. No doubt, shrewd as he was, he guessed Theo had mentioned something of the sort to me this morning, but in any event, he was going to make no bones of his feelings on the subject.

'Charles was never invited because he lacked courage and fire, and his wherewithal, in any case, was not up to scratch. Theo has fire and courage, all right, but he's a scoundrel who might well bring the association into disrepute. And his wherewithal is no better than his father's, I'm afraid.'

'And never will be unless he has the advantages the association can offer its members,' I persisted. 'Why don't you at least give him a chance?'

Mr Paterson laughed. Actually laughed.

'And why don't you, my dear Davina, stick to what you are good at – growing babies and being nice to your husband – and leave business matters to those who understand them.'

I was mortified – and annoyed.

'You cannot blame me for speaking on Theo's behalf!' I flared. 'He is family to me, after all. And a small family it is, all aging and dying.'

'And you cannot blame me for wanting as little as possible to do with them, Davina,' he countered. 'Family loyalties and business do not make good bedfellows. I don't trust Theo, and I have no intention of inviting him to join the Venturers simply because he introduced me to his beautiful cousin and suggested I marry her. If he thought it would be his entrée, then he was, I am afraid, much mistaken. Now, let's forget the wretched fellow and enjoy what remains of our evening.'

His hand covered my knee. I managed to move away, hoping he would put my reticence down to his dismissal of Theo, and not realize it was because of revulsion. Whatever his faults, I did not think he deserved to be hurt so.

To be honest, though, I do not think he even noticed my rejection of him. He was too full of ardour – and strong liquor. I took my leave of him and went to my room, but to my dismay, not so long afterwards, I heard his tread on the boards and my door opened.

He came into the room carrying a candle. He was wearing his nightshirt, which did not become him. In his fine clothes he was quite an imposing figure; in his nightshirt he reminded me of a fat old woman. But he had it in mind to do things to me that no fat old woman would do.

He lit my own candle, which I had snuffed, from the one he was carrying, and set them one each side of the bed. Then he lowered his not inconsiderable weight on to the mattress and reached for me.

'Mr Paterson . . .' I protested.

'Don't be like that,' he chided me, scrabbling up the hem of my nightgown. 'It's been a long time, Davina.'

'Because, if you remember, I am carrying your child!' I said with what hauteur I could muster whilst trying, without much success, to keep my nightgown about my knees.

'But the danger time is passed now, surely,' he said. He yanked his own nightgown up, and I felt him between my legs.

Suddenly I could not bear it. I had hated it before, from the very first time, and schooled myself to submit because I must. Now, with the sensuous dreams of Richard Wells' hard, strong body fresh in my mind, I simply could not bear it. I pushed him away with all my might.

'Stop it!' I cried. 'Stop it at once! The worst of the danger time might be over, but I have been feeling poorly all day, and what you intend might well be disastrous.'

He hesitated. 'You did not say you were unwell, Davina! You never said—'

'Because I did not want to worry you!' I said, pressing home my advantage. 'I have lost my uncle today, and it has upset me a great deal. I don't know what effect *that* will have on me, let alone you forcing yourself upon me. Do you want me to lose the child? Because if you do, you are going the right way about it. And I swear you'll have no one but yourself to blame if I tell you in the morning that I have miscarried!'

'You are leading me a merry dance, my dear!' Frustration made his voice angry, but he released me anyway. I think that though he doubted what I was saying, yet he was afraid to put it to the test. 'You tempt me all evening, and then turn cold on me, just when I'm ready to exercise my husbandly rights. I thought when I married a young wife I would have a willing partner, but I see now that I was wrong.'

'It's for the sake of the baby!' I cried. 'How can you be so selfish?'

'Me? Selfish? Are you sure, my dear, that is not the pot calling the kettle black? Are you sure you are not using your condition as an excuse to deny me?' He moved abruptly. 'No, don't bother to answer that. I don't want you to lie, but I don't think I want to hear the truth either. Very well, for now, I'll leave you in peace. But don't think this is the end of the matter. Oh dear me no!'

The mattress sprang up as his weight lifted from it and he took up his candle and padded furiously across the floor.

'I shall go downstairs and console myself with a large brandy,' he said, and the door closed after him.

My breath came more easily, my heartbeat returned to its normal rhythm. But the sick revulsion did not leave me. I had managed to avoid his attentions for tonight, but for how much longer would I be able to do so? Until my baby was born, perhaps – if I was lucky. After that I would have no excuse at all. But I would feel no differently towards him, I knew.

171

Tears pricked my eyes. I closed them against the tears. But I did not put out the candle. I did not want to be in the dark tonight. I could not understand what it was I was afraid of. I only knew I did not want to be in the dark tonight.

I was woken by the sound of screaming. For a moment I thought that unearthly, piercing cry was a part of one of my vivid dreams, though tonight I could remember none. Then, as I lay staring into the shadows cast by the candle, it came again, and I knew it was as real as the ticking of the mantle clock and the moaning of the wind, which had risen and was roaring in the chimney. And the screams were coming from somewhere within the house.

Without a second's thought I thrust aside the covers and swung my feet to the floor, reaching for my wrapper, which lay across the back of the chair beside my bed. Then I grabbed up the candle and went out on to the landing.

I half thought I would meet Mr Paterson emerging from his room next door to mine, yet at the same time I felt that not much time had elapsed since he had left me, saying he was going downstairs for a glass of brandy. I made my way to the head of the stairs and down to the little landing where the stairs crooked at right angles to lead down to the entrance hall.

A small sliver of light lay across the tiled floor, indicating that the drawing-room door was ajar, and Mr Paterson indeed still up and about. I could not understand why he had not come to investigate. The screams had quietened now to a low anguished wail and they seemed to be coming from the parlour on the opposite side of the hall.

I hesitated for a moment, disorientated by sleep, and frightened. As I did so the parlour door burst open and Dorcas came running out. By the light of the candle I could see that the too large dress, which I had not yet managed to have replaced, was hanging loose from one thin ebony shoulder, and she was struggling to hold it around her. She glanced up at me, huge dark eyes wide and terrified in her small face, then ran in the direction of

172

the rear of the house, her bare feet making no sound on the tiled floor.

'Dorcas?' I called in bewilderment. Yet I think, even then, I knew the awful truth. She ignored me and was gone, the door that led to the servants' quarters slamming after her.

I stood as if turned to stone, one hand resting on the bannister, the other holding the candle aloft. And then Mr Paterson was silhouetted in the parlour doorway. He had put on his clothes since leaving me – I suppose he did not think it right to wander about the house in his nightshirt – but his shirt was unbuttoned at the neck and he was straightening his breeches.

I knew then that I had been right about the reason for Dorcas's distress.

I knew it without doubt, though I could scarcely believe it.

'What in heaven's name is going on here?' I demanded.

Mr Paterson looked up and saw me. I suppose I must have looked a little like an avenging angel, standing there on the landing above his head with my candle held high, because for a moment he looked like nothing so much as a guilty schoolboy.

'Davina . . .' Then he recovered himself and began to bluster. 'Why are you down here? I thought you were in bed and asleep!'

'I'm sure you did!' I flared. 'What have you done to that poor child, John?'

'Oh, she's all right,' he said impatiently.

'She is not all right!' I cried. 'She is not all right at all! I could hear her screaming at the top of the house.'

'Africans weep and wail at the least thing,' he blustered. 'She is all right, I tell you. I didn't hurt her.'

'You raped her!' I cried. I was so shocked and angry I had thrown all caution to the winds. 'You raped her, did you not? You might as well admit it, for I know that it is so!'

'And what if I did?' Suddenly Mr Paterson was angry too, because he was ashamed of himself, I should like to think.

173

'What is a man supposed to do when his wife refuses to have him in her bed for months on end?'

'Don't seek to blame me for your disgraceful behaviour!' I flared. 'What did you do before you married me, in the years following your first wife's death? How many young girls did you rape then? How could you, John? How could you do such a terrible thing? Why, she's little more than a child!'

'She's a slave!' he shot back. 'Only a slave!'

The callousness of those words almost took my breath away.

'She is a human being!' I cried. 'And we are responsible for her! I am shocked, truly shocked!'

'You are hysterical, Davina,' he said coldly. 'Every girl has to lose her virginity at some time and at least she is well cared for here – you see to that. She has food on her plate, a warm bed and a roof over her head. She is one of the lucky ones. Far worse befalls most slaves. Many die on the voyage and are thrown over the side to be food for the fishes. And many are sold to the sugar plantations, where they work until they drop, and then are beaten until they get up again. Their lives are nothing short of hell – and short lives they are too!'

'That's no excuse!' I stormed. 'None at all! To take a young girl like that . . . oh, I'll never forgive you for this – never! That such a thing should happen in my house . . .'

'You would do well to look to the deeds of your own family before you begin castigating me, Davina,' Mr Paterson said coldly. 'As I say, there are many worse fates than Dorcas's – and your own flesh and blood play their part. If you wish to begin preaching and moralizing, I suggest you begin with them, and short shrift you'll get from them, too.'

'What do you mean?' I demanded.

'Oh – go to bed, Davina. It's too late to stand around chewing the fat,' Mr Paterson said impatiently.

'Whatever my family may be guilty of, I trust and pray it is not defiling innocent children!' I snapped. 'As for going to bed – I could not sleep a wink if I had not first tried to comfort poor little Dorcas. And I doubt if I will even then!'

174

I turned away furiously, but Mr Paterson's voice stopped me in my tracks.

'Leave her be!' he ordered. 'Don't dare to interfere, Davina!'

I turned back, my chin high, the angry colour hot in my cheeks.

'I shall do as I think fit.'

'You are my wife, Davina. You will do as I say. And I say leave the girl alone and go to your bed!'

'Make me!' I flashed. 'Perhaps you'd like to rape me too whilst you are about it! Though I can't imagine you would be capable twice in one night.'

Again I turned away and this time he did not try to stop me. As I strode along the passageway to the back of the house I heard him go into the drawing room, heard the chink of crystal on crystal. So – he was turning to the bottle! How very typical! Well, with all my heart I hoped he would take enough to give him a raging headache in the morning!

I found Dorcas in the servants' quarters, and, to my surprise, Thomas was there too, and offering her comfort. He was holding her tenderly and stroking her hair, and over her head his jet-black eyes met mine; they were cold and full of accusation.

I stopped, uncertain suddenly in the face of his unconcealed hostility, and I knew any comfort I could offer would be less well received by Dorcas than the comfort she could receive from her own kind. But there was something I had to do.

'Set the copper to boil, Thomas,' I instructed. 'She needs to bathe.'

He did as I bid, while Dorcas huddled in the corner, arms wrapped around her thin body, head bent in shame. She no longer wept, but her face was anguished and she shook from time to time as if with a fever.

When the water was hot, we bathed her and Thomas left us alone while I douched her, for I wanted to do all I could to ensure Mr Paterson's seed did not take root in her and grow.

175

And all the while she said not a word. She was, I think, in deep shock.

I found her one of my own clean nightgowns, which hung on her even more than the dress she usually wore, and Thomas took her off to her bed, his arm protective around her thin shoulders.

I went back to my own part of the house. A light still showed in the drawing room and I could hear the sound of snoring. Mr Paterson must have fallen asleep over his brandy, I supposed. Well, let him stay there in the chair or on the chaise or wherever he had dozed off. He would be cold and stiff when he woke, and I was glad of it.

I think in that moment I knew that my terrible decision had been made for me. I no longer felt an iota of loyalty to Mr Paterson, and I did not want to stay with him for another night, let alone the rest of my life. The thought of him sharing my bed again was totally repulsive to me, and he had forfeited my affection and my trust.

I was still unsure of the wisdom of going to Richard Wells. For all I knew, he, too, could be a monster. Theo claimed he was, and everything Richard had told me might be a wicked deceit. But at that moment I wanted him more than ever. I would send word to him tomorrow. If he would still have me, I would take my chance.

For what now did I have to lose?

I remained in my room next morning until I was sure Mr Paterson had left for the coffee house. I did not want to see him, did not want to hear whatever explanation or apology he might see fit to offer. I did not want to set eyes on him ever again if I could help it, though I knew that was simply wishful thinking.

When I finally ventured downstairs everything was just as it always was – steaming salvers in the breakfast room, the smell of freshly brewed coffee mingling with the pungent aroma of the braised kidneys. A fire was burning in the grate but it did not warm me; I did not think I would ever be warm again, and my stomach revolted at the thought of food.

'You are a little pale this morning, madam,' Perrett ventured.

I replied: 'I did not sleep well,' and wondered if she knew what had occurred here last night.

Thomas came in to serve me; his eyes were dark and reproachful. Of little Dorcas there was no sign.

'Thomas,' I said when I was sure we were alone. 'Could you take another message for me to Mr Wells, do you think?'

'I am not sure,' Thomas said, cold but impeccably polite, 'whether that will be possible.'

My heart sank. He was holding me responsible for Mr Paterson's wicked behaviour, even though I had done everything I could for Dorcas after the event.

'Thomas,' I said desperately. 'I am as upset as you are by what happened. I had no idea Mr Paterson was capable of such an outrage. Please – you must believe me. I need your help.'

'As I said, ma'am, I am not sure it is possible.'

'Why not?' I demanded. 'You know where to find Mr Wells, don't you?'

'Sometimes,' Thomas replied evasively. 'Sometimes not.'

'Very well then,' I said, making up my mind. 'Would you please have the carriage made ready and take me to Lady Avonbridge's house. I shall call on her this morning.'

'At what time, ma'am?'

'As soon as possible,' I said impatiently. His lack of cooperation coupled with this excessive politeness was making my already taut nerves jangle.

I managed to force down a little breakfast and some coffee, then asked Perrett to help me change into my redingote. The carriage was waiting outside the door – at least Thomas was still following my instructions to the letter.

On the drive to the Clifton woods, I sat nervous and silent. Calling unannounced on someone of Lady Avonbridge's standing was not at all the done thing, but desperate situations call for desperate measures and I felt sure Lady Avonbridge must know where I could find Richard Wells, or at least get a message to him. But when I rang the bell, the butler

177

who answered informed me that Lady Avonbridge was not at home.

My heart sank. This was an eventuality which had not occurred to me.

'When are you expecting her back?' I asked in desperation, and the butler, an elderly man whom I imagined had been in the service of the family all of his life, replied that Lady Avonbridge was in Sussex visiting her sister, and would be away for at least two more weeks.

Two weeks! It seemed to me like a lifetime.

There was nothing for it; I had to return home frustrated and with wretchedness weighing heavily upon me. Never in my life had I felt quite so trapped. But what could I do? Unless Thomas had a change of heart and carried my message for me, I would somehow have to endure my life with Mr Paterson until Lady Avonbridge's return.

Great-Uncle Charles' funeral was to be held two days later, not in the cathedral, but in the Church of St Mar Redclift, just across the river from his home in Queen's Square, and my grandparents were travelling down from Gloucestershire to attend. Grandfather was to assist with the ceremony, Theo told me, and they would be staying on overnight.

At once it occurred to me that this would be an opportunity for me to talk to them about the accusations Richard Wells had made. I trembled inwardly at the prospect, but I knew it must be done. Somehow I had to ascertain where the truth lay.

I thought I might invite them to dine at my home, but relations between me and Mr Paterson were still very strained. Theo said he believed Grandfather would prefer to be in the familiar surroundings of his brother's house. He was, Theo said, very upset by Great-Uncle Charles' unexpected demise.

This made me feel guilty, for I knew that what I planned to say to him and Grandmama would upset him still more. But I refused to be swayed by this. The truth about my forgotten past was too momentously important to me. If they had been honest with me, then they had nothing to fear. If not – well, then, they had to take the consequences of their actions. They

178

must have known, surely, that they could not keep it a secret for ever?

But I was unsure what chance I would have to talk to them alone, with all the comings and goings. Why, Aunt Linnie might even accompany them to Bristol, and I could well imagine her constantly at Grandmama's side, twittering and fussing. Then Theo informed me that only the menfolk were to attend the service and burial, and asked if I would keep Grandmama company for the duration, and I realized that fate had at last dealt the cards in my favour.

Thomas drove me down to Queen's Square on the morning of the funeral. I was shocked by Grandfather's appearance – overnight, it seemed, he had become an old man.

'He has been upset very badly by Charles' death,' Grandmama said to me as the cortège left, the hooves of the black-plumed horses echoing on the cobbles in a slow tattoo, the carriage bearing the coffin clattering behind them. 'Charles was his only brother, and to lose him so unexpectedly . . . well, it reminds one of one's own mortality.'

Her thin, worn face was anxious; she was worrying, no doubt, that grief would bring Grandfather low too, and once again I felt a stab of guilt. But I put it aside determinedly.

'Grandmama – I must talk to you,' I said. 'Something is worrying me a great deal and you are the only person who can clarify things for me.'

She looked at me sharply. 'Is there something amiss in your marriage? Are you not happy with Mr Paterson?'

Had she noticed the coolness between us? I wondered. I did not want to discuss Mr Paterson with her, and she would know soon enough that things were certainly amiss, but neither did I want to lie. I avoided the question entirely.

'It has nothing to do with Mr Paterson.'

'What then? Your pregnancy? You are worried about giving birth?'

'Not exactly.' I took a deep breath. 'Is this my first time, Grandmama? Have I borne a child before?'

If I had struck her she could not have looked more startled, nor more afraid. What little colour was in her face left it in a rush;

179

I thought for a moment she was about to swoon. Her bloodless lips worked, but no sound came. I hardened my heart.

'Grandmama?' I pressed her.

Her breath came out on a little gasp. 'Whatever makes you say such a thing? Is your memory returning?'

If ever I had looked for an answer, that was it. No outright denial, just that simple question: *Is your memory returning?* And the fear and guilt written in her white face.

'No,' I said. 'Not yet. Not in any coherent way. But . . .'

'What then?' She looked momentarily relieved. 'I don't understand where you should have got such an idea!'

'I have been told things,' I said.

'By whom? By Theo?'

'No,' I said. 'Not Theo. Richard Wells.'

For a moment she stared at me blankly, as if the name meant nothing at all to her.

'Richard Wells,' I repeated. 'The man who claims I am the mother of his child.'

'*Him!*' She spat the word. 'Oh dear sweet heaven, Davina, this is beyond belief! Do not tell me that man is still pursuing you! You must not have anything to do with him. He's a terrible man – terrible! Why, Theo says—'

'And yet,' I said, calm and cool-sounding, though a white-hot anger was consuming me, 'you handed my innocent baby over to this *terrible* man! And kept it all from me. I did not know whether to believe it, Grandmama. I found it impossible. How could you do such a thing?'

Her mouth worked. 'It was for the best!' she cried. 'You were so ill, Davina, we thought you would not recover! How could you care for a baby? How could we? And he had ruined you, that dreadful man! The least we could do was to give you a fresh start, should you ever be fit enough. And you have it! A good marriage, another baby on the way – you must put this out of your mind. It's over!'

'It is not over!' I stormed. 'Did you not think that I had a right to know, at least? And my child – what of her need for me?'

'I've already told you, Davina, you were at death's door. Though we prayed for your recovery, there was no guarantee

180

of it – God does not always see fit to answer prayers, however fervently they are offered. And even given that you did recover, what could you give a child? You came to us with nothing. Nothing! And the shame of it!' She wrung her hands. 'The shame, Davina! We couldn't go through all that again! It was for the best, I tell you. For the best!'

'You told him I was dead,' I said. Even now, with the confirmation coming from her own lips, I could scarcely believe my grandmother could have done such a thing. 'You told him I had died in childbirth. That was the most terrible thing of all.'

'To save you from him!' she cried. 'He is evil! Oh, Davina, I can't talk about this any more. I feel ill – very ill.' She swayed. 'You'll kill me, and your grandfather, too, if you go on this way! Is that what you want – to have two more funerals? Oh, please, please say no more about this!'

She pressed her hand to her heart, her breathing ragged, and I realized I must indeed let this go or risk some kind of fatal attack.

'I'll fetch you a glass of water, Grandmama,' I said, and I left her there with the guilt I knew she must always bear.

So, she was my child, little Alice, just as I had known she was all along deep in my heart. And I wanted her so much! My arms ached for her, my mind ran in great swirling circles. I must get a message to Richard somehow – I must! Even if it meant braving the docks again in search of him. Someone must know him, surely! But I could not risk Theo learning of it. Theo had had Richard beaten once, next time he might arrange for worse, to ensure I was kept from him, and Alice would not only be without a mother, but without a father too. I must achieve the meeting with Richard without Theo's knowledge. But how . . . how . . . ?

And then, when the mourners returned from the burial, the solution presented itself to me, for I saw that Dr Thorson was with them. He must have attended Great-Uncle Charles, I supposed, come to the service as a mark of respect for a patient and been invited back for the customary glass of brandy or dish of tea. Now I remembered that he had treated

181

Richard after his beating, and even intimated that he knew him beyond the strictly professional relationship.

Dare I solicit his help? Could I trust him to say nothing to anyone but Richard himself? He was, after all, my doctor too. He had treated me once and would doubtless attend me at my confinement. Surely anything I said to him would be treated with confidentiality – the confidentiality of his Hippocratic oath?

I could not keep from trembling as I passed amongst the mourners with little dishes of sweetmeats. Grandmama sat in a corner, pale still, very pale, but everyone took it to be grief. Only I knew the truth. And she was watching me like a hawk, afraid, no doubt, that I would begin to rail at Grandfather as I had railed at her.

She need not have worried. I knew that would achieve nothing and I had other things on my mind now. Namely, how to approach Andrew Thorson without arousing suspicion.

My chance came when I saw him standing alone. I took my dish of sweetmeats and crossed to him hastily.

'Dr Thorson?'

'Oh, Davina, not for me, thank you!' he said, with his wry little smile. 'I've eaten quite enough already and my housekeeper will have a feast of a meal waiting for me when I get home too.'

'Dr Thorson,' I said in a low voice. 'Do you remember I asked you once before about Richard Wells?'

'Yes.' His eyes were speculative now. I felt he was looking right inside me, seeing what was in my heart. Hot colour rushed to my cheeks; I tried to ignore it.

'Do you ever see him now?' I asked tentatively.

'Not for the last week or so,' he said. 'And I won't be seeing him again for some time.'

'Oh!' I was quite unable to hide my dismay. 'But why?'

And Andrew Thorson replied: 'Richard Wells has sailed on a long voyage. He will not be returning until late spring at the earliest, and he may be gone longer. I would think it will be many months before he is back in England and I, or anyone else in Bristol, sees him again.'

Thirteen

The desolation I experienced then was worse than anything that had gone before. I had come to a decision. I had learned that Alice was indeed my daughter, and that Richard and I must have been lovers, whatever the rights or wrongs, wisdom or folly of the relationship. I wanted with all my heart to see both him and Alice, wanted it with an urgency that burned like a fever in my blood, even though I was not sure that he wanted to see me now that he knew I was expecting Mr Paterson's baby. I had been prepared to go to him and take my chances because I could no longer bear to do otherwise. I no longer felt any responsibility towards Mr Paterson or my grandparents – at least none that would keep me from following my heart.

And now, just when the way was clear, Richard Wells had set out on a voyage that would keep him from me for many months! The cruelty of it was like a chill winter wind that blows suddenly in to remove any hope of warm days, and the bleakness of it was a pit of despair.

I would not see him and I would not see Alice, for I knew that, wherever she was, whoever was caring for her, I could not insinuate myself into her life until I had first come to some arrangement with Richard. He had been right to be concerned about the effect it would have on her if I was to take a place in her affections only to disappear again. I would not do so willingly, of course, but Richard might have other ideas. And he would not, I felt sure, take kindly to returning and finding that I had made contact with her without his permission.

My new baby would be born, too, before his return. The baby to whom I still owed a duty of care.

There was nothing for it. I would have to return to Mr Paterson and make the best of it, for the time being at least. I had no other choice.

The days passed and the weeks, and it seemed to me almost that I had stepped out of time and stopped living. I existed, yes, sleeping and waking and moving through the days with each one indistinguishable from the one before. I discussed menus with Cook, I carried out my duties of overseeing the household, I did a little needlework, stitching linens to make a layette for my baby, and all in this curious hinterland that seemed oddly divorced from reality.

My relations with Mr Paterson remained strained; I could not look at him without feeling disgust, but he was out a good deal by day and, thank heavens, he did not bother me at night. He did not want to risk another humiliating rejection, I supposed, and possibly did not want to remind me of that night. As if I could forget! Even now, when the house was silent and I lay sleepless, I seemed to hear Dorcas's screams and sobs, as if they had somehow become imprisoned in the very walls, and echoed out when there was no other sound to drown them.

At least, mercifully, she seemed to have suffered no lasting harm, physically, anyway. The bath and douche that I had given her must have washed away Mr Paterson's seed, for her thin little body showed no sign of growing thicker about her stomach, though the good food I insisted she should be given had put a little flesh on her thin arms, and her dress no longer hung on her like a sack. I had ordered two new ones for her, but she still wore the old one more often than not. Perhaps this was to hide the silver collar Mr Paterson had had made for her, bearing her name, which I knew she hated, perhaps because she thought she was safer from his unwelcome attentions if she was well hidden beneath folds of fabric.

I did not think Mr Paterson would bother her again, however. I thought that he was truly ashamed of himself – and so he should be! It did occur to me to wonder if perhaps

184

he was visiting the loose women who plied their trade in the mean streets around the docks, and found I could not care very much if he was or not. Just so long as he left me alone, and did not try to force himself on Dorcas, he could do as he liked. And if he caught the pox, it was no more than he deserved.

As I drifted through the days in this strange, abstracted state, something rather curious occurred. Snatches of my past began to return to me.

As first I thought that, like the dreams that came when I was sleeping, the little scenes that entered my head were my own interpretation of the things Richard had related to me, my imagination working with the new food he had provided for my hungry soul. But some of the pictures that came to me had no basis in what he had said. They seemed to belong to an earlier life of which he had said nothing; which he could not even have known about.

Once, when I went to the kitchen to return the day's menus for Cook's attention, the smell of the puddings she was boiling evoked in me the strongest sense of the past, but this time, instead of merely leaving me frustrated, a vision came to me of my mother, standing at a kitchen counter, with a whole array of appetizing ingredients laid out before her. And I, a little child, not much older than Alice, playing on the floor with some cooking implements. My mother said to me: *Do you want to scrape the mixing bowl?* and I jumped up eagerly. She wiped her floury hands on her apron, lifted me up on to a wooden bench, and I ran the spoon around a crock and licked off the delicious fruity mixture, getting a smear of it on to my nose as I did so. And my mother laughed and said I was a messy little creature, and wiped it away, and I was upset because I had wasted a whole precious mouthful.

The picture was so sharp and clear it unlocked a door in my mind and I knew we had not always travelled with the strolling players. Sometimes my mother had found domestic work and we had lived in the servants' halls of great houses.

On another occasion when I woke to find an early and

185

unexpected snowstorm had turned the world outside my window white, I remembered my wonder as a child on making the same discovery. I had climbed up on to the window sill, pressing my nose against the cold glass, looking out at the drifts that had built up against the hedges and lay in a thick crust along a low stone wall, the path and garden all hidden beneath a pristine white blanket, and I had begged to be allowed to go outside and play in it, wade through it, leave my footprints on that unmarked canvas.

And I saw a man I knew was my father, a tall man with a pigtail wig that I loved to tug. His features were unclear, but I knew his eyes were blue and that he laughed a great deal and was kind to me, and let me ride on his shoulders. There was no trace of fear in my feelings for him, only a sense of security, of loving and being loved.

These scenes were, as yet, mere snatches, but the very fact that I felt sure they were real memories gave me the confidence to believe my dreams were real memories too. A sense of almost childlike excitement materialized from deep within me, as if I were right on the brink of something momentous. But it was frightening too.

The journey back to full recall had begun, I felt sure. What would I learn about myself along that journey? Would there be things I would rather not know? Almost certainly there would be. No life can be charmed throughout, no life can be nothing but sweet-tasting pudding mix and pristine new-fallen snow and a loving, laughing father. I must have know sorrow as well as joy, and in all likelihood fear and despair, disappointment and betrayal, though I could imagine nothing worse than the things that had happened to me during the last two or three years.

But there might be. Whatever lies I had been told, whatever doctored versions of the truth, one fact was more or less undisputed. My mother and I had fled to Gloucestershire for refuge. Whether it was a flight from some unspecified danger, as Richard Wells would have it, or a flight from Richard Wells himself, as Theo had claimed, I did not know. The more recent past was as thoroughly hidden from me as ever.

And I could not help fearing, with a weight of sick dread, that when I did at last remember, it would have the power to destroy me all over again.

One day when Mr Paterson was out, as usual, on business, Theo came to call on me.

Though at first he was his usual charming self, yet I knew instinctively this was no mere social visit. Something in his demeanour told me so. I thought he looked older, too, than when I had last seen him, thinner and more drawn. And very soon he came to the point of his visit.

'Do you remember the conversation we had, Davina, on the day Papa died?'

'Yes, of course,' Admittedly, I had given little thought to it since. 'You were concerned about the state of your business affairs, but hoping that things would take a turn for the better.'

'Well, they have not,' Theo said bluntly. 'They are even worse. My best ship, the *Blackbird*, is overdue and my creditors are pressing. To be honest, Davina, I am facing ruin. That is why I am here – to ask you a great favour.'

'Me?' I said, startled. 'But what can I do?'

Theo sat forward eagerly, elbows resting on knees.

'You are John Paterson's wife, and he is one of the richest and most influential merchants in Bristol. Talk to him on my behalf, I beg you. Ask him to make me a loan. It won't be for long – just until the *Blackbird* comes home. I expect her any day, but I can't afford to wait any longer. The root of the trouble is that I foresold her cargo in order to raise money I needed a few months ago. But the main merchant has found cheaper sugar elsewhere. He is demanding reimbursement of his advance, and I am unable to pay.'

I frowned. 'Didn't you have a contract with this man?'

'Of course, but it's already been broken by *Blackbird*'s failure to reach port by the agreed date. Every day I go to the docks, and there is no sign of her. She must come in soon though, and when she does my troubles will be over – for the time being, anyway. I can sell the sugar on again and repay Mr Paterson at once.'

'But . . .' I hardly liked to make things worse by pointing out the obvious, but since he was seeking to involve me, I felt I must. 'Supposing she does not come home, Theo? Supposing that she has foundered and that's the reason she is not here already. What then?'

'Then I truly am ruined,' he said simply.

'But you have insurance surely?' I ventured.

Theo smirked, but there was no warmth or humour in his eyes.

'Not entirely. The middle leg of the return voyage is an expensive one. Africa to the Sugar Islands is a risky trip. I took a chance on it . . .'

'Oh Theo!' I bit my lip. No wonder Great-Uncle Charles had been angry with him. To risk sailing without insurance was a terrible gamble when it might result in not only the loss of the cargo but of the very means to recoup any losses – the ship itself! Then another thought struck me. 'Did you say Africa to the Sugar Islands? That must mean your cargo was . . .' My voice tailed away.

'Yes. Slaves. As many as the master could pack in. Oh, don't look like that, Davina, so disapproving! After all, they are only savages.'

I thought of Thomas and poor little Dorcas.

'Sometimes I think it is we who are the savages,' I said coldly, 'and the way we treat them is less than human. But I don't want to argue with you, Theo. I realize I shall be wasting my breath.'

'I don't want to argue either, Davina.' He leaned forward. 'Will you do it for me? Will you ask Mr Paterson if he will extend me a loan?'

'Don't you think it would be better if you were to ask him yourself?' I suggested.

Theo moved impatiently. 'So, you still haven't forgiven me, then, Davina.'

'Forgiven you?' I repeated, puzzled.

'For having that rat Richard Wells taught a lesson.'

188

'Oh!' I shook my head incredulously. 'That has nothing to do with it, Theo. Why, I never even thought of it! No, I just don't see that it is my place to discuss your financial affairs with Mr Paterson. I know nothing of business – I would not be able to argue the points as you could. I really think . . .'

'He's far more likely to be persuaded by you than by me,' Theo interrupted. 'To be truthful, I don't even think he likes me very much.'

Well, that much certainly was true, I thought. Mr Paterson did not like Theo. My cousin must have seen my hesitation, for he rushed on: 'Davina, do this for me, I beg you! Everything depends on it. My creditor is threatening to have the bailiffs sent in if I do not repay him, and quickly. I could lose everything – even the house. And no one would trade with a man who does not honour his debts. Word would spread like wildfire – damage has already been done, and that is just the beginning. I would not only be ruined, Davina, I would be bankrupt. If you have any regard at all for me – for the honour of your family – use your influence with Mr Paterson on my behalf, I implore you.'

I sighed. I was not at all sure how much influence I had with Mr Paterson where matters of business were concerned – or indeed, in any connection whatever. But distraught as Theo was, desperate as his plight seemed to be, I did not see that I could continue to refuse to do what I could to help him.

'Very well,' I said quietly. 'I'll do as you ask. But truly, Theo, I must warn you I am not overly hopeful as to the outcome.'

I approached Mr Paterson that very evening; after all, from what Theo had said, the matter was of extreme urgency, and, in any case, I did not want to have it hanging over my head for a moment longer than was necessary.

I asked Perrett to help me dress in a rose-pink gown which I knew was one of Mr Paterson's favourites – I was not above using my feminine wiles to get my own way, and though, to be truthful, I thought I looked like a great beached whale with my enormous stomach and swollen breasts, I knew that my condition might well work in my favour, for Mr Paterson was still puffed up with pride at the prospect of becoming a father.

I waited until he had eaten a good meal of roasted partridge, and drunk enough porter to mellow him, and then I took a deep breath and began.

'Theo came to see me today.'

Mr Paterson's features tightened. 'Oh, he did, did he? And what did he want?'

This was not promising, but I pressed on.

'I am worried about him, John. It seems he's having the most dreadful problems. Someone is pressing him to repay a debt, threatening to set the bailiffs on him if he does not settle quickly, and he's not in a position to do so until his ship comes home.'

Best not to mention that she was already overdue, I thought.

'Well, I'm not surprised,' Mr Paterson said. 'He's always sailed close to the wind.' He smiled faintly at his own unintended choice of words.

I toyed with the stem of my wine glass.

'I was wondering whether we couldn't make him a loan, just to see him over this troubling time,' I said tentatively.

Mr Paterson looked frankly amazed.

'Whatever made you think of such a thing, Davina?'

I hesitated. I did not want to admit that Theo had been the instigator of my request. Mr Paterson would be far more likely to agree to it if he thought that it was my own idea.

'I want to help him,' I said. 'He is, after all, family to me. I don't want to see him put out on to the street – he does not deserve that. A little short-term loan is all I am asking. You would scarcely miss it, I'm sure, and it could make the difference between survival and ruin for Theo.'

'I did not get where I am today, Davina, by throwing money away,' Mr Paterson said, rather smugly, I thought. 'What I spend, I spend wisely, and I have always ensured that my investments are sound ones. Theo, I fear, is a bad

190

risk. I rather doubt that I would ever see a loan returned from him.'

'He would pay it back, I'm sure, when the *Blackbird* comes home,' I said.

Mr Paterson's eyes narrowed. 'Oh, it's the *Blackbird* he's waiting on, is it?'

'Yes. She's on her way from the Sugar Islands . . .'

'The price of sugar is dropping,' Mr Paterson said. 'The planters are expanding their estates to produce more and more, the French are exporting to England, and now, I hear, there's talk of *making* it from some kind of root vegetable. As for slaves, Liverpool, where the ships can come and go easily, with no river to negotiate before they can dock, is taking a good deal of our trade. And there are rumblings that a group of dissidents is trying to get the trade stopped altogether. These are difficult times, Davina.'

I bit my lip. Times were even more difficult for Theo. I had not held out much hope of persuading Mr Paterson to make him the loan he so sorely needed, but suddenly it mattered a great deal to me that I should achieve it.

'Well, supposing that he *is* unable to repay you,' I said recklessly. 'Does it matter so much? Couldn't you look on it as a gift? For my sake? It was Theo, after all, who brokered our marriage. It's him you have to thank for the fact that you will soon be blessed with a son and heir.'

Mr Paterson's eyes rested for a moment on my swollen body and that familiar look of pride and satisfaction softened his florid features.

'That's true enough.'

'And I am so very worried about him, John,' I persisted, heartened, and anxious to press home my advantage. 'I have thought of nothing else all day since he told me of his troubles, fretting at the thought of him losing everything. I don't think that can be good for me in my condition, do you? Nor good for our baby either.'

Mr Paterson shook his head and laughed aloud.

'Oh Davina, Davina, what will I do with you? You know

how to wind a man around your little finger and make a fool of him and no mistake!'

'Make a fool of you? Never!' I said, and crossed my fingers in the folds of my gown.

What was planning to leave him if it was not making a fool of him? What was secretly meeting with another man? What was marrying him as a supposed virgin when I was in fact the mother of that other man's child? The catalogue was endless. But for Theo's sake I lowered my eyes demurely and lied.

'Oh, very well!' Mr Paterson said. 'You shall have your loan for Theo if it means so much to you. But a loan it is. If he does not repay me in the given time, then I shall be as ruthless as the creditors who press him now. It will be me setting the bailiffs on him, is that understood?'

'Oh yes . . . Oh John, thank you!'

I rose, made my way around the table to him as swiftly as my bulk would allow, and kissed him.

It was the first time I had done so since the night of Dorcas's rape. He had kissed me, and I had submitted, gritting my teeth against my feelings of revulsion. But I had not kissed him, not once.

Now, however, not only did I feel I owed it to him, I actually wanted to do it. He was not really a bad man. What he had done to Dorcas was unforgivable, of course, but no doubt I should shoulder my share of the blame. I had humiliated him, left him hurt, with his male needs frustrated. And he truly did see Dorcas as being different from a white girl. The fact that he was wrong in this did not alter the fact that it was his deeply held belief. He would never have treated Perrett or any of the other white maids so, I felt sure. And certainly I had made him pay for that act, almost to the point of cruelty.

Now I felt something that was almost tenderness towards him, as one might feel tenderness for a wayward child who has been severely punished.

'Thank you,' I said simply.

He put his arm around my waist, pulling me close so that his head almost rested against the bump that was our unborn child.

192

'You'd better tell Theo to come and see me,' he said roughly.

And so the period of waiting began again, seeming more endless than ever.

I was growing impatient with my ungainly girth, the extreme discomfort that kept me awake at nights and prevented me from doing much by day. I could not go out – it was not seemly to be seen in public with my condition so blatantly obvious, and I had no energy or inclination for it in any case. Not only were the sleepless nights taking their toll on me, my joints were all swollen too, making the slightest movement painful and difficult. And my face was swollen, so puffed and ugly I felt ashamed – I, who had not for one moment thought that I might be vain. It is very easy to take one's looks for granted, I realized. It is only when they disappear that we discover just how important they had been to us all the time.

'It was not like this before,' I thought, and realized with a shock that I was experiencing another memory – my first pregnancy. Anxious concerning the circumstances, I might have been, concerned for what the future held, maybe, but not physically impaired as I was now, not bloated and stiff and headachy and sick. No, I had not suffered so before, I felt sure.

The pains began on a dark March day when leaden skies hung over the Clifton heights and rain lashed down into the river gorge beneath, and I recognized them at once.

'Perrett,' I said faintly, pressing both hands to my back where the muscles were contracting with a force that felt fit to tear me apart. 'Would you please send for Dr Thorson?'

Mr Paterson had insisted Andrew Thorson should be in charge of the birth. He believed, of course, that this was my first child, I thought, acquiescing with his request. But I had also secured the services of one of the most highly regarded midwives in Bristol, for though Andrew Thorson might be a qualified physician, he always seemed so young to me, and I thought I would be far more at ease with an older, experienced woman to attend me.

She was the first to arrive, bustling in and taking charge. I was thankful indeed to see her, for my pains were already frequent and hard, and I had been a little frightened that my baby might choose to put in an appearance with only Perrett, who was clearly far too young to have any knowledge of what was required, to assist me.

Sure enough, Mistress Hobbs, as she liked to be known, took one look at me and confirmed what I had already known – that it would not be long before my baby was born.

'Have you been in labour long?' she asked, looking at me questioningly as she set out the things she would need.

'A few hours,' I lied.

'You should have sent for me before this,' she scolded. 'Never mind, I'm here now. But if Dr Thorson doesn't make haste, he'll miss the birth and he won't be too pleased at missing out on his fee, I'll be bound.'

I did not think Dr Thorson was the one to be too concerned about such things, and I certainly had more on my mind than worrying about it! All I could think of was bearing the pains, and then the overwhelming urge to push and push and push my baby out into the world.

Though it was a cold day, the heat from the fire in the bedroom grate made the room oppressively hot; Mistress Hobbs, her sleeves rolled up to her elbows, was perspiring profusely, and I was perspiring too – I could feel the beads of sweat running down my face and trickling between my heaving breasts. And all the while I felt as if I was being torn in two.

How could I have forgotten something like this? I wondered fleetingly.

I had. But now I remembered, and that other experience seemed to be happening to me all over again. The sea of pain, and myself adrift in it.

I looked up and saw, not the lofty ceiling of my room here in Clifton, but the wooden beams that straddled the rectory rooms end to end. The voice urging me to push was not Mistress Hobbs' strident voice, but one with a softer, Gloucestershire burr, the face that hovered over me anxiously not her round red one, but older, thinner, with anxious eyes.

I heard Grandmama's voice: *Is she strong enough? Can she deliver the baby?*

And that soft Gloucestershire voice: *Of course she'll do it! Of course she will! You're doing fine, my dear. Not much longer now. Bear up, there's a good girl. I've never lost a mother yet, and I won't lose you.*

The pain swallowed me whole, it was as if I was floating up amongst the beams on the ceiling, looking down at my tortured body.

Push now! Push!

I pushed. Again and again. And suddenly there was a different pain, like a red-hot knife, and a rush of warmth between my legs, and a little muling cry. And the voice said: *You have a little girl!* And the pain was gone, and I felt nothing but joy and relief.

And then I heard my grandmother say: *Take her away!*

'No!' I cried. 'No – let me have her! Give her to me!'

And my grandmother said to the midwife: *It's best she doesn't hold her, or even see her. And if ever you say one word of this, God will strike you dumb.*

Who will suckle the mite? the midwife asked. *You can't leave her to starve!*

And my grandmother said: *It's all arranged, never fear. The arrangements are made with one we can trust until we can find a home for the child. Take her away now.*

'No!' I cried again. 'My daughter! I want my daughter!'

And I was back in the pain with the tears wet on my cheeks, going through it all again, and the next voice I heard belonged to Mistress Hobbs.

'Whatever are you talking about, Mrs Paterson? You haven't got a daughter! You have a son. A fine healthy boy if ever I saw one.'

'Oh!' I was back in my bedroom in Clifton, Mistress Hobbs was wrapping my baby in the length of clean, washed sheet that had been waiting, placing him in my arms. I looked down at his little red wrinkled face, his cap of dark hair, shining with the moistures of birth, and felt the love well up in me.

But alongside my joy and triumph, alongside my sense of achievement and the overwhelming instinctive mother's love for this perfect little being, come from her body and now out in the wide world, innocent, vulnerable, needy, alongside all that was a grief and a longing for that other baby whom I had never held in my arms.

And I knew that if I had a dozen more children, nothing could make up for that loss. She would still be there in my heart. My firstborn. A little girl with fair hair and a sunny smile who scarcely knew me, and certainly did not know that I was her mother.

Dr Thorson arrived soon afterwards. He checked both me and the baby, pronouncing him fine and healthy, and me 'in surprisingly good shape'.

'Why surprising?' I asked, tucking the baby against my breast. Mistress Hobbs had wanted to lay him in the crib; I had refused to let him go. I wanted to have him safe in my arms. No one would take this baby from me.

Andrew Thorson's eyes were sharp and shrewd. 'He came very quickly for a first babe. That's what I find surprising.'

'Oh.' I looked away.

'Well, I think we can ask the proud father to come in now, don't you? He's eager to see his new son – and you, too, of course.' He started towards the door, wiping his hands on a towel.

'Dr Thorson . . .' I said, then broke off, knowing that this was not the time nor the place for the question I was burning to ask, yet afraid the opportunity might not come again.

He looked back at me questioningly. 'Yes?'

'Is there any news of Richard Wells?' I asked urgently.

'None.' His face was devoid of any expression, though he must have been curious, to say the least, at me asking such a thing at a time when I should be thinking of nothing but my baby and husband. I threw caution to the winds.

196

'Will you please tell him when he does return that I must see him?' I said urgently.

Andrew Thorson's eyes narrowed a fraction. 'Are you sure that is wise?'

'Yes!' I said, and then: 'No, I am not at all sure. But please tell him anyway.'

He nodded, just the tiniest inclination of his head.

'I'll call John now, shall I?'

Mr Paterson came into the bedroom so swiftly I was afraid he might have been lurking in the corridor and overheard what I had said to Andrew Thorson. But there was no sign of it on his face or in his demeanour. He looked only every inch the proud father, anxious, eager, a little overwhelmed by the responsibility for the new life there in the room with us.

'Davina! Are you—?'

'I'm fine, John,' I said. 'Very tired and a little sore, but otherwise fine.'

'Good. Good.' He dropped a kiss on my head, smoothed a damp curl away from my forehead, and gazed down at the baby.

'I can scarcely believe it,' he said. 'My son!'

'Do you want to hold him?' I asked.

I thought it was the right thing to say, but I was still reluctant to let my new baby out of my arms, and I was relieved when he took a hasty step backwards, looking nervous and flustered.

'No! No – I'll just look at him, thank you.'

I smiled, feeling once again that strange tenderness for a man I had thought I despised.

'He's beautiful, isn't he?'

'Yes, I suppose so.' Mr Paterson sounded doubtful. 'I don't believe I ever saw a newborn babe before. He's very . . . wrinkled. He is healthy, is he?'

'Perfectly healthy, John,' Dr Thorson said, smiling. 'He's just had a hard time of it, and something of a shock, finding himself in the cold hard world. Have you thought of a name for him yet?'

197

'Yes.' Mr Paterson recovered himself. 'We thought Daniel. Are you still happy with that, my dear?' he asked me.

'Yes,' I murmured. I was growing drowsy now; incredibly, overpoweringly drowsy.

Daniel. It suited him.

Daniel . . . and Alice.

My son, and my daughter . . .

I snuggled little Daniel against my breast and before I knew it, I slept.

Fourteen

I was totally enchanted by my little son, totally absorbed in him. It was as if, having been robbed of my first child's babyhood, I needed to achieve double the wonder and satisfaction from my second. Whilst I was confined to my bed, of course, he was always there, either in my arms or in his crib beside me, and when I was up and about again I refused to let him out of my sight.

Mr Paterson had engaged a nurse, but she soon left, since there was nothing for her to do.

'Mrs Paterson will not even let me bathe the child!' she complained on giving notice. 'I've hardly lifted a finger for him. I think my skills could be put to better use elsewhere.'

Mr Paterson remonstrated with me, urging me to relinquish at least some of Daniel's care to her so that he could persuade her to stay. He thought I was overtiring myself, and that it would damage his social standing if it became known that his child had no nurse. But I was adamant.

'I can manage perfectly well,' I insisted. 'And in any case I have Perrett to help me. I don't like that woman looking over my shoulder all the time and trying to tell me how I should do things. Let her go.'

So she went, and I had Daniel all to myself.

Mr Paterson had taken to spending a great deal more time at home, too, for he was almost as delighted with his son as I was; he dangled his fob watch over the crib to amuse the baby and even pushed him in his carriage around the garden when the weather was good enough. It was a happy domestic arrangement, doting parents and a perfect baby who scarcely ever cried, and I could almost have learned to become content

199

with my lot had it not been for the aching space in my heart for Alice.

Loving Daniel had somehow made me long for her all the more; I wanted her here with us, playing with him, growing with him, bonding with him. She was my child too and until I held them both in my arms I could not rest satisfied.

And all the while, my memory was returning. Not in a rush, nothing so dramatic, simply snippets from the past that presented themselves to me unexpectedly, or the discovery that there was something else I had remembered without even realizing it.

I sang a lullaby to Daniel one evening and knew it was one my mother had sung to me. I watched the birds carrying twigs to build a nest in the hedge outside my window and remembered myself as a child putting out handfuls of moulted dog hair for the birds to take and use. 'Fur makes a warm nest lining,' my mother had said. 'And Horatio doesn't need it any more.' I remembered Horatio – a big black cross-breed who lived in a kennel behind the house where we were living, and my mother working as the cook. Horatio did not have long hair, it seemed quite wiry to me, and I could not imagine how it was possible for him to shed so much and not be entirely bald.

I remembered the places we had gone with the players, barns lit by flares and filled with excited people come to be entertained; I remembered some of the performers – a contortionist, a midget, and – most exciting of all – Percy, the mathematical pig, who could, apparently, with the help of his trainer, count and do simple sums. And I recalled my mother, beautiful, graceful, with the voice of an angel, singing on a makeshift stage whilst the bawdy crowd fell silent to listen and my heart swelled with pride.

I remembered the harbour scene that had come to me in a dream and I knew the blue bay was indeed Watchet, in Somerset. But what Richard and I had said to one another before he sailed away, the exact details of the situation, had faded with the dream and slipped back into the still-fuzzy part of my mind. Frustratingly, I could remember nothing about Richard at all, nor anything that had led up to my accident.

Yes, there were still yawning gaps in my memory, but I was grateful for what I had recalled so far, and heartened that I would, eventually, regain my past completely. And I only hoped that the hidden parts were not remaining hidden to me because remembering them would be more than I could bear.

The message I had awaited with such eagerness arrived on a day in early summer when a light band of haze obscured most of the river gorge and, above it, the trees of the Clifton woods rose as if they were rooted in nothing more substantial than cloud. The air was soft and smelled sweet – no stench rising from the river today, no acrid smell of burning lime. The first flowers were beginning to open in the garden, where I sat, gently rocking little Daniel in his baby carriage, and two blackbirds were busy building a nest in the bushes.

When Thomas handed me the letter, I recognized the writing at once as the same hand that had penned the enigmatic note which had been awaiting me on my return from our wedding tour. Instantly I was all a-prickle, my heart thudding, a lump of nervousness rising in my throat. I tore the letter open.

'If you wish to see me, I shall be at Lady Avonbridge's house at noon tomorrow.'

It was signed simply: 'Richard.'

My heart beat even faster; the lump in my throat threatened to choke me. Oh dear God, he was home, safely home! And he was willing to see me! My spirits leapt and soared, yet at the same time, I was terribly afraid.

At the time I had made my decision, I would have gone to him without a moment's thought. Besides longing to be with him and little Alice, I had been desperate to escape from Mr Paterson. The terrible thing he had done to Dorcas had meant I had no longer cared a fig for the hurt I would cause him. But, in the intervening months, things had changed. Mr Paterson had treated me with great kindness, I had Daniel, and for all that my marriage was far from perfect, we were a family. Richard and the little fair-haired girl seemed like a distant memory. There was about them the same sense of unreality that I felt for the memories of my childhood that I was now experiencing. That day in the garden when I had first seen Alice seemed so long ago, as if it belonged in another life, or was simply a dream with no substance to it at all. This was my world now.

And yet . . . and yet . . .

The yearning was beginning in me again, fermenting, bubbling in my veins, aching in my heart, an irresistible force. I had to see him. I had to see Alice. As for the commitment . . . I would think about that later.

Thomas was standing a discreet distance apart, inscrutable as ever.

'Thomas . . .' There was a little tremble in my voice. 'I would like you to have the carriage ready for me in the morning. We shall be visiting Lady Avonbridge.'

And, as if he had no inclination of what that visit meant, Thomas replied evenly: 'As you wish, ma'am.'

I had never left Daniel in his short life and I could not leave him now. It would have immediately aroused suspicion, and in any case, he might need to be fed. I would not leave him anyway. He was a part of me now, his life was my life, and I needed Richard to know that.

As I made ready, my mind was in a whirl, my emotions seething. Daniel must have sensed it, for he became fretful, which was most unlike him. Again and again I had to break off in my preparations to try to soothe him, but I was not my usual calm self, and instead of dropping off to sleep in my arms, he wriggled and squirmed as if he had a colic, which only added to my agitation. Supposing he should become ill? With my heightened emotions, such a thing seemed only too likely, and I fretted that perhaps I was bringing down a judgement on both of us by my deceitful behaviour.

I had wanted to look my best, but dealing with Daniel left me very little time. Nevertheless, I was not too displeased with the image that looked back at me from the mirror. I had regained my figure, though I thought my waist a little thicker than it had been before, and the gloss had returned to my hair. I settled a little cap upon it, dressed Daniel warmly, for there was a chilly breeze today to remind me that summer had not yet arrived, and we were ready.

As we crossed the river, I drew my cape around his face, worried as to what pestilence there might be abroad in the stinking air, then, as we climbed once more towards Lady Avonbridge's house, I lifted him up to show him the trees and the river snaking below.

'See the boats!' I said to him. 'Your papa has boats like those.' And then I felt frightened all over again to think that, although Mr Paterson would always be his papa, very soon he might play very little part in his life.

It was not yet noon when we reached Avonbridge Hall. We had made good time; in my anxiety not to be late, we were, in fact, early. In spite of this, I had hoped Richard might be waiting for us as he had before, but when a maid showed us into the parlour, it was Lady Avonbridge herself who came to greet us.

'He's not here yet,' she said bluntly. 'He said noon, I believe.'

'Yes . . .' I scarcely knew what to say; I was not totally comfortable in such grand company at the best of times, and now I felt more awkward than ever.

'So, this is your son,' Lady Avonbridge said, glancing, without much interest, at Daniel. 'Well, he looks healthy enough.' She raised her eyes to mine, looking at me narrowly. 'I hope you are not going to hurt Richard again. I hope you have not come here simply to play with his emotions. He deserves better than that.'

'No . . . I . . .'

'Men are so very easily hurt,' she went on frankly. 'And deeply. Especially men like Richard. He does not wear his heart on his sleeve, and to the outside world he gives every appearance of being hard – ruthless, even – with no feelings at all. But he is the more vulnerable for it. When a man like

Richard gives his heart, he gives it completely, and the woman who holds it has the power to destroy him where an adversary never could.'

Again I felt a pang of guilt, not for Richard, but for Mr Paterson. The same could be said of him, I rather thought. A hard-dealing businessman, with the confidence and authority that came with money and power. But I knew another side of him. I knew that I could command him and hurt him. I had done so in the past, and I could so easily do so again.

Oh, dear Lord, I had never wanted to hurt anybody! Yet, one man was going to be hurt, dreadfully, before this was over, and it would be my doing.

Voices in the hall arrested my attention – a voice I recognized at once. His voice! My heart came into my mouth with a great leap. My feelings must have been transparent, for Lady Avonbridge moved to the door.

'He's here; I'll leave you.' She stopped, looked back. 'Don't you have a nursemaid for that child?'

'No, I care for him myself,' I said. There was a little uneven catch in my voice.

'Shall I send a maid to take him and look after him while you talk?' she asked.

'No. He's asleep. If I could just lie him down on the chaise . . .'

She sniffed. 'Just as long as he does not puke or wet on it.'

'I'll lie him on my cloak,' I said. 'He won't make any mess, I promise you.'

'Very well.' She left the room. I heard her say something to Richard, telling him where he could find me, no doubt, for a moment later the door opened again and he was there.

Though I had often pictured him in the early days, I had almost forgotten the effect his appearance could have on me. The weatherbeaten face, lined, I thought, more deeply than before, the strong jaw, the hazel eyes, the dark, natural hair, pulled into a pigtail on the nape of his neck. His tall athletic frame, his broad shoulders, his slim hips and long poweful legs clad in creamy buckskin. The sheer animal magnetism that sparked between us. The warmth. The joy. That same joy I had felt the first time he had accosted me outside the hot well.

In that moment I forgot everything, forgot my torment, forgot my indecision, forgot little Daniel, lying asleep now in my arms, forgot Alice and my longing for her.

I could think of nothing but that this was the man I loved and had always loved, the man who said he loved me. Whatever he was, whatever he might have done, it did not matter. Nothing mattered but that he was here and we were together again.

'Rowan,' he said, and it sounded right, so right.

And I could only reply, with my heart in my eyes: 'Richard.'

In that moment I wished I had allowed Lady Avonbridge to send a maid for Daniel; he would have come to no harm, and it might even have been good for him to experience the attention of others besides myself. And I wanted – oh, how I wanted! – to be in Richard's arms. Yet here I stood, the baby cradled against my chest, gawping at him like a moonstruck calf.

'You came,' he said. 'I thought you might not.'

'I sent word with Dr Thorson to say I would.'

'But that was some time ago. It occurred to me that you might well have had time to reconsider. After all – ' he glanced at Daniel – 'things are different for you now.'

I did not tell him how close I had come to settling for my life with Mr Paterson. I did not mention the heart-searching that had kept me awake at nights, when I had wondered if I should remain with Mr Paterson for the sake of Daniel's future. I could say nothing of the terrible guilt I felt at the prospect of shaming my husband by abandoning him, and depriving him of the son he adored.

'It has been a long time,' I said instead. 'I heard you were in the Sugar Islands. Why did you go there? Did you accept an appointment as a sea captain once more?'

Richard declined to answer, asking me instead a question of his own.

205

'Have you recovered your memory at all, Rowan?'

'To a certain extent, yes,' I said. 'I have begun to recall the early part of my life. There are still great gaps, but I believe it is all coming back to me little by little.'

'And me? You remember me?'

'I know I loved you. I remember living in Watchet. And I remember saying goodbye to you and watching you sail away. But I don't remember where you were going and I don't remember much of what happened afterwards – or, indeed, before. Just little snatches, and they come mostly in dreams – and frightening ones at that. A fire . . . A terrible fire . . . The coach accident . . .' I closed my eyes briefly. 'And I have remembered giving birth to Alice,' I went on. 'And my grandmother having her taken from me. That is the most terrible memory of all. I have even wondered whether it was being forcibly parted from her that caused me to lose my memory, and not the accident at all. Is that possible, do you think? That it was simply too much for me to bear, and I shut it all out?'

He shook his head, shrugging helplessly. 'I don't know, Rowan. It is possible, I suppose. I just don't know.'

'How is she?' I asked, eager now for news of my daughter. 'Is she well? Is she . . . ?' I scarcely dared ask. 'Is she here today, with you?'

A smile lifted the corners of his mouth. 'So many questions, Rowan! You haven't changed. The answer to the first is yes, she is well, and growing fast. And to the second, no, she is not here with me today. I need to have your answer first. That you are prepared to leave John Paterson and come to us – not just for an hour, or a day, but for always. If you are, then I shall buy a house for us and we can live together, as a family.'

The thought of it melted me. A family. Not a family held together by convenience and duty, but by love. But I could take nothing for granted.

'And Daniel?' I said. 'I have him to think of now, too.'

'And Daniel, too, of course. He is your child, just as Alice is. He needs you just as she does.'

'I thought,' I said haltingly, 'that you might not be prepared to take another man's child.'

'Rowan,' he said. 'I would take on every child in Bristol if that were the price to be paid for having you with me.'

My heart soared. In that moment I did not stop to think his words might be yet more proof of the obsession with me which Theo had described. The rosy cloud of happiness to be here, with the prospect of a future with him and Alice before me, obscured all else, made me forget my indecisions and the obstacles that still had to be overcome, made everything seem possible.

'You will come to us, won't you?' he asked, his hazel eyes mesmerizing me.

And I nodded. 'Yes. Oh yes!'

His face softened to a smile.

'Then for the love of God put that baby down and let me kiss you!'

I laid Daniel down, still sleeping, on my cloak in the curve of the chaise, and he kissed me.

He kissed me, and it was everything it had been in my dreams. The taste of his mouth, the scent of his skin, the hard pressure of his body, his hunger, my hunger. His arms were about me, holding me close, awakening all the excitement that began in the very core of me and spread through every vein like wildfire through dry brush, sensitizing me, making me alive with desire. And yet at the same time it was like coming home after a long, long journey. So familiar. So warm. So precious.

The muscles of his back were hard beneath my hands; I clung to him as a drowning man might cling to one who offers him salvation. And indeed, he was offering me just that. Salvation from the wilderness of the last years, salvation from a loveless marriage and a future of bearing children for a man who, for all his kindness to me, I found physically repellent.

And yet, at the same time, it was as if those last years had been stripped away, had never been at all, and I was remembering, with my mind as well as my body, the loving we had shared.

I knew exactly how it felt to lie with him, our bodies entwined, with no clothing to come between. I knew the way our skin, moist with the flush of passion, cleaved together, the way every mound and hollow of our bodies fitted together, my face in the crook between his shoulder and throat, our legs entwined. I knew the touch of his hands and his lips on my breasts, my stomach, my most hidden secret places. I knew the taste of his skin and the glory of his body filling me. I knew all the delights of our lovemaking, from the delicious, tantalizing anticipation of the wooing through the urgency when we moved in unison, upwards and still upwards until I thought I would die of the pleasure and the overpowering need, to the pinnacle so high that I could not help but cry out, and the plateau of dreamy contentment and satiated completeness where I luxuriated afterwards, loving with all my heart, and knowing that I was loved in return.

How could I ever have forgotten such bliss? But, of course, I had not. The memory of it had been there all the time, and though the mists had obscured it from my consciousness, yet my body had remembered, and my senses, and had been drawn to him, this man with whom I had shared so much.

A great deal was still lost to me, there was still some long way to go before my memories were complete, but this much I knew. He had been my lover before, and he would be again, for my feelings for him were too strong to be denied.

And as if that were not enough, he was also the father of my firstborn. He had loved and cared for her and raised her, and for that, too, I loved him.

I could not wait for us to be all together, yet for the moment the whole of my world had shrunk to the circle of his arms about me, his lips on mine. And the fierce joy was leaping in me, and anything seemed possible.

And then Daniel cried, a hiccuping whimper that fast became a persistent wail. We drew apart, me turning to my little son, Richard smiling ruefully.

'You'd better attend to him before Lady Avonbridge has

us thrown out. She is not much enamoured of babies, I think – though when they become children she is rather good with them.'

I went to pick Daniel up; the moment he was in my arms the crying stopped.

'He's usually very good,' I said apologetically.

'He sensed someone other than him had your attention, I suspect,' Richard said. 'Men can be very possessive, you know, and from a very early age.'

A tiny shard of unease pricked at the bubble of my happiness.

'And you?' I said. 'Are you possessive?'

'Well, of course I am!' he replied easily. 'Don't you remember? But I'm happy enough to share you with a babe now that we have the rest of our lives together to look forward to.'

The glow returned, but with it the realization that we had as yet planned nothing that would make our lives together a reality.

'What are we going to do?' I asked.

'You, I think, have decided to leave your husband and come to me,' he said, as if it were already a fait accompli.

'And live where?' I asked, ever practical.

'I feel sure her ladyship would be willing for you to come here for the time being,' he replied easily. 'She is a good friend of mine, and since I have no home of my own in Bristol at present, I think she would be happy for you to make use of the same rooms that she puts at my disposal – so long as Daniel is as good a child as you say he is!'

I bit my lip. I was still a little in awe of the great lady.

'Wouldn't it be better to wait until we have a house of our own to go to?' I suggested tentatively.

Richard frowned. 'You want to wait? It could be weeks, or even months, before I can find a suitable property and complete a deal. These things take time, and I want to be sure we are both happy with the house we choose for our home. It's important for the children, too, that they are settled

209

and able to put down roots. We don't want to be continually moving them from pillar to post.'

I could see the logic of his argument, and although I was still not entirely comfortable with the idea of living here as Lady Avonbridge's guest, neither did I want to prolong my life as Mr Paterson's wife a moment longer than could be avoided.

'I don't want to wait,' I said. 'Now that my mind is made up. Only . . .'

I broke off, flooded suddenly by nervousness at the enormity of what I had to do.

'Tell him immediately, then,' Richard said. 'Or if you can't face that, simply pack a few things and leave. Better yet, do not return at all. Write a letter, and let Thomas deliver it. I'll provide you with everything you need from this moment on.'

I hesitated. It was a tempting suggestion. But, for all that I dreaded facing Mr Paterson with my decision, I felt I owed it to him to speak of it to him face to face. Besides, if Thomas delivered a letter for me, goodness only knows how Mr Paterson would have reacted. Upset and angry as I felt certain he would be, he might well take out his feelings on Thomas, blaming him for driving me here and carrying the message home. I had heard him threaten on several occasions to have Thomas whipped, and I could not bear to think that he might be punished for my wrongdoing.

'No,' I said. 'I must tell him myself.'

Richard's face was set. 'Very well, but do it without delay. I cannot bear to think of you in that house with him, under his thumb. Your place is here, with me.'

'I know it,' I said. At that moment, if he had asked me to accompany him to the ends of the earth, I would have gone with him. 'I shall speak to Mr Paterson this very evening.'

'Then I shall come for you myself tomorrow,' Richard said. 'John Paterson may well not be willing to allow you the use of his carriage to run away from him, and you cannot walk the streets alone. I'll be outside the house at ten, waiting for you. And for the love of God, be careful until then.'

Daniel was stirring restlessly again, his mouth opening like a small bird's whilst he struggled to reach my breast, hidden, of course, beneath my gown.

'Daniel needs to be fed,' I said. 'He's hungry and I think I should go now.'

'I feel sure Lady Avonbridge would place a room at your disposal,' Richard suggested.

I shook my head. From tomorrow on I would have to accustom myself to feeding Daniel here, at Avonbridge Hall, but for the moment I felt I would be more comfortable attending to him in the familiar nursery.

Richard kissed me again, lightly this time, but warmly, so warmly, then accompanied me to the door.

'Till tomorrow then.'

My heart skipped a beat, nervous excitement forming a lump in my throat.

'Till tomorrow.'

He walked with me to the carriage and he and Thomas acknowledged one another. Once again I found myself wondering how they knew one another on such apparently friendly terms. But I did not wonder for long. I had far too many other things on my mind.

Richard handed me into the carriage and for just a moment I leaned on him, loving the strength of his arm beneath mine, wishing he could hold me close once more, tantalized to a state of burning desire by the knowledge that he could not. At least, not yet. After tomorrow there would be all the time in the world for the sensual moments and expressions of love I craved. For now I must try to be patient and enjoy the anticipation of our future together.

Thomas flicked the reins; the horses moved off. I turned, raising my hand in farewell. He was standing there, watching me go, just as once I had watched him.

I kept looking back long after his rugged, weatherbeaten features had become nothing but a blur, and his tall strong

211

figure was just a dark shape against the light-coloured stone of the house.

With all my heart I hoped we need never be parted again.

As we neared home, I was surprised to see a carriage that looked like Theo's pulling away from outside Mr Paterson's house. As it approached, I could see I was right, and I raised my hand in greeting. But Theo seemed not to notice me. He drove past us at a brisk pace, staring straight ahead, his face like thunder.

I frowned, puzzled. Had Theo been to see me, and found me out? But if so, why had he cut me dead? Or had he been to see Mr Paterson? Well, he would almost certainly have found him out, too. At this time of day Mr Paterson was invariably at his office. I found it all very strange, but at the same time I was rather relieved that I had not met Theo face to face. Knowing him, he might well have asked some awkward questions as to where I had been, and put two and two together in a way Mr Paterson never would.

Theo was going to be very angry with me, I knew, but I couldn't help that. Sooner or later he would have to know that I intended leaving my husband for Richard Wells, but not until I was ready – and certainly not until I had told Mr Paterson. I should not like my husband to hear of it from anyone but me – and in private.

I went into the house, Daniel in my arms, quiet for the moment. The carriage drive had rocked him back to sleep again but I knew that would not last long and I was just hurrying up the stairs to the nursery when the parlour opened and, to my surprise, Mr Paterson appeared.

'Davina! Where have you been?' he asked.

This was not the moment for the truths I had to admit to. At any moment Daniel would waken again.

'For a drive,' I said, and, overtaken by cowardice, I added: 'I thought the fresh air would do Daniel good.'

'Hmm.' Mr Paterson's face was set. 'You just missed that cousin of yours.'

'Theo has been here?' I said, pretending ignorance.

'I sent for him,' Mr Paterson said grimly. 'I don't like the things I have been hearing concerning his activities.'

'What do you mean?' I asked. Daniel was beginning to stir. I rocked him gently.

'The bloody fool has been engaging in illicit trade,' Mr Paterson said bad-temperedly. 'He has been selling slaves to the Spanish plantations, and that's against the law of the land these days. He's courting ruin, Davina, and disgrace. I should never have made him that loan, and I never would if I hadn't been persuaded by you. I'm calling it in. I can't have my name linked with a lawbreaker such as him. My own reputation is too important in this town.'

He was, I could see, beside himself with fury, and I was overcome with guilt. From the quarrel I had overheard between Great-Uncle Charles and Theo when I had first come to Bristol, I had known that Theo's dealings were not as straightforward as they should have been, and perhaps I should never have interceded with Mr Paterson on his behalf. But whatever he had done, he was family, and I had wanted to help him.

'Oh John, I'm sorry . . .' I murmured.

'And so you should be!'

At that moment Daniel awakened with a hungry, lusty yell.

'I must feed him,' I said apologetically. And fled to the nursery, where, for a little while, I could be alone with my son – and my thoughts.

Fifteen

By the time I had fed Daniel and settled him, Mr Paterson had left to return to his office and I knew I would have to wait a while longer before I could tell him of my decision.

One part of me was glad of the reprieve, another was prickling with impatience to say what had to be said and move on to the next part of my life. It seemed to me that I was standing on the very edge of a precipice, poised for flight, and I was both excited by, and afraid of, what lay ahead.

This, I thought, as I gently rocked Daniel's crib, must have been how my mother had felt when she had run away from her home and her parents to be with my father. Like her, I would face the disapproval of society, for it was a scandalous thing I was set upon, abandoning the husband whom I had vowed in the sight of God to love, honour and obey, in order to live in sin with a man I could never wed. Like her I would doubtless be ostracized by decent people. Like her I would have to bear the guilt of knowing I had hurt and shamed those who loved me. And yet, like her, I knew I must follow my heart, be true to myself and the man I loved. And besides that . . .

'Did you know that you have a big sister?' I whispered softly to Daniel. 'She is called Alice and she is the most beautiful little girl in the whole world. She does not know yet that she has a mother, let alone a baby brother. It will be such a surprise for her! But she will grow to love you, as you will love her. And I shall be able to hold her as I hold you. My children, both together. Richard will take care of us all. And we shall be so happy!'

Set against that rosy dream, nothing that I might have to face seemed of importance. My two children and my lover were the whole world to me. I sat beside Daniel's crib looking down at his pink, innocent, sleeping face and gathering my courage for what I had to do.

I had been denied moments such as this with Alice, but I would make up for them. From tomorrow on, no one would ever come between me and my beloved children ever again.

Or so I thought. But I was wrong. How could I have been so foolish and naive? How could I have failed to foresee the result of my being honest with Mr Paterson regarding my intentions? If I had possessed a more devious mind, if I had planned my escape more cunningly, perhaps things would have been different. But somehow I doubt it. There are some things in this life that one can never change, and one of them is a man's inalienable right to be master in his home, head of his household. I had forgotten, to my cost, that Mr Paterson owned me and Daniel just as he owned his house, his horses and his slaves. And any court in the land would back that ownership.

But he reminded me soon enough, and in no uncertain terms.

I broached the subject after we had eaten our evening meal, trembling at the prospect, yet determined.

'I must talk to you, John.'

He gave me a straight, severe look.

'If it's about that cousin of yours, you may as well save your breath, Davina. My mind is made up on the subject. I won't have my name coupled with that of a man who deals illegally with the Spanish.'

'No,' I said. 'It's not about Theo. It's about us.'

'Us?' he repeated blankly. 'What do you mean – us? And why are you in such a state, Davina? Good gracious, you are like a cat on hot bricks!'

'John.' I crossed to him, sitting on the footstool beside his chair and taking his hand in mine. 'I want you to know that I am very grateful to you for marrying me, and grateful too for all your kindness to me. But . . .'

'What are you talking about?' He put my hand aside

215

impatiently and reached for the brandy decanter. 'Marrying you suited me. And why should I not be kind to you? You are my wife.'

'John, listen to me, please!' I begged. 'I know I am about to hurt you dreadfully and I am so, so sorry for that. If there was any other way . . . but there is not. That is why you must let me say what I have to, and try to understand.'

I had his attention now; though he concentrated on filling his glass with brandy, there was a heaviness about his features suddenly, a wariness, as if somehow he had always known that this moment would one day come, and he wanted to delay it as long as possible.

'Go on,' he said, and took a long draught of the brandy.

'You know that when I married you I had no recollection of my past life,' I said. 'If I had, I would never have agreed to become your wife. I'm not sure, even, that you would have wanted me to. My memory has returned to a certain extent over the last few months, and I have to tell you that I was not the pure, innocent girl you thought me. Before the accident that took my memory and almost killed me, I had lived, unwed, with a man, and had a child by him.'

'Oh, is that all!' Mr Paterson snorted. 'Well, I guessed that much.'

'You did?' I was astounded. 'You never said . . .'

'Why would I? What would it have achieved?'

'You *knew*? And you didn't mind?'

'My dear girl, I'm not a fool! I knew something was being kept from me by your family, and it did not take me long to work out what it was. It's the reason they were so anxious to marry you off, I dare say – to try to protect your reputation – though I'm certain my business connections had a good deal to do with it as far as Charles and Theo were concerned. He's been disappointed on that score – I've made sure of that. I don't like a man who uses a pretty woman like a chip in a game of poker – and tries to take me for an old fool to boot. But for the rest – I let it pass. Put it to the back of my mind. So long as no one else knows, where's the harm been done? I've a pretty young wife and a son and heir, and I'm well satisfied. As far as I'm concerned, my dear, the past is the past, and that's an end to it.'

'But . . . it's not,' I said faintly.

He frowned. 'Not what?'

'It's not over and done with,' I said desperately. 'I have met again the man I loved, I have seen my child. It's not over and done with at all!'

'What are you saying?' Mr Paterson set his brandy down so hard upon the occasional table beside him that I thought for a moment he had cracked the fine crystal. Strange that at such a time such an inconsequential thought could have occurred to me. 'They are here – in Bristol?'

'Yes,' I said. 'He is staying with Lady Avonbridge. I was not entirely honest with you about my trip out this morning. In truth, I went there to see him.'

Mr Paterson swore. 'God's teeth, Davina!' His face now was like thunder. 'You took my carriage this morning and went to meet this man?'

'Yes,' I said, frightened but defiant.

He swore again. 'And is this man by chance that bounder Richard Wells?'

'Yes,' I whispered.

'Sweet Jesus – I'll have him run out of town! He's nothing but a troublemaker in any case. And Lady Avonbridge – to allow such a thing under her roof – I'd never have thought her capable of condoning anything so improper! Why, she's been my guest here! I've entertained her with my good food and wine . . . I shall certainly not be doing so again!'

He seemed to remember suddenly the last occasion on which Lady Avonbridge had been in his house.

'She was here at the reception I gave before our marriage!' He was almost spluttering with outrage. 'And Richard Wells with her! You saw him then!'

'Yes.'

'God's teeth! I have been a bigger fool by far than I ever imagined! You and your lover, under my nose, in my own house! Well, it won't happen again, madam, you can be sure of that. My hospitality will not be abused a second time. And you will have your wings clipped too. The carriage will no longer be at your disposal. You'll stay here, inside these four walls, except when you are with me.'

'No,' I said.

'What do you mean – no?' He gripped my shoulder, shaking me. 'You are my wife, Davina, and you will do as I say!'

I pulled myself free. 'No, John, you don't understand. I won't stay within these four walls, because I will not be here at all. Don't you see, that's what I'm trying to tell you! I have to go to Richard and my daughter. I don't want to hurt you, truly I don't, but I love him and I love my daughter, though I scarcely know her. She is mine, she needs me – and I need her. My place is with her, John – and with Richard.'

The wind seemed to go out of his sails. He slumped, looking for a moment like a broken man. 'You are saying you wish to leave me?'

'Yes,' I said, quietly but firmly. 'That is exactly what I am saying.'

'*Leave me!*' he repeated. He reached for the decanter, refilled his glass, downed it in one gulp.

'I am so sorry,' I whispered.

And suddenly he was angry again, the fury filling him like a roaring gale.

'You think I'd let you *leave* me?' he demanded. 'Make a fool of me for the whole of Bristol to see? You must be mad to even consider such a thing!'

'Perhaps I am,' I said. 'But it's what I must do, John. I must go to Richard and Alice. And you cannot stop me, whatever you might say. My mind is made up.'

'I can stop you, my lady! You are my wife!'

'You'd hold me here like a prisoner? You'd lock the doors and bar the windows? I don't think so, John. See reason, please . . .'

'Reason!' he exploded. '*You* tell *me* to see reason, when you are proposing to walk out of a life of comfort to become a social outcast? To go to a troublemaker who will no doubt end his days murdered in the gutter or floating in the docks?

Oh, he's in line to come into a title one day, I know . . . Is that the attraction?'

'No, of course not . . .'

'But I doubt he'll live that long, given the number of enemies he's made for himself. And, to share his uncertain existence, you would leave your home, your husband, your son . . . ?'

'Of course I would not leave Daniel!' I cried. 'He's just a baby! He'll come with me!'

'Oh, you think so, do you?' Mr Paterson thundered. 'Well, there, madam, you are certainly mistaken. You are quite right that I can hardly keep you here by force. I cannot chain you to your bed, and if you choose to walk out, then, damnation take it – just go! But if you think I would allow you to take my son . . .'

'But he needs me!' I protested, very frightened suddenly. 'He's still at my breast!'

'I'll find a wet nurse for him. There'll be no problem there. I mean it, Davina, if you take my son from this house, I'll have the law on you before you can lift a finger. He will be returned to me with the law of the land on my side – and you . . . I'll have you thrown into jail to ensure his safety!'

I was shaking now from head to foot, not just my limbs, but every bit of me. My throat was dry, my lips numb. Perhaps I was reliving that other occasion when my child had been torn from my arms, though, if so, it was not a conscious thought. I was beyond that.

'You wouldn't . . .' I managed to whisper.

'Oh, I most certainly would!' Mr Paterson replied, and I was in no doubt but that he meant what he said. 'Go, Davina, if you must, but in the certain knowledge you will never see your son again!'

I knew, of course, in that moment, that he had won. That I had no choice – no choice at all. I could not abandon my baby son. Alice might need me, yes, but Daniel needed me more. Alice had never known me – she was well and happy enough with the life Richard had made for her. I would enrich her life, I hoped; I would be there for her when she fell and scraped her hands and knees, when she had an earache or a toothache; when she woke in the night from a bad dream, I would dry her tears and sooth her back to sleep. I would listen to her problems, little ones, now, easily solved; and in the years to come, as she grew, I would try to help her through the bigger ones which I could not solve, only comfort and advise. I would share her joys and her triumphs; I would watch her grow from child to woman with pride and love. But if I was not there, she would turn to those who already cared for her, and they would be there for her just as they always had been. Perhaps sometimes she would feel an ache of longing for the mother she had never known, but it would be just that, a little ache that would soon be forgotten, for what she had never had she could not truly miss.

Daniel, on the other hand, was but a tiny defenceless babe. He still suckled at my breast, he knew the smell of my skin, the feel of my arms about him, the sound of my voice when I talked to him and softly sang him to sleep. He had never been parted from me for a single day of his life; he would look for me, and pine. No wet nurse could take my place; her milk might fill his little belly and satisfy his hunger, but his warm safe world would be a barren, empty place.

For all that I had no doubt that Mr Paterson loved him, he was not a man capable of showing that love. Though in the early days he had sometimes wheeled Daniel around the garden in his baby carriage, that novelty had worn off. I had never once seen him cuddle Daniel, and when he cried, Mr Paterson became instantly impatient. He would see that his son lacked for nothing where worldly possessions were concerned, I knew, but worldly possessions are not everything – far from it!

As for the values he would pass on – they were certainly not ones I wished Daniel to accept without question. A ruthless attitude where business and money were concerned, an obsession with being first in the pecking order, the careless belief that one man could own another, body and soul, and there was nothing wrong in that, these were not ideas I wanted

220

my son indoctrinated with. And though I had put it to the back of my mind, I had never forgotten Mr Paterson's treatment of poor little Dorcas, either. He had used her shamefully because she was his and she was there. He had dismissed her as beneath consideration because, as he had reminded me, she was 'only a slave'. I did not want Daniel exposed to such views with no one to temper them. Supposing, when he became a young man, his father should suggest to him that he cut his teeth by raping some young black slave?

No, I could not leave Daniel. It was unthinkable. And therefore I must stay. Mr Paterson had made the decision for me, as, it seems, men always have the power to do. With his ultimatum he had made me a prisoner even more surely than if he had indeed put locks on the doors, for which I had no key, and bars at the windows. Somehow I would have found a way to escape. But the ties with which he had bound me were stronger by far. The bond of a mother with her child. Fine as gossamer yet indestructible. He had left me no choice at all. I must stay.

I cried more tears that night than I can ever remember crying in the whole of my life before. I cried them into my pillow and on to Daniel's defenceless, downy head as I cradled him to my breast. I cried with passion, the sobs tearing deep within me, and I cried softly, the tears sliding down my cheeks, tears of bitter disappointment and tears of despair. And when the grey light of dawn began to creep over the horizon, I heard the patter of raindrops on the window and knew that the sky was weeping too. For my lost hopes, for my lost child, for my lost love, for my lost future.

I took care, however, that Mr Paterson should not see my tears. My pride would not allow it. I faced him over the breakfast table, pale and drawn, but dry-eyed.

He had not gone to the coffee house for his breakfast this morning. He wanted, I suppose, to be sure that I would take heed of his warnings before leaving me alone. If I had decided to make a run for it, taking Daniel with me, there is no doubt he could have sent the constables after us, recovered his son, and had me thrown into jail for child-stealing as he had threatened; but it would cause him a great deal of trouble which he no doubt wished to avoid, and cause a scandal that would have been the talk of the town. So he took his breakfast at home and seemed in no hurry to leave afterwards. He barely spoke to me, and when he did, his voice was cold and hard, and the things he said unpleasant.

'Tidy your hair, can't you, Davina? Strands will end up in the butter!' Or, 'That cousin of yours will have to sell his house to pay his debts to me and to others, no doubt, but don't think, just because he is related to you, I shall relent, or offer him a roof over his head.' And: 'Is that Daniel I hear crying? No – don't leave the table. Let the maid attend to him. You will only upset him the more. Your face this morning would turn the milk sour.'

And so would yours! I wanted to retort, but I did not. I bit my tongue, knowing that the more I antagonized Mr Paterson, the longer this unpleasantness would last and the worse it would be for me and for Daniel. I had to live with this man for the rest of my life; better that it should not be a battleground.

At last he left the table and went to his study, and I was free to go to my own rooms.

Perrett was dangling Daniel on her knee and entertaining him with a rattle.

'You don't look well at all this morning, Mrs Paterson,' she said when I went to take him from her. 'You go and have a lie down. I'll look after Daniel. He's fine with me, aren't you, my cherub?'

'I know he is. He's very fond of you, Perrett,' I said, taking him all the same. 'But it will soon be time for him to be fed.'

'Oh not yet, surely . . .' She broke off, knowing it was not her place to argue, but looking at me oddly, just the same.

'Perrett,' I said, a little sharply. 'I am perfectly well, I assure you, and I am sure you have things to do.'

'Yes, madam.' She bobbed a curtsey and left the nursery. I had affronted her, I knew, and I was sorry for that, but I needed my son in my arms, and I needed to be alone.

I sat in the low chair that I used for nursing and offered Daniel my breast, more for my own need than his, for, as Perrett had rightly said, it would be an hour or more before it was time for his next feed. I held him close, taking comfort from the slightly sleepy and intermittent pull of his little rosebud mouth on my nipple, and breathed in the sweet baby smell of him.

'You are all I have now, Daniel,' I murmured. 'All I will ever have. But it will be enough for me. It must!'

And, from somewhere in the past, came the echo of my words.

You are all I have now, Rowan. But it is enough, and I knew it was my mother, speaking to me when I, too, was just a child. Older than Daniel, yes – a little girl with unruly curly hair, dressed in a cheap cotton gown and a pinafore, but still a child nonetheless. And I recalled the solemnity I had felt, and the sadness.

My father was gone. Gone for ever. Never again would he play the fool with me, letting me ride on his back whilst he crawled around on all fours pretending to be a horse. Never again would he make the beautiful haunting music I loved to hear, playing his fiddle whilst my mother danced with me in her arms, round and round, faster and faster, until we collapsed, breathless, giddy, laughing. Never again would he perform his amazing tricks to amuse me, never again nurse me in his lap as we travelled from place to place and I fell asleep with my head against his chest and the rhythmic clip-clop of the horses' hooves in my ears and the sway of the carriage lulling me to sweet dreams.

I had stood beside my mother at the grave side, holding tight to her hand as his coffin was lowered into the cold, dark earth, bewildered, lost, unutterably sad, hearing the priest intoning phrases which were meaningless to me, but sounded more mournful than anything I had ever heard. My mother had tossed a blood-red rose down into the gulf to rest upon the plain wood box that hid him for ever from my view, and urged me to do the same. I had not wanted to drop my flower, it had seemed to me that, as long as I held it in my small moist hand, it was not finally over; there was still hope. I had cried: *No, no! I want Papa's flower! I want Papa!* and she had not forced me to part with it, but allowed me to take it home with me, where I slept with it under my pillow until it was squashed and faded and the petals dropped, and then I had tied them into a corner of a kerchief, and the faint haunting perfume was, to me, some morsel of comfort, a talisman that I carried with me wherever I went.

And: *We must not be too sad, Rowan*, my mother had said. *He wouldn't want us to be sad. We have to be joyful for him*, and I thought it was strange that she should talk of being joyful with the tears running down her cheeks. And I wound my arms around her neck and pressed my face to hers, and she said: *Thank God for you, my darling little one! You are all I have now. But it is enough. Many people have lived their whole lives and never known such love and happiness as I have known. And though he is gone, I still have my memories. And I still have you.*

I thought now of her words.

I, too, had known love and happiness, and though my memories were still incomplete, they were there, just sleeping, and they were returning to me. And I had Daniel. It was what I must cling to.

The sound of a clock striking somewhere interrupted my reverie.

Dear God, was it already ten o'clock? The hour when Richard had said he would come for me?

In a panic I jumped up and ran to the window. And there, outside, was the carriage and Richard himself, tall, strong, purposeful, striding up the steps to the front door, disappearing from my sight beneath the stone balustrade that overhung it, his knock reverberating throughout the house.

I ran from the nursery on to the landing. Mr Paterson must have answered Richard's knock, for as I scurried towards the head of the stairs, I heard his voice, loud and belligerent.

'She's not coming with you, Wells. She's had a change of heart.'

And Richard's reply: 'You can't keep her here by force, Paterson.'

'She is remaining with me of her own choosing.' Mr Paterson again. 'Now, get off my doorstep and desist from bothering me and my wife, or I swear you'll be sorry.'

'I am going nowhere, Paterson, until I have seen Rowan. What have you done to her, you bastard? Beaten her? Tied her up?'

'I need to do none of those things,' Mr Paterson said coldly. I heard his footsteps on the tiled floor of the hall and he called up the stairs: 'Mrs Paterson? Come down here! I know you're skulking and listening! Come and tell your paramour that you will be remaining here, with me. Come on now!'

My feet faltered on the stairs, I held Daniel tightly to me with one hand whilst the other gripped the bannister rail as if for dear life.

Mr Paterson was at the foot, waiting for me. He gripped me roughly by the arm and thrust me forwards. Richard took a step towards me. It was all I could do not to pull away from my husband's grasp and run into his arms.

'Tell him!' Mr Paterson roared. 'Tell him yourself of your decision.'

My lips were dry; my mouth worked, but no sound came.

'Tell him!' Mr Paterson repeated harshly.

'I cannot come with you,' I whispered.

'Rowan – you can! He cannot prevent you!'

In my arms, Daniel whimpered.

'I cannot come with you,' I said again.

'You know your place is with me!' His voice was low, urgent. For a moment it was as if we were quite alone.

My heart was in my eyes; I prayed that he could see it, pleading with him to understand.

'Tell him to leave you alone. Go on – tell him!'

'Please, Richard,' I whispered. 'Please forget me! I am Mr Paterson's wife. I cannot come with you.'

'Now are you satisfied?' Mr Paterson grated. 'You've seen

225

her and she has told you of her decision. Now – get out of here before I call a constable and have you arrested. Go on – leave my house! And leave my wife alone!'

For a moment longer Richard stood there, as if trying to decide whether he should take me by force, rip me from Mr Paterson's grasp and carry me bodily to the carriage. I could bear it no longer; it was more than flesh and blood could stand, being forced to look the man I loved in the face and send him from my life for ever.

'For the love of God, Richard!' I cried. 'For my sake and Daniel's, do as he says, and go!'

His face hardened then, his mouth an angry line, his eyes narrow slits in the weatherbeaten face I loved. His hands were balled to fists at his side, his powerful shoulders tight and oddly threatening. Then: 'If that is what you want, Rowan, then so be it,' he ground out. And turned on his heel.

Mr Paterson did not, as I had expected, drag me immediately back into the house. With that unforgiving hand gripping tight to my elbow, he made me stand there and watch as Richard strode down the steps and climbed up into the carriage. He made me stand and watch as the reins clipped sharply against the horses' sleek handsome backs and the carriage began to roll forward. He made me stand and watch it move away down the street.

Then, and only then, he pushed me back into the hall and slammed the door so hard that the glass rattled.

'Good,' he ground out. 'Now perhaps the bastard will understand. But if ever he comes near you again, Davina, if ever I think for one moment that you are cuckolding me with him . . . well, you know, I think, what will happen. Do I make myself clear?'

'Yes,' I whispered.

'Now – get to your room,' he ordered, as if I were a wayward child.

I went, creeping back up the stairs on legs that felt heavy as lead. I had denied my love, I had denied my daughter, I had been forced to utter words that had torn me apart. Now, I must somehow get my grieving over and done with, put it to the back of my mind as if it had never been, and attempt for Daniel's sake to rebuild my relationship with Mr Paterson.

It was ironic, I thought, that whilst my past had been hidden in a cloudy veil, I had been able to accept the life he had offered me.

I had always known the return of my memory might be painful for me, even as I had desperately wanted it. But I had never, for one instant, realized just how painful it would be. To glimpse what had been and what might yet be, to see my child and have her torn from me for a second time, was a torture so exquisite I thought it was more than I could bear.

But somehow, for Daniel's sake, I must. I had already blighted enough lives. I must not blight his too.

Sixteen

For the next two or three days Mr Paterson never left the house. He was, I suppose, as yet unwilling to trust me not to try to make my escape and take Daniel with me.

I could not, of course, have gone far – Thomas had been instructed that I was no longer to have use of the carriage, and it would have been impossible for me to walk all the way over to the Clifton woods even without a baby in my arms. With him, I most certainly would not attempt such a thing. I would never expose his delicate lungs to the pestilence and disease that hung in the air near the river, which I would have to cross on foot, and I knew that when Mr Paterson caught up with me, as he surely would, he was more than likely to implement his threat to have me thrown into prison and remove Daniel from my care for ever.

No, I dared not risk such a thing, and Mr Paterson must have known it. But perhaps he was not confident that Richard would not return to try once more to persuade me to go with him, though thought that most unlikely. What, after all, could he hope to gain from it? I had told him, face to face, that I could not – would not – go with him, and there had been a dreadful finality about the set of his shoulders as he stomped away. No, I did not think Richard would return to try to persuade me to change my mind. I had made my decision and it was not in his nature to wheedle and plead. He was too proud a man, used to controlling his own destiny, not dependent on the whims of others. For I knew he might feel he had been made to look a fool, and that, I felt certain, was not something he was likely to risk a second time, though I

228

hoped with all my heart that he understood that in reality I had no choice at all.

On the fourth day, however, when I came down for breakfast, I found that Mr Paterson had already eaten, and saw that he was dressed for going out. My numb misery was punctuated by a feeling of relief. His surly presence these last days had been oppressive; it seemed to permeate the whole house, even the nursery, where I escaped whenever I could to sit with Daniel.

'I've business that has to be attended to,' he informed me. 'I hope you can be trusted, Mrs Paterson.'

Not once since I had told him of my intention to leave him had he called me Davina, but always Mrs Paterson, presumably to remind me that I was his wife, his chattel, as if I needed reminding!

'I shall have little opportunity to be anything but trust-worthy,' I replied stiffly. 'And in any case, I have my baby to care for.'

He nodded brusquely. 'I'm glad that you seem to be accepting where your responsibilities lie,' he said. 'But I shall not be gone long. Thomas will drive me to my office and wait whilst I do what I have to do. I have told Cook to expect me back for a midday meal, and I shall expect you to share it with me.'

'Naturally,' I replied, though I was disappointed. I had hoped to have the best part of the day to myself.

'Good.' He strode to the door, paused, turned back. For just a moment the mask of cold fury that had hardened his features whenever he looked at me these last few days dropped away, and I caught a glimpse of the anguish that lay beneath it. 'We'll get through this, Mrs Paterson,' he said.

'Will we?' My tone was harsh. It was not what I had meant to say. I knew that he was hurting just as I was, and that it was my fault. I knew that I had failed to keep my side of the bargain that is marriage, and caused him great pain. But I could not bring myself to admit it, or bend to him even a little. His good points were all obscured from me now. I looked at him and saw, perhaps unfairly, a man who had trapped me into marriage. I saw a man who had raped a defenceless African girl and dismissed it as unimportant because she was only a slave. I saw a man who had resorted to the greatest cruelty imaginable – threatening a woman with the loss of her child – in order to keep me with him. And I felt nothing but hatred and scorn.

I would never forgive him, nor forget, and I wished I had the courage to tell him so. But for Daniel's sake I had to try to make this home of his bearable, if not happy. So I said nothing, though I think the curl of my lip and the coldness in my eyes might have been a clear expression of my feelings.

He turned then and left the room and the house. I sat down to pick at my breakfast. And I had no way of knowing that I would never see him again.

It was shortly after midday, and Cook had the meal ready and waiting. I had spent the morning wheeling Daniel around the garden, since it was a fine bright day and I thought the fresh air would do him good.

The birds were busy looking for worms, and though I knew he was too young to understand, I had pointed them out to him.

'Look, see that, Daniel? That thrush with the wriggly thing in his beak? I believe he has babies in the nest and is taking it home for their dinner! Watch, now! He's going into the bush! Very soon we may see those little ones learning to spread their wings!'

Daniel gurgled and flapped his plump little hands as if he, too, were trying to learn to fly, and I laughed, the first time I had laughed or even so much as smiled since telling Richard I could not go with him.

I had fed Daniel, as always, finding comfort and something like peace in his rhythmic sucking, and then took him to the parlour to await Mr Paterson's return.

He was late, and Cook was, I imagined, becoming anxious that the meal was spoiling, for several times I heard Dorcas come along the hall and go to the dining-room window, sent by Cook, no doubt, to look out and see if there was

230

any sign of him. But she was nowhere in evidence when I heard the clatter of hooves and, a moment later, the front door opening. I got up with the intention of setting Daniel in his crib, and to my astonishment, saw Thomas in the hall.

I think I knew in that first startled moment that something was very wrong. Thomas never used the front door, and of Mr Paterson there was no sign. Moreover, Thomas's face, usually so implacable, wore an expression that might almost, under other circumstances, have appeared comical. His eyes were very wide, displaying the whites all around the coal-black centres, his lips thrust outwards, his jaw slack.

'Thomas!' I said. 'Whatever—?'

'It's Mr Paterson!' His voice was hoarse.

'What is wrong with Mr Paterson?' I asked. 'Has there been an accident? Is he ill?'

'You'd better sit down, ma'am.' Thomas ushered me back into the parlour, solicitous as ever in spite of his own obvious distress.

'Why should I sit down?' I demanded. I was very frightened now, and beginning to tremble. 'What is it, Thomas?'

Thomas wrung his hands.

'Oh, Mrs Paterson . . . he's dead! He's been murdered!'

For a moment I simply could not take it in. Mr Paterson *dead*? *Murdered*? I stared at Thomas, shock robbing me of all my senses.

'What are you talking about?' I asked dully, and then, more shrilly: 'What are you talking about, Thomas?'

'Mr Paterson,' Thomas said. 'In his office. He's been killed, ma'am.'

'Killed? How?'

'Bludgeoned. His head broke open. Oh, Mrs Paterson . . .'

Thomas put his hands to his own head, bowing it to his chest and rocking his body to and fro. Any display of emotion was so totally unlike him that I could no longer be in any doubt but that what he said was true, unbelievable as it seemed, and suddenly, surprisingly, I was icy calm.

231

I laid Daniel down in his crib, crossed to the drinks table and poured some brandy into a glass.

'Here,' I said. 'You'd better have this.'

He made no move to take it. I took him by the elbow, steered him towards a chair, sat him down, and put the glass into his hand.

'Go on, drink it!' I instructed him. 'Do as I say, Thomas. It will make you feel better.'

Obediently he raised the glass, drinking a little with lips that shook so much that I heard his teeth rattle against the crystal and some of the brandy ran in a glistening trickle down his chin.

'Now tell me,' I said urgently. 'Tell me everything.'

Haltingly, as if shock had robbed him of the English language he usually spoke so fluently, he told me.

He had called at the quayside premises to collect Mr Paterson as he had been told to do, but Mr Paterson had not made an appearance. After waiting some time, Thomas had taken it upon himself to go inside and look for him.

He had called from the doorway, and when there was no reply, climbed the stairs to the first floor room where Mr Paterson had his office. And there he had found him, slumped over his desk, wig awry, as though asleep. At first, Thomas had thought he had been taken ill and collapsed – then he had seen the blood. Matted in his wig and in his own hair beneath it, congealing on his collar, splattered across the ledgers on which he had been working. The base of his skull had been shattered by some heavy object, very likely the heavy trivet which held the fire irons, for they were all scattered about the grate. And he was dead. Quite dead.

As I listened, I had to hold on tightly to the unnatural calm that had descended upon me. When he stopped speaking, sinking his head once more into his huge, black hands, I refilled his brandy glass and poured a little for myself, sipping it jerkily and feeling the warmth burn my throat and permeate my veins.

'What did you do then, Thomas?' I asked, though I think I already knew. 'Did you run to raise the alarm?'

Thomas gave a little shake of his head.

'No, ma'am,' he answered, as I had expected. 'I drove straight home. I didn't know what else to do.'

I set down my brandy glass. 'Then we must call a constable at once. Mr Paterson cannot be left there like that. And we have to find out who has done this terrible thing.'

'I think I have a clue,' Thomas said. 'It may assist the law in apprehending the murderer.' He fished in his pocket and brought out a leather coin pouch. 'This lay on the stairs – I saw it on my way up to the office and picked it up. I think whoever killed Mr Paterson may have dropped it as he fled.'

He held the pouch out. I took it, and the remains of my composure drained out of me as I looked at it, washed away on a tide of horror and disbelief.

There were initials stamped in gold lettering on the pouch. And those initials were *R.W.*

R.W. Richard Wells.

The blood seemed to drain from my body.

Oh, there must be others in this town who shared the initials R.W. but how many of them would have reason to wish Mr Paterson dead?

In a flash I saw it all, as vivid as a scene from one of the stage plays I had watched my parents perform when I was a child. Richard, calling on Mr Paterson to try to reason with him. Mr Paterson dismissing him with the same cold hauteur as when he had come to the house to take me with him, returning to his desk, and taking up his pen to show Richard that the interview was over, impress upon him the irrelevance and unimportance of his plea. And Richard, in a flash of fury, grabbing up the heavy brass trivet and bringing it crashing down on the base of Mr Paterson's skull.

Or perhaps he had gone there having the intention of killing Mr Paterson clear in his mind. Perhaps he had seen Mr Paterson go into his office, known he was alone, and seized his chance. For he knew full well it was Mr Paterson who stood between us. As long as he lived, Mr Paterson would keep me with him by refusing to allow me to take Daniel, and I would never abandon my little son. With my husband dead, I would be free. Free to go to him with no fear of losing my child, free, even, to marry him.

It would, of course, be cold-blooded murder, not even mitigated by provocation. Was Richard capable of such a thing? I did not know, but I thought of the hard masculinity of him, that slightly dangerous air which I, to my shame, found so fatally attractive, and thought that perhaps he was.

My heart was beating now like a trapped bird within my chest, my mind chasing in wild, scarcely coherent circles.

I did not love my husband; these last days I had come close to hating him. I would never grieve for him as a wife should; I was too glad to be free of him. But oh, I did not wish him dead, and in such terrible circumstances! And the thought that he might well have died at my lover's hand was insupportable, both because it made me as guilty as if I had struck the blow which killed him, and because I knew that I could never find true happiness with a man who could do such a thing, for whatever reason.

I looked once more at the pouch with the tell-tale initials stamped upon it.

'I'll take care of it, Thomas,' I said, slipping it into the pocket of my gown. 'I must go and tell Cook and the others what has happened. And you must go and find a constable or a watchman and ask him to go to the office without delay.'

As I crossed the hall to the kitchen, where, if I was not much mistaken, I would find a row of curious ears pressed to the crack in the door, the pouch seemed to burn a hole in my pocket.

I had not yet decided what I should do with it, whether I should show it to an officer of the law, or dispose of it so thoroughly that it would never be seen again. With all my heart I prayed that my terrible suspicions were wrong; that the pouch belonged to some other man who shared Richard's initials, or that, if it was indeed Richard's, there was some innocent explanation for it being on the stairs to Mr Paterson's office.

But at that moment, numb with shock and horror, I was quite unable to think of one.

I was still in the kitchen when there came a hammering at the front door.

'Answer it please, Perrett,' I said, but by the time she had wiped her eyes on her apron – all the servants, with the understandable exception of Dorcas, the slave, were very upset by the news I had brought them – there was the sound of a commotion in the hallway.

I ran to the door and saw a group of men milling about. Two or three of them were attempting to drag Thomas out of the front door and down the steps. All of them were shouting obscenities.

'What is going on?' I cried.

A burly man I recognized as a constable of the port stepped forward towards me.

'Mrs Paterson, a most serious thing has occurred. Your husband has been beaten to death in his office at the quay.'

'Yes, I know, but—'

'And there is no doubt his slave is responsible.'

'Thomas!' I cried. 'No – you are making a terrible mistake! Thomas would never—'

'He was seen running from the scene,' the man went on. 'He thought to secure his freedom, no doubt, or take revenge for some imagined ill-treatment. You can't trust these savages.'

'Oh, don't be ridiculous!' I cried. 'Thomas found Mr Paterson dead! He came straight home . . .'

The man smirked. 'We'll see what the magistrate has to say about that! He ran here, no doubt, because he knew we were after him. You'd not be defending him, Mrs Paterson, if you could see what he's done to your husband – not that I'd want any lady to have to look on such a grizzly sight. You'd be thanking us, and paying these men a goodly reward for their trouble!'

At that very moment the volume of the commotion outside increased to a crescendo, and through the open door I saw

Thomas break free from his captors and pound off along the street, the mob close on his heels.

The constable swore, then turned back confidently to me.

'They'll catch him again, have no fear of that. He may have been strong enough – and quick enough – to take them by surprise once, but he won't do it again. He'll be in a place of safety before the hour is out, mark my words – unless he's lynched first. The men are in an ugly mood, I can tell you.'

'Oh dear God!' I whispered.

In the parlour, no doubt awakened by all the commotion, Daniel had begun to cry lustily.

'You'd best get a male relative to take care of things for you,' the constable advised me. 'What has to be done is no job for a lady. Is there someone who can help you?'

'There's my cousin Theo . . .' I managed.

'Theo Grimes?' The constable's eyes narrowed. 'Well, you'd better get hold of him right away. He'll know what has to be done.' He strutted importantly to the door and I followed. There was no sign now of Thomas or his pursuers, but my throat closed as I imagined the chase, as fervent as any fox hunt, and with violent death just as likely an outcome.

In a state of total gibbering shock, I went to Daniel, picked him up and rocked him in my arms, clinging to him as the only breath of sanity in a world gone mad.

My husband murdered. Thomas hunted for the crime. And the pouch bearing the initials R.W. in the pocket of my gown.

With the arrival of the constable and the mob, it had gone completely from my mind. Now I remembered it and burned with guilt. I should have shown it to the constable. I should have told him it was proof of Thomas's innocence. But was it? Even if he had listened to me – and I doubted that he would – the pouch proved nothing. Convinced of Thomas's guilt as he seemed to be, the constable would doubtless have argued that I had only the slave's word for it that he had discovered the pouch on the stairs leading to Mr Paterson's office.

Was it possible, I wondered distractedly, that the constable was right? Might my husband have met his death at the hand of his trusted servant? Though I had never seen him anything but deferential and loyal, was it possible that something had finally caused him to snap and lash out at all the indignities that had been visited upon him? There were enough of them, in all conscience, to drive any man to the limits of his endurance, especially one as fiercely proud as Thomas. The threats to have him whipped if he stepped out of line, the silver collar and stupid livery he was forced to wear, simply the knowledge that he was owned, body and soul, all this must have been festering for years beneath that impassive exterior. And I remembered, too, the fury and hatred I had seen in his eyes on the night Dorcas had been raped. If he had killed Mr Paterson in his bed that night I would not have been surprised.

Could it be that some final act of callousness or display of mastery by my husband had suddenly ignited the fire that smouldered in Thomas, fanning it to a blaze as the bellows fan the smouldering embers of a parlour fire? The men who had come to take him had seemed utterly convinced of his guilt. Had they perhaps heard some kind of a struggle taking place immediately prior to Thomas running from the office? Certainly he had been in a terrible state when he arrived home – more upset than I would have expected, given his hatred of Mr Paterson . . .

I caught myself up sharply. What on earth was I doing? Was I trying to make a case for Thomas having struck the fatal blow because I *wanted* him to be guilty – found it a preferable scenario to the one I had envisaged earlier – better by far than believing my beloved Richard was responsible for the wicked deed?

The thoughts whirled around and around in my tortured brain like a flock of birds startled by the shot from a gamekeeper's gun.

What should I do? Should I take the pouch to a magistrate? If I did, I might be incriminating the man I loved, and who might yet be entirely innocent. If I did not, I could be betraying Thomas and leaving him to a terrible fate – if it had not already overtaken him. I did not know what to do, and the indecision was tearing me apart.

There was only one person who could show me the right way, I thought, and that was Richard himself. A great wave of longing for him washed over me, yes, even though I still harboured the fear that he might have been the one responsible for my husband's murder. I longed for him to tell me it was not so, longed for him to take this terrible burden from my shoulders.

And Richard knew Thomas and respected him, too. He had sympathy as I did for what slaves endured. If Thomas had indeed lost his head and bludgeoned Mr Paterson to death in a moment of madness, Richard would know best how to represent his interests; he would speak up for him. If he had not, if Richard himself had been responsible, I could not believe he would let an innocent man suffer for his actions. And if, as I prayed, it had been neither of them, but some ruffian from the docks, intent only on stealing what he could from Mr Paterson's office and his person, then he would know how to present that to the magistrate too.

But I did not know how I could get to Richard. My only point of contact with him was through Lady Avonbridge, and I had no way of getting to her house. I could not drive the carriage, and I could not walk so far. What was I to do?

A hammering at the door interrupted my thoughts; I froze still as a statue, heart pounding as my shattered nerves leaped and twanged and I wondered in panic – *What now?*

I heard Perrett go to answer it, then the sound of a man's voice. Relief flooded me. I ran into the hall.

'Oh Theo!' I cried. 'Thank God you're here! The most terrible thing . . .'

And: 'I know,' he said. 'I came as soon as I heard. Don't worry, Davina, I'm here to take care of everything.'

He came into the parlour, poured himself a brandy, and asked me for the details of what had happened. He had been working at his books in his own warehouse office, he told me, when news had reached him that Mr Paterson

238

had been discovered dead, and he had come straight away to offer me his assistance. He had even thought I might not yet have heard the news, and he could have been the one to break it to me.

'I didn't like the thought of you hearing it from strangers,' he said, patting my hand. 'I am your own flesh and blood and I hoped to be here for you.'

'That's kind, Theo . . .' Tears pricked my eyes, the first since all this had begun. 'But I didn't hear it from strangers. I heard it from Thomas. It was he who found Mr Paterson, or at least, that's what he told me. But the constable came, and a gang of men acting as vigilantes, and they tried to take Thomas away. He went on the run, but he's likely been captured by now, and I don't know what they will do to him . . .'

'Thomas?' Theo exclaimed. 'They tried to take *Thomas*?'

'Yes. They seemed convinced it was he who—'

'I don't believe it!' Theo interrupted me. 'Thomas was devoted to poor John!'

Hardly devoted, I thought, but I did not want to go into all that. Instead I said: 'I can't believe it of him either. Not really . . .'

'What proof do they have?' Theo demanded.

'None that I know of. Just that he was seen running away . . .'

'They have the wrong man, I'm sure of it!' Theo said forcefully. 'A proper search must be made of John's premises. I wish now I had gone in myself when I heard the news, but I was so anxious to get to you. I hope no one conceals evidence for their own purposes. I can't believe the murderer can have been there and left no clue as to his identity!'

The pouch seemed to burn a hole in my pocket. This was my opportunity to tell Theo what Thomas claimed to have found. But I knew that if I did so, Theo would take it directly to the constable or the magistrate, only too ready to assume guilt on Richard's part. After all, had he not already warned me just how ruthless Richard could be in his pursuit for me? Oh yes, he would certainly go directly to the magistrate. I

239

had to speak to Richard first, give him the opportunity to explain . . .

'I'll go to John's office at once, and see if I can discover any clue,' Theo said, turning for the door.

'No!' I reached out and caught at his sleeve.

Theo looked at me, perplexed. 'Why not?'

'Because . . .' I was thinking frantically.

Theo's carriage was here, outside the house. It could provide me with a means of transport to get to Lady Avonbridge's house, and thence to the interview I so much wanted with Richard. But I could not tell Theo that. He disapproved totally of Richard, would never hear of me going to him. No, I had to think of another excuse – and quickly!

'I want to go there myself,' I said.

'What! Davina – the scene of a murder is no place for a lady . . .'

'But it is my duty,' I said. 'I have to see the scene for myself, Theo.' I drew myself up. 'It is my duty,' I repeated. 'I am – was – his wife. Please, lend me your carriage . . .'

'I think it most inadvisable, Davina. But if you are set upon it, I will come with you.'

'No!' Again I spoke sharply. 'No – the best thing you can do for me, Theo, is to take care of Daniel for me. He has never been parted from me for a single moment since he was born, and I cannot conceive of leaving him now with anyone who is not family. Please . . . do this for me. I shall not be long gone.'

For a moment I thought Theo would continue to reason with me, or even refuse my request. His eyes narrowed, his face thoughtful. Then, to my surprise, he nodded.

'Very well, Davina. If you insist. I must warn you this will be upsetting for you in the extreme, however.'

'I know it, but it is what I must do,' I lied.

He took my hand. 'Remember I am here for you. When you return, I shall be here for you. And have no fear, I shall take very good care of both you and Daniel. Hold on to that. I shall take good care of both of you from this moment on. You need never be afraid or alone ever again.'

240

The misting tears filled my eyes. I pressed the hand that held mine and felt bad that I was deceiving the cousin who was one of my few relatives in the whole wide world.

'Thank you, Theo,' I murmured. 'You are good to me indeed.'

And, full of emotion as I was, set upon my quest as I was, I failed to notice the look on his face, the strange light in his eyes, that would have warned me, had I seen it, that Theo cared for me a great deal more than I had realized, and that the comfort and support he promised me went far beyond cousinly duty.

Seventeen

I took the carriage. I instructed Theo's coachman to drive
me direct to Avonbridge Hall. He looked, I admit, a little
surprised, but he said nothing. He was a servant of the old
school, used to doing as he was bid without question.

My heart was beating fast with nervousness, my thoughts
churning. It was almost too much to hope for that I should find
Richard there, I knew, but at least Lady Avonbridge should
be able to tell me where I could find him. I hoped against
hope that she would not tell me he was at the docks. If that
were the case, it might very well be that he had indeed gone
to Mr Paterson's office and killed him, either in a temper, or,
worse, in cold blood, driven on by his determination that we
should be together.

The thought made me shudder afresh. However strong our
love and our desire to be together, nothing could ever justify
murder. Mr Paterson's blood would be upon my own hands;
the guilt would be with me until my dying day. And though
there would be nothing now to keep us apart, I could not love
and live with a man who had done such a thing – and I could
not be content for him to raise my children either.

But I did not know yet that it was so, I told myself. And
until I did there was no point tormenting myself with it. But
it was there in my mind, all the same, and I leaned forward
to ask the coachman to make the best possible speed.

My knees were trembling as I climbed down from the
carriage, my hand, too, as I raised it to knock at the great
front door of Avonbridge Hall. A butler came to answer;
he looked down his nose at me when he saw I had no
calling card to present, but nonetheless went off to inform

his mistress that I was there, and returned, a few moments later, to show me into the drawing room. As I entered, Lady Avonbridge herself, imposing as ever, rose to greet me, but there was no warmth or friendship in that greeting.

'Mrs Paterson! This is quite a surprise.'

In spite of my nervousness – Lady Avonbridge intimidated me even at the best of times – I kept my head high.

'I am very sorry to call on you unannounced, and I hope it is not inconvenient. But it is imperative I should speak with Richard, and I have no idea how to find him except through yourself.'

'Indeed!' She surveyed me with hauteur. 'I'm not sure that I should help you, Mrs Paterson. I warned you once before that you should not play with Richard's emotions, asked you not to hurt him again, but you paid no heed. You chose to raise his hopes of a reconciliation only to dash them. You elected to remain with your husband rather than come to Richard and your daughter.'

'I had no choice,' I said. 'My husband issued me with an ultimatum – if I went with Richard, I would never see my son again.'

She sniffed. 'You chose your husband's son over the daughter you have with Richard.'

'Yes,' I said, spirited suddenly. 'And if you can't see why, then I really don't have the time to explain it to you.'

A corner of her mouth quirked. 'Not so meek, I see, Mrs Paterson.'

'I'm sorry,' I said. 'I don't mean to be impolite, but really time is of the essence. I must speak with Richard urgently.'

'And does your husband know that you are here?' she asked archly.

'My husband is dead,' I said.

I saw the surprise flicker over her face, then she sniffed again, pressing her fingertips together and looking at me with disconcerting directness.

'I see. So now that you have lost one protector you are looking for another.'

The last remnants of my patience snapped. 'Lady Avonbridge, I know that you are a good friend to Richard, but—'

'He is not here,' she interrupted me. 'You have had a
wasted journey, I'm afraid.'

My heart sank. 'Can you not tell me where I can find
him?'

She gave a light laugh. 'I can tell you – for all the good it
will do you. Richard is in London. He left this morning.'

Relief coursed through me. If he had left for London this
morning . . .

'Thank God!' I whispered faintly.

And then it came to me in a flash. What Lady Avonbridge
had told me meant nothing. Nothing at all. Richard might
well have left the house this morning to go to London, but
he could easily have gone to the docks first. He could have
gone to Mr Paterson's office, killed him, and been well out
of the way by the time the alarm was raised. On his way to
London – a perfect alibi. And a perfect hiding place, too, if
anyone pointed the finger of suspicion . . .

'Oh!' I gasped, as all my doubts were resurrected, and
pressed my hands to my mouth.

'Rowan.' It was the first time Lady Avonbridge had called
me by my given name, but I scarcely noticed. 'Rowan – would
you care to enlighten me as to what all this means?'

Her tone was kinder than before, there was less hostility
in her gaze. And suddenly I saw her for what she was. A
woman with great influence in this town. A woman of means.
A woman of integrity and courage. A woman I could trust
with the truth.

'Lady Avonbridge,' I said, 'my husband did not simply
die. He was murdered this morning as he sat at his desk.
Someone broke his head with a heavy instrument. Our
slave, Thomas, has been accused of the crime and is no
doubt languishing at this very moment in some stinking
cell – if he has not already been taken by a lynch mob.
But before they came for him, he showed me something
which he claimed to have found on the stairs leading to Mr
Paterson's office.'

244

I pulled the pouch from my pocket, held it out to her with the lettering uppermost.

'It's Richard's, isn't it?'

She took it from me, turning it over in her beringed hands. 'It certainly looks like it.'

'So, what was it doing on the stairs to Mr Paterson's office?' I demanded. 'Why was he there, if not for—'

'Not so fast!' Lady Avonbridge interrupted once more. 'This pouch is no proof at all that Richard was on your husband's premises this morning or at any other time. It has not been in his possession for a long while. Do you remember the beating he took from a gang of thugs? The pouch was stolen from him then. I know that to be the case because its loss affected him more deeply than did the beating. "My bones will heal," he said to me, "but my pouch, which was given to me by my grandmother to mark a special birthday, is gone for ever." No, I am certain as can be that, whoever dropped that pouch, it was not Richard. And equally certain he will be delighted to have it back in his possession.'

My mouth was dry suddenly. Was she speaking the truth, or attempting to protect Richard?

'Whoever attacked Richard stole his pouch,' Lady Avonbridge went on. 'There was a good deal of money in it, which is doubtless long gone, but it seems to follow that the same ruffians are to blame for your husband's demise. Thieves and vagabonds, willing to beat or kill for what they can get.'

'Yes!' I said it eagerly, relief returning. She was right, of course. It had been ruffians who had beaten Richard senseless, for all that they had done so at Theo's instigation. Doubtless they had been only too ready to take what they could get by way of extra payment. And those same men would prey on any victim whom they thought might be worth their efforts. Mr Paterson was known in the city as a man of means. If he had been alone in his office he might well have seemed an easy target and fallen victim to their evil greed.

But it seemed Richard had never mentioned to Lady Avonbridge that he knew who had been behind the terrible beating he had taken – to protect me, perhaps . . .

'He led you to believe the attack was simple robbery, did he?' I asked.

'I assumed it to be,' she agreed. 'Though there are plenty of men in this town who would be glad to see him incapacitated, or even dead.'

Her words shocked me. 'Richard?' I asked in disbelief.

'Oh yes.' She smiled slightly. 'Richard is much hated for his crusade, I'm afraid, and has made many enemies.'

'His crusade?' I repeated, puzzled. 'What do you mean, his crusade?'

'Has he never spoken of it to you, then?' Lady Avonbridge asked.

I shook my head. 'Since our reaquaintance, there has never really been the time nor the opportunity to talk much,' I said. 'And there is still a great deal I do not remember.'

'And have you never wondered where it is he goes, what he does?' she asked, looking at me in frank amazement.

'Of course I wonder,' I admitted. 'But I know he is a sailor, and I assumed—'

'He *was* a sailor,' Lady Avonbridge corrected me. 'It is some years now, however, since he followed that calling. Richard works now for the abolition of the slave trade. He travels the country, organizing meetings. He distributes pamphlets, he conjoins like-minded people in an effort to bring pressure to bear on Parliament and have the laws of the land changed. Here, in Bristol, he is the leader of a group who meet regularly to formulate plans and strategies. They are a motley group, lawyers, wheelwrights – your own doctor, Andrew Thorson, is one of their number, I believe. And there are even one or two slaves who sometimes manage to attend the weekly meetings when they can slip out unnoticed. They are not in a position to contribute much, of course, but the contact, and the knowledge that Englishmen are working on their behalf, gives them hope.'

'That is how Thomas comes to know Richard, then!' I said.

'Indeed. Thomas goes to the meetings whenever he can, and has been able to provide useful background information

246

regarding the trade. Though Richard, of course, has seen it for himself, and been so repelled by it that he felt he had to give over his life to working for its abolition and freedom – or at least more rights – for the poor souls taken against their will and sold into purgatory.'

'Yes!' I said, her words stirring faint memories. 'Yes, I do remember something of it! But if he is no longer employed as a sea captain, how does he make a living? There can be no money in fighting for the rights of poor slaves . . .'

Lady Avonbridge smiled slightly. 'As you may or may not know, Richard's family is well-to-do, and they support him in his mission. And I . . . I do what I can too. He has my backing and the use of my house. It's little enough, but it eases my social conscience, and provides a safe haven for him to work from. For what he is doing is dangerous, make no mistake of it. The fortunes of this city were built upon slavery, and though the rich merchants no longer need to trade in human life to support their extravagant habits, they are greedy. They don't want the calm waters of their millpond ruffled by the likes of Richard. If he met his death in a back alley some dark night, they would no doubt dance on his grave.'

I shivered.

'Some of his enemies would stop at nothing,' Lady Avonbridge went on. 'Richard has always known that. He had only just begun his mission when he first met and fell in love with you, but he knew he was set upon a dangerous course. It was for that reason that he installed you in the little house in Watchet – well away from his enemies in the city of Bristol. He did not want any possible repercussions to fall on you. But it was not far enough, it seems. Richard believes the fire which destroyed your home was the work of arsonists seeking their revenge upon him.'

A chill whispered over my skin. I smelled again the dense, acrid smoke, heard the crackle of the hungry flames, as I had done on occasion since it had come to me in the dreams that had been the beginning of my memory reawakening.

Our house burned around us, forcing us to flee, and

setting in motion the whole terrible chain of events which had followed – the work of Richard's enemies?

But no, there was something wrong with that theory, something I could not put my finger on, something I still could not remember, no matter how hard I tried. Maybe it was not something I had ever truly known, merely surmised or suspected, and that was why it eluded me, yet at the same time whispered to me that whatever Richard might think, I did not truly believe we had been the victims of disgruntled slave traders and their henchmen.

'Rightly or wrongly, Richard blamed himself for your fate,' Lady Avonbridge continued. 'It made him all the more determined to continue his campaign. He did not want you to have died – as he believed – in vain. And besides his work here, in England, he has sailed for the far corners of the earth, gathering evidence of the atrocity that is slavery, and seeking evidence to bring to justice those who flaunt what laws already exist. His most recent voyage, to the Sugar Islands, was one such mission. He suspected there are those who trade slaves to the Spanish, who are known to be the cruellest masters of all. The poor souls sold to the plantations there live but short and wretched lives, whipped to continue working until they drop and die like flies in the terrible conditions they are forced to endure. He has that evidence now, and has gone to lay it before those who can act upon it. There is one slave trader in this town who will shortly find himself in conflict with the authorities – one whom he has been at odds with for some time, and whose wickedness he is sworn to put an end to.' Her eyes met mine, holding my gaze steadily. 'I think I should tell you – that trader is your own cousin, Theo Grimes.'

A wave of shame overcame me. I had known that Theo dealt in slaves. I had even known he was flouting the law of the land by trading with the Spanish. But somehow I had failed to grasp the full implications of it – that what he was engaged in was even more wickedly cruel than the trade as I had witnessed it, besides being illegal. Perhaps I had been too concerned with my own affairs; perhaps because he was my own flesh and blood I had tried to blot it out from my mind. It is not a pleasant thing to believe ones own flesh and blood can be guilty of something so abhorrent, and I had perhaps been too ready to think the best of Theo and put an acceptable complexion on the aspects of his character I did not care for. I had tried to make excuses for the beating he had arranged for Richard. I had pleaded with Mr Paterson to save him from ruin . . .

Oh dear God! A sudden terrible thought came into my mind. Leaving thieves and vagabonds aside, there was someone else besides Richard and Thomas who had a motive for wanting Mr Paterson dead. Theo! Mr Paterson was calling in the loan he had made him, and Theo was not in a position to repay it. If Mr Paterson insisted, as he had told me in no uncertain terms he intended to do, then Theo would be ruined. Was he capable of murder? Certainly he had arranged for Richard to be beaten and threatened . . .

The pouch! Yet another dreadful thought assailed me, turning my blood to ice. Both Lady Avonbridge and I had jumped to the conclusion that the men who had attacked Richard had also murdered Mr Paterson, and had dropped the pouch in their haste to escape from the scene of the crime. Now it occurred to me that perhaps the pouch being dropped on the stairs was no accident. Was it possible it had been left there deliberately with the intention of incriminating Richard? If Richard was arrested and charged with murder, Theo would have nothing more to fear from him. He would no longer be free to work against the evil trade, and if he was discredited, labelled a common criminal, hanged even, the evidence he had gathered against Theo would never be presented in a court of law.

No wonder he had agreed to me visiting the scene of the murder! When I had told him of Thomas's arrest and made no mention of the pouch, he must have been puzzled and dismayed. He must have thought it had not yet been found – and he had hoped that I would discover it! Why, he had even bidden me to look around carefully for any clues, not knowing that all the while the pouch was burning a hole in my pocket!

Surely, though, he must have known I would recognize the initials? Did he trust me to hand the pouch over to the authorities and incriminate the man I loved? But then, he was under the impression that that was all over now, and that I had been deterred by his warnings about Richard being a danger to me. Perhaps he had thought I would take the pouch as final proof that Richard was indeed a dangerous man – one who could bludgeon my husband to death in cold blood.

Had Theo called once more upon his thugs – or was the truth even worse? He had been at the docks this morning. Perhaps he had gone to see Mr Paterson in his office to beg him once more to give him time to repay the loan, and when Mr Paterson had refused, he had battered him to death with his own trivet, dropped the pouch on the stairs to divert attention, and then come to me to offer his assistance. What was it he had said? *I shall take good care of both you and Daniel from now on . . . You need never be alone or afraid again . . .*

I gasped as the full implication of it hit me. *I will take good care of both you and Daniel from now on. You and Daniel.* Daniel – the heir to Mr Paterson's wealth. Daniel – a mere babe in arms. Theo had not made the promise out of the goodness of his heart, or even from concern for me. He meant to worm his way into our lives to such an extent that he would be responsible for Daniel's inheritance. The wealth that had eluded him in spite of the marriage he had arranged between me and Mr Paterson was now within his grasp.

Oh dear God, was it really possible that my own cousin could hide such a black heart beneath the charming manner he showed to the world? Could he really be so wicked? I could still scarcely believe it, and yet . . .

As I stood there, thoughts churning, something very odd happened. With a blinding flash, a door in my memory opened. I was remembering, truly remembering, that last desperate journey with my mother. In reality, not in dreams, I felt the rock of the carriage, the discomfort it caused me in my delicate condition, the anxiety as to what was to become of us all. I recalled the abrupt halt on the lonely road and the face at the window – the face of the man who would fire

250

the fatal shot that would send us careering towards disaster. For the first time, I saw it clearly, and knew why I had felt a frisson of surprise on seeing it. For it was not the face of some unknown highwayman at all. It was the face of my cousin Theo.

The blood drained from my face; my heart seemed to stop beating. Theo! It was not Richard I had been trying to escape from – it was Theo! When he had talked of a man obsessed, it was himself he had been describing! It was Theo who had been behind the burning of the cottage in the hope of driving me back into his arms, and when my mother and I had fled, he had followed us and held up the carriage with the intention of abducting me. But everything had gone awry. Shots were fired, the horses bolted, my mother was killed and I was badly injured. And worst of all, I was pregnant with Richard's child. How shocked Theo must have been when he discovered it! He had turned against me then, and for a while, no doubt, had despised me with the same fervour as he had loved me. And then he had seen his chance to use me as a pawn in his ambition to become a Merchant Venturer, and at the same time take his revenge on Richard – by arranging for me to marry Mr Paterson.

Now, for some reason, he had once more become obsessed with me. And, even more so, with the life of luxury I represented. He saw everything he desired within his grasp. And I had played into his hands more neatly than he could ever have hoped. Into my mind's eye came the picture of Theo bidding me goodbye at my door, with little Daniel in his arms. I had handed my son into the care of a heartless schemer, a slave trader, a murderer.

'Rowan?' Lady Avonbridge's voice, tinged with anxiety, impinged on the dreadful pictures my mind was conjuring up. 'Are you well? Has all this been too much for you?'

'I must go home at once!' I said.

'Wouldn't you like to see Alice?' she asked. 'Richard left her with me. She is upstairs with her nurse . . .'

Longing tugged at me briefly. But for the moment my

251

greatest concern was Daniel. Alice was safe here, and happy. Daniel . . . Daniel was with the man who had betrayed me.

'I must go at once!' I repeated. 'But, if Richard returns, please tell him I need him. Desperately. And with urgency.'

Then, waiting for nothing more, I ran from the house.

When I came running out, Theo's driver looked almost as startled as Lady Avonbridge had done.

'Take me home, please!' I instructed, breathless with haste and anxiety.

'To Queen's Square, madam?' he enquired politely.

'No – to Clifton, of course!' I snapped. 'And please make haste!'

Never had the journey seemed so long. I knotted my hands in my skirts, picking at my fingers and trying to decide the best course of action.

Daniel was my priority. First, I must get him away from Theo. Then I could go to a magistrate, hand the pouch over, and tell him my story. It would be enough, I hoped, to free Thomas, if indeed his pursuers had captured him. Beyond that, I did not know what I would do. I only prayed Richard would come home soon. But, for the moment, I could think of nothing but holding Daniel safe in my arms.

Just why I was so afraid for him I did not know. However dangerous Theo might be – and I was suddenly utterly convinced that he was very dangerous indeed – he would certainly not harm Daniel. The boy and his inheritance were Theo's passport to a life of luxury. Yet the very thought of my son in Theo's care was enough to drive me to a frenzy of anxiety.

The carriage drew up outside the house that I had come to call my home. I climbed down hastily, not waiting for Theo's driver to help me, and ran inside.

There was no sign of Theo or of Daniel. Not in the parlour; not in the drawing room. I ran up the stairs to the nursery. Perrett was there, folding a pile of clean sheets.

'Where is Daniel?' I demanded.

252

'Why, Mr Theo took him out,' she replied. 'Took him out in the carriage.'

Her eyes, I noticed, were red, and had I not been so demented with anxiety I would have been touched to think that the servants, at least, were upset by Mr Paterson's death.

'But *I* had the use of Mr Theo's carriage!' I cried.

'He took Mr Paterson's and drove himself. He put Daniel in the Moses basket on the seat beside him.'

'Where was he going?' I demanded.

'To the docks. To Mr Paterson's office, to look for you. He felt bad that he had allowed you to go alone, and quite right too!' Perrett said. 'Haven't you seen him?'

I did not wait to answer or explain myself. I ran from the nursery, down the stairs, and out of the house. Perrett called after me, thinking, no doubt, that I had been unhinged by the shock of Mr Paterson's death, but I ignored her. Nothing was of the slightest importance but finding Theo – and Daniel.

Theo's carriage was still drawn up at the door, the coachman standing with the horse, rubbing his neck.

'The docks!' I instructed. 'Please take me to my husband's warehouse without delay!'

I sank back in the seat, trembling from head to toe. My imagination was running wild, my thoughts racing. What would I do if I could not find Theo? Supposing he was not at the docks – what then? Panic closed my throat. I was never going to see my little son again! I tried to still my fevered imaginings, but without much success. Losing a child was too real for me. I knew exactly how it felt. And the terrible events of the day overlaid everything with the sense of living a nightmare.

Down Park Street we went, too slowly – oh, far too slowly! The stench of the river rose to greet us and I pressed a handkerchief to my mouth and nose, for the smell, always nauseating, was making my quaking stomach heave.

The docks were busy, as always. A ship was unloading, orders were shouted, barrels rolled along the cobbles, rigging was being inspected and repaired, sail makers pulled tattered

253

canvas from lockers to spread on the quayside. Sailors lounging to yarn moved aside to let us pass, and at last – at last! – we were drawing up outside Mr Paterson's warehouse.

I jumped down, ran inside and up the stairs to the office, not even stopping to wonder if the body of my husband would still be there, slumped at his desk. My only concern was to find Theo – and Daniel. But the office, like the warehouse, was deserted. Mr Paterson's body had been removed, and there was only a dark stain of congealed blood to show where it had lain. Of Theo and Daniel, there was no sign.

Back down the stairs I ran, demented almost in the extremity of my anxiety. Back down the stairs and on to the quayside, looking around wildly. And then, a little further along, I saw Mr Paterson's carriage pulled up outside Theo's own warehouse. How could I not have seen it before? The bustle on the quay had hidden it from me, I supposed – or I had been too blinded by my panic to notice. Relief coursed through me in a hot flood tide. I ran along the quayside, oblivious to the stares and muttered comments of the sailors and dock workers, through the door and up the stairs. I was breathless, my heart pumping madly.

I threw open the door to the office and sobbed with the release of tension.

They were there, Theo bending over some paperwork on the desk, Daniel – still in his Moses basket – on the floor beside him. Theo locked up, surprise – and suspicion – written all over his handsome face.

'Davina! Where have you been?'

I did not answer. I ran to the basket and picked up Daniel, holding him tight.

'Oh Daniel! Thank God – oh, thank God!'

'Where have you been?' Theo repeated. 'You said you intended coming to the docks.'

And with a recklessness born of my boundless joy and relief, I cried: 'I know all about you, Theo! You've been deceiving me! I've remembered – it was you who held up the carriage and caused the accident – I saw your face at the window! And it was you who fired the cottage, too, wasn't

254

it? You tried to convince me it was Richard I should fear, and all the time it was you!'

Theo's face was startled – and thunderstruck. 'Have you gone mad, Davina?'

'Mad? No! For the first time I am seeing things as they really are. You have been using me to further your ambitions, and when that didn't work, when you faced ruin because Mr Paterson was demanding the repayment of his loan, you had him killed! And tried to lay the blame for that too at Richard's door!'

Theo straightened, moving out from behind the desk. 'You *are* mad! Why should you think such a thing?'

'Because of this!' Blazing with all my pent-up emotion, I pulled out Richard's pouch and held it towards him in the palm of my hand. 'Do you see the initials on it? *R.W.* – Richard Wells. Thomas found it on the stairs when he discovered Mr Paterson's body, left there, no doubt, in an effort to incriminate him. But this pouch was stolen from Richard when your ruffians attacked and beat him. Did they bring it to you as proof they had done the deed you asked of them – after they had stolen the money it contained, of course? Or were you there when he was beaten senseless? Did you take it from him yourself as a trophy of war?'

Theo laughed suddenly. 'Oh Davina, I have underestimated you! What a woman! Oh yes, I should have married you myself when I had the chance! But you were more valuable to me as a passport to riches – or so I mistakenly thought. Yes, you are right, of course. I *was* there to watch Wells beaten – and much pleasure it gave me too. To defile you, my beautiful little cousin, and then to dare to try to insinuate himself into your life again, and risk everything I have worked for . . . Oh, it gave me great pleasure, and every time I looked at that pouch, it reminded me of him lying there in the gutter. But the time came when it would be more use to me as evidence against him. It's true, everything you say. Yes, it was me who struck the blow that killed that tight-fisted husband of yours, and I would have enjoyed it even if it had not been a means to gain control of all his wealth, through you and Daniel. He

255

thought himself better than me. He thought he could sneer at me, humiliate me, and get away with it – well, I showed him different. He deserved to die – and I'm glad I was the one to strike the fatal blow. But nobody but you will ever know it. I shall not admit it outside these four walls, and the pouch will condemn Richard Wells.'

'We'll see about that!' I cried. 'No less a person than Lady Avonbridge will confirm it was stolen from him long ago. I intend going to the magistrate without delay and I shall tell him everything.'

I turned for the door, but Theo was there before me, barring my way.

'Oh no, Davina!' His voice was low and dangerous suddenly, a tone I had never heard him use before. 'Oh no, my love, you are not going anywhere!'

Eighteen

In that moment I realized just how rash I had been. The moment Daniel was safe in my arms, I should have turned and fled straight to the magistrate. Instead I had allowed my tongue to run away with me – and now I was in terrible danger.

The noise of the quayside sounded very far away suddenly. I could expect no assistance from the outside world. Not from the seamen and dock labourers, who would imagine my cousin was comforting me in my grief, not from Theo's coachman, who was paid to think nothing at all. I was quite alone with a man who was so obsessed with his ambition that he was prepared to stop at nothing to achieve it.

'Theo!' I said, striving to keep my voice level. 'Please stand aside and let me pass. You are frightening me!'

'Oh Davina!' He reached out a hand and caught a lock of my hair which had, as usual, come loose from its pins. 'I'm sorry. It was never my wish to frighten you, or harm you in any way. I only ever wished to love you. You must know that, if your memory is returning. You must know what we were to each other before you ran off with that damnable man. You hurt me dreadfully, you know, by choosing to go with him. And when I discovered you were to bear his child . . . Can you not imagine how I felt? The torment you put me through? For a while I could scarcely bear to look on you. But I forgave you. That is the measure of my love for you! I forgave you even that. Don't you see, I wanted you so much!'

'So why did you arrange for me to marry Mr Paterson?' I asked. 'If you cared for me so deeply, why did you not ask me to be your wife?'

Theo sighed. 'Oh, it was too good an opportunity to pass up – or so I thought. An entrée at last to the closed circle of the Merchant Venturers. Prosperity within my grasp . . . And John Paterson an old man. I knew that one day in the not too distant future you would be a widow, and then we would be together. I would have you, and I would be rich. I could have it all! And when Daniel was born – well, better yet! I knew that John's fortune was safe, for Daniel would inherit, not some obscure male relative. And who better to take care of it for him than his mother's husband? The successful and respected merchant, Theo Grimes! Oh, this last year has been very difficult for me, I grant you, seeing you wed to another man, but I have comforted myself that it would not be for long. And now that time is come – the time I have waited for so patiently.' His face contorted with sudden anger. 'But you are spoiling it all with your wild talk of running to the magistrate. I can't let you do that, surely you can see that?'

The panic was drying my throat, threatening to overwhelm me. Theo was mad. Truly mad. Though he had certainly concealed his obsessions cunningly these last years, even if he had not, I could never have guessed at the twisted reasonings of his warped mind. There was no rhyme nor reason to his actions, either prior to my accident or since, looked at from the mind of a normal, healthy human being. But to Theo there had been some kind of logic in it all. He craved wealth and position, and he craved me, and he had worked out one dreadful scheme after another in his pursuit of the objects of his craving. No doubt when he had killed Mr Paterson this morning it had seemed to him that everything was at last falling into place. He would have his fortune, and he would have me. And perhaps in that lay my salvation. For he had just shown me what I must do and say to bring myself – and Daniel – to safety.

'Oh, I was only joking, Theo!' I said, trying to sound convincing. 'Surely you didn't really think I would betray you? You are my cousin, after all, and I am very fond of you. Even more so now, when I see how clever you have been! You, me, and Daniel – living in comfort on Daniel's inheritance. Why, I can't think of anything that would please me more!'

His face softened, his fingers played again with my wayward curl, and a tiny spark of hope flickered within me.

'Oh Davina, Davina, I so much wish I could believe you! But you made a fool of me once – how do I know you won't do so again?'

'I won't!' I cried passionately. 'Oh please, Theo, let's go home. And I shall never so much as think of Richard Wells again.'

It was the wrong thing to say. As if the very mention of his rival's name were a fuse to a gunpowder keg, Theo exploded.

'You see? You cannot help but drag him into it! Oh, I should have had him finished off in the gutter that night! I don't know what possessed me to let him live! And now . . . It's him you want, I know it! You almost had me fooled – but I can't trust you where he's concerned, can I? He came between us before, and he'll do it again.'

'No . . .'

'Don't lie to me!' Theo snarled. 'You'd be off to the magistrate the first chance you had! You'd spurn me and betray me. You must see – I can't allow that. No, I can't allow that.' And he pushed me roughly back into the room.

'Theo!' I cried desperately. 'Be sensible, please! You can't keep me here for ever!'

He laughed, the laugh of a madman, and again I wondered how I had failed to see that madness beneath his charming exterior.

'What's to stop me?' he asked, smiling – actually smiling! 'Oh, not for ever, I grant you, but long enough. Long enough for you to be truly mine, long enough for me to do to you all the things I have yearned to do for so long. The things other men have done, and I have been denied . . .'

His fingers were stroking my throat, the light of lust burning in his eyes.

'Oh yes, we'll have such times, you and I! And when I have had my fill of you, well, it won't be hard to dispose of

259

you. There's enough dark water out there to drown a hundred men and no one notice, let alone one little girl who was so demented by her husband's murder that she chose to end her own life. And no one will ever defile you or take you from me ever again . . .'

A wash of icy fear ran through me. He would do it, I knew. And the madness would make poetry of it in his deranged mind.

'Theo,' I begged desperately. 'Let me go, please! You can have whatever you want – I mean it, truly! For Daniel's sake, if not for mine, let us go!'

'Ah yes, Daniel!' Theo looked down at my baby, who was, miraculously, sleeping in my arms. 'Oh, you need not worry about Daniel, Davina! I will take good care of him, have no fear. He will be my ward. I am, after all, the only relative he has – apart from your grandparents and poor, simple Aunt Linnie, and they are all much too old to take a baby. And everyone will say how kind and selfless I am to take on your child and raise him. Now, why don't you put him back in his cradle? We don't want to frighten him, do we? And you and I, my dear, have unfinished business . . .'

'No!' I sobbed. My grasp tightened on Daniel; he stirred and opened his eyes, clear blue, unwinking. 'No, I won't put him down! I won't let you have him!'

'Would you rather I threw him into the docks with you?' Theo snarled. 'Oh, it's all right, Davina, don't look so worried. Of course I would never do such a thing! Not when he is heir to Mr Paterson's fortune – and my passport to the wealth that is his by right. But it would be best if we don't fight over him. Lay him down, my dear. That way we shall be sure he will not be hurt. Neither of us want that, do we?'

'Oh dear God!' I sobbed.

'Lay him down!' Theo ordered again. 'I will have him, Davina, one way or the other, make no mistake of that!'

His tone left me in not the slightest doubt but that he meant what he said, and I realized I had no choice. If he had to tear Daniel screaming from my arms, he would do it. Though my every instinct cried out against it, I knew that the best thing I could do now was to relinquish Daniel gracefully and pray that even now there was some way I could talk myself free and fetch help. At least Daniel was in no immediate danger. He was too valuable to Theo for that.

Steeling myself, I crossed to the cradle and laid Daniel down. He whimpered a protest and stared up at me reproachfully with those wide blue eyes. My heart filled with love and my eyes with tears. I looked down at him and wondered if ever I would hold him in my arms again. Then Theo's hand was gripping my arm, pulling me roughly away from the cradle.

'Good! I'm glad you've seen sense! Now, what am I to do with you? I'd like to kiss you, my dear, but one thing would lead to another and time is short. I don't want anyone asking awkward questions, though you did play into my hands wonderfully well, insisting you drove alone to the docks. Just right for the image of a woman demented by grief – though you and I both know grief was the last thing you were feeling.' He broke off, looking at me curiously. 'Where did you go, Davina?'

'You think I'd tell you now?' I shot at him, aware that, if I told him the truth, he might well decide I should die sooner rather than later. As it was, there was always the chance that someone might come looking for me. Though, if I were missing, and later found drowned, my hasty flight from Avonbridge Hall without explanation might well be taken for yet more evidence that I was unhinged for one reason or another.

'I rather think our little liaison will have to wait until another day. You have not yet accepted the situation, I'm afraid,' Theo said. 'Until you do, I must put you somewhere secure . . . Somewhere from where you cannot escape and run off to tell tales.'

'You are quite mad, Theo!' I cried defiantly. 'You'll never get away with this!'

He yanked me towards him so that his face was just inches from mine.

'We'll see about that!' he ground out. 'And don't ever, ever call me mad! Do you understand?'

As I flinched from pain and fear, he twisted my arm behind my back with such violence I thought it would be wrenched from the socket, and pushed me bodily across the room and out the door. I heard Daniel wail and could do nothing about it, for Theo was forcing me down the stairs, jerking me upright each time I stumbled.

I could not understand where he was taking me – not back on to the quayside, surely? Then, at the foot of the stairs, he turned me back, away from the sliver of daylight, and into a dark, narrow passage, where I found myself face to face with a heavy wooden door. With his free hand, Theo fumbled with the bolts and drew them back. As the door swung open, the fetid smell that rose to meet me made my stomach heave. The river smell – but even worse. The smell of excrement and sweat and fear and, not water, but dank earth. As I gasped, a wave of faintness threatening, Theo forced me forward on to a flight of steep stone steps, leading downward.

And then his hand was no longer restraining me but was in the small of my back. A sharp push and I lost my balance, falling headlong down the steps. My head cracked against stone, I felt a moment's sharp pain. And then the blackness closed in as it had done once before.

Consciousness returned through swirling mists of nausea and pain and I lay for a moment, still stunned and unable to move, as if the crashing fall had shocked my entire body into some kind of paralysis. My head throbbed unbearably and something wet and warm was trickling down my face. Tentatively, I raised a hand to touch it; my fingers came away sticky, and I knew it was blood.

For a moment I could not think where I was, or how I came to be here, and experienced a flash of sheer panic. Oh dear God, not again! Please, please, not again!

And then, with a rush, it all came back. I was in the cellar beneath Theo's dockside warehouse. He had incarcerated me here. And he had Daniel!

I tried to get up then, too quickly, and a fresh wave of dizziness overcame me, forcing me back to the dank stone floor. I tried to breathe deeply, but the fetid cellar air only turned my stomach and I vomited violently. But at least, I realized, I had not broken any bones when I fell. Though my hands burned as if the skin had been scraped from them and the whole of my body felt as if a huge rock had fallen on it, miraculously I seemed otherwise unharmed.

I tried again to struggle to my feet, and this time did so, leaning my hands against the rock walls of my prison. It was pitch black in the cellar, no chink of light to show me how large it was or even in which direction lay the flight of steps down which I had fallen, for in trying to rise, I had stumbled around and now I was completely disorientated.

Panic rose in me again. Somehow I fought it down, inching along the walls, trying at least to get my bearings. My fingers encountered a heavy iron ring set into the rock; my slippered toes kicked into a length of chain. It had been used, presumably, to secure the poor slaves and ensure they did not attack the slave master when he came to feed them and select the ones he would take for sale. Under any other circumstances, my heart would have bled for them, cold, afraid, robbed of their freedom and far from their native shores, awaiting their fate in this evil hellhole. But for the moment I could think of nothing but my plight – and my baby in the hands of a man maddened by greed, lust, and ambition.

At last – at last! – I was back at the steps. I climbed them on all fours, broad ledges cut into the rock, then straightened to run my hands over the wood of the door, seeking a handle. I found it, but as I had feared, it refused to turn beneath my fevered hands. Theo had locked it, of course. He had no intention of letting me escape so easily.

Trapped! Trapped for ever in the stinking darkness. Powerless to get to my baby son. Once again the panic threatened to overcome me, once again I fought it down.

I began to hammer on the door and shout for help at the top of my voice, though I had little hope of attracting attention. With all the bustle and noise on the quayside, why should anyone take the slightest notice of a few thuds coming from a merchant's cellar? And my voice would be lost amongst the shouts of the seamen, the cries of the hawkers. Despair rose in a knot in my throat; I sobbed with it, then renewed my efforts, shouting and banging with all my might.

And suddenly, miraculously, I heard a scraping sound on the other side of the door – the sound of the bolts being drawn! The door gave under my frenzied thrust and I stumbled and almost fell into blinding daylight and blessed fresh air, gasping and sobbing.

'However did you come to get locked in there?' a man's voice was asking.

'He's got my baby!' I screamed, and without even stopping to thank my rescuer I ran frantically out on to the quayside.

At first I could see no sign of Theo and I feared he was long gone. I had no idea how long I had been locked in the cellar and I could not imagine he would delay here. Frantic, with no clear idea of what I was doing, I ran along the quayside and into the narrow street beyond, a street lined on either side with mean dark houses that leaned towards one another across the cobbles. Rough women who plied their trade around the docks stared at me from the doorways, a drunk rolled out of a rum shop and almost collided with me. Somehow I avoided him and ran on. And then, with a sob of almost disbelieving relief, I saw Mr Paterson's landaulet drawn up at the roadside and Theo, bold as brass, standing beside it and talking to a man who looked like a sailor.

I picked up my skirts and began to run towards the carriage, screaming Daniel's name as I went. It was, of course, a stupid thing to do, but I was beside myself, beyond coherent thought.

Theo looked round and saw me, and fury distorted his handsome features. He turned to the carriage, hastily climbing up and taking the reins.

'Stop!' I screamed. 'Stop him!'

The whip flashed in his hand; the landaulet began to move forward. Desperation lent my feet wings, and before the carriage could gather any speed I was alongside it, still screaming at Theo to stop. Daniel was in his Moses basket on the seat; I could see him but not reach him.

Theo looked down at me, his face contorted, eyes blazing with madness. He raised his hand, lashing out with the whip – at me. The tip caught my cheek, drawing blood. He lashed out again; this time the whip wrapped itself around my legs, tripping me, and I fell headlong on to the cobbles. And the carriage pulled away, gathering speed.

Somehow I picked myself up, sobbing with desperation. There was no way I would ever catch up with Theo – and Daniel – now. And then, to my utter astonishment, a figure emerged from one of the mean little houses – a tall figure in immaculate blue livery, skin gleaming like polished jet in the sunlight.

Thomas! I had never thought to see him again; thought him either long gone or else thrown into gaol. Yet here he was in my moment of need, throwing himself at the horse's head, catching the bridle! For a terrifying moment I thought he would be dragged along or run down, but the horse knew him well. Instead, the carriage came to a halt.

'Get out of the way, damn you!' I heard Theo yell, now laying about Thomas with the whip, but Thomas stood his ground, head held high and proud, defying Theo as he had never defied any man since he had been driven in chains on to English soil.

I do not believe Theo even noticed me running alongside the carriage again; all his awareness was concentrated on Thomas, and this time I had the sense to do nothing to draw attention to myself. Somehow I hoisted myself up on to the step, and only then did Theo become aware of me, turning with a snarl. But too late. I had Daniel out of his Moses basket and safe in my arms, and I was running back along the street with him, running with no clear idea of where I was going, except to get as far away from Theo as I could.

In a moment Theo leaped down from the landaulet and ran after me. Like me, he must have lost all reason, for if he had stopped to think, he would have known that already it was too late – I was free and I would never, now, allow him any part in the upbringing of my son.

So I ran and he ran after me, back along the street, around the corner on to the quayside. I risked a glance over my shoulder; he was catching me, of course. He was an athletic man, with longer legs than mine, and unimpeded by skirts. As for me, my legs were weak and shaking, my head throbbing, my breath coming in painful gasps.

I darted between a group of men mending sails and another rolling a barrel, expecting to feel his hand on my shoulder at any moment. Instead I heard a yell of fury and I turned again – just in time to see the barrel take Theo's feet from under him, propelling him towards the dock edge. His arms were flailing wildly as he tried to regain his balance, then, with an almighty splash, both the barrel and Theo went over the side into the filthy water, which was running at high tide.

My first reaction was utter shock – how had such a thing happened? My second, of course, relief. Theo would never catch up with me now. By the time he clambered out of the water, I would be long gone, and Daniel with me.

Then I heard a terrible scream that stopped me once more in my tracks. In that first startled moment I could not believe it was Theo who had screamed. It was too shrill a sound to have been made by a man; it was more like an animal in terror or pain. And then realization dawned through the fog created by my reeling senses. A great ship was moored close by the very point where Theo had gone into the water; it rocked and washed with the tide, slapping against the quayside with a force that displaced the scummy water and sucked it down again. Theo had been caught between hull and harbour wall!

Sick horror washed over me in a great cold rush. Whatever he had done, whatever he had planned to do, I could not have wished such a fate on him, or anyone. I stood frozen to the spot, the need for escape gone, paralysed by a terrible fascination, watching as men gathered round the scene and the strange, unreal aura of disaster being witnessed descended upon the docks.

266

Thomas appeared at my side as if from nowhere, staring at the ship that must surely have taken Theo's life. 'Mrs Paterson . . .'

'Oh Thomas, Thomas!' I could find no words to thank him for stopping the carriage, nor indeed for anything. My teeth had begun to chatter, desperation and fear and shock seemed to have robbed me of the power of speech. 'Oh Thomas – Mr Theo!'

'Come away, ma'am.' He touched my arm; there was an urgency in his voice. 'Come away. When they get him out, it won't be a pretty sight.'

'I have to see,' I managed haltingly. Even as I spoke, I was not sure what motive drove me to say that, whether I wanted to be sure that Theo truly was no longer a threat to me, or whether it was because, whatever he had done, he was still my kinsman and in some strange way I felt it my duty to witness his fate.

Somehow the men managed to retrieve Theo from the filthy water. They laid his body on the cobbles, and when no one made any effort to revive him I crept closer, close enough to see that though his eyes were wide open, they saw nothing, and his mouth, still agape from that last terrible scream, would never utter another word. His body was awkwardly crumpled, like that of a roughly discarded rag doll; blood poured from his crushed skull and ran out to mingle with the water that lay in pools on the cobbles.

'He's dead then,' I said flatly, emotionlessly. 'Theo is dead.'

And Thomas replied simply: 'Yes, ma'am.'

Somehow I tore my eyes away from the sodden and bloody bundle of rags and pulped bones that had been my cousin.

'You escaped the constable and his men, then,' I said to Thomas.

'Yes, ma'am.'

'Then will you drive me to Lady Avonbridge's house? We'll all be safe there. Her ladyship's sympathies are such that she will offer you sanctuary until I can lay before the magistrate the evidence that will establish your innocence.'

267

And again he replied with just two words: 'Yes, ma'am.'

Lady Avonbridge must have been surprised indeed to find me back at her door, this time with Thomas in tow, but, as I had expected, she took us both in. She listened to all I had to say, making no unnecessary interruptions, though her expression grew more and more grim. When I had finished, she turned to Thomas, assuring him he need have no further fear of arrest so long as he remained under her roof. If allegations were made against him, she personally would speak up for him, and no magistrate in the city would dare to go against her.

Towards me, her manner remained brisk – she had not yet forgiven me, I think, for causing Richard such heartache – but it was tempered now with something as close to kindness as I thought she was capable of showing me.

'I'll put a room at your disposal, Rowan. Your baby looks as if he's hungry again. And I'll have hot water sent up for you to wash – you are in a filthy state, and that cut on your head needs cleaning and dressing.'

'Thank you.' I had almost forgotten the cut; though my temple was still throbbing, I had grown so used to headaches over the years, they had become almost a way of life for me.

'As for Alice,' she went on, 'I think it might be better to wait until Richard is here before you see her. I don't want her alarmed in any way, and it is for Richard to decide how this should be approached.'

I nodded. Truth to tell, though I longed to see my little daughter again, I could not help but agree that this was not the right time. Not only must I be a dreadful fright to look at, I was exhausted physically, mentally and emotionally. I could give no guarantees as to how I would react in front of her, and my senses would, for the moment, take no more.

A maid showed me to the room Lady Avonbridge had allocated me. I washed myself, I fed Daniel, and settled him. Then I lay down on the great four-poster bed with him beside me, and though for a little while the terrifying events of the day spun round my head like a flock of startled birds, they seemed to be going further and further away, and I was drifting, drifting.

I slept.

Nineteen

'Rowan.' The voice was soft, a part of some dream. Someone was holding my hand; it felt good and safe. Lips touched my face, fingers brushed a stray lock of hair from my forehead, their touch gentle, soothing the insistent throbbing in my temple.

I opened my eyes, still drowsy, and saw him there, and for a blissful moment it was as if the last years had never been at all. Rather it was as if I was waking in my bed in our little house in Watchet to find Richard home from his voyage; as if everything that had happened between his leaving me there and my awakening to find him at my side had been some fevered dream. Then Daniel whimpered and I knew it had been real, all of it, in every unbelievably terrifying detail.

'Richard!' I whispered. 'Oh Richard, I am so sorry . . .'

'For what?' His voice was rough, yet at the same time tender. 'It is I who should be sorry, Rowan, for leaving you at the mercy of those who would use you, not just once, but twice. I shall never forgive myself.'

'You had to go,' I said. 'It was what you had set out to do. And I am glad – and proud – that you fight for the rights of those who cannot fight for themselves.'

'You know? You have remembered?'

'Lady Avonbridge told me. But yes, I am beginning to remember for myself too.'

It was true. I was remembering. Richard's brave mission, the love we had shared, Theo's mad obsession with me. Everything. I had not yet had time to examine my memories in detail, but I knew they were there now, waiting for me when I had the time to explore them.

270

'That is good,' he said. 'But, oh Rowan, I should have been here for you! No matter what, you are the most important thing to me in the whole world. The most precious. I should have been here for you.'

'It doesn't matter now,' I said. 'It's all over now.'

And that, too, was true. I was safe. Daniel was safe. And terrible though the events were that had made it possible, there was nothing now to come between Richard and me. My body ached from the punishment it had taken this day, my heart ached for John, struck down before his time by my own cousin. But my soul yearned only for my one true love.

'Please hold me,' I whispered.

He clambered on to the great four-poster bed, lay down beside me, and wrapped his arms around me. With Daniel still tucked into the crook of my arm, I turned my face into Richard's shoulder, with the fine lawn of his shirt soft against my cheek and the faint familiar scent of his skin in my nostrils, and knew contentment and something closer to peace than I had known in a very long time.

He did not ask me then, but later he did. 'Have you come back to me, Rowan?'

I looked at him, puzzled that he even needed to ask.

'Of course! Surely you must know that?'

His hazel eyes were shadowed, his expression a little rueful.

'I have learned, my sweet, through bitter experience, to take nothing for granted. As John's widow, and the mother of the heir to his fortune, your future is assured. You have a fine house, servants, wealth . . . all I can offer you for the foreseeable future is a little cottage such as the one I took for you before, and a host of enemies made by me through working for the cause.'

'For heaven's sake!' I exclaimed. 'What do servants and a fine house matter to me?'

'They are your son's birthright.'

'The most important thing for any child is a happy family!'

I said. 'And in any case, all those things will be waiting for him. I shall not spend a penny piece of his inheritance, and when he is grown he can do as he likes with it. But I hope that the upbringing we can give him will mean that he will use it wisely.'

A sudden worrying thought assailed me. 'You haven't changed your mind, have you? You are still willing to take him?'

'Of course I have not changed my mind! The very idea! I shall treat Daniel as if he were my own son – and teach Alice to look upon him as her brother. She will love him, I know – a real live doll for her to play with.'

A little nerve of anticipation at the thought of the happy days ahead jumped in my throat.

'Just so long as she doesn't chase him around when he begins to crawl, as she chases that poor cat!' I joked.

'Undoubtedly she will. It will be up to you to teach her to be gentle and patient with him.'

'Yes.' I raised my eyes to Richard's. 'May I see her now? Can we tell her who I really am?'

And: 'Yes,' he said. 'If you are ready, I'll take you to her.'

We found Alice in a big, sunny room at the top of the house. She sat astride a wooden rocking horse, her little legs dangling some inches short of the stirrups whilst she held on tight to its mane of real horsehair. Her nurse was with her, steadying her with one hand and gently pushing the horse on its rockers with the other.

As we went into the room, Alice's face lit up.

'Papa! Papa! Look at me – I'm riding!'

Richard laughed. 'I can see you are! But I have brought someone to see you. Do you remember meeting this lady once before?'

Alice fixed me with a solemn blue stare. 'Yes.'

'And you liked her, didn't you?'

'Yes.' That was a little less certain. I felt a lump of nervousness constricting my throat.

'Then I think you should get down from the rocking horse

272

for a moment or two. I have something very important to tell you.'

'Oh Papa . . .'

'Come along now.' He lifted her down, she wound her arms around his neck, blue eyes and hazel were both fixed on me.

'Alice,' Richard said gently, 'have you not asked me sometimes why you have no mama? And I told you that she had to go away? Do you remember that?'

She nodded.

'Well, I am very happy to tell you that she has come back into our lives, yours and mine. This lady is she, Alice. This is your mama. And she is not going to go away and leave us ever again.'

Alice regarded me solemnly. My heart was full. All I wanted was to take her in my arms and make up for the lost years, but I knew I must restrain myself. I must not alarm her; I must not force her in any way. I must wait for her to accept me and build and nurture the bond between us with patience and with love.

'And you have a little brother too,' Richard went on. 'His name is Daniel, and when he is bigger, the two of you will be able to play together. You'll like that, won't you?'

Alice's thumb went into her mouth, then, still puzzled, still wary, she nodded.

'Mm.'

'We are very lucky, are we not, that your mama has come back to us.'

'Mm.' Another long, thoughtful look, then she wriggled impatiently. 'Papa . . .'

'Yes, sweeting?'

'Can I ride my horse again now?'

Richard smiled, all the harsh lines of his face softening with love.

'Yes, sweeting, of course you can.'

He settled her back on the horse, holding her securely in the leather saddle and rocking her gently. And as she laughed with delight, the warmth inside me grew and swelled until I thought I would burst with it.

Yes, I must be patient in gaining her trust and her affection, but I could allow myself that luxury. For did I now not have all the time in the world?

There was a sense of unreality about those first days with Richard as we rediscovered each other and put together the first building blocks that would form the basis of our new life, our family.

Lady Avonbridge had kindly agreed that Daniel and I could stay at the Hall for the time being, for it would not be right for Richard to move into Mr Paterson's house and I could not face the thought of going back there alone. Her own coachman drove me over to Clifton to collect the things we would both need, and I brought Perrett back with me too, to provide continuity in Daniel's care and attend to my own needs. The rest of the servants remained behind to run the house until I had had time to decide what should be done with it.

With my blessing, Richard took care of all the arrangements for the two funerals that had to take place – Mr Paterson's and Theo's both, for there was no one but me left to bury Theo, and I could not countenance throwing the responsibility upon my grandparents' shoulders. But aside from this, he put all his other duties to one side and spent the time with me.

'Are there not things you have to do?' I asked, reluctant to have him out of my sight, yet anxious he was neglecting his self-imposed mission.

'They can wait,' he replied firmly. 'There will be time enough for them when I am sure you are recovered fully from your ordeal.'

And, grateful for his concern, I did not argue.

Lady Avonbridge was very kind in her brusque way, and very discreet. She ensured we were left alone, and we spent many hours talking – and simply holding hands, for we could scarcely believe that, after so much, we were truly together once more.

274

With my newly recovered memory, I was able to tell Richard what had occurred with regard to Theo whilst he, Richard, was away on that fateful voyage, leaving myself and my mother in Watchet.

He knew, of course, that Theo had attempted to woo me before he and I had met. Our troupe had been performing in Bristol, and he had recognized my mother and made himself known to her. At first, she had been pleased. 'I never thought any of my family would ever speak to me again,' I recall her saying. But her pleasure soon turned to consternation when she realized he was taking far more interest in me than she thought suitable.

'He is your own cousin, Rowan,' she had said. 'And in any case, he is far too old for you. I don't care for the life he leads, either.'

I had laughed at that. Considering that *we* were the ones who led what most people judged to be a less than respectable life, I thought it amusing that she should criticize the habits of a man who had followed his father into the trade. And in any case I had not taken Theo's attentions seriously. To me, he was simply a rather exciting diversion. He flattered me, he spent money on me, he was fun to spend a little time with, and nothing more.

It was only when we moved on and Theo kept appearing at the venues we were playing around the countryside that I began to realize his interest was more serious than I had thought – or wished for. I told him in no uncertain terms that there could never be anything between us, and, when I met and fell in love with Richard, I thought, mistakenly, that was the end of the matter.

I was, of course, wrong; Theo refused to give up so easily. He tried to warn me off Richard, telling me he was nothing but a troublemaker and an adventurer. He even used the very words that he was later to attribute to Richard.

'If I cannot have you, no one else will.'

I was frightened, but defiant. What, after all, could he do to me with Richard to protect me? And it was, in any case, I thought, an empty threat. Mere words. Again, I was wrong.

Whether Theo was indeed behind the firing of our cottage at Watchet, I shall never know for certain. It may well be that it was indeed Richard's enemies who were responsible, but certainly my mother believed that it was Theo who set the torch.

'He is a dangerous madman,' she said, beside herself with anxiety. 'He believes that if you no longer have a roof over your head, you will have to accept his offer. He's obsessed with you, Rowan, and now that he has found you again, he'll never let you go.'

'But I am having Richard's child!' I had objected. 'Surely if he knew that . . .'

'I fear it would only serve to madden him the more,' Mama had said. 'God alone knows what he would do, Rowan. And we have nowhere to live, nowhere we can be safe from him.'

'Can we not return to the strolling players?' I suggested.

'In your condition? No! And in any case, he'd find you, and they would be able to offer you no protection. No, there's only one place you would be safe – one place where he would not dare touch you . . . I shall have to swallow my pride, take you to my parents' home, and plead with them to take us in and give us refuge until Richard returns.'

I had not known what to make of that – though, in truth, the idea of a family rather appealed to me. And I was, in any case, in no position to argue. And so we set out on that last fateful journey, by hired carriage.

Night was falling when we reached the rectory; my first sight of it was not encouraging. In the grey half-light it looked a bleak, oppressive place. My mother bid the coachman wait and we approached the front door along a path overhung with heavy foliage. She was nervous, I could tell, for she walked briskly yet stiffly ahead of me, her head erect, her shoulders set, and she hesitated for a moment before rapping sharply on the door.

My grandfather himself answered. With the dull glow of the lamp behind him and the last dim light of the day on his face he made a forbidding figure.

276

'Yes?' he said. 'How can I help you?'

I realized that we were to him merely dark, shadowy figures.

'Papa,' my mother said. 'It's me – Elizabeth.'

There was a long silence. He did not open his arms to her; there was to be no killing of the fatted calf here.

'Elizabeth,' he said at last, quite tonelessly. 'And who is this?'

'This is Rowan, my daughter. Papa . . . we need your help . . .'

Another long silence while his eyes ran over me in the half light and I almost shrank under his fierce, critical scrutiny. Then: 'So I see. I always knew it would come to this, Elizabeth.'

'Papa . . .'

'Your daughter, I see, is no better than you. She is shaming you as you shamed me.'

'Papa, please! I am proud to call Rowan my daughter! Don't judge her. You have no knowledge of her circumstances.'

'No shame!' he boomed. 'No shame then, and none now. Well, it's no use coming running home now that things have gone wrong for you. I won't allow this household to be sullied and used so. You made your choice long ago, and it seems this daughter of yours has made hers. With as little honour and decency! And she, like you, must take the consequences.'

'Papa . . .'

'Fornication, Elizabeth, is a sin I cannot – will not – condone. How could I? It is against the laws of God which I preach. What would my parishioners say if my own family is shown to be as wicked as the inhabitants of Sodom and Gomorrah? You have sinned grievously, and so has your daughter, and until you are prepared to confess, do penance, and resolve to live a pure life, well, there is no place for you here.'

My mother was now trembling, I knew it, even though she stood tall and straight.

'I understand, Papa.'

277

'Elizabeth – you have never understood, nor tried to . . .'

'Oh, I have, believe me! You call yourself a man of God, Papa, but you have not one ounce of Christian charity in your veins. You pray each day to be forgiven your trespasses, as you forgive those who have trespassed against you. But you don't know the meaning of forgiveness! Don't worry, we won't trouble you any further.' She touched my arm. 'Come, Rowan!'

I was angry then. Angry not for myself, but for my mother, who had humbled herself to ask for her father's mercy, and found none.

'How can you treat your own daughter so?' I cried. 'Don't you know what it cost her to come to you? Well, may your God forgive you for your heartlessness, for I surely never will!'

And so we returned to our carriage and set out on that fateful last journey.

There were still things I did not know, of course. I did not know how Theo had come to accost our carriage, or why. I was only certain that he had done so. His face at the window was something which, now that I had remembered it, I could never forget.

All this I told Richard, and he listened, grim-faced.

'I knew he was a rotten apple,' he said. 'I did not realize, though, the extent of his madness. If I had, I would never have left you for a moment.'

'We could not have lived like that,' I said. 'I would not have wanted it so. And neither would you. There are things you had to do – you would quickly have come to resent me as a millstone around your neck if I prevented you from working for the abolition of the slave trade.'

'You a millstone, Rowan? Never!'

'You would not be the man you are if you were robbed of your purpose in life,' I said. 'You would not be the man I love. And I am as anxious as you to see an end to this most barbaric practice. It is abhorrent, Richard. It is evil. It has to be stopped.'

Richard sighed, running a hand around his jawline.

278

'Sometimes, Rowan, I despair of being able to make the slightest difference. Those who make the laws are in the pockets of the wealthy traders – they have a vested interest in ensuring the money continues to roll in.'

'Things *will* change!' I said passionately. 'They must! When enough right-minded people are prepared to stand up and be counted, Parliament will have to listen! And, in the meantime, we must all do what we can.' I paused. 'I have been thinking, Richard. I want to give our slaves their freedom.'

'Thomas?'

'And Dorcas too.' I bit my lip. I could not bring myself to tell Richard of what Mr Paterson had done to Dorcas; I was too ashamed, and, strangely, protective of his reputation now that he was no longer here to defend it himself. 'But I am not sure how to go about it,' I continued. 'I could, of course, simply let them go, but I would like to ensure it as their legal right in case it should ever be challenged. Do you think it could be arranged?'

Richard nodded thoughtfully. 'As part of John Paterson's estate, they belong, of course, not to you, but to Daniel. But the trustees could no doubt make a decision. I'll talk to some of the lawyers sympathetic to our cause. There are several in our group.'

'And where would they go, Thomas and Dorcas, if they were free?' I asked anxiously. 'That's something else that has been worrying me. I'd like to be able to offer to keep them on as paid servants – Thomas is a rock – but I don't think it would be right somehow. They would never *feel* free, would they – living in the household where they were owned body and soul?'

'I quite agree,' Richard said seriously. 'The choice would be theirs, of course, but I would suggest London. There are a goodly number of freed slaves living and working there. Don't worry any more, Rowan, I shall make sure they have a place to go; and the wherewithal to start a new life. We owe Thomas a good deal.'

'We owe him everything!' I said. 'If he had not stepped

in to stop Theo getting away with Daniel, I dread to think what might have happened!'

'And he will be well rewarded,' Richard promised.

I nodded. All charges against Thomas had been dropped now, of course. The magistrate had agreed that Theo was responsible for John's murder and, since Theo was himself dead, the matter ended there.

'Oh Richard . . .' I whispered. Thinking about that terrible day had brought it all back to me with dreadful clarity, and I shuddered as I thought what might have been.

'Come here, my love,' Richard said.

I went into his arms, and as he held me and kissed me the demons gradually receded once more, and I told myself I must learn to live with them, and be grateful.

Sometimes remembering can be painful and distressing. But I knew, from bitter experience, it is far preferable to having no memory at all.

There was something else I had to do. I had to make my peace with my grandparents.

One fine day, Richard drove me to Gloucestershire. We took Alice and Daniel with us, Daniel in his Moses basket, Alice squashed into the seat between us to ensure she did not tumble down.

I was very nervous. I was not at all sure how my grand-parents would receive us – I thought that history might repeat itself, and that, like myself and Mama when we had sought refuge, I might not be allowed beyond the front door. But it was Grandmama who answered my knock – a Grandmama who looked small and frail, startled and guilty, and she even asked if Richard and the children wanted to come in too.

'No, they will wait for me outside,' I said. This was something I had to do alone.

She took me through to the parlour. Grandfather was seated in the big wing chair. He, too, looked older and more frail. Aunt Linnie was there too, dozing as usual. When she heard my voice she woke with a start, un-certain, I think, as to whether to be pleased to see me or apprehensive at the scene she feared my visit would precipitate.

'Davina! Oh, Davina! What a surprise . . .'

'Rowan,' I corrected her gently. 'My name is Rowan.'

'Rowan? Oh yes! Oh dear, oh dear . . .'

'Linnie!' my grandfather snapped. 'Be quiet, do! Or else leave the room.'

But Aunt Linnie had no intention of missing anything. She sank back, hands pressed to her mouth.

'Grandpapa, Grandmama,' I said. 'I have come to tell you that I am going to be married again, after a decent interval. To Mr Richard Wells.'

'Married – again? Married *twice*?' Aunt Linnie, who had never been married at all, burst out in astonishment and admiration.

'Linnie!' my grandfather admonished her.

'Richard is the father of my little girl,' I went on, as if the interruption had never happened at all. 'You have met him, of course – when you entrusted her to his care.'

Grandmama wrung her hands. 'Oh Davina, I do so hope that you are doing the right thing! We really do not know what to think about this Richard Wells. Theo always said . . .'

'I am afraid Theo misled you for reasons of his own,' I said. 'He was the one from whom Mama and I were fleeing. I know it is so, because I have, thankfully, recovered my memory. And I know exactly what happened when we came here. It is not as you told me at all. Grandfather saw my condition and refused to take us in.'

I turned my gaze towards my grandfather. 'How could you do it? How could you behave so cruelly towards your own daughter?'

Grandfather sat stony-faced, saying nothing.

'He regretted it,' Grandmama said. 'He regretted it at once. Theo was here, visiting, and we asked him to ride after you and bring you back. But everything went terribly wrong. The coachman thought he was a highwayman, no doubt. He refused to stop, and poor dear Theo . . .'

I cringed. Poor dear Theo indeed! But I said nothing. I

doubted I would ever know the truth of what was in his deranged thoughts that night, but there was nothing to be gained from causing my grandparents more distress. I had to try to put the past behind me now.

'We are so truly sorry, Davina,' Grandmama said. 'Not a day has passed when we haven't thought of what happened and wished we could somehow change things. And we did try, in our own poor way, to do our best for you. When Theo came to tell us of the accident, we took you in and cared for you . . .'

And took my child from me, and hoped I would never know . . .

But again, I said nothing of it. The time for recriminations was past, and I did truly believe that, misguided though they had been, they truly had believed that they were acting in my best interests.

'I have been so afraid,' my grandmother went on, 'that we had lost you too. I couldn't have borne that, Davina. You are all we have left now – you and your little ones. Please say you can find it in your heart to forgive us. We haven't long left in this world, and—'

'We shall answer before God,' my grandfather said. There was a regret and a humility in his voice that I had never heard before.

'Grandmama, Grandfather, I have been very lucky,' I said. 'I have two fine healthy children, and I have the love of a good man. I want to put the past behind me now, and I would like you to share in my happiness. I shall come to see you as often as I can – if you are willing, that is.'

'Oh, Davina, we should like nothing better . . .'

When I left, the three of them accompanied me to the door.

'Oh!' Aunt Linnie gasped when she saw Richard. 'What a very handsome man! More handsome by far than Mr Paterson! Though he was very kind . . .' she added regretfully.

I kissed them all and promised again to visit very soon.

Then I turned and walked to the carriage, where my happiness and my future awaited me.

* * *

282

We were married, Richard and I, when a decent interval had elapsed following Mr Paterson's death. Richard acquired a darling little house for us in a village on the outskirts of Bristol, and continued to work for the cause.

Thomas and Dorcas were given their freedom and, as Richard had suggested, moved to London, where there was a growing community of freed slaves and African sailors. They maintained contact with us, however, and I was delighted to hear they had married and started a family of their own. The hardships and ignominies they had shared had formed a bond between them, it seemed, which had blossomed into love.

There is a saying, I believe, that unless you have never known great sadness, you can never be truly happy. I pray that it may be so for Thomas and Dorcas, for it is certainly true for me. I value so greatly every moment spent with my husband and my children, for I know the agony of being apart from them. And I treasure my memories, for, having been without a past for so long, I know how important each and every one is, happy and sad alike, for each one represents a part of my life, and is a legacy for the future.

This is my world, the destiny I almost forfeited. Every morning when I rise and watch the sun coming up over the hills, I embrace the day, every night I look at the stars and say a prayer of gratitude.

For my life, for my little ones, for the fate which brought me back to Richard.

My one and only love.

1807

*H*e stood on the Clifton heights, looking down on the river that wound its way between the wooded walls of the gorge beneath. Sun sparkled on the water today, a ferry crossed and re-crossed the river, a sailing ship was being towed in on the tide. But it was not a slaver. Not today, nor tomorrow, nor ever again would the ships bring in their human cargo of misery. The trade had been abolished by an act of Parliament and Bristol had seen the last slaving voyage.

He had played his part, he knew, and he was glad. It had almost cost him the woman he loved, but he knew that if he had his time over again, he could not do differently. He could not have lived with his conscience if he had not fought to bring an end to the barbarity, and he knew his beloved Rowan could not either. They had been lucky, so lucky, and it seemed all they had endured had only brought them closer together.

But today, looking at the sun on the water, he knew only an enormous sense of relief that it was over. He could devote himself to his family now with an easy mind.

The running sore that was the evil of the slave trade had been banished for ever.